DRAGONFIRE

Bink was a standing target as the dragon opened its gullet to spew fire at him—but the diving griffin crashed into the dragon's snout as the flame emerged. The snout met the ground, and the dragon's head was bathed in the backblast.

The griffin snatched Bink up, and with Chester galloping below them, they made for the refuge of a wide crevice in the ground—but the dragon followed.

Suddenly the centaur skidded to a halt.

"Don't stop!" Bink cried. "The monster's right behind us!"

"Some escape route," Chester said bitterly. "We'd better turn and fight the dragon."

Then Bink saw with a rush of horror what had stopped Chester . . .

Also by Piers Anthony
Published by Ballantine Books:

THE SOURCE
OF MAGIC

Piers Anthony

A Del Rey Book

BALLANTINE BOOKS • NEW YORK

A Del Rey Book
Published by Ballantine Books

Copyright © 1979 by Piers Anthony Jacob

Library of Congress Catalog Card Number: 78-61817

ISBN 0-345-33555-4

Manufactured in the United States of America

First Edition: February 1979
Twenty-second Printing: October 1985

Cover art by Doug Beekman

Contents

XANTH

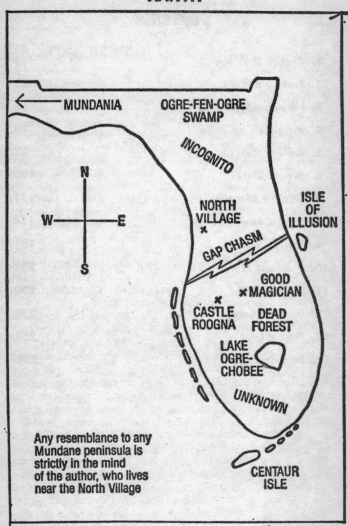

MUNDANIA ←

OGRE-FEN-OGRE SWAMP

INCOGNITO

N
W —— E
S

NORTH VILLAGE ×

GAP CHASM

ISLE OF ILLUSION

GOOD × MAGICIAN

CASTLE ROOGNA ×

DEAD FOREST

LAKE OGRE-CHOBEE

UNKNOWN

CENTAUR ISLE

Any resemblance to any Mundane peninsula is strictly in the mind of the author, who lives near the North Village

Chapter 1. Closet Skeleton

The magic-sniffer ambled toward Bink, its long limber snout snuffling industriously. When the creature reached him it went into a frenzy of enthusiasm, snorting out flutelike notes, wagging its bushy tail, and prancing in a circle.

"Sure, I like you too, Sniffer!" Bink said, squatting to embrace it. The creature's snout kissed his nose wetly. "You were one of the first to believe in my magic, when—"

Bink paused, for the creature was acting strangely. It had stopped frisking and become subdued, almost frightened. "What's the matter, little friend?" Bink asked, concerned. "Did I say something to hurt your feelings? I apologize!"

But the sniffer curled its tail between its legs and slunk away. Bink stared after it, chagrined. It was almost as if the magic had been turned off, causing the thing to lose its function. But Bink's talent, like all others, was inherent; it could not dissipate while he lived. Something else must have frightened the sniffer.

Bink looked about, feeling uneasy. To the east was the Castle Roogna orchard, whose trees bore all manner of exotic fruit, vegetables, and sundry artifacts like cherry bombs and doorknobs. To the south was the untamed wilderness of Xanth. Bink remembered how that jungle had herded him and his companions here, seeming so menacing, way back when. Today the trees were basically friendly; they had only wanted a Magician to stay and make Castle Roogna great again. King Trent had done that. Now the consider-

1

able power of this region exerted itself for the benefit of the kingdom. Everything seemed to be in order.

Well, on with his business. There was to be a ball tonight, and his shoes were badly worn. He proceeded to the edge of the orchard where a stray shoe-tree had rooted. Shoes liked to move about, and often planted themselves in out-of-the-way places.

This one had several ripe shoes. Bink inspected individual ones without plucking them, until he was sure he had found a pair that fit him. Then he twisted them off, shook out the seeds, and put them carefully on his feet. They were quite comfortable, and looked nice because they were fresh.

He started back, walking with exaggerated motion to break in the shoes without scuffing them, his mind still nagged by the episode with the magic-sniffer. Was it an omen? Omens always came true, here in the Land of Xanth, but it was seldom possible to understand them properly until too late. Was something bad going to happen to him? That really seemed unlikely; Bink knew it was no exaggeration to assume that serious evil would have to fall on all Xanth before Bink himself was harmed. So it must be a misreading. The magic-sniffer had merely suffered a fit of indigestion, and had to scoot off.

Soon Bink was within sight of his home. It was a fine cottage cheese just off the palace grounds, which he had moved into when he married. The rind had long since hardened and lost the better part of its flavor, and the walls were fine-grained creamy-yellow petrified cheese. It was one of the most tasteful cottages extant, but since he hadn't hollowed it out himself he didn't see fit to brag about it.

Bink took a deep breath, nerved himself, and opened the front rind-door. A sweetish waft of seasoned cheese blew out, together with a raucous screech.

"That you, Bink? About time! Where did you sneak off to, right when there's work to be done? You have no consideration at all, do you!"

"I needed shoes," he said shortly.

"Shoes!" she exclaimed incredulously. "You *have* shoes, idiot!"

His wife was much smarter than he, at the moment, for Chameleon's intelligence varied with the time of the month, as did her appearance. When she was beautiful, she was stupid—in the extreme, for both. When she was smart, she was ugly. Very smart and very ugly. At the moment she was at the height of the latter phase. This was one reason she was keeping herself secluded, virtually locked in her room.

"I need good-looking ones, tonight," he said, mustering patience. But even as the words were out he realized he had phrased it badly; any reference to good looks set her off.

"The hell you do, dunce!"

He wished she wouldn't keep rubbing in his inferior intelligence. Ordinarily she was smart enough not to do that. Bink knew he was no genius, but he wasn't subnormal either; *she* was the one who was both. "I have to attend the Anniversary Ball," he explained, though of course she already knew that. "It would be an insult to the Queen if I attended sloppily dressed."

"Dolt!" she screamed from her hideaway. "You're attending in costume! No one will see your stinking shoes!"

Oops, that was right. He had made his trip for nothing.

"But that's all too typical of your selfishness," she continued with righteous ire. "Bugging off to the party to have a good time while I suffer home alone, chewing on the walls." That was literal; the cheese was old and hard, but she gnawed on it when she got angry, and she was angry most of the time now.

Still, he tried to be positive. He had only been married a year, and he loved Chameleon. He had known at the outset that there would be good times and bad times, and this was a bad time. A very bad time. "Why don't you come to the ball too, dear?"

She exploded with cynical wrath. "Me? When I'm like this? Spare me your feebleminded sarcasm!"

"But as you reminded me, it's a costume party. The Queen is cloaking every attendee in a disguise of her choosing. So no one will see—"

"You utter moronic nincompoop!" she bawled through the wall, and he had heard something crash.

3

Now she was throwing things, in a genuine temper tantrum. "How can I go to a party in *any* guise—when I'm nine months pregnant?"

And that was what was really bothering her. Not her normal smart-ugly phase, that she had lived with all her life, but the enormous discomfort and restriction of her pregnancy. Bink had precipitated that condition during her lovely-stupid phase, only to learn when she got smarter that she had not wanted such a commitment at this time. She feared her baby would be like her—or like him. She had wanted to find some spell to ensure that the child would be positively talented, or at least normal, and now it was up to blind chance. She had accepted the situation with extremely poor grace, and had not forgiven him. The smarter she got, and the more pregnant she got, the more intense her ire became.

Well, soon she would be over the hump, and getting prettier—just in time for the baby. It was due in a week or so. Maybe the baby would be normal, perhaps even strongly talented, and Chameleon's fears would be laid to rest. Then she would stop taking it out on him.

If, however, the baby were abnormal . . . but best not even think of that. "Sorry, I forgot," he mumbled.

"You *forgot!*" The irony in her tone cut through his sensitivities like a magic sword through the cheese of the cottage. "Imbecile! You'd like to forget, wouldn't you! Why didn't you think of that last year when you—"

"I have to go, Chameleon," he muttered, hastily retreating out the door. "The Queen gets upset when people are tardy." In fact it seemed to be the nature of women to get upset at men, and to throw tantrums. That was one of the things that distinguished them from nymphs, who looked like women but were always amenable to the idle whims of men. He supposed he should count himself lucky that his wife did not have a dangerous talent, like setting fire to people or generating thunderstorms.

"Why does the Queen have to throw her ridiculous pointless dull party now?" Chameleon demanded. "Right when she *knows* I can't attend?"

4

Ah, the logic of women! Why bother to try to understand it. All the intelligence in the Land of Xanth could not make sense of the senseless. Bink closed the door behind him.

Actually, Chameleon's question had been rhetorical. They both knew the answer. Queen Iris took every opportunity to flaunt her status, and this was the first anniversary of that status. Theoretically the ball was in honor of the King, but actually King Trent cared little for theatrics and would probably skip the festivities. The party was really for the Queen—and though she could not compel the King to attend, woe betide the lesser functionary who played hooky tonight! Bink was such a functionary.

And why was this so? he asked himself as he trod glumly on. He was supposed to be an important person, the Royal Researcher of Xanth, whose duty it was to probe the mysteries of magic and report directly to the King. But with Chameleon's pregnancy, and the necessary organization of his homestead, Bink had not gotten around to any real research. For that he had only himself to blame, really. He should indeed have considered the consequence of impregnating his wife. At the time, fatherhood had been the last thing on his mind. But Chameleon-lovely was a figure to cloud man's mind and excite his—never mind!

Ah, nostalgia! Back when love was new, carefree, uncomplicated, without responsibility! Chameleon-lovely was very like a nymph—

No, that was a false feeling. His life before he met Chameleon had not been all that simple, and he had encountered her three times before he recognized her. He had feared he had no magic talent—

He shimmered—and suddenly his appearance changed. The Queen's costume had arrived. Bink was the same person, mentally and physically, but now he looked like a centaur. The Queen's illusion, so he could play the game she had devised, in her infinite capacity to generate minor mischief. Each person had to guess the identities of as many others as possible before making his way to the palace ballroom, and there was a prize for the one who guessed the most correctly.

5

In addition, she had set up a mock-maze-hedge around Castle Roogna. Even if he did not play the people-guessing game, he would be forced to thread his way through the giant puzzle. Damn the Queen!

But he had to go through with it, as did everyone else. The King wisely did not interfere with household matters, and gave the Queen considerable play on her tether. With resignation Bink entered the maze and began the laborious chore of threading his way through the network of false paths toward the castle.

Most of the hedge was illusion, but enough of it was anchored in reality to make it safest simply to honor the maze, rather than barging through. The Queen would have her fun, especially on this important First Anniversary of the King's coronation. She could get uglier than Chameleon when not humored.

Bink whipped around a corner—and almost collided with a zombie. The thing's wormy face dripped earth and goo, and the great square eye-sockets were windows of putrefaction. The smell was appalling.

Morbidly fascinated, Bink stared into those eyes. Far within their depths there seemed to be a faint illumination, as of moonlight on a haunted plain or glow-fungus feeding on the corpse's rotting brain. It was as if he could see through twin tunnels into the very source of its foul animation, and perhaps to the root of all the magic of Xanth. Yet it was nightmare, for the zombie was one of the living dead, a horror that should be quickly buried and forgotten. Why had this one ripped free of its unquiet grave? The zombies normally roused themselves only in defense of Castle Roogna, and they had been passive since King Trent took over.

The zombie stepped toward him, opening its fossil mouth. "Vvooomm," it said, laboring to make the putrid gas that was its only breath form a word.

Bink backed away, sickened. He feared little in the Land of Xanth, for his physical prowess and magic talent made him one of the most subtly formidable people in the kingdom. But the peculiar discomfort and disgust entailed by dealing with a zombie unnerved him. He spun about and ran down a side avenue, leaving the undead thing behind. With its

6

decayed articulation of bones and moldy flesh it could not match his speed, and did not even try.

Suddenly a gleaming sword rose up before him. Bink halted, amazed by this second apparition. He saw no person, no connections, just the weapon. What was the purpose of this illusion?

Oh—it must be another cute little trick of the Queen's. She liked to make her parties exciting and challenging. All he had to do was walk through the sword, calling the bluff of this *ad hoc* interference.

Yet he hesitated. The blade looked terribly real. Bink remembered his experience with Jama, as a youth. Jama's talent was the manifestation of flying swords, solid and sharp and dangerous for the few seconds they existed, and he tended to exert his talent arrogantly. Jama was no friend of Bink's, and if he were in the area—

Bink drew his own sword. "On guard!" he exclaimed, and struck at the other weapon, half expecting his blade to pass through it without resistance. The Queen would be pleased her bluff had worked, and this way he was taking no risk, just in case—

The other sword was solid. Steel clanged on steel. Then the other weapon twisted about to disengage from his, and thrust swiftly at his chest.

Bink parried and stepped aside. This was no temporary blade, and no mindlessly flying thing! Some invisible hand guided it, and that meant an invisible man.

The sword struck again, and again Bink parried. This thing was really trying to get him! "Who are you?" Bink demanded, but there was no answer.

Bink had been practicing with the sword for the past year, and his tutor claimed that he was an apt student. Bink had courage, speed, and ample physical power. He knew he was hardly expert yet, but he was no longer amateur. He rather enjoyed the challenge, even with an invisible opponent.

But a serious fight . . . was something else. Why was he being attacked, on this festive occasion? Who was his silent, secretive enemy? Bink was lucky that that person's spell of invisibility had not affected the sword itself, for then he would have had an awful time

7

countering it. But every item of magic in Xanth was single; a sword could not carry its necessary charms of sharpness and hardness and also be invisible. Well, it was possible, for anything was possible with magic; but it was highly unlikely. At any rate, that weapon was all Bink needed to see.

"Halt!" he cried. "Desist, or I must counter you."

Again the enemy sword slashed at him ferociously. Bink was already aware that he faced no expert; the swordsman's style was more bold than skilled. Bink blocked the weapon off, then countered with a half-hearted thrust to his opponent's exposed midsection. There was only one place that midsection could be, visible or not, for a certain balance and position were essential in swordplay. Bink's strike was not hard enough to maim, but was sufficient to—

His blade passed right through the invisible torso without resistance. There was nothing there.

Bink, startled, lost his concentration and balance. The enemy sword thrust at his face. He ducked barely in time. His instructor, Crombie the soldier, had taught him such avoidance; but this escape was at least partly luck. Without his talent, he could have been dead.

Bink did not like to depend on his talent. That was the point in learning swordsmanship: to defend himself his own way, openly, with pride, without suffering the private snickers of those who assumed, naturally enough, that mere chance had helped him. His magic might stop or blunt an attack by having the attacker slip on a littered fruit rind; it didn't care about his pride. But when he won fairly with his sword, no one laughed. No one was laughing now, but still he did not like being attacked by a—what?

It must be one of the magic weapons of the King's private arsenal, and it was consciously directed. No way this could be the action of the King, however; King Trent never played practical jokes, and permitted no tampering with his weapons. Someone had activated this sword and sent it out to do mischief, and that person would shortly face the formidable wrath of the King.

That was little comfort to Bink at the moment, though. He didn't want to seem to hide behind the protection of the King. He wanted to fight his own battle and win. Except that he would have some problem getting at a person who wasn't there.

As he considered, Bink rejected the notion that a distant person could be wielding this weapon. It was magically possible, but as far as he knew he had no enemies; no one would want to attack him, by magical or natural means, and no one would dare do it with one of the King's own swords, in the garden of Castle Roogna.

Bink fenced with the enemy sword again, maneuvered it into a vulnerable position, and sliced through the invisible arm. No arm was there, of course. No doubt about it: the sword was wielding itself. He had never actually fought one of these before, because the King didn't trust the judgment of mindless weapons, so the experience was a novel one. But of course there was nothing inherently odd about it; why *not* do battle with a charmed sword?

Yet why should such a sword seek his life, assuming it was acting on its own? Bink had nothing but respect for bladed weapons. He took good care of his own sword, making sure the sharpness charm was in good order and never abusing the instrument. Swords of any type or creed should have no quarrel with him.

Perhaps he had inadvertently affronted this particular sword. "Sword, if I have caused you distress or wronged you, I apologize and proffer amends," he said. "I do not wish to fight you without reason."

The sword cut ferociously at his legs. No quarter there!

"At least tell me what your grievance is!" Bink exclaimed, dancing away just in time.

The sword continued its attack relentlessly.

"Then I must put you out of commission," Bink said, with mixed regret, ire, and anticipation. Here was a real challenge! For the first time he took a full offensive posture, fencing the sword with skill. He knew he was a better man than it.

But he could not strike down the wielder of that weapon, because there was none. Nobody to pierce, no hand to slice. The sword showed no sign of tiring; magic powered it. How, then, could he overcome it?

This was more of a challenge than he had supposed! Bink was not worried, because he found it hard to worry about a skill less than his own. Yet if the opposition were invulnerable—

Still, his talent would not allow the sword to hurt him. A sword wielded by a man in ordinary fashion could damage him, because that was mundane; but when magic was involved, he was safe. In Xanth, hardly anything was completely unmagical, so he was extremely well protected. The question was, was he going to prevail honestly, by his own skill and courage, or by some fantastic-seeming coincidence? If he didn't do it the first way, his talent would do it the second way.

Again he maneuvered the sword into a vulnerable position, then struck it across the flat of the blade, hoping to snap it off short. This did not work; the metal was too strong. He had not really expected such a ploy to be effective; strength was one of the basic charms built into modern swords. Well, what next?

He heard the clop-clop of someone approaching. He had to wrap this up quickly, or suffer the embarrassment of being rescued. His talent didn't care about his pride, just his body.

Bink found himself backed up against a tree—a real one. The hedge-maze had been superimposed on existing vegetation, so that everything became part of that puzzle. This was a gluebark tree: anything that penetrated the bark was magically stuck to it. Then the tree slowly grew around the object, absorbing it. Harmless, so long as the bark was intact; children could safely climb the trunk and play in its branches, as long as they did not use cleats. Woodpeckers stayed well away from it. So Bink could lean against it, but had to be careful not to—

The enemy sword slashed at his face. Bink was never sure, afterward, whether his inspiration came before or after his action. Probably after, which meant that his talent was in operation again despite his effort to avoid that. At any rate, instead of parrying this time, he ducked.

The sword passed over his head and smacked into the tree, slicing deeply into the bark. Instantly the

10

tree's magic focused, and the blade was sealed in place. It wrenched and struggled, but could not escape. Nothing could beat the specific magic of a thing in its own bailiwick! Bink was the victor.

"'Bye, Sword," he said, sheathing his own weapon. "Sorry we couldn't visit longer." But behind his flippancy was a certain grim disquiet: who or what had incited this magic sword to slay him? He must, after all, have an enemy somewhere, and he didn't like that. It wasn't so much any fear of attack, but a gut feeling of distress that he should be disliked to that extent by anyone, when he tried so hard to get along.

He ducked around another corner—and smacked into a needle-cactus. Not a real one, or he would have become a human pincushion; a mock one.

The cactus reached down with a prickly branch and gripped Bink by the neck. "Clumsy oaf!" it snorted. "Do you wish me to prettify your ugly face in the mud?"

Bink recognized that voice and that grip. "Chester!" he rasped past the constriction in his neck. "Chester Centaur!"

"Horseflies!" Chester swore. "You tricked me into giving myself away!" He eased his terrible grip slightly. "But now you'd better tell me who *you* are, or I might squeeze you like this." He squeezed, and Bink thought his head was going to pop off his body. Where was his talent now?

"Fink! Fink!" Bink squeaked, trying to pronounce his name when his lips would not quite close. "Hink!"

"I do *not* stink!" Chester said, becoming irritated. That made his grip tighten. "Not only are you homely as hell, you're impertinent." Then he did a double take. "Hey—you're wearing my face!"

Bink had forgotten: he was in costume. The centaur's surprise caused him to relax momentarily, and Bink snatched his opportunity. "I'm Bink! Your friend! In illusion guise!"

Chester pondered. No centaur was stupid, but this one tended to think with his muscles. "If you're trying to fool me—"

"Remember Herman the hermit? How I met him in the wilderness, and he saved Xanth from the wiggle

11

swarm with his will-o'-the-wisp magic? The finest centaur of them all!"

Chester finally put Bink down. "Uncle Herman," he agreed, smiling. The effect was horrendous on the cactus-face. "I guess you're okay. But what are you doing in my form?"

"The same thing you're doing in cactus form," Bink said, massaging his throat. "Attending the masquerade ball." His neck did not seem to be damaged, so his talent must have let this encounter be.

"Oh, yes," Chester agreed, flexing his needles eloquently. "The mischief of Good Queen Iris, the bitch-Sorceress. Have you found a way into the palace yet?"

"No. In fact, I ran into a—" But Bink wasn't sure he wanted to talk about the sword just yet. "A zombie."

"A zombie!" Chester laughed. "Pity the poor oaf in *that* costume!"

A costume! Of course! The zombie had not been real; it had merely been another of the Queen's illusion-costumes. Bink had reacted as shortsightedly as Chester, fleeing it before discovering its identity. And thereby encountering the sword, which certainly had not been either costume or illusion. "Well, I don't much like this game anyway," he said.

"I don't go for the game either," Chester agreed. "But the prize—that is worth a year of my life."

"By definition," Bink agreed morosely. "One Question Answered by the Good Magician Humfrey—free. But everyone's competing for it; someone else will win."

"Not if we get hoofing!" Chester said. "Let's go unmask the zombie before it gets away!"

"Yes," Bink agreed, embarrassed by his previous reaction.

They passed the sword, still stuck in the tree. "Finders keepers!" Chester exclaimed happily, and put his hand to it.

"That's a gluebark; it won't let go."

But the centaur had already grasped the sword and yanked. Such was his strength there was a shower of bark and wood. But the sword did not come free.

"Hm," Chester said. "Look, tree—we have a gluebark in Centaur Village. During the drought I watered it every day, so it survived. Now all I ask in return is this sword, that you have no use for."

The sword came free. Chester tucked it into his quiver of arrows, fastening it in place with a loop of the coil of rope he also carried. Or so Bink guessed, observing the contortions of the cactus. Bink had put a hand to his own sword, half-fearing a renewal of hostilities, but the other weapon was quiescent. Whatever had animated it was gone.

Chester became aware of Bink's stare. "You just have to understand trees," he said, moving on. "It's true of course; a centaur never lies. I did water that tree. It was more convenient than the privy."

So this gluebark had given up its prize. Well, why not? Centaurs were indeed generally kind to trees, though Chester had no particular love for needle-cactuses. Which was no doubt why the Queen in her humor had imposed this costume on him.

They came to the place where Bink had encountered the zombie, but the awful thing was gone. Only a slimy chunk of dirt lay in the path. Chester nudged it with one forehoof. "Real dirt—from a fake zombie?" he inquired, puzzled. "The Queen's illusions are getting better."

Bink nodded agreement. It was a disquieting note. Obviously the Queen had extended the illusion greatly —but why should she bother? Her magic was strong, far beyond the talents of ordinary people, for she was one of the three Magician-class citizens of Xanth. But it had to be a strain on even her power to maintain every detail of every costume of every person attending the masquerade. Bink and Chester's costumes were visual only, or it would have been difficult for them to converse.

"Here is a fresh pile of dirt," Chester remarked. "Real dirt, not zombie dirt." He tapped at it with a cactus foot that nevertheless left a hoofprint. "Could the thing have gone back into the ground here?"

Curious, Bink scraped at the mound with his own foot. There was nothing inside it except more dirt. No zombie. "Well, we lost him," Bink said, upset for a reason he could not quite fathom. The zombie had seemed so real! "Let's just find our way into the palace, instead of making fools of ourselves out here."

Chester nodded, his cactus-head wobbling ludicrously. "I wasn't guessing people very well anyway," he admitted. "And the only question I could ask the Good Magician doesn't have any answer."

"No answer?" Bink asked as they turned into another channel.

"Since Cherie had the colt—mind you, he's a fine little centaur, bushy-tailed—she doesn't seem to have much time for me anymore. I'm like a fifth hoof around the stable. So what can I—?"

"You, too!" Bink exclaimed, recognizing the root of his own bad mood. "Chameleon hasn't even had ours yet, but—" He shrugged.

"Don't worry—she won't have a colt."

Bink choked, though it really wasn't funny.

"Fillies—can't run with them, can't run without them," Chester said dolefully.

Suddenly a harpy rounded a corner. There was another scramble to avoid a collision. "You blind in the beak?" Chester demanded. "Flap off, birdbrain."

"You have a vegetable head?" the harpy retorted in a fluting tone. "Clear out of my way before I sew you up in a stinking ball with your own dull needles."

"Dull needles!" Chester, somewhat belligerent even in the best of moods, swelled up visibly at this affront. Had he actually been a cactus, he would have fired off a volley of needles immediately—and none of those darts looked dull. "You want your grimy feathers crammed up your snotty snoot?"

It was the harpy's turn to swell. Most of its breed were female, but this one was male: more of the Queen's rather cutting humor. "Naturally," the birdman fluted. "Right after you have the juice squeezed out of your pulp, greenface."

"Oh, yeah?" Chester demanded, forgetting that centaurs were not common brawlers. Harpy and cactus squared off. The harpy was evidently a considerably larger creature, one that never had to take any guff off strangers. That odd, half-musical mode of speech—

"Manticora!" Bink exclaimed.

14

The harpy paused. "One point for you, Centaur. Your voice sounds familiar, but——"

Startled, Bink reminded himself that he was in the guise of a centaur at the moment, so that it was himself, not Chester, the creature addressed. "I'm Bink. I met you when I visited the Good Magician, way back when——"

"Oh, yes. You broke his magic mirror. Fortunately he had another. Whatever became of you?"

"I fell upon evil times. I got married."

The manticora laughed musically. "Not to this cactus, I trust?"

"Listen, thing——" Chester said warningly.

"This really is my friend, Chester Centaur," Bink said quickly. "He's the nephew of Herman the hermit, who saved Xanth from the——"

"I knew Herman!" the Manticora said. "Greatest centaur there ever was, even before he gave his noble life for his country. Only one I know who wasn't ashamed of his magic talent. His will-o'-the-wisps led me out of a dragon warren once. When I learned of his death, I was so sad I went out and stung a small tangle tree to death. He was so much better than those hoof-headed equines of the common herd who exiled him——" He broke off. "No offense, Cactus, you being his nephew and all. I may have a target to sting with you, but I would not affront the memory of that remarkable hermit."

There was no surer route to Chester's favor than praise of his hero-uncle, as perhaps the manticora knew. "No offense!" he said instantly. "Everything you said is true! My people exiled Herman because they thought magic in a centaur was obscene. Most of them still do. Even my own filly, as nice a piece of horseflesh as you'd care to——" He shook his cactus-head, becoming aware of the impropriety. "They *are* hoofheads."

"Times are changing," the manticora said. "One day all the centaurs will be flaunting their talents instead of flouting them." He made a gesture with his harpy wings. "Well, I must go identify some more people, not that I need the prize. It's merely a challenge."

He moved on. Bink marveled again at the humor of

15

the Queen, to costume as a harpy such a formidable creature as a manticora, who possessed the head of a man with triple jaws, body of a lion, wings of a dragon, and tail of a monstrous scorpion. Certainly one of the most deadly monsters of the Land of Xanth —rendered into the likeness of one of the most disgusting. Yet the manticora was bearing up with grace, and playing the game of charades and costumes. Probably he felt secure in the knowledge that he had a soul, and so he cared little for appearances.

"I wonder if I have a magic talent?" Chester mused, sounding a trifle guilty. The transition from obscenity to pride was indeed a difficult one!

"If you won the prize, you could find out," Bink pointed out.

The cactus brightened. "That's right!" This was evidently the unanswerable question Chester had had in mind, unvoiced. Then the cactus dulled. "But Cherie would never let me have a talent, not even a little one. She's awfully prudish about that sort of thing."

Bink remembered the filly's prim attitude, and nodded. Cherie Centaur was one fine figure of a filly, and well able to handle the general magic of Xanth, but she could not abide it in any centaur. It reminded Bink of his own mother's attitude about sex in young humans. For animals it was natural, but when something like a wild-oats nymph was involved—well, Chester did have a problem.

They turned another corner—corners abounded in this infernal maze—and there was the palace gate, shining beyond the drawbridge over the moat. "Let's get over there before the maze changes!" Bink exclaimed.

They ran toward it—but even as they did, the hedge-pattern shimmered and fogged. The awful thing about this puzzle-pattern was its instability; at irregular intervals it shifted into new configurations, so that it was impossible to solve it methodically. They were going to be too late to break out.

"I'm not stopping now!" Chester cried. The sound of cactus-galloping became louder. "Get on my back!"

Bink didn't argue. He made a leap for the prickliest portion of the cactus, grimacing in half-expectation

16

of a crotchful of needles. He landed neatly on Chester's back, which felt quite equine. Phew!

At the feel of that impact, Chester accelerated. Bink had ridden a centaur before, when Cherie had kindly given him a lift—but never a powerhouse like this! Chester was husky even by centaur standards, and now he was in a hurry. The huge muscles pulsed along his body, launching him forward with such ferocity that Bink was afraid he would be hurled off as fast as he had landed. But he clutched two handfuls of mane and hung on, confident that his talent would protect him even from this.

Few residents of Xanth were aware of Bink's talent, and he himself had been ignorant of it the first twenty-five years of his life. This was because of the way the talent clouded itself, hiding from publicity. It prevented him from being harmed by magic—but anyone who knew this could then harm him by mundane means. So Bink's talent shrouded itself in seeming coincidence. Only King Trent, besides Bink himself, knew the truth. Good Magician Humfrey probably suspected, and Chameleon had to have an idea.

A new hedge formed between them and the gate. It was probably illusion, since they had just seen the gate. Chester plunged through it—and sent branches flying. No illusion; this time it must have been the gate that was the illusion. The Sorceress Queen could make things disappear, by creating the illusion of open space; he should have remembered that before.

What drive this creature had! Invisible foliage tore at Bink like the winds of a tempest, but he clung tight. Another barrier appeared; Chester veered to follow a new channel that went his way, then smashed past another cross-hedge. Once this centaur got moving, pity the man, beast, or plant that got in his way!

Suddenly they were out of the maze and at the moat. But Chester's veer had brought him to it twenty paces to the side of the drawbridge, and there was no room to make a course correction. "Hang on!" Chester cried, and leaped.

This time the thrust was so great that Bink ripped a double handful of mane out of the centaur's hide and

17

still slid off the rear. He tumbled end over end and splashed into the moat.

Immediately the moat-monsters converged, jaws gaping eagerly. They were ever alert; they would have been fired, otherwise. A huge serpent looped down, each glistening tooth as long as one of Bink's fingers. From the other side a purple croc opened its gnarly proboscis, showing off teeth that were even longer. And directly under Bink, rising from the swirling moat-mud, came a behemoth, its back so broad it seemed to fill the entire moat.

Bink thrashed madly in the water, trying to swim to safety, knowing that no man could escape any one of these monsters, let alone all three. The behemoth came up, lifting him half out of the water; the croc came across, its jaws parting cavernously; the serpent struck with lightning velocity from above.

And—croc and serpent collided, their teeth throwing off sparks as they clashed. Both monsters were shunted aside by the mass of the rising behemoth— and Bink slid down that lifting slope as on a greased skid, away from the teeth and safely to the stone-lined inner wall of the moat. An amazing coincidence—

Ha. That was his talent operating, saving him once again from his own folly. Trying to ride a galloping centaur that looked like a cactus—he should have picked his way out of the maze the way the others were doing. He was just lucky that both centaurs and moat-monsters were magical, so that his talent could function.

Chester had landed safely, and was on hand to haul him out of the moat. With one hand the centaur lifted Bink clear, hardly seeming to exert himself. But his voice shook. "I thought—when you fell among those monsters—I never saw anything like—"

"They weren't really hungry," Bink said, preferring to disparage the significance of the event. "They were just playing with their food, and overdid it. Let's go on inside. They must be serving the refreshments by now."

"Hey, yes!" Chester agreed. Like all powerful creatures, he had a chronic appetite.

"Hay, yes," Bink muttered. But it was not a good pun; centaurs did not eat hay, despite what detractors might imply.

They moved to the castle—and the illusions faded. The spell was off, here; they were themselves again, man and centaur. "You know, I never realized how homely my face was, until I saw it on you," Chester said musingly.

"But you have an exceedingly handsome posterior," Bink pointed out.

"True, true," the centaur agreed, mollified. "I always said Cherie didn't become my mate for my face."

Bink started to laugh, but realized his friend was serious. Also, they were at the entry now, and others were within earshot.

The guard at the palace gate frowned. "How many did you guess, Bink?" he inquired, pad poised for a note.

"One, Crombie," Bink said, indicating Chester. Then he remembered the manticora. "Two, rather."

"You're out of the running, then," Crombie said. "The leading contestant has twelve." He glanced at Chester. "You?"

"I didn't want the prize anyway," the centaur said gruffly.

"You folk haven't been trying," Crombie said. "If I'd been out there, instead of stuck here running errands for the Queen—"

"I thought you liked this palace job," Bink said. He had first encountered Crombie when the man soldiered for the prior King.

"I like it—but I like adventure better. The King's okay, but—" Crombie scowled. "Well, you know the Queen."

"All fillies are difficult," Chester said. "It's their nature; they can't help it, even if they wanted to."

"Right you are!" Crombie agreed heartily. He was the original woman-hater. "And the ones with the strongest magic—who else would have dreamed up this idiocy of a masquerade? She just wants to show off her sorcery."

"She hasn't got much else to show off," Chester said. "The King pays no attention to her."

"The King's one smart Magician!" Crombie agreed. "When she's not making mischief like this, this palace guard duty is dull as hell. I wish I were out on a man's mission, like the time when Bink and I—"

Bink smiled reminiscently. "Wasn't that Technicolor hailstorm something? We camped out under the quiescent tangle tree—"

"And the girl ran off," Crombie agreed. "Those were the days!"

Surprised, Bink found himself agreeing. The adventure had not seemed like fun at the time, but in retrospect it had a certain twilight luster. "You told me she was a threat to me."

"And she *was*," Crombie said. "She married you, didn't she?"

Bink laughed, but it was a trifle forced. "We'd better get on in before the refreshments are gone." He turned—and almost stumbled over another little mound of dirt. "You have moles around the palace?" he inquired with a certain edge.

Crombie squinted at the dirt. "That wasn't there a moment ago. Maybe a magic mole was attracted by the party. I'll notify the head grounds keeper, when I get offshift."

Bink and Chester moved on in. The palace ballroom had been decorated by Queen Iris, naturally. It was an undersea setting, with streamers of seaweed rising from the rocky deeps, and brightly colored fish swimming through, and barnacles on the walls. Here and there were subaqueous beaches of fine white sand, which shifted location magically, so that if a person stood still the scenery would come to him. A large serpentine sea monster coiled around the entire area, its pulsing, convoluted coils showing here and there in lieu of the walls.

Chester glanced around. "She's a bitch, and she shows off, but I have to admit her magic is impressive. But I'm worried about the quantity of food; if there isn't enough—"

There turned out to be no danger of a shortage. The refreshments were mountainous, and under the personal guard of Queen Iris. She had a picklepuss on a little leash. Whenever someone had the temerity to take a delicacy, the picklepuss pickled it. "No one eats until the grand prize is awarded," Iris announced, glaring about. Since she had garbed herself as a warrior-queen-mermaid, complete with spiked crown, trident, and powerful tail, and the points of the trident glistened with a coating of slime that was probably illusion too but just might possibly be genuine poison, this was an effective enough deterrent even without the picklepuss.

Bink and Chester separated, mixing with the other guests. Just about every creature of note in Xanth was present, except for Chester's filly Cherie, who was no doubt still wrapped up in the colt, and Bink's Chameleon, wrapped up in her misery. And the Good Magician Humfrey, who never socialized voluntarily.

Bink spotted his father Roland, down from the North Village. Roland was careful not to embarrass him by any overt show of affection. They shook hands "Nice shoes, son."

This was nevertheless a miscue, after the scene with Chameleon. "Fresh from the tree," Bink said awkwardly.

"What have you been doing these past few months?" Bubbles rose from Roland's mouth as he spoke, quivering spherically as they sought the surface of the ocean. When Queen Iris put on an illusion, it was some illusion! Ordinary citizens, with their motley individual magic talents, could only look upon the works of the Sorceress and despair. Which was, of course, why the Queen was putting on this show.

"Oh, practicing with the sword, tilling the garden, that sort of thing," Bink said.

"I understand Chameleon is expecting momentarily."

"That, too," Bink said, again experiencing the frustration of his situation.

"A son will help fill the house."

Provided it turned out to be a normal, talented son. Bink changed the subject. "We have a delicate young lady-slipper plant just blossoming; I think it will bear its first pair of slippers soon."

"The ladies will be pleased," Roland said gravely, exactly as if this were significant news. Suddenly Bink

21

realized that he had very little to show for his past year. What had he accomplished? Virtually nothing. No wonder he felt out of sorts!

The illumination dimmed. It was as if dusk were falling, causing the sea to darken, too. But the diffused daylight was replaced by nocturnal fluorescence. The flotation sacs on the seaweed glowed like little lamps, and the neon-coral was brightly outlined in assorted colors. Even the puffy sponges emitted wan beams. The animal life had sharper light, with electric eels flashing searchlight beams, and assorted fish shone translucently. The overall effect was bewilderingly beautiful.

"If only her personality were as excellent as her taste," Roland murmured, referring to the Queen.

"We shall now award the door prize," Queen Iris announced. She glowed most of all: streams of light emanated from the points of her crown and trident, and her beautifully bare mermaid torso was clearly outlined. She was the mistress of illusion; she could make herself as lovely as she chose, and she chose well.

"I understand it was a marriage of convenience," Roland continued. Though no Magician himself, Roland was the King's regent north of the Gap, and did not hold royalty in awe. "It must be extremely convenient at times."

Bink nodded, slightly embarrassed by his father's evident appreciation of the well-displayed if illusory charms of the Queen. The man was bordering on fifty, after all! Yet it had to be true. The King professed no love for the Queen, and governed that temperamental woman with a subtly iron hand that amazed those who had known Iris before her marriage. Yet she thrived under that discipline. Those who knew the King well understood that not only was he a more powerful Magician than she, he was also a stronger person. In fact, it looked as if the magic Land of Xanth had its most effective King since the Fourth Wave Reign of Roogna, the builder of this castle-palace. Already formidable changes were occurring; the magic shield that had protected Xanth from intrusion had been removed, and Mundane creatures

22

were allowed to cross the border. The first to cross had been the members of the King's former Mundane army; they had been settled in wilderness regions and were becoming productive citizens of Xanth. The requirement that each citizen demonstrate a magic talent had been abolished—and to the amazement of some conservatives, chaos had not resulted. People were becoming known and respected for their total qualities, not just the accident of their magic. Selected parties were exploring nearby Mundania, where no magic existed, and outlying guard posts were being established so that no invasion could happen by surprise. The King had not destroyed the shieldstone; he would restore the shield if it were ever needed.

At any rate, Bink was sure King Trent had an eye for all things good and useful, including the flesh of fair women, and the Queen was his to command. She could and would be anything the King wished, and he would not be human if he did not avail himself of this, at least on occasion. The question was, what did he want? This was common palace speculation, and the prevailing opinion was that the King wanted variety. The Queen seldom appeared in the same guise twice.

"Palace Guard, your report," the Queen demanded peremptorily.

Soldier Crombie came forward slowly. He was resplendent in his palace uniform, every inch the soldier in a kingdom that hardly needed soldiers. He could fight well and savagely with sword or bare hands and did not like serving as lackey to a woman—and he showed it. Therefore she enjoyed ordering him about. But she could not push him too far, for his loyalty was to the King, and the King's favor lay on him.

"The winner—" Crombie began, consulting his notes.

"No, not that way, idiot!" she exclaimed, blotting him out with a cloud of diffusing dye. More illusion, of course, but quite effective. "First you give the runner-up, *then* you give the winner. Do something right, for a change."

Crombie's scowling face emerged from the thinning dye. "Women!" he muttered with caustic freighting.

23

The Queen smiled, enjoying his ire. "The runner-up, with nine correct identifications, is—" He scowled again. "A woman. Bianca of the North Village."

"Mother!" Bink breathed, surprised.

"She always did enjoy guessing games," Roland said with pride. "I think you inherit your intelligence as well as your looks from her."

"And my courage and strength from you," Bink said, appreciating the compliment.

Bianca walked sedately to the stage area. She was a handsome woman who in youth had been beautiful, and unlike the Queen she was genuine. Her talent was the replay, not illusion.

"So the distaff proves itself again," the Queen said, smirking at Crombie the woman-hater. "The prize is—" She paused. "Doorman, fetch the second prize. You should have had it ready."

Crombie's scowl became truly ominous, but he walked to a cabinet half concealed by seaweed and brought out a covered container.

"The prize is," the Queen repeated, then whipped off the cover. "A potted snapdragon!"

There was a murmur of well-meaning awe and envy from the ladies present as the plant's several flower-heads flexed about on their stems, snapping viciously. Snapdragons were very good for eliminating insect and animal pests, and served as useful guards for houses. Woe to the intruder who stepped in or near such a plant! But they did not take readily to potting, so that a special and rather difficult spell was necessary to confine them. Thus wild snapdragons were common enough, but potted ones rare and much prized.

Bianca showed her pleasure as she accepted the plant, turning her face away with a smile as a little dragon-head snapped at her nose. Part of the potting process included a spell to render the plant harmless to its owner, but it took a while for it to get to know that owner. "It's beautiful," she said. "Thank you, Queen Iris." Then, diplomatically: "You're beautiful too—but not the same way."

The Queen snapped her teeth in mock imitation of the snapdragon, then smiled graciously. She craved the recognition and praise of such established and reputable citizens as Bianca, for Iris had lived in semi-exile for years before assuming the crown. *"Now the top winner, servitor,"* she said to Crombie. "This time give it some flair, if you have any."

"The winner, with thirteen correct identities," Crombie drawled without flair, "is Millie the ghost." And he shrugged as if to express bemusement at yet another female success. He had made the count, so he knew the contest wasn't rigged. However, it was generally understood that the men had not been trying very hard.

The pretty, young-seeming ghost floated up. She was in her fashion both the youngest and the oldest of Castle Roogna's inhabitants. She had been in her teens when she died over eight hundred years before. When Bink first saw her she had been a formless blob of vapor, but since the occupancy of the castle by mortals she had shaped up until her outline was as firm and sightly as that of any living woman. She was a very sweet ghost, well liked by all, and there was applause at her victory.

"And the grand prize is—" The Queen spread her hands dramatically. "This certificate for one free Answer by the Good Magician Humfrey!" There was background fanfare, punctuated by magically augmented applause, as she handed the paper to the ghost.

Millie hesitated. Having no physical substance, she could not carry the certificate.

"That's all right," the Queen said. "I'll just write your name on it, and Magician Humfrey will know it's yours. In fact, he's probably watching us in his magic mirror at this moment. Why don't you ask your question now?"

Millie's reply was inaudible, for she could hardly speak above a ghostly whisper.

"Don't be concerned; I'm sure everyone will be glad to help," the Queen said. "Here—we'll write it down on the magic slate, and Magician Humfrey can respond in the same way." She gestured at Crombie. "Flunky, the slate!"

Crombie paused, but his curiosity made him go

along with it. He fetched the slate. The Queen conscripted the nearest centaur, who happened to be Chester (who had been trying without success to sneak a cookie from the refreshment stand without having it pickled), to transcribe the ghost's inaudible words. Centaurs were literate; many of them were teachers, so writing chores fell naturally to them.

Chester did not like the Queen's attitude much better than Crombie did, but he also played along. What possible Question could a ghost have for the Magician? He wrote in flourishing capitals: HOW CAN MILLIE LIVE AGAIN?

There was more applause. The guests liked that Question. It was a challenging one—and the Answer, given publicly, might provide insights for them all. Usually Magician Humfrey's Answers cost the asker a year's service, and were given only to the one who asked. This party was getting interesting!

The words disappeared as if erased by an invisible sponge. Then the Magician's Answer showed: THE REQUIREMENTS ARE 3REE: 1RST—YOU MUST HAVE THE TRUE WILL TO BECOME MORTAL.

It was evident that Millie did. She gestured imploringly at the slate to continue, so that she could know whether the other requirements were similarly easy—or impossible. Technically, as the common saying went, nothing was impossible with magic, but in practice some spells were prohibitively difficult. Bink yearned with her: he had once longed as ardently for a magic talent, upon which his citizenship, welfare, and self-respect then depended. To one who had died prematurely, but not expired, what a tremendous hope mortality might be! Of course, if Millie lived, she would also die, in due course. But really she would be completing the life she had started, so many centuries ago. As a ghost she was in hiatus, unable to affect her destiny materially, unable to love and fear and feel.

Well, no, Bink corrected himself. Obviously she did feel—but not in the fashion physical people did. She could not experience bodily pleasure or pain.

2COND, the slate continued, YOU MUST HAVE A

26

SPELL DOCTOR RESTORE YOUR TALENT TO OPTIMUM POTENCY.

"Is there a spell doctor in the house?" the Queen inquired, looking about, her points flashing. "No? Very well, errand boy—point out the nearest spell doctor."

Crombie started a snarl, but again was overcome by curiosity. He closed his eyes, spun about, and extended his right arm. It came to rest pointing northeast.

"That would be the Gap Village," the Queen said. There was a spell on the Gap that rendered the giant crevice that separated Xanth into the northern and southern sections unmemorable, but a spot counterspell had been applied to the Castle so that inhabitants and visitors could remember such things. The King would have had trouble governing properly if he could not remember so critical a feature of the landscape as the Gap! "Where is our transporter?"

"On my way, Your Highness," a man said. He sighted along the line Crombie was pointing out, concentrated—and suddenly an old woman stood before them. She looked about, bewildered by the people and water, for they were still in the undersea illusion.

"You are a spell doctor?" the Queen demanded.

"Yes," the old woman agreed. "But I don't do no doctoring for foolish people sunk in the ocean. Especially when I get yanked from my laundry without a—"

"This is King Trent's Coronation Anniversary Celebration Ball," the Queen said haughtily. "Now you have a choice, old crone: doctor one spell for us, and have the run of the party and all the food and fun you want, in a costume like this—" The old woman was abruptly garbed like a matron of honor, courtesy of the Queen's illusion magic. "Or *don't* doctor the spell, and this creature will pickle you." She held up the picklepuss, who hissed eagerly.

The old woman, like Crombie and Chester, looked rebellious, but decided on the expedient course. "What spell?"

"Millie's spell," the Queen said, indicating the ghost. The spell doctor studied Millie, then cackled. "It is

27

done," she said, smiling broadly so that all four of her teeth showed.

"I wonder what is so funny?" Roland murmured. "Do you know what Millie's talent is?"

"Ghosts don't have talents," Bink said.

"Her spell in life. It must be something special."

"Must be. I guess we'll find out, if she can fulfill the third requirement."

3IRD, the slate continued. IMMERSE YOUR SKELETON IN HEALING ELIXIR.

"We have plenty of that," the Queen said. "Lackey—"

The soldier was already on his way. In a moment he returned with a bucket of elixir.

"Now—where is your skeleton?" the Queen demanded.

But at this point Millie balked. She seemed to be trying to speak, but was unable.

"A silence spell!" the Queen exclaimed. "You aren't permitted to tell where it is! That's why it has remained hidden all these centuries!"

Millie nodded sadly.

"This is better yet!" the Queen said. "We shall have a treasure hunt! In which closet is Millie's skeleton? A special prize to whoever finds it first!" She pondered fleetingly. "I'm out of regular prizes . . . I know! The first date with Millie the mortal!"

"But what if a woman finds it?" someone asked.

"I'll have my husband the King change her into a man for the occasion," the Queen said.

There was an uneasy laugh. Was she joking—or serious? As far as Bink knew, the King could transform anything living into any other thing living—of the same sex. But he never used his talent capriciously. So it must be humor.

"But what about the food?" Chester demanded.

"That's it!" she decided. "The women have already proved their superiority, so they'll be barred from the treasure hunt. They'll start in on the refreshments while the men go look for—" But she saw Chester swelling up, and realized she was going too far. "Oh, all right, the men can eat too, even those with appetites like horses. But don't touch the Anniversary cake. The King will serve that—when the treasure hunt is over." She looked momentarily pensive, which was unusual for her; was she sure the King would perform?

The cake was magnificent: tier on tier of scintillating icing embroidered with a huge number 1, crowned with a magically lifelike bust of King Trent. The Queen always promoted the King's glory, because her own glory was a reflection of it. Some poor chef had spent a lot of effort organizing the magic for this ornate pastry!

"Picklepuss, stand guard over that cake, and pickle anybody who durst touch it," the Queen said, fastening the end of the puss's leash to the leg of the cake's table. "Now, men—on with the treasure hunt!"

Roland shook his head. "Skeletons in closets are best left undisturbed," he remarked. "I believe I will go congratulate your mother." He glanced at Bink. "You will have to represent our family in the treasure hunt. You don't have to search too hard." He made a little gesture of parting and moved off through the glowing currents of the sea.

Bink stood in place a moment, reflecting. It was evident his father knew there was something wrong, but was not commenting directly.

And what *was* wrong? Bink knew he had a good life, now, with a fine if variable wife and the favor of the King. Why did he dream of adventures in far places, of using the sword whose art he had been studying, of danger and even death, though he knew his talent would protect him from all genuine threats? What was the matter with him? It somehow seemed he had been happier when his future was in doubt— and that was ridiculous.

Why wasn't Chameleon here? She was near term, but she could have attended the Ball if she had wanted to. There was a magic midwife on the palace staff.

He decided. On with the treasure hunt! Maybe he could prove himself by locating that skeleton in the closet!

Chapter 2. Treasure Hunt

Now he had a challenge, however superficial. He had to start with his brain. Millie was not necessarily in a closet *per se*. Her bones had to be somewhere in the palace demesnes, because her ghost was here—but that could be anywhere within the moat or even the garden. Away from the regularly traveled sections. Unless the bones were buried under a floor or between walls. That seemed unlikely; the structure of the palace was quite solid, buttressed by durability spells; it would be a major undertaking to breach any floor or wall. Presuming that Millie had died suddenly, under suspicious circumstances (otherwise she would not have become a ghost), the murderer would have had to hide her body quickly, surreptitiously. No rebuilding of walls to conceal it! Old King Roogna would not have tolerated such a thing.

Where could a body have been hidden in minutes —so well as to withstand the scrutiny of centuries? The King's renovations had covered every part of Castle Roogna, converting it to the royal palace of the present kingdom; the restorative artisans could not have missed anything like this. So the feat seemed mechanically impossible. There could be no skeletons in these closets.

Bink saw that other men were already busy rummaging in all the closets. No use to compete directly with them, even if the skeleton were there.

Mechanically impossible—ah, there was the clue! Not magically impossible! The bones must have been transformed to something else, something innocuous, misleading. The question was, *what?* There were a thousand artifacts in the palace, and any one could be it. Yet transformation was major magic, and what Magician would be fooling around with a mere chambermaid? So her bones might after all remain in their natural state, or perhaps dissolved in solvent or ground up into powder. Regardless, there should be some clue to their identity, if only it could be correctly fathomed. Yes, a most intriguing puzzle!

Bink walked up to the refreshment table. There were tarts and donuts and cookies and cakes and pies and assorted beverages. Chester was stuffing himself. Bink circled the table, searching for something interesting. As he neared the Anniversary cake, the picklepuss hissed at him warningly. It was cat-bodied, with a snout that was green and prickly like a pickle, and its eyes were moist with brine. For a moment he was tempted to advance on it, to try his magic against its magic. He could not be harmed by magic, yet surely the feline would try to pickle him. What would happen?

No—he was not a juvenile daredevil compelled to prove himself by foolish exploits. Why force his talent to labor unnecessarily?

He spotted a smiling-face cookie and picked it up. As he brought it to his mouth, the smile became an O of horror. Bink hesitated, knowing this was merely another of the Queen's illusions, but loath to bite anyway. The cookie screwed its face in anticipation of the awful end; then when the bite did not come, slowly reopened one icing-dab eye.

"Here, puss—you take it," Bink said, extending the cookie to the leashed creature. There was a faint *zoop!* and the cookie was pickled, one of its eyes opened, the other closed. Now it reeked of brine. He set it down on the floor, and the picklepuss slunk forward and took the pickle-cookie in its mouth. Bink no longer felt hungry.

"Your spell is ailing," said a woman beside him. It was the old spell doctor, enjoying her unexpected participation in the proceedings. The party was theoretically open to all, but few garden-variety citizens had the nerve to attend. "But it is too potent for me to fix. Are you a Magician?"

"No, just a strongly talented nonentity," Bink said, wishing that were as facetious as it was intended to sound.

She concentrated. "No, I am mistaken. Your spell is not sick, just balked. I think it suffers from lack of exercise. Have you used it in the last year?"

"Some," Bink said, thinking of his recent escape from the moat-monsters. "Not much."

"You have to use magic, or you lose it," she said wisely.

"But what if there is no occasion to use it?"

"There is always an occasion for magic—in Xanth."

That hardly seemed true, for him, here in the palace. His talent protected him from most harm—but so did the favor of the King. So his talent got little exercise, and might indeed be getting flabby. His fight with the animated sword had been the first real occasion for his talent to manifest in some time, and he had sought to avoid invoking his magic there. So his moat dunking was about it. He remained a little wet, but the undersea decor concealed that. Would he have to seek danger, to keep his talent healthy? That would be ironic.

The woman shrugged and moved on, sampling other delicacies. Bink looked about—and caught the ghostly eye of Millie.

He went to her. "How is it proceeding?" he inquired politely.

At close range, the ghost was audible. Perhaps the movement of her white lips helped. "It is so exciting!" she exclaimed faintly. "To be whole again!"

"Are you sure being mortal is worth it?" he asked. "Sometimes when a person achieves his dream, it sours." Was he really addressing her—or himself?

She gazed at him with sympathy. He could see the other guests milling about beyond her, for she was translucent. Milling through Millie! It was slightly hard to focus on her. Yet she was beautiful in a special way: not merely her face and figure, but her sheer niceness and concern for others. Millie had helped Chameleon a lot, showing her where things were, what fruits were edible and what were dangerous, explaining castle protocol. It was Millie who had inadvertently shown Bink himself another facet of the Magician Trent, back when Bink had believed the man to be evil. "It would be so nice if you found my bones," Millie said.

Bink laughed, embarrassed. "Millie, I'm a married man!"

"Yes," she agreed. "Married men are best. They are—broken in, experienced, gentle, durable, and they do not talk gratuitously. For my return to life, for the first experience, it would be so nice—"

"You don't understand," Bink said. "I love my wife, Chameleon."

"Yes, of course you are loyal," Millie replied. "But right now she is in her ugly phase, and in her ninth month with child, and her tongue is as sharp as the manticora's stinger. Right now is when you need relief, and if I recover my life—"

"Please, no more!" Bink exclaimed. The ghost was striking right on target.

"I love you too, you know," she continued. "You remind me of—of the one I really loved, when I lived. But he is eight hundred years dead and gone." She gazed pensively at her misty fingers. "I could not marry you, Bink, when I first met you. I could only look and long. Do you know what it is like, seeing everything and never participating? I could have been so good for you, if only—" She broke down, hiding her face, her whole head hazing before his eyes.

Bink was embarrassed and touched. "I'm sorry, Millie, I didn't know." He put his hand on her shaking shoulder, but of course passed right through it. "It never occurred to me that your life could be restored. If I had—"

"Yes, of course," she sobbed.

"But you will be a very pretty girl. I'm sure there are many other young men who—"

"True, true," she agreed, shaking harder. Now her whole body was fogging out. The other guests were beginning to stare. This was about to get awkward.

"If there is anything I can do—" Bink said.

Millie brightened instantly, and her image sharpened correspondingly. "Find my bones!"

Fortunately that was not easily accomplished. "I'll look," Bink agreed. "But I have no better chance than anyone else."

"Yes, you do. You know how to do it, if only you put your marvelous mind to it. I can't tell you where they are, but if you really try—" She looked at him with ardent urgency. "It's been so many centuries. Promise me you'll try."

"But I—what would Chameleon think if—"

Millie put her face in her hands. The stares of the other guests hardened as the ghost's outline softened. "All right, I'll try," Bink promised. Why hadn't his talent protected him from this? But he knew the answer: his magic protected him from physical, magical harm. Millie was magical but not physical—and what she intended for him when she became physical would not ordinarily be construed as harm. His talent had never concerned itself with emotional complications. Bink would have to solve this triangle by himself.

The ghost smiled. "Don't be long," she said, and drifted off, her feet not touching the floor.

Bink spotted Crombie and joined him. "I begin to comprehend your view," he said.

"Yes, I noticed her working you over," Crombie agreed. "She's had her secret eye on you for some time. A man hardly has a chance when one of those vixens starts in on him."

"She believes I can locate her bones first—and now I have to try. Really try, not just dawdle."

"Child's play," Crombie remarked. "They're that way." He closed his eyes and pointed upward at an angle.

"I didn't ask for your help!" Bink snapped.

"Oops, sorry. Forget where I pointed."

"I can't. Now I'll have to look there, and sure as hell her bones will be there. Millie must have known I'd consult you. Maybe that's her talent: knowing things ahead of time."

"Why didn't she skip out before she was murdered, then?"

Good question. "Maybe she was asleep, when—"

"Well, you're not asleep. *You* could skip out. Someone else will find her, especially if I give him the hint."

"Why don't you find the bones?" Bink demanded. "You could follow your finger and do it in an instant."

"Can't. I'm on duty." Crombie smiled smugly. "I have woman problems enough already, thanks to you."

Oh. Bink had introduced the woman-hater to his former fiancée, Sabrina, a talented and beautiful girl Bink had discovered he didn't love. Apparently that introduction had led to an involvement. Now Crombie was having his revenge.

Bink set his shoulders and followed the direction indicated. The bones had to be somewhere upstairs. But maybe they still would not be obvious. If he did his honest best but could not locate them—

Yet would it be so bad, that date with Millie? All that she had said was true; this was a very bad time for Chameleon, and she seemed fit only to be left alone. Until she phased into her beautiful, sweet aspect, and had the baby.

No, there lay ruin. He had known what Chameleon was when he married her, and that there would be good times and bad. He had only to tide through the bad time, knowing it would pass. He had done it before. When there was some difficult chore or problem, her smart phase was an invaluable asset; sometimes they saved up problems for her to work on in that phase. He could not afford to dally with Millie or any other female.

He oriented on the room that lay on the line Crombie had pointed. It was the Royal Library, where the lore of centuries was stored. The ghostly skeleton was there?

Bink entered—and there sat the King. "Oh, sorry, Your Majesty. I didn't realize—"

"Come in, Bink," King Trent said, fashioning a warm smile. He looked every bit the monarch, even when half slumped over the table, as now. "I was meditating on a personal problem, and perhaps you have been sent to provide the answer."

"I lack the answer to my own dilemma," Bink said, somewhat diffidently. "I am ill-equipped to comment on yours."

"Your problem?"

"Chameleon is difficult, and I am restless, and some-

35

one is trying to kill me, and Millie the ghost wishes to make love to me."

King Trent laughed—then stopped. "Suddenly I perceive that was not a joke," he said. "Chameleon will improve and your restlessness should abate. But the others—who seeks your life? I assure you there is no royal sanction for that."

Bink described the episode with the sword. Now the King was thoughtful. "You and I know that only a Magician could actually harm you by such means, Bink—and there are only three people of that class in Xanth, none of whom wishes you ill and none of whom possesses the talent of animating swords. So you are not really in danger. But I agree, this could be very annoying. I shall investigate. Since you made the sword captive, we should be able to trace down the root of its imperative. If someone has co-opted one of the weapons of my arsenal—"

"Uh, I think that is where it came from," Bink said. "But Chester Centaur spotted it and took it—"

"Oh. Well, let's let that aspect drop, then; the alliance of the centaurs is important to me, as it has been to every King of Xanth throughout history. Chester can keep the sword, though I believe we shall turn off its self-motivating property. But it occurs to me that there is a certain similarity here to your own magic: whatever opposes you is hidden, using other magic than its own to attack you. The sword is not your enemy; it was merely the instrument of the hostile power."

"Magic like my own . . ." Bink repeated. "I suppose that could be. It would not be identical, since magic never repeats in Xanth, but similar—" He looked at the King, alarmed. "That means I can expect trouble anywhere, from anything, all seeming coincidental!"

"From a zombie, or a sword, or moat-monsters, or a ghost," the King agreed. "There may be a pattern here." He paused, considering. "Yet how could a ghost—?"

"She is to be restored, once I find her skeleton—and that may be in this room. What bothers me most is that I find myself tempted."

"Millie is a very fetching figure of a slip of a

woman," King Trent said. "I can well understand the temptation. I suffer temptation myself; that is the subject of my present meditation."

"Surely the Queen can fulfill any, uh, temptation," Bink said cautiously, unwilling to betray how freely palace speculation had dwelt on this very subject. The King's private life should be private. "She can make herself resemble any—"

"Precisely. I have not touched the Queen or any other woman, since my wife died." To King Trent, the word "wife" meant only the woman he had married in Mundania. "Yet there is pressure on me to provide an heir to the throne of Xanth, by birth or adoption, in case there should be no suitable Magician available when that time comes. I sincerely hope there *is* a Magician! I feel obliged to make the attempt, nevertheless, since this was one of the implied stipulations I agreed to when assuming the crown. Ethically this must involve the Queen. So I shall do it, though I do not love her and never shall. The question is, what form shall I have her assume for the occasion?"

This was a more personal problem than Bink felt prepared to cope with. "Any form that pleases you, I should think." One big advantage the Queen had was the ability to assume a new form instantly. If Chameleon had been able to do that—

"But I do not wish to be pleased. I want to accomplish only what is necessary."

"Why not combine them? Let the Queen assume her most provocative illusion-form, or transform her to it yourself. When there is an heir, change her back. There is no wrong in enjoying your duty, is there?"

The King shook his head. "Ordinarily, this would be true. But mine is a special case. I am not sure I would be potent with a beautiful woman, or *any* woman— other than one who closely resembled my wife."

"Then let the Queen resemble your wife," Bink said without thinking.

"My concern is that this would degrade the memory I cherish."

"Oh, I see. You mean if she was too much like your wife, she might seem to replace her, and—"

"Approximately."

That was an impasse. If the King could only be potent with his dead wife, and could not abide any other woman resembling her physically, what could he do? This was the hidden aspect of the King that Millie had shown Bink, way back when: his continuing devotion to his prior family. It had been hard, after that, to think of such a man as evil; and indeed, King Trent was not evil. He was the finest Magician and perhaps the finest man in Xanth. Bink would be the last to wish to disrupt that aspect of King Trent's being.

Yet the problem of an heir was a real one. No one wanted a repetition of the shambles resulting from lack of a well-defined royal line. There had to be an heir to serve until a suitable Magician appeared, lending continuity to the government.

"We seem to have a similar dilemma, Your Majesty," Bink said. He tried to maintain the proper attitude of respect, because of the way he had known Trent before he was King. He had to set a good example. "We each prefer to remain loyal to our original wives, yet find it difficult. My problem will pass, but yours—" He paused, struck by dubious inspiration. "Millie is to be restored by having her skeleton dipped in healing water. Suppose you were to recover your wife's bones, bring them to Xanth—"

"If that worked, I would be a bigamist," King Trent pointed out. But he looked shaken. "Still, if my wife could live again—"

"You could check how well the procedure works, as they try it on Millie," Bink said.

"Millie is a ghost—not quite dead. A special case, like that of a shade. It happens when there is pressing unfinished business for that spirit to attend to. My wife is no ghost; she never left anything unfinished, except her life. To reanimate her body without her soul—"

Bink was beginning to be sorry he had thought of the notion. What horrors might be loosed on Xanth if all bones were renovated indiscriminately? "She might be a zombie," he said.

"There are serious risks," the King decided. "Still, you have provided me food for thought. Perhaps there is hope for me yet! Meanwhile, I certainly shall not have the Queen assume the likeness of my wife. Perhaps I shall only embarrass myself by trying and failing, but—"

"Too bad you can't transform yourself," Bink said. "Then you could test your potency without anyone knowing."

"The Queen would know. And to fail with her would be to show weakness that I can hardly afford. She would feel superior to me, knowing that what she has taken to be iron control is in fact impotence. There would be much mischief in that knowledge."

Bink, knowing the Queen, could well appreciate that. Only her respect for, and fear of, the King's personality and magic power held her in check. His transforming talent would remain—but the respect she held for his personality would inevitably erode. She could become extremely difficult to manage, and that would not be good for the Land of Xanth. "Could you, er, experiment with some other woman first? That way, if you failed—"

"No," the King said firmly. "The Queen is not my love, but she is my legal spouse. I will not cheat her—or any other member of my kingdom, in this or any other respect."

And there was the essence of his nobility! Yet the Queen might cheat *him,* if she saw her opportunity, and knew him to be impotent. Bink didn't like that notion. He had seen King Trent's reign as the onset of a Golden Age; how fraught it was with liabilities, from this vantage!

Then Bink had another inspiration. "Your memory of your wife—it isn't just your memory of her you are preserving, it is your memory of yourself. Yourself when you were happy. You can't make love to another woman, or let another woman look like her. But if two other people made love—I mean, the Queen and a man who did not resemble you—no memories would be defiled. So if the Queen changed your appearance—"

"Ridiculous!" the King snapped.

"I suppose so," Bink said. "I shouldn't have mentioned it."

"I'll try it."

"Sorry I bothered you. I—" Bink broke off. "You will?"

"Objectively I know that my continuing attachment to my dead wife and son is not reasonable," the King said. "It is hampering me in the performance of my office. Perhaps an unreasonable subterfuge will compensate. I will have Iris make me into the likeness of another man, and herself another woman, and as strangers we shall make the attempt. Do you just indulge in the courtesy of maintaining the secret, Bink."

"Yes, of course, by all means," Bink said, feeling awkward. He would have preferred to have the King devoid of human fallibilities, while paradoxically respecting him *for* those weaknesses. But he knew this was a side of the King no other person saw. Bink was a confidant, uncomfortable as the position might be at times.

"I—uh, I'm supposed to locate Millie's bones. They should be somewhere in this library."

"By all means. Continue your pursuit; I shall seek out the Queen." And the King rose abruptly and departed.

Just like that! Bink was amazed again at the alacrity with which the man acted, once he had come to a decision. But that was one of the qualities that made him fit to rule, in contrast to Bink himself.

Bink looked at the books. And suddenly realized: Millie's skeleton could have been transformed into a book; that would account for its neglect over the centuries, and for Millie's frequent presence here. She hovered often by the south wall. The question was, which book?

He walked along the packed shelves, reading titles from the spines of the tomes. This was an excellent library, with hundreds of texts; how could he choose among them? And if he found the proper one, somehow, how could it be restored? It would have to be transformed first back into the skeleton—and that was Magician-class magic. He kept running into this: too much magic was involved here! No inanimate transformer was alive today, as far as he knew. So Millie's quest looked hopeless after all. Yet why, then, had the

Good Magician told her to use mere healing elixir? It made no sense!

Still, he had promised to try, though it complicated his personal situation. First he had to find the book; then he could worry about the next step.

The search took some time. Some texts he could eliminate immediately, such as *The Anatomy of Purple Dragons* or *Hailstones: Magic vs. Mundane*. But others were problematical, like *The Status of Spirits in Royal Abodes* or *Tales for Ghosts*. He had to take these out and turn over the pages, looking for he knew not what.

More time passed. He was not getting anywhere. No one else came here; apparently he was the only one following this particular lead. His guess about the books must have been wrong. There was another room above this one, in a turret, and Crombie's line intersected it too. Maybe there—

Then he spotted it. *The Skeleton in the Closet.* That had to be it!

He took down the book. It was strangely heavy. The cover was of variegated leather, subtly horrible. He opened it, and a strange, unpleasant odor wafted up, as of the flesh of a zombie too long in the sun. There was no print on the first page, only a mélange of color and wash suggestive of the remains of a flattened bug.

Quickly he closed the book. He no longer had any doubt.

The bucket of elixir was downstairs in the ballroom. Bink clasped the book in both arms—it was too heavy to hold in one arm for any length of time—and started down.

He met another zombie, or perhaps the same one as before. It was hard to tell them apart! It was coming up the stairs. This one he knew was real, because the Queen had not extended the masquerade illusion inside the palace, and no illusion at all upstairs. Now Bink suspected the one in the garden had been real too. What were the zombies doing out of their earthy resting places?

"Back off!" Bink cried, protecting the book. "Get out of the palace! Return to your grave!" He advanced

41

menacingly on the zombie, and it retreated. A healthy man could readily dismember a zombie, if he cared to make the attempt. The zombie stumbled on the stair and fell, toppling with grisly abandon down the flight. Bits of bone and goo were scattered on the steps, and dark fluid soaked into the fine old wood. The smell was such as to make Bink's stomach struggle for sudden relief, and his eyes smarted. Zombies did not have much cohesion.

Bink followed it down, pursing his lips with distaste. A number of zombies were associated with Castle Roogna, and they had been instrumental in making it the palace of the King. But now they were supposed to lie safely in their graves. What ghastly urgency brought them into the party?

Well, he would notify the King in due course. First he had to see to Millie's skeleton. He entered the ballroom—and found that the subaquatic motif was gone. The normal pillars and walls had returned. Had the Queen lost interest in her decorations?

"I've got it!" he cried, and the guests collected immediately. "What happened to the water?"

"The Queen left suddenly, and her illusion stopped," Chester said, wiping crumbs of green cake from his face. It seemed refreshments had been real enough, anyway. "Here, let me help you with that book." The centaur reached down with one hand and took it easily from Bink's tiring grasp. Oh for the power of a centaur!

"I meant the healing water, the elixir," Bink said. He knew what had happened to the Queen, now that he thought about it! The King had summoned her.

"Right here," Crombie said, bringing it out from under a table. "Didn't want crumbs to fall in it." The bucket was now on the floor beside the Anniversary Cake.

"That doesn't look like a skeleton," the manticora said.

"Transformed—or something," Bink explained. He opened the book while Chester supported it. There was a general murmur of awe. Some magic!

The spell doctor peered at it. "That's not a transfor-

42

mation. That's topology magic. I never saw such an extreme case before."

Neither had the others. "What is topology magic?" Crombie asked.

"Changing the form without changing it," she said.

"Old crone, you're talking nonsense," Crombie said with his customary diplomacy around the sex.

"I'm talking *magic,* young squirt," she retorted. "Take an object. Stretch it out. Squish it flat. Fold it. You have changed its shape but not its nature. It remains topologically similar. This book is a person."

"With the spirit squished out," Bink said. "Where's Millie?"

The ghost appeared, silent. She remained under the geas, unable to comment on her body. What a terrible fate she had suffered, all these centuries! Flattened and folded into a book, and prevented from telling anyone. Until the Queen's charade-contest prize had coincidentally opened the way.

Coincidentally? Bink suspected his talent was at work.

"Should the Queen supervise the restoration?" the manticora asked.

"The Queen is otherwise occupied, and must not be disturbed," Bink said. Actually it was the King he was protecting. "We'd better proceed without her."

"Right," Chester said, and dumped the book into the bucket.

"Wait!" Bink cried, knowing it was already too late. He had contemplated a gentle immersion. But perhaps this was best.

The dunked book shimmered. Millie the Ghost made an almost soundless shriek as she was drawn toward the bucket. Then the book inflated, absorbing elixir rapidly, opening and unfolding as its tissues filled out. The pages became human limbs and the heavy jacket a human head and torso, flattened horrendously but already bulging into doll-like features. Grotesquely it convulsed into a misshapen mannikin figure, swelling and firming into the semblance of a woman.

Millie the ghost, still trying to scream, floated into the mass, her outline merging with that of the forming body. Suddenly the two phased completely. She stood

43

knee deep in the bucket, as lovely a nymph as could be desired, and an astonishing contrast to what they had just seen. "I'm whole!" she exclaimed in wonder.

"You certainly are," Chester agreed. "Someone fetch her some clothing."

There was a scramble. A form came forward bearing a decayed robe. It was a zombie. Women shrieked. Everyone scrambled to avoid it.

Crombie charged forward, scowling. "You rotters can't come in here! Out, out!"

The zombie retreated, backing toward the Anniversary Cake. "Not that way!" Bink cried, again too late. The zombie came within range of the picklepuss, who snarled.

There was a *zoop!* and the zombie was pickled. Squirting putrid juices, it fell into the cake. The picklepuss struck again, pickling the entire cake as the zombie disappeared into it. Pickled icing flew outward explosively, spattering the guests. The picklepuss broke free of its leash and bounded onto the refreshment table, pickling everything it passed. Women screamed again. It was one of the foolish, enchanting mannerisms they had.

"What is going on here?" a strange young man demanded from the main doorway.

"Stand back!" Bink snapped. "The damn Queen's damn pickler is on the loose!" Now he saw a comely young woman behind the stranger. They were evidently gate-crashers.

Crombie was dashing up. "I'll get those idiots out of the way!" he cried, drawing his sword.

The picklepuss preferred to introduce itself, and to clear its own way. It bounded directly at the strangers. There was a zap—but this time it was the puss who was pickled, in a fashion. It landed on the floor, surprised, then flapped its wings and took off. It had become a deerfly, a delicately winged miniature deer.

"My cake!" the strange young woman cried.

Then Bink caught on. "The Queen!"

"And King!" Crombie agreed, appalled. "In illusion-costume."

What had Bink called the Queen, in his distraction? And Crombie had drawn his sword against the King.

But Queen Iris was already at the cake. "Pickled—with a zombie in it! Who did this thing?" In her outrage she let her illusion slip. She appeared before the crowd in her natural form, and revealed the King in his. Both were in dishabille.

Crombie the woman-hater nevertheless suffered a seizure of gallantry. He sheathed his sword, whipped off his jacket, and put it about the Queen's shoulders, concealing her middle-aged torso. "It is cool here, Highness."

Bink hastily proffered his own jacket to the King, who accepted as if this were a quite ordinary occasion. "Thanks, Bink," he muttered.

Millie stepped out of the bucket, gloriously naked and not cold at all. "I fear I did it, Your Majesties. The zombie came to help me, and the picklepuss got loose—"

The Queen gazed for a long moment on Millie's splendor. Then she glanced down at herself. Abruptly King and Queen were clothed royally again, she rather resembling Millie, he in his natural likeness, which was handsome enough. Bink knew, as did everyone present, that both were in borrowed jackets, with embarrassing portions of their anatomy uncovered, but now there was no sign of this. And, in another moment, Millie was also clothed in illusion, garbed like the chambermaid she was, yet still very pretty.

Bink nodded to himself. It seemed his suggestion about the King changing his own image for lovemaking had been effective. Except that the commotion surrounding Millie's restoration had interrupted it.

The Queen surveyed the ruin of the refreshments. Then she glanced obliquely at the King. She decided to be gracious. "So it worked! You are no longer a ghost!" She studied Millie again, appraisingly. "But you should be dressed for the occasion; this is not a workday for you." And Millie appeared in a fetching evening gown, glassy slippers, and a sparkling tiara. "Who found your skeleton?"

Millie smiled radiantly. "Bink rescued me."

The Queen looked at Bink. "Your nose seems to be into everything," she murmured. Then, more loudly: "Then Bink gets the prize. The first date with—"

She broke off, as well she might. Behind her, the pickled zombie had risen out of the cake. Even pickling could not kill a zombie; they were half pickled by nature. Clots of briny flesh dropped along with the pickled cake. One amorphous glob had dropped on the Queen's shoulder, passing right through the illusion-dress and lodging who-knew-where. This was the cause of the interruption in her speech.

Furious, the Queen whirled on the zombie. "Get out of the palace, you hunk of decay!" She shot a look at the King. "Trent, transform this monster! It ruined my cake!"

But King Trent was thoughtful. "I think the zombie will depart of its own volition, Iris. Procure another date for Millie; I have need of Bink's services in another capacity."

"But Your Majesty—" Millie protested.

"Make the substitute look like Bink," the King murmured to the Queen. "Bink, come to the library."

In the library, King Trent spoke his mind. "Here in Xanth we have a hierarchy of magic. As the most powerful Magician, I am King, and the most powerful Sorceress is my consort. The Good Magician Humfrey is our eldest statesman. But you, Bink—you are anonymous. You have equivalent magic, but it is secret. This means you don't have the status your talent deserves. Perhaps this constitutes a threat to your welfare."

"But there is no danger—"

"Not true, Bink. Whoever sent that sword constitutes a threat to you, though probably not a great one. However, your talent is powerful, not smart. It protects you from hostile magic, but has a problem with intangible menaces. As we know, your situation at home is not ideal at the moment, and—"

Bink nodded. "But as we both also know, that will pass, Your Majesty."

"Agreed. But your talent is not so rational, perhaps. So it procured for you what it deemed to be a better woman—and I fault its ethics, not its taste. Then it balked when you realized the mischief this would cause. So it stopped you from having your date with Millie. The reanimation of the zombie was part of this.

46

Probably the zombie was supposed to help you locate the skeleton, but then it had to reverse its initiative. There is no knowing what mischief might have resulted if Millie and the Queen had insisted on completing your date; but we do know the havoc would have seemed to be coincidental, because that is the way your talent operates. We might have had the whole palace collapse on our heads, or some unfortunate accident might have rendered Millie into a ghost again."

"No!" Bink cried, horrified.

"I know you would not wish that on so nice a creature. Neither would I. This is the reason I interceded. We must simply accept the fact that you can not date Millie, though your talent brought her back to life. I believe I have solved that problem for the nonce. It is obvious that Millie's talent is sex appeal; that accounts for her original untimely demise in ghost-generating circumstances. She shall not lack for male company—other than yours."

"Sex appeal!" Bink exclaimed. "That was why the spell doctor was so amused! She knew what sort of trouble there would be when she restored the spell! And that's why I was so tempted by her offer, despite—"

"Precisely. I felt it too—and I had just completed my liaison with the Queen, thanks to your suggestion. Here, your jacket." And the King gravely handed it back.

"It's my fault all the palace will know—"

"That I am virile as well as Kingly," Trent finished. "This is no shame. Now Iris will never know the weakness I might otherwise have shown. Obviously at such a moment, I should not have felt any attraction to another woman. I did feel it near Millie. So I knew magic was involved. But you, with a difficult home situation, and Millie's evident desire for you—Bink, I think we need to get you out of this region for the duration, at least until we get Millie settled."

"But Chameleon—I can't leave her alone—"

"Have no concern. I shall invite her to the palace, to be attended by my own staff. In fact I think Millie herself would be an excellent maid for her, until we

47

find a better situation. All we need to do is remove you from the stress and temptation that necessarily attend your presence here. Because your talent is powerful but disruptive to palace life, I am providing it guidance. Bink, I am directing you to commence your royal mission: to locate the source of the magic of Xanth."

King Trent paused, and Bink waited. Nothing happened. "I think my talent concurs," Bink said at last.

"Good," the King said, relaxing visibly. Only he knew the peril in trying to go against Bink's talent. "I shall assign you any facilities you require. Someone to protect you, since you may have to intrude on hazardous territory and face unmagical threats, and someone to guide you—" He snapped his fingers. "Chester the Centaur! His situation is very like yours, and you are friends. You can ride him, and you could not have a finer ally in danger."

"But the centaurs are not men; he may not choose to go."

"It is true that my power becomes nominal, in the case of the centaurs. I can not order him to accompany you. But I think he will go as far as Good Magician Humfrey's castle."

"Why?" Bink asked, perplexed.

"Because only Humfrey can tell him what his magic talent may be."

The King certainly kept up on things! "But that Answer would cost him a year's service!"

The King shrugged. "No harm in talking with Humfrey, though. Chester may go along with you, just to keep you company, and incidentally chat with the Good Magician while you are there."

Slowly Bink smiled. "And Cherie Centaur would never need to know!"

"You might discuss that aspect with Chester, at any rate." The King pondered momentarily. "And Crombie—he can point the way for you."

"I don't think Crombie could keep up with Chester," Bink said. "No man can match a centaur's steady speed over ground. And Chester would not want to carry two people—"

48

"Easily solved! I shall transform Crombie into a form that can keep up. A dragon—"

"That would frighten people and attract attention—"

"So it would. Very well, a griffin. There are a few tame ones, so people would not be too curious. That will deprive him of speech, but give him the power of flight: a fair exchange. And there is hardly a better fighting animal than a griffin, weight for weight. With a centaur and a griffin accompanying you, there should be no mundane threat you need fear." He paused again. "Even so, I think you had better consult Humfrey for specific advice. There might be more here than we have bargained on."

Bink found himself filling with excitement. Adventure, again! "Your Majesty, I'll find the source of magic for you; when can I start?"

"Tomorrow morning," King Trent said, smiling. "Now go home and tell your wife about your preemptive mission. But don't mention Millie the ex-ghost."

"I won't!" Bink agreed, smiling too. About to go, he thought of something else. "Do you know there is a magic mole hanging around the grounds?"

The King accepted this communication gracefully. "I had not been made aware of that. I have no objection, so long as it does not disturb the zombies' graves." Then he did a double take. "That zombie—"

"There was another in the gardens, where the pile of dirt was. Maybe the same one."

"I will institute an investigation in due course." He fixed Bink with a tolerant stare. "Any other important intelligence to impart?"

"Uh, no," Bink said, abruptly embarrassed. What was he doing, telling the King of such a minor matter? He had lost all sense of proportion!

Chapter 3. Nickelpede Chase

In the morning they commenced the mission: three males with woman-problems. All professed to be glad to get away from their situations and into adventure. Crombie especially liked his new form; he spread his wings frequently and took little practice flights.

Indeed, the soldier had much to be pleased about. His lion's legs were powerfully muscled, and his eagle's head was handsome with penetrating eyes, and the feathers of his wings were glorious. The plumage of his neck was blue, and on his back it was black, and on the front red, and the wings were white. A prettier monster could hardly be found in Xanth.

But this was the wilderness: no playground. The moment they departed Castle Roogna, the hostile magic closed in. Most of the paths in this vicinity had been charmed by order of the King, so there was little danger to travelers who did not stray from them. But Good Magician Humfrey was never keen on company, so there was no direct path to his castle. All roads led *away* from it, magically. That meant no safe passage.

Fortunately Crombie's talent of location could keep them going the right way. Periodically the soldier-griffin paused, closed his eyes, extended one wing or forepaw, spun about, and came to rest pointing. Crombie's directional sense was never wrong. Unfortunately it did not take note of the inconveniences of straight-line travel.

The first thing they ran into was a clump of hell's bells. The vines of the plants reared up, their bells ringing stridently. The tintinnabulation became deafening—and disconcerting. "We have to get out of here!" Bink cried, but knew he could not be heard above the noise. Chester had his hands to his ears and he bucked about, kicking at individual bells—but for every one he smashed, a dozen clanged louder.

Crombie spread his wings and flapped violently. Bink thought he was taking off, but instead the griffin dug all four clawed feet into the massed vines and hauled them violently upward. The vines stretched and the clangor of the bells became shrill, then muted. The tension prevented them from swinging properly, so they could not ring.

Bink and Chester took the opportunity to scramble out of the clump. Then Crombie let go and flew up, out of range of the bells. They were free of the hazard, but it was a warning. They could not simply barge ahead as if treading the King's highway.

They continued on, carefully skirting the tangle trees and noose loops. Now Crombie checked often for the nearest dangers as well as for the proper direction. In some cases they had to turn aside from seemingly innocuous places, ripping through itchweeds and sliding turf. But they trusted Crombie's talent; better itching and sliding, than some ignominious death.

Adventure did not seem quite as exciting, now that they were back in the thick of it. Or the thicket of it, Bink thought. There were many grimy little details and inconveniences that one tended to forget in the comfort of home or palace. Bink's thighs were getting sore from bouncing on the centaur's back, and he was uncomfortably sweaty.

When they got hungry, Crombie pointed out a soda tree growing in a patch of sugar sand. Chester took a sharp stone and poked a spigot-hole in the tree's trunk so that they all could drink from the spouting soda. It looked like blood, a shock at first; but it was actually strawberry-flavored. The sugar sand was too sweet, so it was possible to eat only a little. Crombie pointed out a breadfruit tree, and that was much better. The loaves were just ripe, so that they steamed warmly when opened, and were delicious.

Just when the three were feeling confident again,

51

danger came questing for them. Crombie's talent operated only when invoked; it was not an automatic alert. In this case the threat was a hungry dragon of medium size, land-bound and fire-breathing: about the worst enemy in Xanth except for a large dragon. Such monsters were the lords of the wilderness, and were the standard against which all other viciousness was measured. Had this been the largest variety, they would have been lost. As it was, against this middle range, a man and a griffin and a centaur had a fighting chance.

Still, why had the dragon come after them? Normally dragons did not attack men or centaurs. Dragons fought them, but only when they had to. Because though the dragon was lord of the wilderness, the numbers and organization and weapons of men and centaurs made them more formidable than most dragons preferred. Some men, like the King, had magic that could finish any dragon. Normally people and dragons left each other alone.

That anonymous enemy—could he have sent the dragon? Just a little nudge in the dragon's small, hot brain—and the result would seem like a normal wilderness accident. Bink remembered the King's analysis: that his enemy's magic was very like his own. Not identical, of course. But similar. Therefore insidious.

Then his eyes spotted a little mound of dirt, seemingly freshly deposited. The magic mole here? All Xanth must be infested with the creatures!

Both Crombie and Chester had fighting hearts. But Bink ultimately depended on his secret talent. The trouble was, that protection did not necessarily extend to his two friends. Only by joining the fray directly could Bink hope to help them, for then his talent might have to save them all to save him. He felt guilty about this, knowing that his courage was false; they could die while he was charmed. Yet he could not even tell them about this. There was a lot of this kind of magic in Xanth; it was as if magic liked to clothe itself in superfluous mystery, by that means enhancing itself in the manner of a pretty woman.

At any rate, they were caught in a level clearing:

the dragon's ideal hunting ground. There were no large trees to provide either shelter or escape, and no local magic they could draw on fast enough. The dragon was charging, a shaft of fire jetting from its mouth. One good scorch from that flame would be enough to roast a man entire. Dragons found roasted man very tasty, it was widely rumored.

Chester's bow was in his hands, an arrow nocked. He was well provisioned with bow, arrows, sword, and a length of pliant rope, and knew how to use them all. "Keep clear of the flame!" he yelled. "He's got to build up a bellyful between shots. When you see him start to heave, dodge sidewise!"

Good advice! Any creature the size of a dragon was likely to be a trifle slow maneuvering, and that jet of fire needed careful aiming. In fact they might be safest close to the monster, so that they could dodge around it too quickly for it to orient. Not *too* close, for the dragon's teeth and claws were devastating.

Crombie, however, also possessed claws, and his beak was as good in its fashion as teeth. He had the advantage of flight. He could maneuver faster than the dragon despite his mass, though of course his weight was only a fraction of that of the dragon. But he was not a natural griffin, so would not be able to react with the same speed and precision as a true one.

Bink himself was the weak link in the defense—or so it would naturally seem to the others. "Bink, stand back!" Chester cried as Bink charged forward. Bink had no way to explain to the centaur his seeming foolishness.

The dragon slowed as it came within a dragon's-length, its eye on its most formidable opponent: the griffin. Crombie emitted a shriek of challenge and looped toward the dragon's tail. As the monster's head turned to follow him, Chester fired an arrow into its neck. The shaft was driven with the power only a centaur could muster, but it merely bounced off the dragon's metallic scales. "Have to get a shot into its mouth—when there's no fire," Chester muttered.

Bink knew how dangerous that was. A clear shot into the mouth could be had only by standing more or less in front of the dragon while it opened its orifice—

and normally it only did that to bite or fire. "Don't risk it!" he cried. "Let Combie find us an escape!"

But Crombie was out of hearing, and busy, and in any event the ornery centaur was not in a mood to retreat. If they did not attack the dragon at their convenience, the dragon would demolish them at its convenience.

Bink moved in with his sword, seeking a vulnerable spot. The closer he got, the larger the dragon seemed. Its scales overlapped; they might be proof against most arrows, but maybe not against a blade angled up between them. If he could penetrate the armor in the vicinity of a vital organ—

Crombie dived at the dragon, screaming shrilly. The dive-bombing of a griffin was a thing not even a dragon could afford to ignore. The dragon whipped about, its whole body coiling smoothly, its head striking upward in a circle to intercept the griffin. The huge jaws gaped, but it was not quite set for fire; it intended to bite off a wing or head if it could. Its neck was bowed toward Bink, who was not regarded as a threat.

Chester shot an arrow into that mouth, but his angle was bad and the missile ricocheted from a tooth. Crombie came close, talons extended, banking to avoid those gaping jaws and score on an eye. Bink ran in close, and rammed his charmed point into the splayed scales beneath the neck.

The dragon's body was about as thick as Bink was tall, and each scale was the diameter of a spread-fingered hand, glossy blue and fringed with iridescence. Each edge was sharp as a knife. As Bink's blade sank in, those beautiful, deadly scales slid closer to his hand. Abruptly he realized that his hand could be sliced apart before his sword did critical damage to the monster. It was indeed a futile thing for a man to attempt to slay a dragon!

Bink's thrust, however, hurt, as the prick of a thorn could hurt a man. The dragon whipped about to focus on the annoyance. Its neck bent in an S-curve to bring the snout to bear on Bink. That snout seemed twice as large from this vantage. It was the height of his waist, and coppery, with two nostril-valves that hinged inward to prevent air from being expelled. The dragon breathed in through its nose and out through its mouth; probably a snootful of flames would destroy the delicate nasal passages, so the system had to be fail-safe. Below, the lips were burnished and lighter in color, as if alloyed with some sterner metal, able to tolerate the furnace heat of the dragon's breath. The teeth were stained scorch-brown, with black soot in the crevices.

The eyes were situated on the sides of the dragon's cranium, but the muzzle was channeled so that the creature could look directly forward to see where its fire struck. At the moment those eyes were on Bink, who stood there with one hand on the hilt of his sword embedded in the lower curve of the S-bend of the neck. Dragons varied in intelligence, like all creatures, but even a stupid dragon would be quick enough to connect Bink with the injury in such a circumstance. The nostril-valves closed with little pings. The mouth cracked open. Bink was about to be thoroughly scorched.

He froze. All he could think of was his sword: it was a good weapon, charmed to be always sharp and light in his hand, a gift from the King's arsenal. If he dodged out of the way, he would have to leave that faithful blade embedded in the dragon's neck, for there was not time to lever it loose. He did not want to lose it, so he hung on—and was unable to move out of the projected path of flame.

A roaring developed in the belly of the dragon. The throat opened into a round tube, ready to eject the column of fire. Bink was a standing target.

Then an arrow swished over Bink's still shoulder and down that open throat. A perfect shot by the centaur!

Too perfect. Instead of penetrating the softer lining of the deep gullet and punctuating a vital organ, the arrow disappeared into the stirring flame. Now that flame came out, a deadly shaft of golden light, destroying the arrow, hurtling toward Bink's head.

And the griffin crashed into the dragon's snout, bearing it down just as the fire emerged. The snout met the ground at Bink's feet. There was something like an explosion. The dragon's head was bathed in the backblast, and a small crater was gouged out of the earth. The griffin just missed having a wing scorched. Bink was left standing there, sword in hand, at the smoking rim, unscathed.

The griffin snatched Bink in his claws as the dragon reoriented. They were momentarily airborne as a second blast of fire passed beneath Bink's dangling feet.

Crombie could not support Bink's weight long on the ground, let alone airborne. "Find an escape!" Bink cried. "Use your talent!"

Surprised, the griffin dropped Bink in a pillow bush and performed his direction-pointing routine in midair. Meanwhile the dragon coughed out several dusty fireballs, sprayed particles of soot, cleared its pipe, and charged after them. Chester galloped beside it, trying to get in another good shot. It was evident that this dragon was too tough for the three of them together.

Crombie's right wing pointed to the side. "Squawk!" he cried.

Chester looped back and cruised by. "On my back!" he cried.

Bink leaped, and sprawled across the centaur's rump. He started to slide off, grabbed wildly, caught a handful of mane, and righted himself while the centaur galloped on, head held low. Bink almost tumbled forward, but clasped his knees tightly and held on.

He looked up—and saw the dragon charging headlong at them. The monster must have looped back too! "Chester!" Bink screamed in panic. "It's in front of us!"

"Front, hell!" the centaur yelled from behind him. "You're facing backward, dodo."

Oops. So he was. The dragon was following them, trying to catch up. Bink was holding onto Chester's handsome tail. No wonder the head had seemed low!

Well, it was a good way to watch the dragon. "The monster's gaining," Bink reported. "Where's Crombie pointing?"

"That's where I'm going!" Chester called back. "But I don't know how far it is!" His evident ire was understandable; he did not like fleeing an enemy, even so formidable a one as a dragon. If it weren't for Bink, the centaur would not have retreated at all.

Crombie had indicated the direction, but could not

know whether they would be able to reach the place of safety in time. Suppose the dragon caught them first? Bink feared his talent would have to come into operation again.

"That was the bravest thing I ever saw in a man," Chester called. Obviously he felt centaurs had elevated standards of bravery. "You stood right in front of the dragon's mouth, attracting his attention, and you kept absolutely still so I could get a clear shot around you. You could have been fried."

Or skewered by the centaur's arrow. But centaurs seldom missed their targets. "That wasn't bravery," Bink replied. "I was too terrified to move a muscle."

"So? And what about when you spiked your sword into old firesnoot's neck?"

That had resembled bravery. How could Bink explain that the protection provided by his devious talent made such acts easier? Had he really believed he might get killed, he might never have had the nerve. "I only did what you two were doing: attacking. To save my hide."

Chester snorted derisively and charged on. The dragon continued to gain. Had it been a flying one, they would have been lost—except that the flying dragons were smaller, and consequently less powerful. But *any* dragon was real trouble, unless the one being attacked had nullifying magic.

Now the dragon was coming within torching range. There was dirt on its nose, but its fires remained stoked. It opened its mouth—

Chester dropped into a hole. "Hang on!" the centaur cried belatedly. "It's a crevice too broad to leap!"

Evidently so. Bink narrowly avoided doing a somersault over Chester's tail, hung on, and landed with gut-jarring impact. The walls rose up rapidly on either side. They must have approached this chasm obliquely, so that it was easy to rush down inside it. This must be the escape Crombie had indicated. Indeed, the griffin was angling down to join them.

But the dragon followed them into the crack. Its long, sinuous body was well adapted to this type of aperture. There was no crevice a centaur could hide in that would be too narrow for the dragon. That made

57

Bink uncertain; could this be a diversion, and not the escape route?

Suddenly Chester skidded to a halt. "Don't stop!" Bink cried. "The monster's right behind us!"

"Some escape route that featherbrain picked for us," Chester muttered with disgust. "We'd better fight the dragon."

"We'll have to," Bink said, turning around to face the centaur's head. "We can't outrun it—"

Then he saw what had stopped Chester. "Nickel-pedes!" he cried with new horror.

The dragon saw the nickelpedes too. It skidded to a halt and tried to turn about—but the crevice was too narrow for effective circling. It might have looped up and over its own body, but that would have meant exposing its neck again, where it had already been stung.

Crombie came to land between them. "This was your way out, birdbrain?" Chester demanded as the nickelpedes scuttled close, forming living barricades wherever there were shadows, cutting off any likely escape.

"Squawk!" the griffin replied angrily. He understood both the language and the insult perfectly, though he could not reply in kind. He stood up, wings furled so they would not bang against the close walls and get smudged. He closed his eyes, whirled awkwardly, and pointed with a forepaw. But the paw was not firm; it wavered across half a circle.

A few bold nickelpedes attacked. Each was girt with about five hundred legs and a single set of pincers, and each had a taste for fresh meat. A single nickelpede could be killed, with a certain amount of effort and unpleasantness; a hundred were insurmountable without extraordinary armor or magic. But the attempt had to be made, for if there was one thing worse than being roasted by a dragon, it was being gouged by nickel-pedes.

The dragon youped. A nickelpede had clamped on its smallest front claw and was gouging out a disk of substance nearly an inch across. The dragon's claws were iron, but the nickelpede's pincers were nickel hardened by magic; they could gouge from almost anything. Chester chuckled grimly.

Then the centaur leaped high, emitting a cry like a neigh. Another nickelpede had scooped out a piece of one hoof. Chester came down, stomping the little monster hard. But the nickelpede scuttled to the side, avoiding the blow—while others attacked Chester's remaining hooves. And the dragon chuckled.

But their predicament was not funny. The crevice was deep, with a level footing below sheer vertical stone walls. It was too deep for Bink to jump out of. He might have made it by standing on Chester's back —but how would the centaur himself get out? The dragon could lift its head that high—but not its forefeet. Only the griffin might escape—except that the narrowness of the cleft prevented him from spreading his wings far enough. He had glided into a landing, but taking off required more vigorous action and lift. With Chester's help he might get high enough—but again, what about Chester? They were trapped as much by the situation as by the walls.

Very soon they would all be food for the swarm, if they didn't get out of here. Yet the bulk of the dragon blocked the exit. At this stage the dragon was fidgeting about, trying to hoist its body off the ground so that it would not get gouged in a tender place, while the nickelpedes went gleefully for its feet. Chester was performing similarly. So was Crombie, who could not fly at the moment. And Bink himself, whose extremities were the most tender of all. Where was his talent now?

"It's only the sunlight that holds them back," Chester said. "When the sun moves over, they'll all be on us."

Bink looked at the line of shadow. At the moment the sun was high, and there was only a small shadowed area. But that area was packed with the pinching monsters. Only one nickelpede in a hundred ventured forth into the light, scuttling across to the shadow of someone's body—but even so, there were a dozen or more coming.

Then Bink had an inspiration. "We must cooperate!" he cried. "All together—before we all get eaten together!"

"Of course," Chester said. "But how do we get rid of the dragon?"

"I mean cooperate *with* the dragon!"

Chester, Crombie, and the dragon looked at him, mutually startled. All of them were still dancing in place. "A dragon's too dumb to cooperate, even if it wanted to," Chester objected. "Even if there were any point. There's just a pilot light in the monster's brain. Why help it eat us?"

"There would have to be a truce," Bink said. "We help it, it doesn't eat us. The dragon can't turn about, it can't lift its body off the ground for any length of time. So it is vulnerable, just as we are. But it can fight the nickelpedes much better than we can. So if we protect its flank—"

"Flame!" Chester exclaimed. "Nickelpedes hate light—and flame has lots of light!"

"Right," Bink said. "So if we protect its dark side, and its feet—"

"And its back," Chester added, glancing at Crombie. "If it will trust us—"

"It has no choice," Bink said, moving toward the dragon.

"It doesn't *know* that! Watch out—it'll scorch you!"

But Bink, protected by his magic, knew he would not get scorched. He walked up to the nose of the dragon and stood before the copper nostrils. Wisps of smoke drifted up from them; there was a little leakage when the system was idle. "Dragon," he said, "you understand me, don't you? You can't talk, but you know we're all in trouble now, and we'll all get gouged to pieces and consumed by the nickelpedes unless we help each other fight them off?" And he jumped to avoid the onslaught of another nickelpede.

The dragon did not respond. It just looked at him. Bink hoped that was a good sign. He drew his sword, sighted at the nickelpede between his feet, and impaled it neatly on the point. The thing clicked its pincers as Bink lifted it, undead, and it strove to get at anything gougeable. From this vantage the pincers were circular; a nickelpede normally clamped onto its target with a few hundred legs and scooped inward to cut away a shallow disk of flesh. Horrible!

"I can nullify one nickelpede at a time," Bink continued, showing his captive to the dragon's right eye.

60

"I could sit on one of your feet and protect it. My friend the centaur could defend your tail. The griffin is actually a transformed soldier, another friend; he could watch for enemies dropping on your back, and crunch them in his beak. We can help you—if you trust us."

"How can we trust *it?*" Chester demanded.

Still the dragon did not react. Was it stupid, or comprehending? As long as it listened, Bink had to assume that all was reasonably well. "Here's what we have to do," he continued hurriedly, as the shadow advanced and the nickelpedes grew bolder. Three were coming at Bink's own feet now; it would be hard to spear them all in time. "The three of us must climb over you to get to your tail and back feet. Crombie will perch on your back. So you will have to let us pass, and tolerate our weight on your body. We'll do what we can to keep your scales intact. But the main job is yours. Once we get clear, you scorch the whole mass of nickelpedes in the crevice before you. Fry them all! They don't like light, and will clear out. Then we can all back out of here. Agreed?"

The dragon merely stared at him. Had it really comprehended? Chester took a hand. "Dragon, you know centaurs are creatures of honor. Everyone knows that! I give my word: I will not attack you if you let me past. I know Bink; even though he is a man, he is also a creature of honor. And the griffin—" He hesitated.

"Squawk!" Crombie said angrily.

"Crombie is also a creature of honor," Bink said quickly. "And we assume you are too, dragon."

Yet the dragon still stared at him. Bink realized he would have to gamble. The dragon might be too stupid to comprehend the nature of their offer, or it still might not trust them. It was possible it had no way to respond. They would have to gamble on the last alternative.

"I am going to climb over your back," Bink said. "My friends will follow me. The truce will hold until we all get out of this crevice."

Truce. He had learned to appreciate this mode of compromise over a year ago, when he and Chameleon had made truce with the Evil Magician. That arrangement had saved them all from disaster in the wilderness. It seemed no enemy was too awful to deal with in time of sufficient peril.

He addressed the silent dragon again. "If you don't believe me, scorch us now, and face the nickelpedes alone."

Bink walked boldly around the dragon's head to the base of the neck where the front legs projected. The dragon did not scorch him. He saw the wound he had made in the neck, dripping ichor that a nickelpede was greedily eating as it landed. The little monster was gouging disks out of the stone floor to get every last bit of the delicacy puddling there. The nickelpedes had to be the most rapacious monsters for their size in all the Land of Xanth!

Bink sheathed his sword after wiping off the impaled nickelpede, then stretched up his hands and jumped. His head and chest cleared the top of the leg, and he was able to scramble over the scales. Because they were lying flat, they did not cut him—so long as he did not rub them the wrong way. The dragon did not move. "Come on, Chester, Crombie!" he called back.

Prompted by his call and the encroaching nickelpedes, the two creatures followed. The dragon eyed them warily, but held its flame. Soon the three assumed their battle stations. Just in time; the nickelpedes had massed so thickly that the shadowed walls were bright with their highlights. The shadow was advancing inexorably.

"Blast out the passage ahead!" Bink yelled to the dragon. "We're protecting your flank!" And he drew his sword and speared another nickelpede on the point.

The dragon responded by belching out a tremendous wash of fire. It scorched the whole crevice, obscuring everything in flame and smoke. It was as if a bolt of lightning had struck. Nickelpedes screeched thinly as they fell from the walls, burning, some even exploding. Success!

"Very good," Bink said to the dragon, wiping his tearing eyes. There had been a fair backlash of hot gas. "Now back out." But the creature did not move.

"It can't back," Chester said, catching on. "Its legs don't work that way. A dragon never retreats."

62

Bink realized it was true. The dragon was limber, and normally it twined about to reverse course. Its legs and feet were structured for forward only. No wonder it had not expressed agreement to Bink's proposal; it could not perform. Without words, it could not explain; any negation would have seemed to be a refusal of the truce. Even a really intelligent creature would have been in a dilemma there, and the dragon was less than that. So it had shut up.

"But that means we can only advance deeper into the crevice!" Bink said, appalled. "Or wait until dark." Either course was disaster; in complete darkness the nickelpedes would be upon them in a mass, and gobble every part of their bodies in disk-chunks called nickels. What a horrible fate, to be nickeled to death!

The dragon's flame would not last forever; the creature had to refuel. Which was what it had been trying to do at the outset, chasing them. The moment its fires gave out, the nickelpedes would swarm back in.

"The dragon can't be saved," Chester said. "Get on my back, Bink; I'll gallop out of here, now that we're past the obstruction. Crombie can leap from its back and fly."

"No," Bink said firmly. "That would violate our truce. We agreed to see the whole party safe outside."

"We did not," the centaur said, nettled. "We agreed not to attack it. We shall not attack it. We shall merely leave it."

"And let the nickelpedes attack it instead?" Bink finished. "That was not my understanding. You go if you choose; I'm finishing my commitment, implied as well as literal."

Chester shook his head. "You're not only the bravest man I've seen, you're the man-headedest."

I.e., brave and stubborn. Bink wished it were true. Buoyed by his talent, he could take risks and honor pledges he might otherwise have reneged on. Crombie and Chester had genuine courage; they knew they could die. He felt guilty, again, knowing that he would get out of this somehow, while his friends had no such assurance. Yet he knew they would not desert him. So he was stuck: he had to place them in terrible peril—

to honor his truce with an enemy who had tried to kill them all. Where was the ethical course?

"If we can't go back, we'll just have to go forward," Chester decided. "Tell your friend to get up steam."

The irony was unsubtle—but Chester was not a subtle centaur. In fact, he was an argumentative brawler. But a loyal friend. Bink's guilt remained. His only hope was that as long as they were all in this fix together, his talent might extricate them together. Might.

"Dragon, if you would—" Bink called. "Maybe there's an exit ahead."

"Maybe the moon isn't made of green cheese," Chester murmured. It was sarcasm, but it reminded Bink poignantly of the time in his childhood when there had been what the centaurs called an eclipse: the sun had banged into the moon and knocked a big chunk out of it, and a great wad of the cheese had fallen to the ground. The whole North Village had gorged on it before it spoiled. Green cheese was the best—but it only grew well in the sky. The best pies were in the sky, too.

The dragon lurched forward. Bink threw his arms about its ankle to keep from being dislodged; this was worse than riding a centaur! Crombie spread his wings partially for balance, and Chester, facing the rear, trotted backward, startled. What was a cautious pace for the dragon was a healthy clip for the others.

Bink was afraid the crevice would narrow, making progress impossible. Then he would really have a crisis of conscience! But it stabilized, extending interminably forward, curving back and forth so that no exit was visible. Periodically the dragon blasted out the path with a snort of flame. But Bink noticed the blasts were getting weaker. It took a lot of energy to shoot out fire, and the dragon was hungry and tiring. Before long it would no longer be able to brush back the nickelpedes. Did dragons like green cheese? Irrelevant thought! Even if cheese would restore the fire, there was no moon available right now, and if the moon were in the sky, how could they reach it?

Then the crevice branched. The dragon paused, perplexed. Which was the most promising route?

Crombie closed his griffin eyes and spun as well as

he could on the dragon's back. But again his wing pointed erratically, sweeping past both choices and finally falling, defeated. Crombie's spell was evidently in need of the spell doctor—at a most inopportune time.

"Trust the bird-head to foul it up," Chester muttered.

Crombie, whose bird hearing evidently remained in good order, reacted angrily. He squawked and walked along the dragon toward the centaur, the feathers of his neck lifting like the hackles of a werewolf.

"Relax!" Bink cried. "We'll never get out if we quarrel among ourselves!"

Reluctantly, Crombie moved back to his station. It seemed to be up to Bink to decide on the route.

Was there a chance the two branches looped around and met each other? If so, this was a handy way to get the dragon turned about, so they all could get out of here. But that seemed unlikely. At any rate, if it were this way, either path would do. "Bear left."

The dragon marched into the left one. The nickelpedes followed. It was getting harder to drive them off; not only was the shadow advancing, the oblique angle of the new passage made a narrower shaft for the sunlight.

Bink looked up into the sky—and discovered that things were even worse than they had seemed. Clouds were forming. Soon there would be no sunlight at all. Then the nickelpedes would be bold indeed.

The passage divided again. Oh, no! This was becoming a maze—a deadly serious one. If they got lost in it—

"Left again," Bink said. This was awful; he was guessing, and it was getting them all deeper into trouble. If only Crombie's talent were operative here! Strange how it had failed. It had seemed to be in good order until they entered the crevice. In fact, it had pointed them here. Why had it sent them into a region that blanked it out? And why had Bink's own talent permitted this? Had it failed too?

Suddenly he was afraid. He had not realized how much he had come to depend on his talent. Without it

65

he was vulnerable! He could be hurt or killed by magic.

No! He could not believe that. His magic had to remain—and Crombie's too. He just had to figure out why they were malfunctioning at the moment.

Malfunctioning? How did he know they were? Maybe those talents were trying to do their jobs, but weren't being interpreted correctly. Like the dragon, they were powerful but silent. Crombie merely had to ask the right question. If he asked "Which road leads out of the maze?" it was possible that any of them did —or none. What would his talent do then? If he demanded the specific direction of out, and the escape route curved, wouldn't his pointing appendage have to curve about, too? There was no single direction, no single choice; escape was a labyrinth. So Crombie was baffled, thinking his talent had failed, when perhaps it had only quit in disgust.

Suppose Bink's talent was aware of this. It would not worry; it would show him a way to make Crombie's talent operate, in due course. But it would be better if Bink figured that way out himself, because then he could be sure that all of them escaped. That way, both friendship and honor would be preserved.

So now the test of his mettle was upon him. How could he solve the riddle of the balked talent? Obviously straight direction was not the answer to the question of out. Yet Crombie's talent was directional. He asked where something was, and it showed the direction. If direction were not the answer in this case, what was—and how could Crombie identify it?

Maybe he could use Crombie's talent to find out. "Crombie," he called around the dragon's body. "Where is something that will get us out of here?"

The griffin obligingly went through his routine, to no avail.

"It's no good," Chester grumbled. "His talent's soured. Not that it ever was much good. Now if *I* had a talent—"

Crombie squawked, and the tone was such that it was obvious that the centaur had been treated to a rich discourse on prospective orifices available for shoving such a talent. Chester's ears reddened.

"That's what you're along to find out," Bink reminded him. "Right now, Crombie's all we have. I think there's a key, if I can only find it in time." He paused to skewer another nickelpede. The things died slowly, but they didn't attack after skewering. They couldn't; their companions gobbled them up immediately. Soon it would not be possible to concentrate on anything but nickelpedes! "Crombie, where is something that will show us how to get out of here?"

"You just asked that," Chester grumbled.

"No, I modified the language slightly. Showing is not the same as—" He stopped to watch the griffin. For a moment it seemed Crombie's talent was working, but then his wing wavered back and forth and gave up.

"Still, we must be getting warm," Bink said with false hope. "Crombie, where is there something that will stop the nickelpedes?"

Crombie's wing pointed straight up.

"Sure," Chester said, disgusted. "The sun. But it's going behind a cloud."

"At least it proves his talent is working."

They came to another fork. "Crombie, which fork will bring us fastest to something that will help us?" Bink asked.

The wing pointed firmly to the right. "Hey, it actually worked!" Chester exclaimed mockingly. "Unless he's faking it."

Crombie let out another vile-sounding squawk, almost enough in itself to scorch a few nickelpedes.

But now the cloud covered the sun, sinking the entire cleft in awful shadow. The nickelpedes moved in with a multiple clicking of satisfaction and anticipation and garden-variety greed. "Dragon, take the right fork!" Bink cried. "Blast it out ahead of you, and *run*. Use up your last reserves of fire if you have to. We're on to something good." He hoped.

The dragon responded by shooting out a searing bolt of flame that illuminated the passage far ahead. Again the nickelpedes squeaked as they died. The dragon galloped over their smoking corpses, carrying Bink and Chester and Crombie along. But it was tiring.

Something sparkled in the dim passage ahead. Bink

67

inhaled hope—but quickly realized it was only a will-o'-the-wisp. No help there!

No help? Suddenly Bink remembered something. "That's it!" he cried. "Dragon, follow that wisp!"

The dragon obeyed, despite Chester's incredulous neigh. It snorted no more flame, for its furnace was almost exhausted, but it could still run at a respectable pace. The wisp dodged about, as wisps had always done, always just at the verge of perception. Wisps were born teases. The dragon lumbered through fork after fork, quite lost—and suddenly emerged into a dry riverbed.

"We're out!" Bink cried, hardly believing it himself. But not yet safe; the nickelpedes were boiling out of the chasm.

Bink and Chester scrambled away from the dragon and up and out of the gully, and found themselves in the ashes of an old burn. Crombie spread his wings and launched into the sky with a squawk of pure relief. The nickelpedes did not follow even the dragon; they could not scuttle well through ashes, and might get caught by returning sunlight. The party was safe.

The dragon collapsed, panting, in a cloud of ashes. Bink walked around to its snout. "Dragon, we had a good fight, and you were winning. We fled, and you pursued, and we all got caught in the cleft. We made a truce to escape, and you honored it well and so did we. By working together we saved all our lives. Now I would rather have you as a friend than an enemy. Will you accept friendship with the three of us before we part?"

The dragon looked at him. Finally, slowly, it inclined its nose slightly forward in an affirmative nod.

"Until we meet again—good hunting," Bink said. "Here, we can help you a little. Crombie, where is the nearest good dragon-prey—something even a tired dragon can nab?"

Crombie spun in the air and flung out a wing as he fell. It pointed north—and now they heard the thrashing of something large, probably caught in a noose-loop bush. Something fat and foolish, who would die a slow death in the loops if not dispatched more mercifully by the scorch of a dragon.

"Good hunting," Bink repeated, patting the dragon on its lukewarm copper nose and turning away. The dragon started north.

"What was the point in that?" Chester asked in a low tone. "We have no need of a dragon's friendship."

"I wanted it amicable, here," Bink said. "This is a very special place, where peace should exist among all creatures of Xanth."

"Are you crazy? This is a burnout!"

"I'll show you," Bink said. "We'll follow that wisp."

The will-o'-the wisp was still present, hovering not quite close enough to overtake. "Look, Bink," Chester protested. "We lucked out on that wisp—but we dare not follow it any farther. It'll lead us into destruction."

"Not this one," Bink said, following it. After a moment Chester shrugged, gave a what-can-you-do? kick with his hind hooves, and followed. Crombie glided down to join them.

Soon the wisp stopped at a glowstone marking a grave. As they approached, the stone lit up with the words HERMAN THE HERMIT.

"Uncle Herman!" Chester exclaimed. "You mean this is the place he—?"

"The place he saved Xanth from the wiggles," Bink said. "By summoning many creatures with his wisps, then setting a salamander-fire to burn the wiggles out. He gave his noble life in that effort, and died a hero. I knew the wisp would lead us here, once I recognized the burnout, because you are his kind and kin and the wisps honor his memory. Crombie's talent located the wisp, and the wisp—"

"Uncle Herman, hero," Chester said, his face twisting into an unfamiliar expression. The belligerent centaur was unused to the gentle emotions of reverence and respect. Almost, it seemed there was a forlorn melody played by a flute, enhancing the mood.

Bink and Crombie withdrew, leaving Chester to his contemplation in privacy. Bink tripped over a pile of dirt that hadn't been there a moment ago and almost fell headlong; that was the only sour note.

Chapter 4. Magician's Castle

Good Magician Humfrey's castle was the same as ever. It stood tall and slender, with stout outer ramparts and a high inner tower topped by embrasures and parapets and similar accouterments normal to castles. It was smaller than Bink remembered, but he knew it had not changed. Perhaps the problem was that his memory of the interior made it larger than his memory of the exterior. With magic, it was possible that the inside really was larger than the outside.

The magic access routes had been changed, however, and the hippocampus or water-horse was gone from the moat, its time of service expired. There was surely another creature standing guard inside, in lieu of the manticora Bink had known: the one at the Anniversary party. Even monsters had to give a year of their lives as fee for the Good Magician's Answers, and they normally performed as guardians of the castle. Humfrey did not appreciate casual intrusions.

As they came to the moat, the nature of the new guardian became apparent. Monster? Monsters! The water teemed with serpentine loops, some white, some black, sliding past each other interminably.

"But where are the heads, the tails?" Chester inquired, perplexed. "All I see are coils."

The three of them stood by the moat, pondering. What could a whole fleet of sea serpents have wanted to ask the Good Magician, needing his Answer so badly that all were willing to pay the fee? How had they gotten here? It seemed it was not for Bink and his friends to know.

Fortunately, this was not a hazard he had to brave.

70

Bink was on the King's business, and would be admitted to the castle as soon as he made his presence known. "Magician Humfrey!" he called.

There was no response from the castle. Doubtless the Good Magician was buried in a good book of magic, oblivious to outside proceedings. "Magician, it is Bink, on a mission for the King!" he called again.

Still no response. "The old gnome must be hard of hearing," Chester muttered. "Let me try." He cupped his hands before his mouth and bellowed: "MAGICIAN: COMPANY!"

The bellow echoed and re-echoed from the battlements, but the castle was silent. "He should be at home," Bink said. "He never goes anywhere. Still, we can check. Crombie, where is the Good Magician?"

The griffin went through his act and pointed—directly toward the castle. "Must be beyond it," Chester said. "If your talent's not on the blink again."

Crombie squawked, his blue hackle-feathers rising again. He stood on his hind feet and made boxing motions with his front feet, challenging the centaur to fight. Chester seemed quite ready to oblige.

"No, no!" Bink cried, diving between them. "We don't want to make a bad impression!"

"Hell, I wanted to make a good impression—on his feathery face," Chester grumbled.

Bink knew he had to separate the two combative creatures. "Go around to the other side of the castle and get another fix on the Magician," he told Crombie.

"Triangulate," Chester said.

Triangulate? Bink, accustomed to his friend's surly manner, had forgotten how educated centaurs were. Triangulation was a magical means of locating something without going there directly. Chester had a good mind and a lot of background information, when he cared to let it show.

The griffin decided that the word was not, after all, a scatological insult, and flew to one side of the castle and pointed again. Toward the castle. No question about it: the Magician was home.

"Better fly in and notify him we're here," Bink said. "We don't want to mess with those moat-monsters."

Crombie took off again. There was a small landing

area between the moat and the castle, but no opening in the wall, so the griffin mounted to the high turrets. But there seemed to be no entry there for a creature of that size, so after circling the tower twice the griffin flew back.

"I remember now," Bink said. "The windows are barred. A small bird can get through, but not a griffin. We'll just have to brave the moat after all."

"We're here on the King's business!" Chester exclaimed angrily. His unhandsome face was excellent for scowling. "We don't have to run the gauntlet!"

Bink was piqued himself. But he knew he could make it through, because of his talent. "It is my responsibility. I'll see if I can navigate the castle obstacles and get his attention, then he'll let you in."

"We won't let you brave that moat alone!" Chester protested, and Crombie squawked agreement. These two might have their rivalry, but they knew their ultimate loyalty.

This was awkward. They had no magical protection. "I'd really rather do it alone," Bink said. "I am smaller than you, and more likely to slip through. If I fall in the moat, you can lasso me and haul me out, quickly. But I could never haul *you* out, if—"

"Got a point," Chester admitted grudgingly. "Crombie can fly across the water, but we already know he can't get in. Too bad he's not strong enough to fly with you."

Crombie started to bridle again, but Bink cut in quickly. "He could carry your rope to me, in an emergency. I really think it is best this way. You can help me most by figuring out what type of monsters are in that moat. Is there anything in the centaur's lexicon about headless serpents?"

"Some—but the coils don't match the pattern. They look more like pieces of a—" Chester broke off, staring. "It *is!* It's an ouroboros!"

"An ouroboros?" Bink repeated blankly. "What's that—a fleet of sea monsters?"

"It is all one monster, a water dragon, clutching its own tail between its teeth. Half of it white, half black. The symbolism is—"

"But there are a score or more segments, all over

72

the moat! Some are in toward the castle, and some out near the edge. Look—there's three lined up parallel. They can't be pieces of the same monster!"

"Yes they can," Chester said wisely. "The ouroboros loops entirely around the castle—"

"But that would account for only a single-file line of—"

"Loops several times, and its head plunges below its own coils to catch the tail. A little like a mobius strip. So—"

"A what?"

"Never mind. That's specialized magic. Take my word: that thing in the moat is all one monster—and it can't bite because it won't let go of its tail. So if you're good at balancing, you can walk along it to the castle."

"But no segment shows above the water more than five feet! I'd fall in, if I tried to jump from segment to segment!"

"Don't jump," Chester said with unusual patience, for him. "Walk. Even coiled several times around the loop, the thing is too long for the moat, so it has to make vertical convolutions. These can never straighten out; as soon as one subsides, another must rise, and this happens in a progressive undulation. That's how the ouroboros moves, in this restricted locale. So you need never get wet; just follow one stage of the thing to the end."

"This makes no sense to me!" Bink said. "You're speaking in Centaurese. Can't you simplify?"

"Just jump aboard the nearest loop and stay there," Chester advised. "You'll understand it once you do it."

"You have more confidence in me than I do," Bink said dubiously. "I hope you know what I'm doing."

"I trusted you to get us out of the nickelpede crevice Crombie got us into," Chester said. "Now you trust me to get you across that moat. It isn't as if you've never ridden a monster before."

"Squawk!" Crombie cried, pointing a wing at the centaur. Bink smiled; he *had* been riding the centaur. Score one for the soldier.

"Just don't fall off," Chester continued evenly. "You'd get crushed by the coils."

"Um," Bink agreed, sobering. Even with his talent backing him up, he didn't like this. Walking the back of a moving sea monster? Why not walk the wings of a flying roc, while he was at it!

He cast his gaze about, as he tended to do when he sought some escape from what he knew he could not escape—and spotted another mound of earth. Angrily he marched a few paces and stepped on it, pressing it down.

But when a convenient loop offered, Bink jumped across to it, windmilling his arms in the fashion of a mill-tree to regain his balance. The segment of monster sank somewhat beneath his weight, then stabilized pneumatically. Though glistening with moisture, the white skin was not slippery. Good; maybe this walk was possible after all!

The flesh rippled. The section in front of him subsided into the water. "Turn about!" Chester called from the bank. "Stay with it!"

Bink turned, windmilling again. There, behind/before him, the loop was extending. He stepped along it, hurrying as the water lapped at his heels. This was like a magic highway, opening out ahead of him, closing behind him. Maybe that was the basic principle of such one-way paths; they were really the backs of monsters! Yet though the serpent seemed to be moving toward Bink's rear, the loop stayed in place, or drifted slightly forward. So he was walking fairly swiftly, to make rather slow progress. "I'll never get across this way," he complained. "I'm not even walking toward the castle."

"You'll get there," Chester called. "Keep your feet going."

Bink kept walking, and the centaur and griffin moved slowly around the moat to keep pace. Suddenly a loop developed between him and his friends. "Hey, I've crossed to an inner loop—and I never left this one!" Bink exclaimed.

"You are spiraling inward," Chester explained. "There is no other way to go. When you get to the inner bank, jump off."

Bink continued, rather enjoying it now that he had his sea legs and understood the mechanism. There was

74

no way he could avoid reaching the other shore, so long as he kept his place here. Yet what an ingenious puzzle it was; could he have solved it without Chester's help?

Abruptly the segment narrowed. He was coming to the end of the tail! Then the head of the ouroboros came in sight, its teeth firmly clamped to the tail. Suddenly nervous again, Bink had no alternative but to tread on that head. Suppose it decided to let go the tail, just this once, and take him in instead? The big dragon eyes stared briefly at him, sending a chill through his body.

Then the head was past, continuing its undulation into the water, and Bink was treading the massive neck, broad as a highway after the slender tail. Apparently this dragon, serpent, or whatever was independent of air; it could keep its head submerged indefinitely. Yet how did it eat, if it never let go of its tail? It couldn't be eating itself, could it? Maybe that had been its Question for the Magician: how could it let go of its tail, so it could consume the idiots who walked along its length? No, if it had the answer to that, it would have gobbled up Bink as he passed.

"Jump, Bink!" Chester called.

Oops—had the serpent changed its mind, let go, and come to gobble? Bink looked back, but saw nothing special. Then he looked ahead—and discovered that the body was twisting down and under the adjacent leg of the spiral. No more highway! He leaped to shore as his footing ended.

Now he was at the outer rampart of the castle. He looked for the great doorway he had encountered on his first approach to this castle, back before Trent was King—and found a waterfall.

A waterfall? How had *that* gotten here? He traced it upward and saw a ledge; the water issued from somewhere out of sight, to course down over the frame of the door.

Was there an aperture behind the sheet of water? Bink did not relish getting wet here, after traversing the whole moat dry, but he would have to look. He removed his clothing and set it aside, so that it would

not get soaked, then nudged cautiously into the waterfall.

The water was cool but not chill. There was a small
air space behind it. Then the wood facing of the door.
He explored the surface with his hands, pushing here
and there, but found no looseness anywhere. There
was no entrance here.

He backed out of the fall, shaking his head to clear
it of drip. Where could he go from here? The ledge
circled the castle, but he knew the wall was solid stone
throughout. There would be no access to the interior.

Nevertheless, Bink made the circuit, verifying his
suspicion. No access. What now?

He suffered a surge of anger. Here he was on the
King's business; why should he have to go through all
this nonsense? The old gnome-Magician thought he
was so clever, putting a maze around himself! Bink had
just about had it with mazes. First the Queen's, then
the nickelpede crevice, now this.

But at heart Bink was a practical man. In due course
the pressure of his anger ceased, like the steam of a
relaxing dragon. He came to look at the waterfall
again. This was no mountain, with natural drainage.
The water had to be raised by mundane or magical
means to an upper level, then poured out. Surely it
was a circulatory system, drawn from the moat and
returning to it. Could he swim in where the water was
sucked up?

No. Water could go where he could not. Such as
through a sieve. He could drown, if his body got stuck
in the water channel. Not worth the risk.

The only other direction was up. Could he climb?

Yes he could. He now noted little handholds in the
wood at the edge of the waterfall. "Here I come," he
muttered.

He climbed. As his head poked over the sill, he
froze. There on the roof squatted a gargoyle. The water
issued from its grotesque mouth.

Then he realized that this monster, like the
ouroboros, should not be dangerous if he handled it
properly. The gargoyle, assigned to water-spouting
duty, would be unlikely to chase him.

Bink clambered to the surface of the small roof. He

76

surveyed the situation from this firmer footing. The gargoyle was about his own height, but it was mostly face. The body was so foreshortened as to represent no more than a pedestal. The head was so distorted that Bink could not tell whether it was man, animal, or other. Huge eyes bulged, the nose was like that of a horse, the ears flared out enormously, and the mouth took up fully a third of the face. With the water pouring out like a prolonged regurgitation.

Behind the monster the wall of the castle resumed. There were no handholds, and even if he could scale it, he saw only barred apertures above. No particular hope there.

Bink contemplated the gargoyle. How had it gotten up here? It had no real hands or feet to use to climb the way Bink had. Was there a door behind it? That seemed reasonable.

He would have to move the monster away from that door. But how? The thing had not attacked him, but its attitude might change if he molested it. The gargoyle was more massive than he; it might shove him right off the roof. Too bad he didn't have his sword to defend himself; that was with his clothing, back beside the moat.

Should he climb back down to get it? No, he was sure that would not be wise; it would give away his intent. The gargoyle could move over and crunch his fingers as he ascended with the weapon.

Maybe he could bluff it. "Move over, foulface; I am on a mission for the King."

The gargoyle ignored him. That was another thing that was getting to Bink: being ignored. "Move, or I'll move you myself!" He stepped toward the monster.

No reaction. How could he back down now? Trusting his talent to protect him, Bink moved in beside the gargoyle, staying clear of the river of water spouting from its mouth, and applied his hands to its surface. The grotesque face felt like stone, completely hard. It was heavy, too; shove as he might, he could not budge it.

This monster was defeating him—and it hadn't even noticed him!

Then Bink had a bright idea. Sometimes creatures

were vulnerable to their own specialties. The gargoyle's specialty was ugliness.

Bink stood before it, straddling the river. "Hey, homely—here's what you look like!" He put his fingers in the corners of his mouth to stretch it wide while he bugged his eyes.

The gargoyle reacted. It pursed its lips to funnel the water toward Bink. Bink jumped nimbly aside. "Nyaa!" he yelled, puffing out his cheeks to make another ludicrous face.

The monster shuddered with rage. It shot another blast of water at him. Bink was tagged by the fringe of it, and almost washed off the ledge. This was, after all, a chancy business!

He opened his mouth and stuck out his tongue. "Haa!" he cried, unable to form anything much better while holding the expression.

The gargoyle was infuriated. Its mouth opened until it took up half the face. But with the opening that large, the water emerged at low pressure, dribbling down the ugly chin.

Bink dived forward—directly into that mouth. He scrambled upstream against the slowly moving water —and emerged into a reservoir tank within the castle. In a moment he had stroked to the surface and climbed out. He was inside!

But not yet safe. A cactus cat perched at the edge of the reservoir. It was about half Bink's height, with a normal feline face, but its fur was composed of thorns. On the ears the thorns were very large and stiff, like slender spikes. But the cat's real weapons were on its front legs: knifelike blades of bone projecting from the front, scintillatingly sharp. These obviously could not be wielded endwise like daggers, but would be devastating as slicers.

The thorn-fur was horizontally striped, green and brown, and this pattern carried over into the three tails. A pretty but dangerous creature; one that no cognizant person would pat casually on the head saying "Nice kitty."

Was this another guardian of the castle, or merely a houseguest? Cactus cats normally ran wild, slicing up cactus with their blades and feeding on the fermenting sap. Needle cactuses fought back, however, shooting their needles into anything that annoyed them, so they were natural enemies to the cactus cats. Encounters between the two were said to be quite something! But there was no cactus of any kind here. Maybe this was an animal soliciting an Answer from the Good Magician.

Bink tried to skirt it, but the cat moved lithely to the only apparent exit and settled there. So it seemed he would have to force the issue, regardless.

Suddenly Bink got mad. He had had enough of these obstructions. He was no mere supplicant, he was here on the King's business! "Cat, get out of my way!" he said loudly.

The animal began to snore. But Bink knew it would come awake instantly and violently if he tried to sneak past it. Cats were ornery that way. This creature was playing cat and mouse with him—and that made him madder yet.

But what could he do? He was no needle cactus, with hundreds of sliver-thorns to launch. How could he strike at this insufferable cat?

Needles. There were other missiles than needles.

"Then pay the consequence!" Bink snapped. He leaned over the reservoir and sliced his hand across its surface, scooping out a fierce splash of water. The droplets arched across the room and splatted against the wall beside the sleeping cat.

The creature rose up with a screech of sheerest feline fury. Sparks radiated from its ears. Most cats hated water, other than small tame amounts for drinking, and desert cats were enraged by it. The thing charged Bink, its forelimb blades gleaming.

Bink scooped another volley of liquid at it. The cat leaped straight up in horror, letting the splash pass under. Oh, it was ecstatically angry now!

"We can handle this two ways, Cactus," Bink said calmly, his hand ready by the water. "Either I can soak you down thoroughly—or you can stand and let me pass. Or any combination of the two."

The cat snarled. It looked at Bink, then at the water. Finally it affected loss of interest, in the manner of balked felines, and stalked to the side, all three tails standing stiffly.

"Very good, Cactus," Bink said. "But a word to the cunning: if I were to be attacked on the way, I should simply have to grab my antagonist and plunge into the pool and drown him, whatever the mutual cost. That would be inconvenient, and I hope it does not become necessary."

The cat pretended not to hear. It settled down again to sleep.

Bink walked toward the door, affecting a nonchalance similar to that of the cactus cat, but was wary. Fortunately he had bluffed it out; the cat did not move.

Now he was past the hurdles. He explored the castle until he located the Good Magician Humfrey. The man was gnomelike, perched on top of three huge tomes so as to gain the elevation he needed to pore over a fourth. He was old, perhaps the oldest man in the Land of Xanth, with skin wrinkled and mottled. But he was a fine and honest Magician, and Bink knew him to be a kindly individual under all his gruffness.

"Magician!" Bink exclaimed, still irked by the challenge of entry. "Why don't you pay attention to who's visiting! I had to run your infernal gauntlet—and I'm not even coming as a supplicant. I'm on the King's business."

Humfrey looked up, rubbing one reddish eye with a gnarled little hand. "Oh, hello, Bink. Why haven't you visited me before this?"

"We were yelling across the moat! You never answered!"

Humfrey frowned. "Why should I answer a transformed griffin who squawks in a manner that would make a real griffin blush? Why should I acknowledge the bellow of an ornery centaur? The one has no Question, and the other doesn't want to pay for his. Both are wasting my time."

"So you were aware of us all the time!" Bink exclaimed, half-angry, half-admiring, with a little indefinable emotion left over. What a personality this was! "You let me struggle through the whole needless route—"

"Needless, Bink? You come on a mission that will cost me an inordinate amount of time, and will threaten the welfare of Xanth itself. Why should I encourage you in such folly?"

"I don't need encouragement!" Bink cried hotly. "All I need is advice—because the King thought that was best."

The Good Magician shook his head. "The King is a remarkably savvy customer. You need more than advice, Bink."

"Well, all I need from *you* is advice!"

"You shall have it, and without charge: forget this mission."

"I can't forget this mission! I'm on assignment for the—"

"So you said. I did tell you that you needed more than advice. You're as ornery as your friends. Why didn't you leave that poor dragon alone?"

"Leave the poor—" Bink started indignantly. Then he laughed. "You're some character, Magician! Now stop teasing me and tell me why, since you obviously have been well aware of my progress, you did not let us into the castle the easy way."

"Because I hate to be disturbed for minor matters. Had you been balked by my routine defenses, you could hardly have possessed the will to pursue your mission properly. But as I feared, you persevered. What started as a minor diversion with a shapely ghost has become a serious quest—and the result is opaque even to my magic. I queried Beauregard on the matter, and he got so upset I had to rebottle him before he had a nervous breakdown."

Beauregard—that was the bespectacled demon corked in a container, highly educated. Bink began to feel uncomfortable. "What could so shake up a demon?"

"The end of Xanth," Humfrey said simply.

"But all I'm looking for is the source of magic," Bink protested. "I'm not going to do anything to harm Xanth. I love Xanth!"

"You weren't going to install the Evil Magician as

81

King, last time you were here," Humfrey reminded him. "Your minor personal quests have a way of getting out of hand."

"You mean this present mission is going to be worse than the last one?" Bink asked, feeling both excited and appalled. He had only wanted to find his own talent, before.

The Magician nodded soberly. "So it would seem. I can not fathom in what precise manner your quest will threaten Xanth, but am certain the risks are extraordinary."

Bink thought of giving up the quest and returning to Chameleon, ugly and sharp of tongue as she was at the moment, with Millie the nonghost hovering near. Suddenly he became much more interested in the source of the magic of Xanth. "Thanks for your advice. I'm going on."

"Less hasty, Bink! That was not my magic advice; that was just common sense, for which I make no charge. I knew you would ignore it."

Bink found it hard at times not to get impatient with the Good Magician. "Let's have your magic Answer, then."

"And what do you proffer for payment?"

"Payment!" Bink expostulated. "This is—"

"The King's business," the Magician finished. "Be realistic, Bink. The King is merely getting you out of his hair for a while until your home life sweetens up. He can't have you tearing up his palace every time he tries to make out with the Queen. That hardly warrants my waiver of fee."

Only a foolish man tried to argue with a Magician whose talent was information. Bink argued. "The King merely timed the mission conveniently. My job always has been to seek out the source of magic; it just took me a while to get around to it. It is important for the King to have this knowledge. Now that I'm actually on the quest, the authority of the King is behind it, and he can call on your resources if he chooses. You knew that when you helped make him King."

Humfrey shook his head. "Trent has become arrogant in his power. He draws ruthlessly on the talents of others to forward his purposes." Then he smiled.

"In other words, he is exactly the kind of monarch Xanth needs. He does not plead or petition, he commands. I as a loyal citizen must support that exercise of power." He glanced at Bink. "However capriciously it happens to be exercised. Thus my fee becomes forfeit to the good of Xanth, though in this case I fear it is the bad of Xanth."

This capitulation was too sudden and too amiable. There had to be a catch. "What is your Answer, then?"

"What is your Question?"

Bink choked on a mouthful of air. "What do I need for this quest?" he spluttered.

"Your quest can not be successful unless you take a Magician along."

"Take a Magician!" Bink exclaimed. "There are only three Magician-class people in Xanth, and two of them are the King and Queen! I can't—" He broke off, realizing. *"You?"*

"I told you this was going to cost me time!" Humfrey grumbled. "All my arcane researches interrupted, my castle mothballed—because you can't wait a few days for your wife to finish her pregnancy and get sweet and pretty again."

"You old rogue!" Bink cried. "You *want* to come!"

"I hardly made that claim," the Magician said sourly. "The fact is, this quest is too important to allow it to be bungled by an amateur, as well the King understood when he sent you here. Since there is no one else of suitable expertise available, I am forced to make the sacrifice. There is no necessity, however, that I be gracious about it."

"But you could have sought the source of magic anytime! You didn't have to co-opt the quest right when I—"

"I co-opt nothing. It is your quest; I merely accompany you, as an emergency resource."

"You mean you're not taking over?"

"What do I want with leadership? I shall stick to my own business, leaving the pesky details of management and routing to you, until my resources are needed—which I trust will not be soon or often."

Now Bink was uncertain how serious Humfrey was.

Surely a man who specialized in magical information would be seriously interested in the source of magic—but certainly the Good Magician liked his convenience and privacy, as his castle and mode of operation testified. Probably Humfrey was torn between desires for isolation and knowledge, so reacted negatively while doing what he deemed to be the right thing. No sense in aggravating the situation. The man would certainly be an incalculable asset on a quest of this nature. "I am sorry to be the agent of such inconvenience to you, but glad to have your help. Your expertise is vastly greater than mine."

"Umph," Humfrey agreed, trying not to seem mollified. "Let's get on with it. Go tell the troll to let down the drawbridge for your companions."

"Uh, there is one other thing," Bink said. "Someone may be trying to kill me—"

"And you want to know who."

"Yes. And why. I don't like—"

"That is not the King's business. It will have to be covered by a separate fee."

Oh. Just when Bink had begun to suspect there was a decent streak in the Good Magician, he had this confirmation of the man's mercenary nature. One year of service for the Answer? Bink preferred to locate and deal with his enemy himself. "Forget it," he said.

"It is already forgotten," Humfrey said graciously.

Miffed, Bink trekked downstairs, found the troll, and gave it the instruction. The brute winched down the bridge. Where the drawbridge mechanism was Bink did not know, as it had not been apparent from the outside, and the troll stood in a chamber near the center of the castle. There had to be magical augmentation to connect what the troll did to what the bridge did. But it worked, and Chester and Crombie entered at last, emerging from a gate that opened from the center of the castle. How could there be an opening here, with no hole through the wall? The Magician was evidently squandering a lot of magic here! Maybe some clever technician had brought a Question, and constructed this mechanism in fee.

"I knew you'd come through, Bink!" the centaur

said. "What did the old gnome say about your quest?"

"He's coming with me."

Chester shook his head. "You're in trouble."

The Magician came downstairs to meet them. "So you want to know your obscene talent," he said to the centaur. "What fee do you offer the old gnome?"

Chester was for once abashed. "I'm not sure I— centaurs aren't supposed to—"

"Aren't supposed to be wishy-washy?" Humfrey asked cuttingly.

"Chester just came along to give me a ride," Bink said. "And fight dragons."

"Bink will still need a ride," Humfrey said. "Since I am now associated with this quest, it behooves me to arrange for it. I proffer you this deal: in lieu of the customary year's service for the Answer, I will accept service for the duration of this quest."

Chester was startled. "You mean I do have a talent? A magic one?"

"Indubitably."

"And you know it already? What it is?"

"I do."

"Then—" But the centaur paused. "I might figure it out for myself, if it was so easy for you to do. Why should I pay you for it?"

"Why, indeed," the Magician agreed.

"But if I don't figure it out, and if Bink gets in trouble because he meets a dragon when I'm not there—"

"I would love to let you stew indefinitely in your dilemma," Humfrey said. "But I am in a hurry and Bink needs a ride, so I'll cut it short. Undertake the service I require, in advance of my Answer. If you fail to solve your talent yourself, I will tell you at the termination of the quest—or any prior time you so request. If you do solve it yourself, I will provide a second Answer to whatever other question you may ask. Thus you will in effect have two Answers for the price of one."

Chester considered momentarily. "Done," he agreed. "I like adventure anyway."

The Magician turned to Crombie. "Now you are directly in the King's service, so are committed for the duration. He has given you a fine form, but it lacks intelligible speech. I believe it would be better for you to be more communicative. Accordingly, meet another of my fee-servitors: Grundy the Golem." A miniature man-figure appeared, his whole height hardly the span of an ordinary man's hand. He seemed to have been formed from bits of string and clay and wood and other refuse, but he was animate.

The griffin looked at the golem with a certain surprised contempt. One bite of that eagle's beak could sever all four appendages from the figure. "Squawk!" Crombie remarked.

"Same to you, birdbeak," the golem said without special emphasis, as if he didn't really care.

"Grundy's talent is translation," the Magician explained. "I shall assign him to render the soldier's griffin-speech into human speech, so we can better understand him. He already understands us, as so many animals do, so no reverse translation is required. The golem is small enough for any of us to carry without strain, so his transportation will be no problem. Bink will ride the centaur, and I will ride the griffin. That way we shall make expeditious progress."

And so, efficiently, it was arranged. The quest for the source of the magic of Xanth had begun.

Chapter 5. Golem Heights

They stood outside the castle, across the moat, watching while the Magician mothballed his residence. The ouroboros and other creatures under fee had been granted leaves of absence and were already gone. Humfrey fumbled in his clothing, showing a large heavy belt containing many pockets, and drew from this belt a closed vial or narrow bottle. He applied his thumbs to its cork until it popped free.

Smoke swirled out, looming high into the sky. Then it coalesced into the largest moth Bink had ever imagined, with a wingspan that cast the entire castle into shadow. The creature flew up over the castle and dropped a ball. As the ball fell near the highest turret it exploded. Gray-white streamers shot out in a huge sphere, drifting down to touch every part of the castle. Then they drew in tight, and suddenly the whole edifice was sheathed in a silky net, and looked like a giant tent. A cold, bitter odor emanated from it, smelling vaguely disinfectant.

"There," Humfrey said with grudging satisfaction. "That'll keep a hundred years, if it has to."

"A hundred years!" Chester exclaimed. "Is that how long you figure this mission will take?"

"Come on, come on, we're wasting time," the Good Magician grumped.

Bink, astride the centaur, looked across at the griffin. "What he means, Crombie, is that we need to know the direction of the source of magic. The mission should be accomplished in a few days, with your help."

The griffin squawked irately. "Well, why didn't the

old fool say so?" the golem translated promptly. He shared the griffin's back with the Magician, as the two together massed barely half what Bink did.

"Well spoken, soldier," Chester muttered low.

Crombie whirled, almost throwing off his riders. "That way," Grundy said, pointing—around in a continuing circle, his tiny arm settling nowhere.

"Oh, no," Chester muttered. "His talent's on the blink again."

"It is not malfunctioning," Humfrey snapped. "You asked the wrong question."

Bink's brow furrowed. "We had some trouble that way before. What is the right question?"

"It's your job to pursue this quest," Humfrey said. "I must conserve my information for emergencies." And he settled down comfortably amid the feathers of the griffin's back and closed his eyes.

The Good Magician remained his taciturn self. He was out of the habit of helping anyone without his fee, even when he himself might benefit from such help. Now Bink was on the spot again; he had to figure out how to make Crombie's talent work—while the Magician snoozed.

Before, in the nickelpede cleft, Crombie had fouled up because there had been no single direction for escape. Was that the case now—no single source for magic? If so, that would be very hard to locate. But the cynosure of this group was on him; he had to perform, and in a hurry. It was evident that the Good Magician had done him no particular favor by leaving the leadership of the quest to Bink. "Where is the most direct route to the source of magic?"

This time the griffin's wing pointed down at an angle.

So that was why there was no horizontal direction; the source was not across, but down. Yet that was not much help. They couldn't dig down very far, very fast. They would have to get a person whose talent was magic-tunneling, and that would mean delay and awkwardness. This group was already larger than Bink had anticipated. Better to find a natural route.

"Where is there an access to this source, from the surface?" Bink asked.

The wing began to vibrate back and forth. "The nearest one!" Bink amended hastily. The wing stabilized, pointing roughly south.

"The heart of the unexplored wilderness," Chester said. "I should have known. Maybe I should take my Answer now and quit."

Crombie squawked. "Birdbeak says if you take your stupid Answer now, you *can't* quit, horserear."

Chester swelled up angrily. "Birdbeak said that? You tell him for me he has bird droppings for brains, and—"

"Easy," Bink cautioned the centaur. "Crombie needs no translation for your words."

"Actually he called you an ass," Grundy said helpfully. "I assume he meant your rear end, which is about as asinine as—"

The griffin squawked again. "Oops, my error," the golem said. "He referred to your *front* end."

"Listen, birdbrain!" Chester shouted. "I don't need your ignorant opinion! Why don't you take it and stuff it—"

But Crombie was squawking at the same time. The two faced off aggressively. The centaur was bigger and more muscular than the griffin, but the griffin was probably the more deadly fighter, for he had the mind of a trained human soldier in the body of a natural combat creature.

"Squawk!" Bink screamed. "I mean, stop! The golem is just making trouble. Obviously the word Crombie used was 'centaur.' Isn't that so, Crombie?"

Crombie squawked affirmatively. "Spoilsport," Grundy muttered, speaking for himself. "Just when it was getting interesting."

"Never mind that," Bink said. "Do you admit I was correct, Golem?"

"A centaur is an ass—front *and* rear," Grundy said sullenly. "It depends on whether you are defining it intellectually or physically."

"I think I will squeeze your big loud mouth into a small silent ball," Chester said, reaching for the golem.

"You can't do that, muleface!" Grundy protested. "I'm on the dwarf's business!"

Chester paused, seeing the Good Magician stir. "Whose business?"

"This midget's business!" Grundy said, gesturing back at Humfrey with a single stiffened finger.

Chester looked at Humfrey, feigning perplexity. "Sir, how is it you accept such insults from a creature who works for you?"

"Oops," the golem muttered, discovering the trap. "I thought he was asleep."

"The golem has no personal reality," Humfrey said. "Therefore his words carry no personal onus. One might as well get angry at a lump of clay."

"That's telling him, imp," Grundy agreed. But he seemed chastened.

"Let's get on with our quest," Bink suggested as the Good Magician closed his eyes again. Privately he wondered how it was that an unreal construct, the golem, could be in fee to the Magician. Grundy must have asked a Question, and had an Answer—but what could have motivated this magical entity to seek such information?

Then Bink had a minor inspiration as they trekked south. "Crombie, someone or something has been trying to eliminate me. I think that's why the dragon came after us. Can you point out where that enemy is?"

"Squawk!" Crombie agreed. He whirled, and the Good Magician wobbled on his back but did not wake up. When the wing stabilized, it pointed—the same direction as it had for the source of magic.

"It seems," Chester said gravely, "that it is your mission your enemy opposes. Does that affect your attitude?"

"Yes," Bink said. "It makes me twice as determined as before." Though he remembered that the sword had attacked him before he set out on this quest. Had his enemy anticipated him? That would be grim news indeed, implying more than ordinary strategy or magic. "Let's get on with it."

Near the Magician's castle the terrain was fairly quiet, but as they penetrated the wilderness it changed. High brush grew up, obscuring the view, and as they passed it there was a static discharge from the foliage that made hair and fur and feathers and string stand out eerily from their bodies. Overlooking this brush was an antenna, orienting unerringly on the party; Bink had never gotten close enough to one of these things to discover exactly what it was, and did not propose to start now. Why did these antennae watch so closely, yet take no action?

Sweat gnats came, making them all miserable until Humfrey woke, brought out a tiny vial, and opened it. Vapor emerged and spread, engulfing the gnats— then it suddenly sucked back into its bottle, carrying the gnats with it. "Misty was due for feeding anyway," the Good Magician explained, putting away the vial. He offered no further explanation, and no one had the nerve to inquire. Again Humfrey slept.

"Must be nice, being a Magician," Chester said. "He's got the answer to all his problems, in one bottle or another."

"Must be acquisitions from prior fees," Bink agreed.

Then they blundered into a patch of curse-burrs. The things were all over their legs, itching incessantly. There was only one way to get rid of such a burr; it had to be banished by a curse. The problem was, no particular curse could be used twice in a day; each had to be different.

Humfrey was not pleased to be awakened yet again. This time it seemed he had no solution in a vial. "By the beard of my Great-Uncle Humbug, begone!" the Good Magician said, and the burr he addressed fell off, stunned. "By the snout of a sick sea serpent, begone!" And another dropped.

Chester was more direct, for several burrs were tangled in his beautiful tail. "To the grave with you, prickleface! I'll stomp you flat as a nickelpede's nickel! Out out, damned burr!" And three burrs fell, overwhelmed.

"Leave me," Bink said, envying the imagination of the others. "Go itch a dragon!" And his burrs too started falling, though not so readily as those conked by the harder-hitting curses of the others. Bink just didn't have the touch.

Crombie, however, was in trouble. Griffins were not native to this particular region of Xanth, and the burrs evidently did not comprehend his squawks. Then the golem started translating, and they fell in droves. "By the bloody mouths of a field of wild snapdragons, drop your ugly purple posteriors into the nearest stinking privy, sidewise! If your faces were flowers, you'd poison the whole garden! Jam your peppery pink rootlets up your—" The golem paused, amazed. "Is that possible? I don't think I can translate it." But the curse burrs comprehended, and suddenly the griffin's bright feathers were free of them. No one could curse like a soldier!

Still, it was impossible to avoid all the burrs in this area, and by the time they escaped it their curses had become extremely farfetched. Sometimes two or even three curses had to be expended to make a single burr let go.

By this time they were hungry. There was nothing like a good bout of cursing to work up an appetite. "You know this area," Chester said to the Magician before he could fall asleep again. "Where is there something to eat?"

"Don't bother me with details," Humfrey snapped. "I brought my own food—as you would have done too, had you had proper foresight." He opened another vial. This time the vapor emerged to coalesce into a layered cake, complete with icing. The Magician took this from the air, broke out a perfect wedge-shaped slice, and ate that while the remainder of the cake dissolved, misted, and flowed back into its bottle.

"I realize we were remiss in not packing food for the journey," Bink said. "You don't suppose you might share some of that, this one time?"

"Why should I suppose anything like that?" Humfrey inquired curiously.

"Well, we are hungry, and it would facilitate—"

The Magician burped. "Go find your own slop, freeloader," the golem translated.

It occurred to Bink that the Good Magician was not as congenial a companion as the Evil Magician had been, the last time he had braved the wilderness of Xanth. But he well knew that appearances could be deceptive.

Crombie squawked. "Birdbeak says there should

be some fruit trees around. He'll point them out."
And the griffin did his thing, pointing the direction.

In a moment they spied a giant fruit cup. The plant
was the shape of an open bowl, filled to overflowing
with assorted fruits. The party ran joyfully up to it—
and, startled, the fruits erupted upward, filling the air
with color.

"Oh, no—they're winged fruits!" Bink exclaimed.
"We should have sneaked up on them. Why didn't
you warn us, Crombie?"

"You didn't ask, fathead," the golem retorted.

"Catch them!" Chester cried, jumping and reaching
high to snatch an apple out of the air. Bink, half-
dislodged, hastily dismounted.

A ripe peach hovered for a moment, getting its
bearings. Bink leaped at it, catching it in one hand.
The wings fluttered frantically as it tried to escape,
then gave up. They were leaves, green and ordinary,
adapted to this special purpose. He stripped them off
ruthlessly so his food could not escape, and went after
the next.

He tripped over something and fell flat, missing a
bobbing pomegranate. Angrily he looked at the ob-
stacle that had thwarted him. It was another of the
ubiquitous mounds of fresh earth. This time he got up
and stomped it absolutely flat. Then he dashed on
after more fruit.

Soon he had a small collection of fruits: apple,
peach, plum, two pears (of course), several grapes,
and one banana. The last, flying on monstrous vulture-
like wing-leaves, had given him a terrible struggle,
but it was delicious. Bink did not feel entirely easy
about consuming such fruit, because it seemed too
much like living creatures, but he knew the wings were
merely a magic adaptation to enable the plants to
spread their seeds more widely. Fruit was supposed to
be eaten; it wasn't really conscious or feeling. Or was
it?

Bink put that thought from his mind and looked
about. They were on the verge of a forest of standing
deadwood. Humfrey came awake. "I suffer misgivings,"
he volunteered. "I don't want to have to waste my

magic ferreting out what killed those trees. We'd better go around."

"What's the good of being a Magician if you don't use your magic?" Chester demanded testily.

"I must conserve my magic rigorously for emergency use," Humfrey said. "These are mere nuisances we have faced so far, not worthy of my talent."

"You tell 'em, twerp," the golem agreed.

Chester looked unconvinced, but retained too much respect for the Magician to make further issue of it. "It's getting on in the afternoon," he remarked. "Where's a good place to spend the night?"

Crombie stopped and whirled so vigorously he almost dislodged his riders. "Hmph!" Humfrey exclaimed, and the golem dutifully translated: "You blundering aviary feline! Get your catty feet on the ground!"

The griffin's head rotated entirely around until the deadly eyes and beak pointed back. "Squawk!" Crombie said with authority. The golem did not translate, but seemed cowed. Crombie completed his maneuver and pointed a slightly new direction.

"That's not far off the track; we'll go there," Chester decided, and no one contradicted him.

Their route skirted the dead forest, and this was fortuitous because there were few other hazards here. Whatever had killed the forest had also wiped out most of the magic associated with it, good and evil. Yet Bink developed a mounting curiosity about the huge trees they spied to the side. There were no marks upon them, and the grass beneath was luxuriant because of the new light let down. This suggested that the soil had not been poisoned by any monster. Indeed, a few new young shoots were rising, beginning the long task of restoring the forest. Something had struck and killed and departed without other trace of its presence.

To distract himself from the annoyance of the unanswerable riddle, Bink addressed the golem. "Grundy, if you care to relate it—what was your Question to the Magician?"

"Me?" the golem asked, amazed. "You have interest in *me?*"

94

"Of course I do," Bink said. "You're a—" He had been about to say "person" but remembered that the golem was technically not a person. "An entity," he finished somewhat lamely. "You have consciousness, feelings—"

"No, no feelings," Grundy said. "I am just a construct of string and clay and wood, animated by magic. I perform as directed, without interest or emotion."

Without interest or emotion? That hardly seemed true. "You seemed to experience a personal involvement just now, when I expressed interest in you."

"Did I? It must have been a routine emulation of human reaction. I have to perform such emulations in the course of my translation service."

Bink was not convinced, but did not challenge this. "If you have no personal interest in human affairs, why did you come to the Good Magician? What did you ask him?"

"I asked him how I could become real," the golem said.

"But you *are* real! You're here, aren't you?"

"Take away the spell that made me, and I'd be nothing but a minor pile of junk. I want to be real the way you are real. Real without magic."

Real without magic. It made sense after all. Bink remembered how he himself had suffered, as a youth, thinking he had no magic talent. This was the other face of the problem: the creature who had no reality *apart* from magic. "And what was the Answer?"

"Care."

"What?"

"Care, dumbbell."

"Care?"

"Care."

"That's all?"

"All."

"All the Answer?"

"All the Answer, stupid."

"And for that you serve a year's labor?"

"You think you have a monopoly on stupidity?"

Bink turned to the Good Magician, who seemed to have caught up on his sleep but remained blithely

95

silent. "How can you justify charging such a fee for such an Answer?"

"I don't have to," Humfrey said. "No one is required to come to the grasping old gnome for information."

"But anyone who pays a fee is entitled to a decent Answer," Bink said, troubled.

"The golem has a decent Answer. He doesn't have a decent comprehension."

"Well, neither do I!" Bink said. "Nobody could make sense of that Answer!"

The Magician shrugged. "Maybe he asked the wrong Question."

Bink turned to Chester's human portion. "Do you call that a fair Answer?"

"Yes," the centaur said.

"I mean that one word 'care'? Nothing else, for a whole year's service?"

"Yes."

"You think it's worth it?" Bink was having trouble getting through.

"Yes."

"You'd be satisfied with that Answer for your Question?"

Chester considered. "I don't think that Answer relates."

"So you *wouldn't* be satisfied!"

"No, I'd be satisfied if that were my Answer. I just don't believe it is. I am not a golem, you see."

Bink shook his head in wonder. "I guess I'm part golem, then. I don't think it's enough."

"You're no golem," Grundy said. "You aren't smart enough."

Some diplomacy! But Bink tried again. "Chester, can you explain that Answer to us?"

"No, I don't understand it either."

"But you said—"

"I said I thought it was a fair Answer. Were I a golem, I would surely appreciate its reference. Its relevance. This is certainly more likely than the notion that the Good Magician would fail to deliver in full measure."

Bink remembered how Humfrey had told the

manticora that he had a soul—in such a manner that the creature was satisfied emotionally as well as intellectually. It was a convincing argument. There must be some reason for the obscurity of the Answer for the golem.

But oh, what frustration until that reason became clear!

Near dusk they spied a house. Crombie's talent indicated that this was their residence for the night.

The only problem was the size of it. The door was ten feet tall.

"That is the domicile of a giant—or an ogre," Humfrey said, frowning.

"An ogre!" Bink repeated. "We can't stay there!"

"He'd have us all in his pot in a moment, and the fire high," Chester agreed. "Ogres consider human flesh a delicacy."

Crombie squawked. "The idiot claims his fool talent is never mistaken," Grundy reported.

"Yes, but remember what his talent doesn't cover!" Bink said. "We asked for a good place to spend the night; we didn't specify that it had to be safe."

"I daresay a big pot of hot water is as comfortable a place to relax as any," Chester agreed. "Until it becomes too hot. Then the bath becomes—"

"I suppose I'll have to expend some of my valuable magic," Humfrey complained. "It's too late to go wandering through the woods in search of alternate lodging." He brought out yet another little stoppered bottle and pulled out the cork. It was an ornery cork, as corks tended to be, and gave way only grudgingly, so that the process took some time.

"Uh, isn't that a demon container?" Bink asked, thinking he recognized the style. Some bottles were solider than others, and more carefully crafted, with magical symbols inscribed. "Shouldn't you—?"

The Magician paused. "Umph."

"He says he was just about to, nitwit," the golem said. "Believe it if you will."

The Magician scraped a pentacle in the dirt, sat the bottle in it, and uttered an indecipherable incantation. The cork popped out and the smoky demon issued, coalescing into the bespectacled entity Bink recognized as Beauregard.

The educated demon didn't even wait for the question. "You routed me out for this, old man? Of course it's safe; that ogre's a vegetarian. It's your mission that's unsafe."

"I didn't ask you about the mission!" Humfrey snapped. "I *know* it's unsafe! That's why I'm along."

"It is not like you to indulge in such foolishness, especially at the expense of your personal comfort," Beauregard continued, pushing his spectacles back along his nose with one finger. "Are you losing your marbles at last? Getting senile? Or merely attempting to go out in a blaze of ignominy?"

"Begone, infernal spirit! I will summon you when I need your useless conjectures."

Beauregard shook his head sadly, then dissipated back into the bottle.

"That's another feeling spirit," Bink said, uneasy. "Do you have to coop him up like that, in such a little bottle?"

"No one can coop a demon," the Magician said shortly. "Besides, his term of service is not yet up."

At times it was hard to follow the man's logic! "But you had him when I first met you, more than a year ago."

"He had a complex Question."

"A demon of information, who answers the questions you get paid fees for, has to pay you for Answers?"

Humfrey did not respond. Bink heard a faint booming laughter, and realized after a moment that it was coming from the demon's bottle. Something was certainly funny here, but not humorous.

"We'd better move in before it gets dark," Chester said, eyeing the ogre's door somewhat dubiously.

Bink would have liked to explore the matter of the demon further, but the centaur had a point.

They stepped up to the door. It was a massive portal formed of whole tree trunks of hewn ironwood, scraped clean of bark and bound together by several severed predator vines. Bink marveled at this; unrusted ironwood could be harvested only from freshly felled trees, and not even a magic axe could cut those very well. And what monster could blithely appropriate the deadly vines for this purpose? The vines normally used their constrictive power to crush their prey, and they were killingly strong.

Chester knocked resoundingly. There was a pause while the metallic echoes faded. Then slow thuds approached from inside. The door wrenched open with such violence that the ironwood hinges grew hot and the suction of air drew the centaur forward a pace. Light burst out blindingly, and the ogre stood there in terrible silhouette. It stood twice Bink's height, dwarfing even the monstrous door, and its body was thick in proportion. The limbs carried knots of muscles like the gnarly boles of trees. "Ungh!" it boomed.

"He says what the hell is this bad smell?" the golem translated.

"Bad smell!" Chester cried. "He's the one who smells!"

It was true. The ogre seemed not to believe in washing or in cleansing magic. Dirt was caked on his flesh, and he reeked of rotting vegetation. "But we don't want to spend the night outside," Bink cautioned.

Crombie squawked. "Birdbeak says let's get on with it, slowpokes."

"Birdbeak would," Chester grumbled.

The ogre grunted. "Stoneface says that's what he's sniffin', a putrid griffin."

The griffin stood tall and angry, half-spreading his brilliant wings as he squawked. "How'd you like that problem corrected by amputation of your schnozzle?" Grundy translated.

The ogre swelled up even more massively than before. He growled. "Me grind you head to make me bread," the golem said.

Then there was a medley of squawks and growls, with the golem happily carrying both parts of the dialogue.

"Come outside and repeat that, numbskull!"

"Come into me house, you beaked mouse. Me break you bone upon me dome."

"You'd break your dome just trying to think!" Crombie squawked.

"Do all ogres speak in rhyming couplets?" Bink asked when there was a pause to replenish the reservoirs of invective. "Or is that just the golem's invention?"

"That little twit not have wit," the golem said, then reacted angrily. "Who's a twit, you frog-faced sh—"

"Ogres vary, as do other creatures," Humfrey cut in smoothly. "This one does seem friendly."

"Friendly!" Bink exclaimed.

"For an ogre. We'd better go on in."

"Me test you mettle in me kettle!" the ogre growled via the golem. But the griffin nudged on in, and the ogre gave grudging way.

The interior was close and gloomy, as befitted the abode of a monster. The blinding light that had manifested when the door first opened was gone; evidently the proprietor had charged up a new torch for the occasion, and it had already burned out. Dank straw was matted on the floor, stocked cordwood lined the walls, and a cauldron bubbled like volcanic mud over a fire blazing in a pit in the center of the room. There seemed to be, however, no piles of bones. That, at least, was encouraging. Bink had never before heard of a vegetarian ogre, but the demon Beauregard surely knew his business.

Bink, realizing that the constant threats were mostly bluffs, found himself embarrassed to be imposing on the good-natured (for an ogre) monster. "What is your name?" he inquired.

"You lunch; me crunch."

Apparently the brute had not understood. "My name's Bink; what's your name?"

"Me have hunch you not know crunch." The ogre dipped a hairy, grimy mitt into the boiling cauldron, fished about, grabbed, withdrew a gooey fistful, plunked it into a gnarly wooden bowl which he shoved at Bink. "Drink, Bink."

"He means his name is Crunch," Chester said, catching on. "He's offering you something to eat. He doesn't distinguish between meals; all food is 'lunch.' "

"Oh. Uh—thank you, Crunch," Bink said awkwardly. *You lunch; me Crunch*—now it made sense. An offer of food, an answer to a question, rather than a threat. He accepted the glop. The ogre served the others similarly; his huge paw seemed immune to the heat.

Bink looked at his portion dubiously. The stuff was too thick to pool, too thin to pick up, and despite its bubbling heat it hardly seemed dead yet. It was a deep-purple hue, with green excrescences. It smelled rather good, actually, though there was a scalded fly floating in it.

Chester sniffed his serving appreciatively. "Why this is purple bouillon with green nutwood—a phenomenal delicacy! But it requires a magic process to extract the bouillon juice, and only a nutty green elf can procure nutwood. How did you come by this?"

The ogre smiled. The effect was horrendous, even in the gloom. "Me have elf, work for pelf," the golem translated. Then Crunch lifted a log from his stack and held it over the cauldron. He twisted one hand on each end—and the wood screwed up like a wet towel. A thin stream of purple liquid fell from it into the cauldron. When the log was dry, the ogre casually ripped it into its component cords and tossed it into the fire, where it flared up eagerly. Well, that was one way to burn cordwood.

Bink had never before witnessed such a feat of brute strength. Rather than comment, he fished out the fly, dipped a finger into his cooling pudding, brought out a creamy glob and put it gingerly to his mouth. It was delicious. "This is the best food I ever ate!" he exclaimed, amazed.

"You say that, Bink. You think it stink," Crunch growled, flattered.

Crombie squawked as he sampled his bowl. "*You* may stink; this is great," the golem translated.

Crunch, highly pleased by the double compliment, served himself a glob by dumping a bubbling fistful directly into his gaping maw. He licked off his fingers, then took another glob. As the others finished their helpings, the ogre served them more with the same hand. No one saw fit to protest; after all, what magic germs could survive that heat?

After the repast, they settled on the straw for the evening. The others seemed satisfied to sleep, but

101

Bink was bothered by something. In a moment he identified it: "Crunch, among our kind we offer some return service for hospitality. What can we do for you to repay this fine meal and lodging?"

"Say, that's right," Chester agreed. "You need some wood chopped or something?"

"That no good. Have plenty wood," the ogre grunted. He smashed one fist down on a log, and it splintered into quivering fragments. He obviously needed no help there.

Crombie squawked. "Birdbeak says he can point out where anything is. What do you want, stoneface?"

"Want sleep, you creep," Crunch mumbled.

"Not until we do you some service," Bink insisted.

"Take heed, no need!" Crunch closed one fist on a handful of straw, squeezed, and when he let go the straw had fused into one spindly stick. The ogre used this to pick at his gross teeth.

Chester argued caution for once. "We can't force a service on him he doesn't want."

"Maybe he doesn't know he wants it," Bink said. "We must honor the code."

"You sure are a stubborn lout," Grundy said, for once speaking for himself. "Why stir up trouble?"

"It's a matter of principle," Bink said uncertainly. "Crombie, can you point out where the thing Crunch desires is?"

The griffin squawked affirmatively, spun about, stirred up the straw, and pointed. At the Good Magician Humfrey, nodding in the corner, one piece of straw straddling his head.

"Forget it," Humfrey snapped sleepily. "I am not available for consumption."

"But he's a vegetarian!" Bink reminded him. "It can't be that he wants to eat you. Maybe he wants to ask you a Question."

"Not for one measly night's lodging! He'd have to serve me for a year."

"Me have no question, no suggestion," the ogre grunted.

"It does seem we're forcing something unwanted on our host," Chester said, surprisingly diplomatic. That log-twisting and straw-squeezing and wood-splintering

102

had evidently impressed the centaur profoundly. The ogre was clearly the strongest creature this party had encountered.

"There is something Crunch wants, even if he doesn't know it himself," Bink said. "It is our duty to locate it for him." No one argued, though he was sure they all wished he would drop the subject. "Crombie, maybe it isn't the Magician he wants, but something *on* the Magician. Exactly where did you point?"

Crombie squawked with tired resignation. He pointed again. Bink lined up his own finger, tracing the point. "There!" he said. "Something in his crotch." Then he paused, abashed. "Uh, his jacket, maybe."

But the Magician, tired, had fallen asleep. His only answer was a snore.

"Oh, come *on!*" Grundy said. "I'll check it out." And he scrambled up on the Magician, climbing inside his jacket.

"I don't think—" Bink began, startled by this audacity.

"That's your problem," the golem said from inside the jacket. "It must be—this." He emerged, clasping a vial in both arms. For him it was a heavy weight.

"That's the demon-bottle!" Chester said. "Don't fool with—"

But Grundy was already prying out the cork.

Bink dived for him, but as usual was too late. The cork was not ornery this time; it popped off cleanly as Bink grabbed the bottle.

"Now you've done it!" Chester exclaimed. "If Humfrey wakes—"

Bink was left holding the bottle as the demon coalesced, unbound by any magic inscription or incantation. "Some—some—somebody make a—a—" Bink stammered.

Beauregard firmed, standing with a huge tome tucked under one arm. He peered at Bink beneath his spectacles. "A pentacle?" the demon finished. "I think not."

"What have I done?" Bink moaned.

Beauregard waved negligently with his free hand. "You have done nothing, Bink. It was the foolish golem."

"But I set him in motion!"

"Perhaps. But do not be concerned. Rather consider yourself as the instrument of fate. Know that neither the bottle nor the pentacle constrained me; I but honored these conventions to please the Magician, to whom I owed professional courtesy. The agreement was that I should serve in this capacity of reserve-informant until circumstances should free me, by the ordinary rules of demon control. That chance has now occurred, as it was fated. A genuinely bound demon would have escaped, so I am free to go. I thank you for that accident, and now I depart." He began to fade.

"Wait!" Bink cried. "At least answer this nice ogre's Question!"

Beauregard firmed again. "He has no Question. He only wants to sleep. Ogres need plenty of rest, or they lose their meanness."

"But Crombie's talent indicated—"

"Oh, that. Technically there is something, but it is not a conscious desire."

"It will do," Bink said. He had not realized that ogres could have unconscious desires. "Tell us what it is, before you go."

"He wants to know whether he should take a wife," the demon said.

The ogre growled. "What kind of life, if me have wife?" the golem said.

"Now that's interesting," Beauregard said. "A golem, serving fee for an Answer he can not comprehend."

"Who could make sense of a one-word Answer?" Grundy demanded.

"Only a real creature," Beauregard replied.

"That's the point—he's not real," Bink said. "He wants to know how to *become* real."

Beauregard turned to the centaur. "And you want to know your talent. I could tell you, of course, but you would then be in fee to me, and neither of us would want that."

"Why don't you just answer the ogre's question and go?" Bink asked, not quite trusting this too-knowledgeable freed demon.

"I can not do that directly, Bink. I am a demon; he would not accept my answer, rational though it would be. He is of an irrational species, like yourself; you must answer him."

"Me! I—" Bink broke off, not wanting to comment on his present problem with Chameleon.

"I spoke in the plural," Beauregard said, a bit condescendingly. "You and Chester and Crombie should discuss your relations with your respective females, and the consensus will provide the ogre with the perspective he needs." He considered. "In fact, in that context, my own comment might become relevant." And he settled down on the straw with them.

There was a silence. "Uh, how did you—that is, there is a lady ogre—uh, ogress in mind?" Bink asked Crunch.

The ogre responded with a volley of growls, snorts, and gnashings of yellow teeth. It was all the golem could do to keep up the translation, but Grundy rose to the occasion and spouted at the height of his form:

"One lovely bleak morning during thunderstorm warning me wandered far out beyond hail of a shout. Me was in a good mood just looking for food. No creature stirred this far from home; no dragon, no monster, not even a gnome. Me entered a forest huge and tall; the trees were so big me seemed small. The way was so tangled no walker could pass, but it opened like magic a lovely crevasse, with nickelpedes and more delights, and stagnant water rich with blights, and me tramped up to a hidden castle with shroud for flag and scalp for tassel. The wind blew by it with lovely moans, and all the timbers were giant bones. At entrance slept little dragon called Puk, guarding what left meself awestruck: a fountain packed with purple mud, spouting gouts of bright-red blood. Me stared so long me stood in doze, and me mouth watered so hard it drooled on me toes. But me knew such enchantment would be complete the moment me yielded and started to eat. Me wanted to see what further treasure offered itself for the hero's pleasure. And in the center in a grimy sack lay a wonderful ogress stretched on a rack. She had hair like nettles, skin like mush, and she face would make a zombie blush.

She breath reeked of carrion, wonderfully foul, and she stench was so strong me wanted to howl. Me thought me sick with worm in gut, but knew it was love for that splendid slut. Me smashed she in face with hairy fist, which is ogre way of making tryst. Then me picked she up by she left leg and dragged she away, me golden egg. Then whole castle come awake: goblin and troll and green mandrake. They celebrated the union of hero and cute by pelting we with rotten fruit. But on way out we tripped a spell that sounded alarm where evil fiends dwell. They had put castle to sleep for a hundred years, those fiends who hated ogres' rears. They fired a spell of such terrible might we had to flee it in a fright. Me dodged it every way me could, but it caught we good in midst of wood. As it struck me cried 'Me crunch no bone!' and it thought we ogres both had flown. It dissipated in such mighty flash the whole near forest was rendered trash. Now me crunch no bones lest fiends of lake learn they curse have make mistake. Me not want them throw another curse maybe like first and maybe worse. Me love lies stunned within the wood, sleeping away she maidenhood. But one thing now gives me pause: she never did make much applause. All me want to know is this: should me leave or fetch the miss?"

The others sat in silence for a time following this remarkable recital. At last Crombie squawked. "That was a considerable adventure and romance," Grundy said for him. "While I can appreciate the fetching qualities of your lady friend, I must say from my own experience that all females are infernal creatures whose primary purpose in life is to deceive, entrap, and make miserable the males. Therefore—"

The ogre's grunt interrupted the griffin in midsquawk. "Hee hee hee, hee hee hee!" Grundy translated, interrupting himself. "Me fetch she instantly!"

Chester smiled. "Despite my friend's recommendation, I must offer a note of caution. No matter how badly the filly nags the stallion, and how unreasonable she normally seems, there comes a time when she births her first foal. Then the dam no longer has much interest in—"

"She no nag? That is snag," Crunch growled, disappointed.

"But in due course," Bink said, "she is bound to return to normal, often with extremely cutting wit. In any event, I should think some nagging is better than no nagging. So why not rouse your beauty and give her a proper chance? She may make your life completely miserable."

The ogre's eyes lighted like torches.

"I must concur," Beauregard said. "This conversation has been a most intriguing insight into the condition of human, animal, and ogre emotions. What is nagging to humans is applause to ogres. This will do nicely to conclude my dissertation."

"Your what?" Bink asked.

"My doctoral thesis on the fallibilities of intelligent life on the surface of Xanth," Beauregard explained. "I sought information from the human Magician Humfrey, and he assured me that a term of service in his bottle would provide me the insights I required, since a person's nature may best be gauged through the questions he considers most vital. This has indeed been the case, and I am now virtually assured of my degree. That will qualify me to form permanent liaison with my chosen demoness, who would seem to be worth the effort. This causes me to experience a certain demoniac exhilaration. Therefore I present you each with a small token gleaned from my researches."

The demon turned to Chester. "I prefer not to inform you of your magic talent directly, for the reason given above, but will provide a hint: it reflects the suppressed aspect of your character. Because you, like most centaurs, have disbelieved in magic among your kind, whole aspects of your personality have been driven as it were underground. When you are able to expiate this conditioning, your talent will manifest naturally. Do not waste a year of your life for the Answer of the Good Magician; just allow yourself more self-expression."

He turned to Crombie. "You can not escape your fate in this manner. When you return from this quest —if you return—Sabrina will trap you into an unhappy marriage unless you arrange for a more suitable commitment elsewhere before you see her. Therefore enjoy yourself now; have your last fling and do not be concerned for the morrow, for it will be worse than today. Yet marriage is not after all, for you, a fate worse than death; you will know that when you do face death."

He left the crestfallen griffin and oriented on the golem. "The meaning of the Magician's Answer to you is this: people care; inanimate objects do not. Only when you experience genuine feelings that pre-empt your logic will you be real. You can achieve this height only if you work at it—but beware, for the emotions of living things are in many cases extremely uncomfortable."

He turned to Crunch. "I say to you, ogre: go fetch your lady. She sounds like a worthy companion for you, in every respect a truly horrendous bitch." And Crunch was so moved he almost blushed.

Beauregard turned to Bink. "I have never been able to fathom your magic, but I feel its operation now. It is extremely strong—but that which you seek is infinitely stronger. If you persist, you run the risk of being destroyed, and of destroying those things you hold most dear. Yet you *will* persist, and so I extend my condolence. Until we meet again—" He faded out.

The members of the remaining circle exchanged glances. "Let's go to sleep," Chester said. That seemed like the best idea of the evening.

Chapter 6. Magic Dust

In the morning they thanked the ogre and continued on their quest, while Crunch tramped eagerly into the dead forest to rouse his beautiful bride: her with the hair like nettles and skin like mush.

They had new material for thought. Now they knew the cause of the death of the trees—but what of the evil fiends who dwelt in the lake and possessed such devastating curses? Were there Magicians among them, and was the source of magic near them?

Magician Humfrey was particularly thoughtful. Either he had not been entirely asleep during the evening session, or he had drawn on his informational magic to ascertain the situation. He had to know that the demon Beauregard was gone. "What magic," he murmured, "could devastate an entire living forest by the dissipation of a single curse? Why have I not known of this before?"

"You never thought to look," Chester said undiplomatically.

"We're looking now," Bink pointed out. "Magic should be stronger near the source."

Crombie squawked. "Strong magic is one thing. Magician-class curses are another. Let me get another line on it." And he did his act once more.

They were headed in the right direction. The terrain seemed ordinary; large trees glowered at the trespassers while small ones shied away as well as they were able. Fruit flies buzzed about: berries, cherries, and grapefruits hovered as if in search of another salad bowl. Tempting paths appeared through tangled

reaches, which the party avoided as a matter of course.
In Xanth, the easy course was seldom best! There was
a dragon run, with scorch marks on the trees to show
the dragon's territorial limits. The safest place to be,
when pursued by a dragon, was a few paces within
another dragon's marked demesnes; any poaching
would lead to a settlement between dragons.

But soon the way became more difficult. Brambles
with glistening points and ugly dispositions closed off
large sections, and a pride of ant lions patrolled others.
A copse of stinkweeds surrounded the most direct
remaining route, and they were of a particularly large
and potent breed. The party tried to pass through
them, but the stench became so intense that even the
ogre might have hesitated. They retreated, gasping.

They contemplated the alternatives: brambles and
ant lions. Bink tried to clear a path through the plants
with his sword, but every time he made a cut, several
more branches closed in, threatening his body. These
were exceptionally alert brambles, and the sheen on
their points suggested poison. Bink backed off. Once
again he was up against the possibility that his talent
might protect him while letting his friends die.

He approached the ant-lion section. The lion-
headed ants had beaten out good highways throughout,
and ruthlessly eliminated all hazards in their way. All
hazards except the ant lions themselves.

Bink's sword might dispatch one lion, and Chester's
arrows and hooves could handle two or three more,
and as a griffin Crombie could take on as many as
four—but the creatures would attack a dozen at a
time without fear or mercy. Again, Bink himself would
probably emerge intact, by some incredible fluke—but
what of the others?

He turned back—and his eyes wandered skyward,
he saw a path through the trees. The tops of the trees.

He rubbed his eyes. A path in air? Yet why not?
With magic, he reminded himself for the umpteenth
time, all things were possible. The question was, could
men and half-men walk on it? And if they could,
where did it lead?

Still, it seemed to be the most promising route. If
he rode Chester, his talent would not let them get on

the airy path unless it would support them both. The griffin, Magician, and golem weighed much less, so they would be safe if they followed. "I think I see a way," Bink said.

They tried it. They located a place where the magic path looped down within reach of the ground, and Crombie whirled and pointed to discover whether there was any danger along this limited-access highway. There was not. They climbed aboard and followed it up high into the trees. The strange thing about it was that the path was always level, no matter how it looped. The forest turned crazy circles about it, however. At times the sun was underfoot, and at times to one side, while the trees assumed varying angles. Bink, curious, reached out to touch the foliage of one tree whose trunk reached up into the ground above; it was solid. Of course he knew that he was the one who was upside down; the path established its own orientation. Looking back, he could see the griffin marching at a different tilt, and knew that to griffin, Magician, and golem the centaur was the tilted one. Intriguing magic, but harmless. So far.

Meanwhile, he enjoyed the convenience and the view. The path led through the forest, generally high above the ground, and this new view of things was refreshing. Slants of sunlight crossed it, and gently hued columns of mist. It was neither man's-eye nor bird's-eye, but an intermediate and unique perspective. The path passed safely above the ant-lion range, yet below the flying-predator range. Bink observed several small flying dragons, a harpy, and a distant roc, but none flew near the path.

The plants, too, were unusually passive. Constrictor tentacles dangled in the vicinity of the path, but never *on* it, and no branches reached across to block it. Obviously this path was charmed, and that was suspicious; the best paths were almost by definition the worst ones. Bink remembered how easy it had been to penetrate the forest around Castle Roogna, back when it had been derelict, and how hard it had been to escape it. What were they walking into now?

Crombie's talent said there was no danger in the direction the path went—but Crombie's talent could be too literal. To Bink, anything that might delay the completion of his quest was a threat. One simply could not afford to trust strange magic. He'd better ask the Good Magician.

"Of course it's safe, Bink," Humfrey said with irritation. "Do you suppose I would be riding it otherwise?"

Bink hadn't even asked the question yet! The Magician retained his special talent, though his grumpy refusal to use it for the convenience of the party made his company seem at times to be worth little more than that of a harpy. What point was there in having a Magician along, if he never used his magic to facilitate things? Even the Evil Magician had freely pitched in when danger threatened to—

"That is the point, Bink," Humfrey said. "There is no present danger. When the situation changes, I will expend my carefully hoarded magic. You are young, yet; you dissipate your resources heedlessly, and get into scrapes you should have avoided."

Served him right for letting his thoughts flow carelessly! Bink shut up, mentally, and rode on. In due course the path wound down to a pleasant little village, with houses thatched with hay and daubed with colored muds, and neat walkways connecting places of faint interest.

"Do you notice," Chester said, "there is no magic in the local construction? Only mundane materials."

"That's right," Bink said, surprised. "If we're approaching the source of magic, on a magic path, shouldn't there be more magic rather than less?" He turned to the griffin. "Crombie, are you sure this is—?"

Crombie squawked. "Birdbeak is sure this is the right direction," the golem said. "But the village may be a mere item on the way, not the destination itself."

A grizzled old harpy flapped out to meet the party as it reached the foot of the path. All of them braced for trouble, for harpies were notorious. But this one, though suitably hideous, was clean and unaggressive. "Welcome, travelers," she said without even bothering to insult them. A most restrained harpy!

"Uh, thanks," Bink said. "We're looking for—a

112

place to spend the night. We don't mean any mischief." He had never heard of a harpy acting polite, so remained on guard, hand over sword.

"You shall have it," she agreed. "You are all males?"

"Yes," Bink said uneasily. "We are on a quest for the source of magic. Your village appears to lie near this. We—"

"Five males," the harpy said. "What a bonanza!"

"We're not interested in your females," Chester said with some of his normal belligerence.

Crombie squawked. "Not their minds, anyway," the golem translated.

Chester's lip curled with almost equine facility. Bink had to speak at once, before another quarrel brewed. "We shall be happy to do some chore for you, in return for food and safe lodging overnight. Then tomorrow, if you have information about magic—"

"You will have to discuss that with Trolla," the harpy said. "This way, please." And she flapped off, muttering once more: "Men!" with hideous excitement.

"Then again, you may have a point," Chester murmured to Crombie. "If we have fallen into a nest of harpies . . ."

"We may be best advised to get on that aerial path and go back the way we came," Bink finished, glancing back.

But the path was gone. They could not escape that way.

Trolla turned out to be—a female troll. She was almost as ugly as the harpy, but she too was amazingly polite. "I realize you are uneasy, you handsome male visitors," Trolla said. "And you have reason to be. But not because of any of the residents of this village. Allow me to serve you supper, while I explain our situation."

Bink exchanged glances with the others. Both centaur and griffin looked distinctly uncomfortable, but the Good Magician seemed to have no concern.

Trolla clapped her horny hands, and several wood-nymphs came in, bearing platters. Their hair was green, their skin brown, their lips and fingernails red: like flowering trees. But their outlines were human; each was a pert, lithe, full-breasted bare beauty. Each eyed Bink and Humfrey with more than casual interest. "Hunger" might be a better term.

The food was virtually mundane: vegetables and fruits harvested locally, and small dragon steaks. Milkweed pods provided the liquid; it was good milk, but in no way special.

"You may have noted we have used no magic in the preparation of this meal," Trolla said. "We use as little magic as possible here, because there is more magic here than anywhere else on the surface of Xanth. I realize that may not make much sense to you—"

"Quite sensible," Humfrey said, chomping into another steak.

Trolla focused on him. "You must be a Magician, sir."

"Umph." He seemed to be more interested in his food than in her discussion. Bink knew that was deceptive. Humfrey paid close attention to all things magic.

"If you are—if any of you have strong magic—I must caution you to be extremely careful in exerting it," she said. "Please do not misunderstand; this is no threat. We do not want you to feel at all uncomfortable here. It is simply that all magic—well, permit me to make a small demonstration." She clapped her hands, and a nymph entered, as buxom and bare as the others. "Bring a small firefly," Trolla said.

In a moment the nymph returned with the firefly. It was very small—the kind that generated hardly more than a spark, harmless. It squatted on the table, rather pretty with its folded flame-hued wings and insulated legs. "Now observe what happens when I frighten it," Trolla said.

She rapped the table with a hooflike knuckle. The firefly jumped up, startled, and generated its momentary fire. A burst of light and heat emanated from it, and a ball of smoke roiled up toward the ceiling. A spot on the table a handsbreadth in diameter was charred. The firefly itself had disappeared.

"It burned itself up!" Chester exclaimed.

"It did not mean to," Trolla said. "This was a nor-

114

mal Xanth firefly, not acclimatized to this region. Here near the source its magic is multiplied a hundredfold. Thus its little spark became a self-immolating fireball. Until you males become acclimatized, I urge you not to practice your magic in this village. We value your presence, and do not wish you to suffer any mishaps."

Bink looked to Humfrey, but the Good Magician continued eating. "Uh, none of us have inflammatory magic," Bink said, realizing that it was up to him to respond for their party. Yet he wondered: what would his talent do if anything threatened? What it might intend to be a mere "coincidental" amelioration might become much worse. "But it would be best if—if nothing seemed to threaten our welfare."

"There is, unfortunately, a most extreme threat to your welfare," Trolla said gravely. "Because you are males. You must have noticed we have no males in this village."

"We noticed," Bink agreed. "Your nymphs seem quite intrigued by us." Indeed, the nymphs were hovering so close that Bink's elbows tended to bump their soft midriffs as he ate.

"Our problem is this," Trolla continued. "A siren has been luring away our males. Originally we were a normal human village, except for our unique and critical task. Then the siren came and deprived us of our men. Because our job could not be neglected, we undertook at great personal risk the construction of the charmed access route you arrived on, so as to encourage immigration. But the new men, too, were soon taken away from us. We extended our search to non-human people; this was how I myself came here, with my husband the troll. But the awful drain continued; I was soon a widow—and not by the proper route."

Bink felt sudden alarm. Some female trolls ate their husbands. It was said that the only thing a troll was afraid of was his wife—with excellent reason. Was this predaceous female looking for another husband?

"Our village now is composed of every type of intelligent female," Trolla continued. "And a number of supporting animals. The magic access route transports only intelligent creatures, but some animals drift in through the jungle. But the siren—this is what I meant by the danger to you. Once you hear her call, you will disappear into the forest and never return. We would spare you this if we could, but we are helpless unless we resort to unconscionable measures."

"What would those be?" Bink asked nervously.

"We might deafen you so you could not hear her," Trolla explained. "Or geld you, so that you would not react to—"

"Why don't some of you females go out and slay the siren?" Chester asked. "Meaning no offense, madam, but you could probably handle it."

"The siren I would gladly tear apart and consume in bleeding chunks," Trolla said. "But I can not pass the tangle tree. The siren has made a deal with the tangler; the tree lets the males through to her, but grabs the females."

"Then you need to eliminate the tangle tree," Bink said. "With magic as strong here as you've shown, it should be a fairly simple chore. A few fireflies, or some pineapple bombs—"

"This is no ordinary tangle tree," Trolla said. "We have tried to destroy it, but though it is outside our village, it has absorbed enough extra magic to foil our efforts. We are, after all, only females—and the men will not fight it when they are in thrall to the siren."

Bink took a deep breath. "I believe this is the service we can render, in return for your hospitality. To-morrow we shall slay the tangler."

Trolla merely shook her head sadly. "It is kind of you to think so," she said. "But the siren will not per-mit it."

The siren did not know about Bink's talent. Since both siren and tangle tree were magical entities, his magic would protect him against them. Somehow. But considering the possible complications of the enhanced potency of magic here, he would do best to tackle the tree alone. He didn't want his friends being hurt by the backlash. Maybe he could sneak out at night and do it, while the others slept.

Crombie squawked. "What is the village employ-ment, crone?" the golem translated.

"We are situated atop the source-lode of magic," Trolla said. "This is the origin of the magic of Xanth. The dust is highly charged with magic, and were it allowed to accumulate, most of the rest of Xanth would slowly become mundane, while the village would develop a fatal concentration. Thus we must spread the dust about, maintaining a reasonable equilibrium." She looked about. "We seem to have completed our repast. Allow me to show you our operations."

"Umph," Humfrey agreed. Now Bink was sure the Magician was only feigning disinterest, as was his fashion; the conclusion of their quest was at hand! Yet Bink found himself disappointed; he had expected more challenge to the acquisition of this knowledge than this.

Trolla showed them to a large central building fashioned of mundane stone. Inside, it was one huge gravel pit, where small female elves, gnomes, and fairies dug and scraped out sand with their little picks and scoops. They loaded it into wheeled wagons drawn by female centaurs, a manticora, and a small sphinx. Bink's skin prickled when he approached the sand; strong magic was associated with it, no doubt of that! Yet this was the first time he had encountered indeterminate magic. That sand performed no magic of its own, and cast no spells; it merely *was* magic, waiting for direction. Bink was not quite sure he could believe that.

The sand was hauled to another structure, where three huge hephalumphs tromped it constantly into dust. The hephalumphs were animals, normally wild creatures of the wilderness, but these were evidently tame and well cared for, and seemed happy. Then a captive roc-bird blew the dust into the air, employing great sweeps of her monstrous wings. So powerful was this forced draft that small tornadoes formed in the turbulence.

"The Technicolor hailstorms!" Bink exclaimed. "Fallout from this operation!"

"Exactly," Trolla agreed. "We try to feed the dust high into the sky so that it will ride the upper currents all over Xanth before it falls, but localized storms bring it down prematurely. The region immediately downwind of us is untenable for intelligent life; the concentration of airborne dust disrupts the local ecology and leads to madness. Thus there are risks associated with our operation—but we must continue. We should be pleased if you males would remain here, encouraging our females—but we know you must flee before the siren calls. Unfortunately our access route is one-way; we have been too busy recently to construct a departure ramp. You can escape only through the Region of Madness. Yet this is preferable to the siren. We shall help you all we can, but—"

"Not until we render our service," Bink said. "We have assorted talents, and should be able to handle this." But privately he was uneasy; he found it hard to believe that they should prevail where all other men had failed. And he wondered again why the source of the magic of Xanth had remained unknown all these centuries, if the people of this village had known about it all along. Maybe the fact that no one ever seemed to leave this village and live—or maybe the magic dust fogged up other magic, so that things like magic mirrors could not focus on this area. There were probably a lot of secrets in the Land of Xanth that remained to be discovered. . . .

"We shall have a gathering this evening," Trolla said. "Some of our younger girls have never seen a male, and deserve this chance. You will meet everyone, and we shall plan how we can best help you to escape the siren. So far, no way has been found to block off her sound from the males, though we females can not hear it. We can, with your permission, confine you in cages so that you can not respond to—"

"No!" Bink and Chester said together, and Crombie squawked.

"You are true males, always ready for a challenge," Trolla said with sad approval. "In any event, we would have to let you out sometime, and then the siren would get you, so cages are no solution. We need to be rid of the siren!" Her face, for a moment, assumed the aspect of savage hate that was normal to trolls. But then she softened. "I will show you to your lodging, and call for you again at dusk. Please be courteous to our villagers; your presence here is a considerable event, and the girls are untrained in social decorum."

When they were alone, Bink addressed the Magician. "Something is funny here. Will you use your magic to fathom the true situation?"

"Do I have to do everything?" Humfrey grumped.

"Listen, you dwarfish gnome!" Chester snapped. "We've been working our tails off, while you just loaf along."

Humfrey was unruffled. "Anytime you wish to have your payment for your efforts——"

Bink decided he had better intercede, though he had considerable sympathy for the centaur's position. He had not realized there would be so many problems in leadership! "We seem to be at our objective, the source of magic. But it has been too easy, and the villagers are too accommodating. Only you can tell us whether we have in fact completed our quest, or whether we have walked into a man-consuming trap. Surely this is the occasion to employ your magic, if you would be so generous."

"Oh, all right," Humfrey said ungraciously. "You don't deserve it after the way you loosed Beauregard, but I'll take a look."

The Magician drew out a mirror. "Mirror, mirror in my hand, are you the finest in the land?"

The mirror clouded, turning deep red. "Oh, stop blushing!" Humfrey snapped. "I was only testing."

Bink remembered a mirror like this. It answered only in pictures, and somewhat circuitously; a too-direct question about a too-delicate matter could crack it up.

"Are you aware of the source of the magic of Xanth?" the Magician asked.

A picture of a baby appeared, smiling. That evidently meant "Yes."

"Can you tell me the location of that source?" Aside to the others he murmured: "This is the crucial point. At home, the mirror never could reveal this information, but here with stronger magic——"

The baby smiled again. Humfrey echoed that smile, anticipating victory. "Will you tell me that location?"

119

Again the cherubic smile. Bink felt his pulse pounding. He realized the Magician was approaching the subject with extreme caution. The mirror took each question literally, and did not volunteer anything; this circuitous approach insured that the mirror would not be overwhelmed by too abrupt a challenge.

"Please show that location on your screen."

The mirror went dark.

"Oops," Bink murmured. "Is it broken?"

The mirror brightened. A crying baby appeared.

"It tells you no," Humfrey snapped. "Kindly allow me to continue my investigation." He returned to the mirror. "Are you showing me a scene of underground?"

The baby smiled.

"In short, you verify that the source of magic is not in this village we are presently sitting in?"

A big question mark appeared.

"You are saying the source of magic *is* in this village?" the Good Magician asked sharply.

The question mark returned. "Hm, a problem of resolution here," Humfrey muttered. "The mirror can't choose between truths. Anybody have another approach?"

"It's a matter of perspective," Chester said. "If the magic dust is the source, there may be more than one cache of it. More likely, a channel of it, welling up from the depths. Thus the source has a multiple definition, depending on whether you are thinking of the source on the surface, or the source of the source."

"Now there is a creature with a disciplined mind," Humfrey said approvingly. "If only he would discipline it more often instead of quarreling with the soldier." He faced the mirror. "Is the centaur's analysis correct?"

The baby smiled.

"Now," the Magician continued. "Are you aware of the motivation of these villagers?" When he received the smile, he asked: "Do they mean well by us?" The smile confirmed it. Bink felt relief. "And Trolla spoke the truth about the curse of the siren?" Another smile.

Humfrey looked up. "Now it gets difficult," he said,

120

seeming pleased. Bink realized that this man, too, enjoyed a challenge. The magic ability the Good Magician had held in reserve was now being used, and it was good magic. "So far we have merely been confirming what we already knew. Now we must venture into the unknown." He returned to the mirror. "Are you able to tell us how to deal with the villagers' problem?"

The cherub smiled. "Unusually responsive," Humfrey remarked, aside. "The local magic-enhancement is indeed multiplying the mirror's power. We have a major research tool, now, rather than a minor one." He returned once more to the mirror. "How—"

"Are you males ready?" Trolla inquired from the door.

They jumped. Bink was about to explain, then saw Humfrey's quick negative nod. The mirror had disappeared. The Good Magician did not want to reveal the secret of his magic to these villagers. Not just yet.

Well, they had gleaned a lot already, and could resume the use of the mirror when convenient. "That's a pretty dress," Bink said to Trolla. This was no lie; the dress was very pretty, though she remained a female troll. Evidently a festive occasion was in the making. They followed her out.

The center circle of the village had been transformed, nonmagically. A genuine wood bonfire blazed, sending sparks and smoke up to the sky. It was dusk, and the stars were beginning to show. It was as if the sparks went up into the sky to become those stars— and perhaps, Bink thought, the potent magic of this region made that so. The stars had to get up there somehow, didn't they?

The females of the village were lovely in their party apparel. There were many more young ones than had been evident before, and now that their work shift was over they were eager and more than eager to mingle with the strange guests. Bink was surrounded by nymphs, sprites, and human maids, while Humfrey was mobbed by fairies, lady elves, and minionettes. Three fetching centaur fillies attended Chester. A pair of griffin cows eyed Crombie, but they hardly had a chance with this transformed woman-hater. They were, after all, animals. There was even a female golem for Grundy.

Yet how sad the remaining females looked—the manticora, the sphinx, and the harpies. They had no males to cater to.

"Uh, girls—I'm a married man," Bink protested as his covey pressed in.

"She will never know," a buxom blue-maned lass informed him. "We need you more than she does." And she planted a firm kiss on his left eye—the only part of him she could reach, because of the density of other girls.

"Yes, no man leaves this village, except at the call of the singing bitch," a furry beauty added. "It is our duty to hold you here, to save your life. Wouldn't your wife rather have you used than dead?"

Awkward question! How *would* Chameleon feel about that? In her lovely, stupid phase she would be hurt, confused, and forgiving; in her ugly, smart phase she would comprehend the situation and be realistic. So she would accept what had to be accepted, and certainly not want him to die. Still, he had no wish or intent to indulge himself with any of these—

Something distracted him. It was a faint, eerie, but somehow most intriguing sound.

He tried to listen, but the clamor of the girls almost drowned it out. "Please, I want to hear—there is a melody—"

"It is the siren!" a fairy screamed. "Sing, girls, sing! Drown out the bitch!"

They sang, loudly, passionately, and tunelessly. Still, that insidious melody penetrated, the single clear theme cutting through the nearby cacophony, compelling Bink to respond. He started toward it.

Immediately the girls restrained him. They flung their arms about him, dragging him back and down, burying him in their exposed softness. Bink collapsed in a tangle of arms, legs, breasts, and assorted other aspects of distaff anatomy he didn't bother to define.

The girls meant well—but the siren's call was not to be denied. Bink fought, and caught glimpses of other thrashing mounds where his male companions fought similarly. Bink was stronger than any of the nymphs, for they were delicate, shapely things; he did not want to hurt any of them. Yet he had to free himself of their near-suffocating embrace. He heaved them off his body, cuffing their hands loose, shoving wherever his hands made contact. There were eeeks and cries and giggles, depending on the type of contact he made; then he was on his feet, charging forward.

Chester and Crombie and the Magician closed in about him, all riveted to that compelling sound. "No, no!" Trolla cried despairingly behind them. "It is death you seek! Are you civilized males or are you mindless things?"

That bothered Bink. What did he want with a magical temptress? Yet still he could not resist the siren. Her lure had an unearthly quality that caught at the very root of his masculinity, beneath the center of his intelligence. He was male, therefore he responded.

"Let them go, they are lost," Trolla said despairingly. "We tried, as we have always tried—and failed."

Though he was in thrall to the siren, Bink felt simultaneous sympathy for Trolla and the girls. They offered life and love, yet were doomed to be rejected; their positive orientation could not compete with the negative compulsion of the siren. The villagers suffered as horrible a damnation as the men! Was it because they were nice girls, making only promises they could keep, while the siren had no such limit?

Crombie squawked. "As all females always fail," Grundy translated, responding to Trolla's despair. "Though why any of us should bother with this bitch-female call—" The griffin shrugged his wings and charged on.

Did even the golem feel it? He must, for he was not protesting.

They ran down a path that opened magically before them. It was a perfect path, exactly the kind that usually led to something huge, predatory, and stationary, like a tangle tree. But of course this particular tangler would not attack them, because they were males in thrall to the siren. *She* would dispatch them, in her own fashion.

And what might that fashion be? Bink wondered. He could not quite imagine it, but the prospect was wrenchingly exciting. "What a way to go!" he breathed.

The tree came into sight. It was monstrous, even for its kind. Its dangling tentacles were as thick as the legs of a man, and extremely long and limber. Its tempting fragrance surrounded it like an evening gown, making it seem thoroughly desirable. Gentle music emanated from its foliage, no siren call, but nice: the kind of music that made a person want to lie down and listen and relax.

But no veteran of the wilderness of Xanth could be fooled for an instant. This was one of the most deadly life forms available. Even a dragon would not venture near a tangle tree!

The path passed right under it, where the curtain of tentacles parted neatly and the soft sward grew. But elsewhere around the fringe was a developing cone of bleaching bones, the remainders of the tree's past victims. Shapely female bones, Bink suspected, and felt another twinge of guilt.

Yet the siren still called, and they followed. They funneled down to single file, for the path beneath the tree was narrow. Chester galloped first, then Crombie, for their forms were fastest; Bink and the Magician followed as well as they could. There had not been occasion to mount the steeds for faster travel.

Chester paused under the awful tree, and the tentacles quivered with suppressed eagerness but did not grab. So it was true: the siren's song nullified the tangle reflex! The distant music was stronger now, and more compelling: the very essence of female allure. The nymphs of the village had been pretty and sweet, but the siren's promise was vital; it was as if the sex appeal of all womankind had been distilled and concentrated and—

Ahead of Bink, the griffin suddenly halted. "Squawk!" Crombie exclaimed. "What am I doing here?" the golem translated, coming up behind, surprisingly fleet on his feet, considering his size. "The siren is nothing but a damned conniving female out for my blood!"

Literally true, but the others ignored him. Of course the siren was a conniving female, the ultimate one! What difference did that make? The call had to be honored!

The woman-hater, however, decided to be difficult. "She's trying to trap me!" he squawked. "All women are traps! Death to them all!" And he pecked viciously at the nearest thing available—which happened to be the slender extremity of a tentacle.

In a small bird, such a peck would have been a nuisance. Crombie, however, was a griffin. His beak was sword-sharp, powerful as a vise, a weapon capable of severing a man's leg at the ankle with a single bite. The tentacle, in this case, was the diameter of an ankle, and the chomp severed it cleanly. The separated end dropped to the ground, twitching and writhing like a headless green snake.

For a moment the whole tree froze in shock. *No* one took a bite out of a tangler! The truncated upper section of the tentacle welled dark ooze as it thrashed about as if looking for its extremity. The gentle background music soured.

"I think the truce has been broken," Bink said. But he didn't really care, for the song of the siren continued, drawing him on to better things. "Move on, Crombie; you're blocking my way."

But the soldier remained unreasonable. "Squawk! Squawk! Squawk!" he exclaimed, and before Grundy could translate, he nipped off another tentacle, then a third.

The tangle tree shuddered. Then, furious, it reacted. Its music became a deafening blare of outrage, and its tentacles grabbed for the griffin—and the centaur, man, and Magician.

"Now you've done it, birdbrain!" Chester screamed over the noise. He grabbed the first tentacle that touched him and wrung it between his two hands the way the ogre had wrung out the log. Tough as the tentacles were when grabbing, they had little resistance to cutting or compression, and this one was squished into uselessness in a moment.

Suddenly the lure of the siren was drowned out by the rage of the tree, and they were in a fight for their lives. Bink drew his sword and slashed at the tentacles that swept toward him, cutting them off. Beside him Crombie pecked and scratched viciously, all four feet operating. Long cuts appeared in the tentacles he touched, and green goo welled out. But more tentacles kept coming in, from all sides, for this was the very center of the tree's power.

Chester backed up to the trunk and operated his bow. He fired arrow after arrow through the thick upper reaches of the tentacles, paralyzing them. But—

"No, Chester!" Bink cried. "Get away from—"

Too late. The tree's huge maw opened in the trunk, the bark-lips lapping forward to engulf the centaur's handsome posterior.

Bink leaped to help his friend. But a tentacle caught his ankle, tripping him. All he could do was yell: "Kick, Chester, kick!" Then he was buried in tentacles, as firm and rounded and pneumatic as the limbs of the village girls, but not nearly as nice. His sword arm was immobilized; all he could do was bite, ineffectively. That green goo tasted awful!

Chester kicked. The kick of a centaur was a potent thing. His head and shoulders went down, counterbalancing his rear, and all the power of his extraordinary body thrust through his two hind hooves. They connected inside the maw of the tree, against the wooden throat, and the ground shook with the double impact. A few old bones were dislodged from the upper foliage to rattle down to the ground. But the wooden mouth held. Sap juices flowed, commencing the digestion of the centaur's excellent flesh. Chester's instinct would have been sound for any ordinary tree, using the inert trunk as protection for his valuable but vulnerable rear, but it was disaster here.

Chester kicked again, and again, violently. Even this predator-tree could not withstand much of this punishment. Normally its prey was unconscious or helpless by the time it reached the consumption stage, not awake and kicking. Slowly, reluctantly, the bark gave way, and the centaur dragged free. His once-beautiful flank was discolored by the saliva sap, and

126

one hoof had been chipped by the force of its contact with the wood, but at least he was alive. Now he drew his sword and strode forward to help Bink, who was not-so-slowly suffocating in the embrace of the tentacles.

Meanwhile Magician Humfrey had problems of his own. He was trying to unstopper one of his little vials, but the tentacles were wrapping about him faster than the stopper was coming loose. The tree was overwhelming them all!

Crombie had clawed and bit his way to the fringe. Suddenly he broke out. "I'm free, you vegetable monster!" he squawked exultantly. "I'll bet you're another female, too!" He was really uncorking his worst insult! The golem had gotten aboard again, so was available for instant translation. "You can't catch me!"

Indeed the tree could not, for it was rooted. Crombie spread his wings and flew up and away, escaping it.

Yet what of the others? As if enraged even further at the loss, the tree concentrated savagely on the remaining prey. Pythons of tentacles whipped about limbs and bodies, squeezing tight. Chester was trying to help Bink, but dared not slash too closely with his sword lest he slice some of Bink along with a tentacle. Bink, now closest to the trunk, found himself being dragged headfirst toward the dread orifice.

Humfrey finally got his bottle open. Smoke issued forth, expanding and coalescing into—a spiced cheesecake.

"Curses!" the Magician cried. "Wrong vial!"

Chester kicked at the cheesecake. It slid across the turf and into the slavering maw of the tree. The barklips closed about it. He could hardly have made a nicer shot had he been trying for it.

The tree choked. There was a paroxysm of wooden coughing, followed by a sylvan sneeze. Gross hunks of cheese flew out of the orifice.

"The spice on that one *is* a bit strong," Humfrey muttered as he scrambled for another vial.

Now Bink's head was at the maw. The bark was writhing, trying to get the taste of spiced cheese out. This monster liked fresh meat, not processed dairy

127

products. Sap coursed down and dripped from tooth-like knots, cleaning out the maw. In a moment it would be ready for Bink.

Chester was still trying to help, but three tentacles had wrapped around his sword arm, and more looped his other extremities. Even his great strength could not avail against the massed might of the tree. "And the cowardly soldier ran out on us!" he grunted as he fought. "If I ever get my hands on him—" He wrung out another tentacle before his free arm was pinioned.

Humfrey got another vial open. The vapor emerged —and formed into a flying vampire bat. The creature took one look at its environs, squeaked in terror, swore off blood, and flapped away. A single tentacle took one casual swing at it and knocked it out of the air. The tree was really getting on top of the situation.

The last of the cheese cleared. The orifice reopened for business, and Bink was the client. He saw the rows of ingrown knots that served as the monster's teeth, and the flowing saliva sap. Fibers like miniature tentacles extended inward from the mouth-walls, ready to absorb the juices of the prey. Suddenly he realized: the tangler was related to the carnivorous grass that grew in patches in the wilderness! Add a trunk and tentacles to such a patch—

Humfrey got another vial open. This time a basilisk formed, flapping its little wings as it glared balefully about. Bink closed his eyes to avoid its direct gaze, and Chester did the same. The tree shivered and tried to draw away. There was no creature in all the Land of Xanth who cared to meet the gaze of this little lizard-cock!

Bink heard the flapping as the basilisk flew right into the tangler's mouth—and stopped. But nothing happened. Cautiously Bink opened one eye. The tree was still alive. The basilisk had not destroyed it at a glance.

"Oh—a mock basilisk," Bink said, disappointed.

"I have a good remedy for tanglers somewhere," Humfrey insisted, still sifting through his vials. Whenever a tentacle encroached too closely he stunned it with a magic gesture. Bink had not known such gestures existed—but of course he was not a Magician of Information. "They're all mixed up—"

The tentacles shoved Bink into the mouth. The odor of carrion became strong. Helpless, he stared into his doom.

"Squawk!" sounded from beyond the tree. "Charge!"

Crombie had returned! But what could he do, alone?

Now there was a sound as of the rush of many feet. The tangle tree shuddered. The odor of smoke and scorching vegetation drifted in. Bink saw, from the corner of his eye, orange light flaring up, as if a forest fire raged.

Torches! Crombie had marshaled the females of the magic-dust village, and they were attacking the tree with blazing brands, singeing the tentacles. What a brave effort!

Now the tangler had to defend itself from attack by a superior force. It dropped Bink, freeing its tentacles for other action. Bink saw a pretty nymph get grabbed, and heard her scream as she was hauled into the air, her torch dropping.

"Squawk! Squawk!" Crombie directed, and other females rushed to the captive's rescue, forming a screen of flame. More tentacles got scorched, and the nymph dropped.

Bink recovered his sword and resumed hacking, from inside the curtain of tentacles. Now that the tree was concentrating on the outside menace, it was vulnerable to the inside one. With every stroke Bink lopped off another green branch, gradually denuding the tree of its deadly limbs.

"Squawk!" Crombie cried. "Get outside!" the golem translated.

That made sense. If the tree should refocus on the interior, Bink, Chester, and Humfrey would be in trouble again. Better to get out while they could!

In a moment they stood beside the griffin. "Squawk!" Crombie exclaimed. "Let's finish off this monster!" Grundy cried for him.

The ladies went to it with a will. There were about fifty of them, ringing the tree, pushing in with their fires, scorching back every tentacle that attacked. They could have conquered the tree anytime, instead of letting it balk them all these years—had they had the masculine drive and command. Ironic that Crombie the woman-hater should be the organizing catalyst!

Yet perhaps this was fitting. Crombie's paranoia about the motives of women had caused him to resist the siren, finally breaking her spell. Now he was using these females in the manner a soldier understood: as fodder for a battle. They might not have responded as well to a "nicer" man. Maybe they needed one who held them in contempt, who was willing to brutalize them for his purpose.

The tree was shriveling, half its awful limbs amputated or paralyzed. It would take time to kill it, but the victory now seemed certain. Thanks to Crombie, and the brave, self-sacrificing villagers.

"You know, I could get to respect women like these," Crombie murmured as he paused from his exertions to watch the wrap-up proceed. Actually it was squawk-and-translation, but Bink was so used to it now that it made little difference. "They obey orders well, and fight damn near as well as a man, allowing for—" He paused in mid-squawk, listening.

Then Bink heard the siren's call again, no longer drowned out by the battle. Oh, no! He tried to resist it —and could not. The siren had recovered her thrall.

Bink started walking toward that sound. His companions joined him, silently. The villagers, intent on their successful campaign, did not see them depart.

Chapter 7. Deadly Distaffs

The sound of the battle faded behind. The males, Crombie included, moved on down the path, lured by the siren's song. The unearthly quality was stronger now, thrilling Bink's inner fiber. He knew the siren meant death, more certainly than the tangle tree —but what a satisfying death it would be!

It was a good path; nothing interfered with their progress. Soon they arrived at the shore of a small lake. In that lake were two tiny islands, like the tips of mountains mostly hidden beneath the surface. The path led over the water to one of these islands. This was the source of the music of the siren.

They started on the path. Bink thought Crombie might balk again, and in his heart hoped he would while fearing that that hope would be fulfilled, but the griffin did not. Apparently his resistance to females had been compromised by the spirit and sacrifice of the village women, and he could no longer master sufficient suspicion. Indeed, he was the first on the water-path, the water depressing slightly under his claws but supporting his weight. The Magician was second, Bink third, and—

There was an angry bleat from the side. A small creature came charging along the small beach. It was four-legged and woolly, like a sheep, with broad curly horns that circled entirely around its head. Evidently the path crossed this creature's territory, and the animal was taking action.

Chester, in the thing's path, paused. "A battering ram," he remarked, recognizing the species. "Not subject to the siren's call because it is a mere animal. No use to reason with it."

A battering ram! Bink paused, his curiosity momentarily overriding the lure of the siren. He had heard of such creatures, and of their relatives the hydraulic rams, but never encountered one before. As he understood it, they existed only to batter, and they loved it. If there were a door to be broken down, or a castle to be breached, such a ram was invaluable. At other times, they were a nuisance, because they never stopped beating their heads against obstacles.

Chester was far larger than the ram—but it had cut him off from the siren's path. Chester dodged it once, nimbly, but the ram screeched to a halt—a neat trick in sand, even with magic—and whirled to recharge. Chester would have been battered in the rear, had he tried to ignore it—and his rear was his proudest feature, despite the recent staining from the tangler's sap —much handsomer than his face. So he whirled to face the ram, and dodged its charge again.

But there was no end to this. The ram would happily go on forever, screeching up more mounds of sand with each miss, but Chester had a siren call to answer. The ram had to be stopped, somehow.

Bink wondered: his talent could have had a part in saving him from the tangler, as it had used the motives and magic of others freely. Was the ram another device to stop him from reaching the siren? In that case, he should be rooting for the ram, not Chester.

Chester, no dummy, maneuvered between charges until he was directly in front of a large tree. He never took his eye off the ram, lest it catch him by surprise. Next charge would fire the ram right into the trunk that Chester had oriented on peripherally, with luck knocking the animal silly. Or at least starting the process, because it took a lot of knocking to knock a battering ram silly. These creatures were pretty silly to begin with.

Then Bink recognized the variety of tree. "Not that one, Chester!" he cried. "That's a—"

Too late. Why was he always too late? It was getting quite annoying! The ram charged, Chester danced aside, there was a flutelike trill of music, and the ram plowed headfirst into the tree. Such was the force of impact, all out of proportion to the animal's size, that the entire tree vibrated violently.

"... pineapple tree," Bink finished belatedly.

Now the fruits were falling: huge golden pineapples, quite ripe. As each hit the ground, it exploded savagely. That was how this tree reproduced: the detonating fruit sent shrapnel-seeds far across the landscape, where each could generate, with luck and magic, a new pineapple tree. But it was hardly safe to stand too near this process.

One pineapple struck the battering ram on the rump. The ram bleated and spun to face it, rear-scorched and bruised, but of course that was futile. Other fruits were exploding all around. One dropped just before the ram. With a snort of challenge the animal leaped boldly forth to intercept it, catching it squarely on the horns. The resulting concussion really did knock the ram silly; it staggered off, bleating happily.

Meanwhile Chester was doing a truly intricate dance of avoidance, trying to keep his flowing tail and sleek equine haunches out of mischief. He could avoid the pineapples falling to left, right, and front, but those behind were problematical. One dropped almost on his tail; in fact it brushed the elevated top. Chester, in a remarkable maneuver, whipped his entire hind-section out of the way—but in the process brought his head into the location vacated by the tail.

The pineapple exploded. Chester caught the blast right under his chin. His head was engulfed in flame and smoke; then the refuse cleared and he stood there, dazed.

Bink found himself unable to run back along the path, despite his concern for his friend. This was partly because the continuing summons of the siren allowed him to pause but not to withdraw, and partly because the path over the water was one-way. It was firm while he proceeded forward, but was mere water when he tried to go back. The lake was small, but seemed very deep, and he hesitated to trust himself to its reaches. Bad magic tended to lurk in the depths. So he could only watch and call. "Chester! Are you all right?"

The centaur stood there, slowly shaking his head. The explosion had not done much harm to Chester's facial appearance, since that had always been homely, but Bink was concerned about the centaur's fine mind. Had the pineapple damaged his brain?

"Chester! Can you hear me?" Then, as Chester ignored him, Bink understood the problem. The blast had deafened him!

Bink waved his hands violently, and finally Chester took note. "Speak louder—I can't hear you!" Then the centaur realized it himself. "I'm deaf! I can't hear anything!"

At least he seemed to be all right, otherwise. Bink, relieved of much of his anxiety, felt himself again overwhelmed by the continuing call of the siren. He beckoned.

"The hell with the siren!" Chester called. "I can't hear her now. It's stupid to go to her. She means death."

Crombie had been briefly freed of the compulsion, back at the tangle tree, but had been recaptured by the siren. Now Chester had been freed by the intercession of the battering ram. It must be the operation of Bink's talent! But Bink himself was still hooked. He turned about and proceeded toward the island. Crombie and the Good Magician were almost there now, as they had not paused as long as Bink.

Chester galloped along the path, catching up to Bink. His powerful hands picked Bink up by the elbows. "Don't go, Bink! It's nonsense!"

But Bink would not be denied. "Put me down, horserear. I have to go!" And his feet kept walking in midair.

"I can't hear you, but I know what you're saying, and it's not worth listening to," Chester said. "Only one way to stop this before the others are lost."

He set Bink down, then unslung his great bow. The siren was still far away, but there was no archery like that of a centaur. Chester's bowstring twanged, and the deadly shaft arced across the water toward the island and the female figure there.

There was a scream of anguish, and the melody halted abruptly. Chester's arrow had scored. Suddenly

134

they all were freed; the compulsion was gone. Bink's talent had prevailed at last, saving him from harm without revealing itself.

They ran to the island. There lay the siren—the loveliest mermaid Bink had ever seen, with hair like flowing sunshine and tail like flowing water. The cruel arrow had passed entirely through her torso, between and slightly below her spectacular bare breasts, and she was bleeding from front and back. Her torso had collapsed across her dulcimer.

Yet she was not dead. Though the arrow, with that uncanny marksmanship of the centaur, must have pierced her heart, she still breathed. In fact she was conscious. She tilted her beautiful face weakly to look up at Chester. "Why did you shoot me, handsome male?" she whispered.

"He can't hear you; he's deaf," Bink said.

"I meant no harm—only love," she continued. "Love to all men, you—why should you oppose that?"

"What joy is there in death?" Bink demanded. "We have brought to you what you have brought to a hundred other men." He spoke gruffly, yet his heart ached to see the agony of this lovely creature. He remembered when Chameleon had been similarly wounded.

"I brought no death!" she protested as vehemently as she was able, and gasped as the effort pushed a gout of blood from her chest. Her whole body below the shoulders was soaked in bright blood, and she was weakening visibly. "Only—only love!"

Then at last she subsided, losing consciousness. Bink, moved despite what he knew, turned to the Magician. "Is—is it possible she speaks the truth?"

Humfrey brought out his magic mirror. It showed the smiling baby face. "It is possible," he said, wise to the ways of the mirror. Then he addressed it directly: "*Did* the siren speak the truth?"

The baby smiled again. "She meant no harm," the Magician said. "She is not the killer, though she lured men here."

The men exchanged glances. Then Humfrey brought out his bottle of healing elixir and sprinkled a drop on the siren's terrible wound. Instantly it healed, and she was sound again.

The Magician offered Chester a drop of elixir for his ears, but the centaur disdained it. So Humfrey sprinkled it on the centaur's rear, and suddenly it was as beautiful as ever.

"You healed me!" the siren exclaimed, passing her hands wonderingly over her front. "There is not even blood, no pain!" Then, startled; "I must sing!" She reached for her dulcimer.

Chester kicked it out of her reach. The musical instrument flew through the air, smashed, and plunked into the water. "There is the source of her magic!" he cried. "I have destroyed it!"

The source of magic . . . destroyed. Was that an omen?

Experimentally, the siren sang. Her upper torso expanded marvelously as she took her breath, and her voice was excellent—but now there was no compulsion in it. The centaur had, indeed, deprived her of her devastating magic.

She broke off. "You mean that was what summoned all the men? I thought they liked my singing." She looked unhappy.

Apparently she really was the lovely innocent, like Chameleon in her beauty-phase. "What happened to all the men?" Bink asked.

"They went across to see my sister," she said, gesturing toward the other island. She pouted. "I offer them all my love—but they always go to her."

Curious! Who could lure victims away from the siren herself? "Who is your sister?" Bink asked. "I mean, what is her magic? Is she another siren?"

"Oh, no! She is a gorgon, very pretty."

"A gorgon!" Bink exclaimed. "But that is death!"

"No, she would not harm anyone, no more than I would," the siren protested. "She cherishes men. I only wish she would send some back to me."

"Don't you know what the gaze of a gorgon does?" Bink demanded. "What happens to someone who looks upon the face of—?"

"I have looked into my sister's face many times! There is no harm in her!"

Humfrey lifted his mirror again. "It affects men only?" he asked, and the smiling baby agreed.

It seemed the siren really did not know the devastating effect her sister's face had on men. So for years she had innocently lured in males—for the gorgon to turn to stone.

"We shall have to talk with your sister," Humfrey said.

"The path continues to her island," the siren informed him. "What will I do, without my dulcimer?"

"Your voice is pretty enough without any accompaniment, and so are you," Bink said diplomatically. It was true as far as it went; had she a lower portion to match her upper portion, it would have been true all the way. "You can sing *a capella,* without accompaniment."

"I can?" she inquired, brightening. "Will it bring nice men like you?"

'No. But perhaps a nice man will find you, regardless." Bink turned to the Magician. "How can we approach the gorgon? One glance—"

"We shall have to deal with her in the morning," Humfrey decided. Bink had lost track of time. The stars had been emerging at the village, then they had charged into the night of the jungle to battle the tangle tree, thence to this island—where it seemed dusk was only now falling. Did that make sense? Bink had somehow assumed that the sun set all over Xanth at the same instant, but realized that this was not necessarily so. But he had other things to worry about at the moment, and listened to the rest of Humfrey's speech: "Siren, if you have food and bed—"

"I'm not really that kind of female," she demurred.

Bink looked at her sleek fishtail. "Obviously not. We only want a place to sleep."

"Oh." She sounded disappointed. "Actually, I could become that kind, if—" She shimmered, and her tail transposed into two fetching legs.

"Just sleep," Chester said. It seemed his hearing was returning naturally. "And food."

But her indignation had not yet run its course. "After you impaled me with your old messy arrow, and broke my dulcimer?"

"I'm sorry," Chester said shortly. "I have a headache."

As well he might, Bink thought. Why hadn't the ornery creature accepted a drop of elixir for his head as well as for his tail?

"If you were really sorry, you'd show it," she said.

Crombie squawked. "She's setting her hooks into you already, ass," the golem said.

Doubly annoyed, Chester glowered at the siren. "How?"

"By giving me a ride on your back."

Bink almost laughed. Nymphs of any type loved to ride!

"Ride, then," Chester said, disconcerted.

She walked to his side, but was unable to mount. "You're too tall," she complained.

Chester turned his front portion, wrapped one arm about her slender waist, and hauled her up easily. "Eeek!" she screamed, delighted, as her feet swished through the air. "You're so strong!"

Crombie squawked again, and his remark needed no interpretation. She was, indeed, working her wiles on the centaur, needing no siren song.

Chester, not in the best of moods after his encounter with the pineapple, was visibly mollified. "All centaurs are strong." He set her neatly on his back, and walked forward.

The siren grabbed two handfuls of his mane. "My, your shoulders are so broad! And what sleek fur you have. You must be the handsomest centaur of all!"

"From the rear, maybe," he agreed. He began to trot.

"Oooh, that's fun!" she cried, letting go just long enough to clap her hands together girlishly. "You must be the smartest centaur, and the fastest—" She paused. "Could you, maybe, make a little jump?"

Chester, now quite puffed up by her praise, made a tremendous leap. The siren screamed and flew off his back. They were at the edge of the water, since this was a small island, and she plunked into the lake.

"Uh, sorry," Chester said, mortified. "Guess I overdid it." He reached down to fish her out.

Fish her out he did: her legs had changed back into a tail. "No harm done," the mermaid said. "I am quite at home in the water." And she wriggled within

138

his grasp, bringing her face to his and planting a wet kiss on him.

Crombie squawked. "There's no fool like a horse-reared fool," the golem said.

"That's for sure," Chester agreed, now in a good mood. "Just don't tell Cherie."

"Cherie?" the siren asked, frowning.

"My filly. The prettiest thing in Xanth. She's back home, tending our foal. His name is Chet."

She assimilated that. "How nice," she said, disgruntled. "I'd better see to your fodder now, and stall space."

Bink smiled privately. Chester wasn't such a fool after all!

They had a modest repast of fish and sea cucumber, and bedded down in a pile of soft dry sponges. Bink stretched out his feet—and banged into another pile of dirt. This time he was too tired to stomp it flat, so he ignored it.

The siren, having given up on the centaur, nestled down in the dark beside Bink. "Say," he said, remembering. "We have to give service for hospitality!"

Crombie squawked. *"You* give service, noodle-brain," Grundy said. "You're closest to her."

"Service?" the siren inquired, nudging him.

Bink found himself blushing furiously in the dark. *Damn* Crombie's innuendo! "Uh, nothing," he said, and pretended to fall suddenly asleep. Very soon it was no pretense.

In the morning they bade farewell to the siren after taking the time to break up some wood for her cooking fire—a service she appreciated, as she was not much for that sort of thing. They set about braving her sister. "The rest of you must be blindfolded," Humfrey decided. "I will use the mirror."

So he could view the gorgon indirectly, of course. That was the only way to look at such creatures; everyone knew that. Yet why did a mirror work? The image in the glass should be as horrendous as the original.

"Polarization," the Magician explained without being asked. "The magic of partial images."

That didn't clarify things much. But a more important question remained. "What do we do, to stop the——" Bink did not want to use the word "kill" in the presence of the innocent siren. Getting close to the gorgon was one thing; dispatching her while blindfolded was another.

"We shall see," Humfrey said.

They submitted to blindfolding, including the golem. Then they formed a chain to follow the Good Magician, who walked backward on the path between the islands, using the mirror to see ahead. In this case he was not utilizing its magic, but merely the ordinary reflection: the natural magic all mirrors possessed.

It was strange and uncomfortable, crossing the water sightlessly. How awful it would be, to lose forever the power of seeing! What magic was better than the natural senses of life?

Bink's feet felt hard land. "You stand here, facing out," Humfrey told them. "Just in case. I will deal with the gorgon."

Still nervous, Bink obeyed. He felt tempted to rip off the blindfold, turn about, and look at the gorgon —but not strongly tempted. Once he had stood atop a tall mountain and suffered an urge to throw himself off it, similarly; it was as if there were a death urge in him along with the life urge. Perhaps the urge to adventure was drawn from the same wellspring.

"Gorgon," Humfrey said.

Right behind Bink, she answered. "I am she. Welcome to my isle." Her voice was dulcet; she sounded even more attractive than her sister. "Why do you not look at me?"

"Your glance would turn me into stone," Humfrey said bluntly.

"Am I not beautiful? Who else has locks as serpentine as mine?" she asked plaintively, and Bink heard the faint hissing of the snakes. He wondered what it would be like to kiss the gorgon, with those snake-hairs twining around their two faces. The notion was both alarming and tempting. Yet what was the gorgon except the literal personification of the promise and threat embodied in every woman?

"You are beautiful," Humfrey agreed gravely. She

140

must be beautiful indeed, Bink thought, for the Good Magician did not waste compliments. Oh, for a single look! "Where are the other men who came to you?"

"They went away," she said sadly.

"Where did they go?"

"There," she said, and Bink assumed she was pointing. "Beyond those rocks."

Humfrey moved over to investigate. "These are statues," he said, unsurprised. "Statues of men, exquisitely realistic. Carved, as it were, from life."

From life . . .

"Yes," she agreed brightly. "They look just like the men who came to me."

"Does that not suggest anything to you?"

"The men left the gifts behind, pictures of themselves, sculptures. But I would rather have had the men stay with me. I have no use for stones."

She didn't realize what she had done! She thought these were mere images offered as remembrances. Maybe she refused to realize the truth, blocking it out from her consciousness, pretending she was an ordinary girl. She refused to believe in her own magic. What a fateful delusion!

Yet, Bink thought, wasn't this too typical of the thought processes of females? What one among them chose to recognize the mischief her sex worked among men!

But that was Crombie's contention, therefore probably an exaggeration. There might be a little siren and a little gorgon in every girl, but not a lot. There was hardly any in Chameleon.

"If more men come," Humfrey continued with unusual gentleness, "they will only leave more statues. This is not good."

"Yes, there are already too many statues," she agreed naively. "My island is getting crowded."

"The men must not come any more," Humfrey said. "They must stay at their homes, with their families."

"Couldn't just one man come—and stay a while?" she asked plaintively.

"I'm afraid not. Men just aren't, er, right for you."

"But I have so much love to give—if only a man

would stay! Even a little one. I would cherish him forever and ever, and make him so happy—"

Bink, listening, was beginning to appreciate the depth of the gorgon's tragedy. All she wanted was to love and be loved, and instead she sowed a harvest of horrible mischief. How many families had been destroyed by her magic? What could be done with her—except execution?

"You must go into exile," Humfrey said. "The magic shield has been lowered by order of the King; you can pass freely out of Xanth. In Mundania your magic will dissipate, and you will be able to interact freely with the man or men of your choice."

"Leave Xanth?" she cried, alarmed. "Oh, no, I would rather die! I can not leave my home!"

Bink experienced a pang of sympathy. Once he himself had faced exile . . . .

"But in Mundania you would be an ordinary girl, under no curse. You are extremely lovely, and your personality is sweet. You could have your pick of men there."

"I love men," she said slowly. "But I love my home more. I can not depart. If this is my only choice, I beg of you to slay me now and end my misery."

For once the Good Magician seemed shaken. "Slay you? I would not do that! You are the most attractive creature I have ever seen, even through a mirror! In my youth I would have—"

Now a little ordinary feminine artifice manifested. "Why, you are not old, sir. You are a handsome man."

Crombie stifled a squawk, Chester coughed, and Bink choked. She had made a gross exaggeration, if not an outright distortion! Humfrey was a good man, and a talented one, but hardly a handsome one. "You flatter me," the Magician said seriously. "But I have other business."

"Of all the men who have come here, you alone have stayed to talk with me," the gorgon continued. "I am so lonely! I beg of you, stay with me, and let me serve you always."

Now Crombie squawked aloud. "Don't turn about, fool!" the golem cried. "Keep using the mirror!"

"Um, yes," Humfrey agreed. The griffin's hearing

must be acute, Bink thought, to detect the sound of the Magician's incipient turning! "Gorgon, if I were to look at you directly—"

"You would feel obliged to go away, leaving only a stone memento in your likeness," she finished. "I do not understand why men are like this! But come, close your eyes if you must, kiss me, let me show you how much love I have for you. Your least word is my command, if you will only stay!"

The Magician sighed. Was the old gnome tempted? It occurred to Bink that it might not have been disinterest in women that kept Humfrey single, but lack of a suitable partner. The average woman was not interested in a wizened, dwarfish old man—or if she expressed interest, it was likely to be only because she wanted a piece of his formidable magic. Here was a woman who knew nothing of him but his appearance, and was eager to love him, asking only his presence.

"My dear, I think not," Humfrey said at last. "Such a course would have its rewards—I hardly deny it! —and I would normally be inclined to dally with you a day or three, though love be blindfolded. But it would require the resources of a Magician to associate safely with you, and I am on a quest that takes precedence, and may not—"

"Then dally a day or three!" she exclaimed. "Be blindfolded! I know no Magician would have interest in me, but even a Magician could not be more wonderful than you, sir!"

Did she suspect the magnitude of Humfrey's talent? Did it matter? The Magician sighed again. "Perhaps, after my present quest is over, if you would care to visit at my castle—"

"Yes, yes!" she cried. "Where is your castle?"

"Just ask for Humfrey. Someone will direct you. Even so, you can not show your face to man. You would have to wear a veil—no, even that would not suffice, for it is your eyes that—"

"Do not cover my eyes! I must see!"

Bink felt another surge of sympathy, for at the moment he could not see.

"Let me consult," Humfrey said. There was a rustle as he rummaged through his magic props. Then:

"This is not ideal, but it will do. Hold this vial before your face and open it."

More rustling as she accepted the vial that he held out over his shoulder. There was a pop as the cork came out, the hiss of escaping vapor, a gasp, then silence. Had the Magician executed her after all, giving her poison vapor to sniff?

"Companions, you may now remove your blindfolds and turn about," Humfrey said. "The gorgon has been nullified."

Bink ripped off the cloth. "Magician! You didn't—?"

"No, I did her no harm. Observe."

Bink observed, as did the others. Before them stood a breathtakingly lovely young woman with hair formed of many small thin snakes. But her face was —absent. There simply wasn't anything there.

"I applied a spell of invisibility to her face," Humfrey explained. "She can see out well enough, but I regret that no man can look upon her face, since it is the loveliest part of her. But this way it is impossible to meet her gaze. She is safe—as are we."

It was too bad, really, Bink had to agree. She seemed like such a nice girl, burdened with such a terrible curse. Magic was not always kind! The Magician had nullified the curse, but it was disconcerting to look into that vacuum in lieu of her face.

Crombie walked around the island, studying the statues. Some were of centaurs, and some of griffins. "Squawk!" "Look at the damage the bitch has done! She must have petrified hundreds of innocent males. What good is it to nullify her now? It is like closing the house door after the man has escaped." He was evidently thinking more like a griffin, now. That was a danger of prolonged transformation.

"Yes, we shall have to do something about the statues," Humfrey agreed. "But I have expended enough of my valuable magic. Too much, in fact. Crombie, point out where the solution to this problem lies."

The griffin whirled and pointed. Down.

"Hm. Now point out the source of magic, again."

Crombie did. The result was the same. "So I supposed," Humfrey said. "Our quest has more than informational significance."

Another factor fell into place for Bink. This whole escapade with the tangle tree and the devastating sisters had seemed like a diversion from the quest and a serious threat to Bink's welfare, yet his talent had permitted it. Now he saw that his experience related to the quest. Still, it should not have been necessary to expose himself to these dangers in order to reach the source of magic. Something other than his talent must be operating.

He remembered the mound of earth, last night. Did that relate? He really could not fathom how, yet he distrusted coincidental occurrences unless they derived from his talent. If an enemy were—

The Good Magician brought out his mirror again. "Get me the Queen," he said into it.

"The Queen?" Bink asked, surprised.

The mirror fogged, then showed the face of Queen Iris. "About time you called in, Humfrey," she said. "How come you're dawdling there on the gorgon's isle, instead of pursuing your fool quest?"

Crombie squawked angrily. "Don't translate that!" Humfrey snapped at the golem. Then, to the Sorceress: "It is Bink's quest, not mine. We have nullified siren and gorgon, and are proceeding toward the source of magic. Notify the King."

Iris made a minor gesture of unconcern. "When I get around to it, midget," she said.

The visage of King Trent appeared in the mirror behind her. Abruptly she assumed the aspect of a Sweet Young Thing, complete with long braids. "Which will be very soon, Good Magician," she amended hastily. Trent waved jovially and tugged on a braid as the mirror went blank.

"How can she talk on the mirror?" Bink inquired. "It shows silent pictures for everyone else."

"She is mistress of illusion," Humfrey explained.

"Mistress of the King, you mean," Crombie squawked.

"We only think we're hearing her," Humfrey continued. He put away the mirror. "And the King only thinks he can yank at an illusory braid. But illusion has its uses, in whatever capacity."

"I'd like the illusion of reality," the golem said wistfully.

Humfrey returned his attention to the gorgon. "We shall return in due course. I suggest you go comfort your sister, meanwhile. She has lost her dulcimer."

"I will, I will!" the gorgon cried. "Farewell, handsome Sorcerer!" She flung her arms around Humfrey and planted an invisible kiss on his mouth while the snakes snapped at his ears and hissed up a storm. "Hurry back! I have so much love stored up—"

"Um. Just so," the Magician agreed, embarrassed. He brought up a finger to snap away one serpent-hair that was gnawing too vigorously on his earlobe.

The magic path ended at the gorgon's isle, so it was necessary to swim back. They used Crombie's talent to locate a safe route across, avoiding lake monsters; then Bink mounted Chester and Humfrey rode the griffin. It was now midmorning, and the return to the magic-dust village was easy and swift. Hostile magic had not yet had time to move in to replace the prior charm of the path.

The tangle tree was a charred stump. The villagers had really done the job, destroying a long-term enemy. But the village itself was now quiet, with black drapes in the windows; it was in mourning for the last party of males to be lost to the siren.

How suddenly that changed, as those males marched in! "You survived!" Trolla cried, tears of untrollish joy streaming down her horrible face. "We tried to follow you, but could not hear the siren and could not trace the path in the dark. In the morning we knew it was too late, and we had wounded to attend to—"

"We have nullified the siren—and her sister, the gorgon," Bink said. "No more men will go that way. But the men who went before—"

"They are all dead; we know."

"No. They are stone. There may be a way to reverse the spell and restore them. If we are successful in our quest—"

"Come, we must celebrate!" Trolla cried. "We shall give you such a party—"

146

Bink knew the answer to that. "Uh, no thanks. You are very kind, but all we want to do now is get on with our quest. We seek the ultimate source of magic— the source of your magic dust, underground."

"There is no way down there," Trolla said. "It wells up in a solid shaft—"

"Yes. So we will seek elsewhere. If any avenue of access exists, from another direction—"

Disappointed, Trolla accepted the situation with grace. "Which way do you go?"

"That way," Bink said, indicating the direction Crombie had pointed for the resumption of their quest.

"But that's into the heart of the Region of Madness!"

Bink smiled. "Perhaps our access is through madness, then."

"The route past the tangle tree is open now. You could go out that way, and loop about to avoid the madness—"

Bink shook his head in negation, knowing that had that been the best way, Crombie would have indicated it.

"You males are so unreasonable! At least wait a few days. We will stop lofting the magic dust into the air, and the effect will diminish. Then you may traverse the region less hazardously."

"No. We have decided to push on." Bink feared that a few days' relaxation in this village of eager females would be as ruinous as continued dalliance with the siren and gorgon. They had to move on.

"Then we shall provide a guide. She can warn you of the immediate traps, and it is barely possible you will survive until clear of the worst of it. You are already half mad, after all."

"Yes," Bink agreed with a wry smile. "We are males." Neither sex understood the other; that was yet another aspect of the magic of Xanth. He rather liked this tame female troll; apparently almost any monster could be worthwhile once it was possible to know it personally.

The guide turned out to be a very pretty female griffin. "Squawk!" Crombie protested. "Awk! Awk!" she replied archly. "Don't saddle us with a chick like

147

that!" Grundy translated happily. "Who are you calling a chick? I'm a lioness!" "You're a nuisance!" "And you're a bore!" "Female!" "Male!"

"Uh, that's enough translation, Grundy," Bink said. "They're down to ultimate insults." He turned to Trolla. "Thank you for the guide. We'll be on our way now."

All the females of the village lined up to wave goodbye. It was a sad but necessary parting.

The wilderness of Xanth soon abolished sentimentality. The trees were extremely large here, closing in to form a dense jungle. This was the downwind region of the magic dust, as Trolla had warned; magic flourished here. Monstrous pincushions grew at the lowest level, stabbing anyone who passed too near; living stalagmites projected between the cushions, their stony points glistening with moisture that fell on them from above. Oil slicks twined wherever suitable depressions were available. The oil was more slippery than anything else, and at the same time more tenacious. "Those tanker trees shouldn't flush their wastes on the surface," Chester muttered. "They should bury it, the way civilized creatures do."

Yet the higher growths were no more promising; the huge metal trunks of ironwood trees crowded against the burned-out boles of ash. Rust and ashes coated the ground around them. Here and there bull spruces snorted and flexed their branch-horns menacingly. Above, it was worse yet; caterpillar nettles crawled along, peering down with prickly anticipation, and vomit-fungus dangled in greasy festoons. Where was there safe passage?

"Awk!" the guide said, showing the way. She glided past an outcropping of hissing serpentine, between two sharp blades of slash pine, and on over the rungs of a fallen ladder-bush. The others followed, wary but swift.

It was gloomy here, almost dark, though the day was rising onto noon. The canopy overhead, not satisfied with shutting out the sun, now constricted like an elastic band until it seemed to enclose them in one tight bubble. Like elastic? Now Bink saw it *was* elastic, from a huge elastic vine that stretched between and around the other foliage. Elastic was not a serious threat to people carrying swords or knives, but it could be a considerable inconvenience.

There seemed to be few large creatures here; but many small ones. Bugs were all over. Some Bink recognized: lightning bugs zapping their charges (this must have been where the demonstration bug had come from, the one that had burned up in the village), soldier beetles marching in precise formations to their bivouac, ladybugs and damselflies hovering near in the immemorial fashion of easy-virtue females near armies. Almost under Chester's hooves a tiger beetle pounced on a stag beetle, making its kill with merciless efficiency. Bink averted his gaze, knowing that such activity was natural, but still not liking it.

Then he noticed Humfrey. The man was staring as if enchanted: a worrisome sign, here. "Are you all right, Magician?" Bink asked.

"Marvelous!" the man murmured raptly. "A treasure trove of nature!"

"You mean the bugs?"

"There's a feather-winged beetle," Humfrey said. Sure enough, a bug with two bright feathers for wings flew by. "And an owl-fly. And two net-wings!" Bink saw the large-eyed, tufted bug sitting on a branch, watching the two nets hover. How a net-wing flew was unclear, as the nets obviously could not hold air. But with magic, what did it matter? "And a picture-winged fly!" the Magician exclaimed, really excited. "That's a new species, I believe; it must have mutated. Let me get my text." He eagerly fumbled open a vial. The vapor came forth and formed a huge tome that the Magician balanced precariously on the back of the griffin, between the folded wings, as he turned over the pages. "PICTURE-WING," he read. "Pastoral, Still-life, Naturalistic, Surrealistic, Cubist, Watercolor, Oil, Pastel Chalk, Pen-and-Ink, Charcoal—I was right! This is a Crayon-Drawing species, unlisted! Bink, verify this for the record!"

Bink leaned over to look. The bug was sitting on the griffin's right ear, its wings outspread, covered by waxy illustrations. "Looks like crayon to me," he agreed.

"Yes!" Humfrey cried. "I must record it! What a

fantastic discovery!" Bink had never seen the man so excited. Suddenly he realized something important: this was what the Good Magician lived for. Humfrey's talent was information, and the discovery and classification of living things was right in line with this. To him there was nothing more important than the acquisition of facts, and he had naturally been resentful about being distracted from this. Now chance had returned him to his type of discovery. For the first time, Bink was seeing the Magician in his animation. Humfrey was not a cold or grasping individual; he was as dynamic and feeling as anyone—when it showed.

Bink felt a tug at his sword. He clapped his hand to the hilt—and two robber flies buzzed up. They had been trying to steal his sword! Then Chester jumped, almost dislodging him. "Almost stepped on a blister beetle," the centaur explained. "I wouldn't want to pull up with a blistered hoof at this stage!"

The lady griffin glanced back, rotating her head without turning her body, in the way griffins had. "Awk!" she exclaimed impatiently. "Hurry up, shrimp," the golem translated. "We're getting near the madness zone."

"Squawk!" Crombie replied irritably. "We're doing the best we can. Why don't you show us a better path, birdbrain?"

"Listen, cattail!" she awked back. "I'm only doing this as a favor to you! If you numbskulls had stayed at the village where you belonged—"

"Stay in a village of females? You're mad already!"

Then they had to stop squawking and awking to dodge a snake-fly that wriggled through, fangs gaping. This time Chester did step on a bug—a stink bug. A horrible odor wafted up, sending them all leaping forward to escape it. The lady griffin's passage stirred up a motley swarm of deerflies, tree hoppers, tiger moths, and a fat butterfly that splattered the Magician with butter.

One lovely gold bug fluttered up under Bink's nose. "Maybe this is another new one!" he cried, getting caught up in the Magician's enthusiasm. He grabbed for it, but Chester stumbled just then so that Bink missed it. "It's headed toward you, Magician!" he cried. "Catch it!"

But Humfrey shied away. "That's a midas fly!" he exclaimed in horror. "Don't touch it!"

"A midas fly?"

"Everything it touches turns to gold." The fly was now circling the Magician, looking for a place to land.

"But that's wonderful!" Bink said. "We must capture it. We can use gold!"

"Not if we become gold ourselves!" Humfrey snapped. He ducked so low that he fell off the griffin. The midas fly settled down to land in his place.

"Crombie!" Bink screamed. "Watch out!"

Then the lady griffin crashed into Crombie, knocking him out of the way with her leonine shoulder. He escaped—but the midas fly landed instead on her.

Just like that, she was a gold statue. The fly buzzed up and away, no longer a threat—but its damage had been done.

"They're extremely rare, and they don't land often," Humfrey said from the bush he had landed in. "I'm amazed we encountered one. Perhaps it was maddened by the dust." He picked himself up.

"It may have been sent," Bink said. "It appeared near me first."

Crombie rolled to his feet with the litheness of his kind. "Squawk!" "She did it for me—to save my life," Grundy translated. "Why?"

"It must indeed be madness," Chester said drily.

Bink contemplated the statue. "Like the handiwork of the gorgon," he murmured. "Gold instead of stone. Is it possible she can be restored?"

Crombie whirled and pointed. "Squawk!" "The answer lies in the same direction as the quest," Grundy said. "Now birdbeak has personal reason to complete it."

"First we must pass through the madness—without a guide," Chester pointed out.

Bink looked ahead, dismayed. Things had abruptly taken a more serious turn—and they had not been unserious before. "How can we find our way safely through this jungle, even without madness?"

"Crombie will have to point out our best route—

one step at a time," Humfrey said. "Look—there is a walking stick." He indicated the stick, ambling along on two tiny feet at the base, its hooked top wobbling erratically. The huge text was gone; he must have conjured it back into its bottle while Bink had been distracted. He hardly needed it. "Mahogany-handled— a very fine specimen."

Crombie pointed the way, and they went slowly on, leaving the gold lady griffin where she stood. There was nothing they could do for her—except complete their quest, hoping to find the magic that would restore her.

Crombie looked back twice, not squawking; he seemed to be having serious private thoughts. For him, the woman-hater, the female's sacrifice had to be an awful enigma, of more significance than his own near-miss with the golden doom. As a soldier he was used to danger, but not to self-sacrifice.

All too soon, dusk loomed. Glowworms appeared from their tunnels in the ground, and bedbugs were already snoring in their bunks. A confused cockroach crowed, mistaking dusk for dawn. Swallowtails consumed their hind parts and disappeared for the night. A group of sawflies sawed boards for their own nocturnal roosts.

Bink looked about. "Right now, I wouldn't mind being a bug," he said. "They're at home here."

Chester agreed soberly. "I have spent the evening in the open before, but never in the deep wilderness. We will not enjoy this night."

Bink looked at Humfrey. The Magician was still absorbed in his taxonomy. "There's a rhinoceros beetle, trying to bull-doze down houses," Humfrey said. "Those houseflies aren't going to like that!"

"Sir, it will be dangerous to sleep out here. If your magic can help us pick the best spot—"

"Now they're bringing in carpenter ants to shore up the timbers!"

"Maybe something from one of your bottles, some temporary shelter for the night—" Bink continued.

"But that rhino is too stupid to quit! He—"

"Magician!" Bink snapped, losing patience.

Humfrey glanced up. "Oh, hello, Bink. Haven't you

set up for the night yet?" He glanced down again. "Look! They've hired an assassin bug! They're going to get rid of that—"

It was useless. The Magician cared more for information than for safety. Humfrey was no leader, which explained why he had been so ready to leave that chore to Bink. So it was up to Bink, again.

"We'll have to make some sort of shelter," he decided. "And keep watch in turns." He paused, considering the problems. How could they make shelter, when every piece of wood, stone, or foliage would be fiercely protective of its rights? This was the untamed wilderness!

Then his roving gaze spied a prospect: the great curving bones of a defunct monster. He couldn't tell what kind of animal it had been in life, but it must have been larger than a dragon. The bones seemed too solid for a roc, and there was no sign of wings, so probably it had been a grown groundborne sphinx. Ten times the height of a man. The only reason sphinxes did not rule the jungle was their rarity, and disinterest in ordinary matters. Dragons were common, while sphinxes were hardly ever encountered. Bink wondered why that was so, and what could kill a sphinx in its prime. Boredom, perhaps. "Crombie, point out the direction of the closest suitable or adaptable site for our overnight camp," he said, wishing to verify his notion.

Crombie obliged. He pointed toward the bones. Bink's hunch had been right! He was gratified. "We'll gather some blanket leaves and spread them over those bones," he said. "That will make us a decent shelter, and it can serve as a fort in case of attack. Crombie, point us out the nearest blankets."

The griffin pointed—right into the quivering ropes of a predator tree. It was not a tangler, but seemed related; it would hardly be safe to go there! "Well, maybe we can stay on guard better if we can see out," Bink decided. "Chester, why don't you stand the first watch. Wake me up the moment you find yourself getting sleepy, then wake Crombie."

The centaur nodded agreement. He did not inquire about Humfrey's share of the work; obviously the Magician would not be reliable for this.

Chapter 8. Mad Constellations

Bink paused for a call of nature, not of magic—and spied a chunk of wood, so dark and moss-grown that it resembled a rock. Something like that could be useful, in case a monster attacked in the night. The wood seemed to have a nice heft, good for throwing. He squatted to pick it up—and paused, in case it should be enchanted. But his talent would protect him; if the piece were dangerous, he would be unable to touch it.

He picked it up, observing the etched grain of it, brown and green and white and altogether intriguing. It was surprisingly hard and heavy, for wood; he wondered whether it would float or sink in water. He felt a tingle in his hand as he held the chunk. There was some quality about it, something magic, strange and potent. He felt his talent responding, taking nebulous hold, sizing up this thing, as it had once before when he drank from the spring of life. As before, his magic encompassed that of the other thing, and accepted it without penalty. Bink's talent was of Magician stature; he seldom felt its action directly except when it encountered strong or complex opposing magic. Yet—a chunk of wood?

He carried the chunk back to their temporary camp. "I don't know what this is, but it seems to be strongly magical. It may be useful."

Chester took it. "Wood, unusual, durable. This might have come from a very large, old tree. I don't recognize the species, which makes it remarkable. Maybe you could find some of the bark—"

Crombie squawked. "Give it here, horseface. I've seen a lot of wood in my day."

154

Chester stiffened only slightly. "By all means, bird-beak."

Crombie held the chunk in one foreclaw and inspected it closely. "Squawk." "Something odd about this."

"Yes," Bink agreed. "Before you get too involved, will you point out the nearest food for us? We can eat while considering."

Crombie obligingly whirled and pointed. Bink looked, and saw a large glowing fungus. "That must be it. I never ate glow before, but your talent's never wrong." He walked over and reached down to break off a section. The fungus was firm and dry, pale inside, and emitted a pleasant odor.

"Squawk!" Crombie protested to the centaur. "I'm not through with it."

"You've had it long enough, buzzard-brain," Chester said. "My turn now."

Bink had to run to break up yet another quarrel. The trouble with fighting creatures was that they tended to fight! He couldn't turn his back on them even to fetch food. "It's the Magician's turn!" he cried. "Maybe he can identify it." He took back the wood and carried it to Humfrey. "Sir, if you care to classify this rare specimen—"

He had said the magic words. The Magician's attention was attracted. He looked. He blinked. "That's Blue Agony fungus! Get rid of it!"

Oops! Bink had put the wrong hand down, and shoved the fungus under Humfrey's nose. "Sorry. I meant to show you this wood, not the—" He paused. "The fungus is poisonous?"

"Its magic will turn your whole body blue, just before you melt into a blue puddle that kills all the vegetation in the ground where it soaks in," Humfrey assured him.

"But Crombie pointed it out as safe to eat!"

"Ridiculous! It's safe to touch, but the unsafest thing anyone could eat. They used to use it for executions, back in the bad old early Waves."

Bink dropped the fungus. "Crombie, didn't you—" He broke off, reconsidering. "Crombie, would you point out the worst thing we could eat?"

155

The griffin shrugged and pointed. Right toward the fungus.

"You absolute idiot!" Chester exclaimed to the griffin. "Have the feathers in your brains rotted? You just a moment ago pointed it out as safe!"

Crombie squawked angrily. "Bink must have picked up the wrong item. My talent is never wrong."

Humfrey was now examining the piece of wood. "Crombie's talent is always wrong," he remarked absently. "That's why I never rely on it."

Even Chester was surprised at this. "Magician, the soldier is no prize—even I am willing to concede that—but usually his talent is sound."

Crombie squawked, outraged at this qualified endorsement.

"Maybe so. I wouldn't know." The Magician squinted at a passing sweat gnat. "What is that creature?"

"You don't recognize a common sweat gnat?" Bink asked, amazed. "A moment ago you were classifying the most obscure bugs, discovering new species!"

Humfrey's brow furrowed. "Why should I do that? I know nothing about bugs."

Man, griffin, and centaur exchanged glances. "First Crombie, then the Magician," Chester murmured. "It must be the madness."

"But wouldn't that affect all of us?" Bink asked, worried. "This is more like a misfire of talents. Crombie pointed out the worst food instead of the best, and Humfrey switched from knowledge to ignorance—"

"Right when the chunk of wood switched hands!" Chester finished.

"We'd better get him away from that wood."

"Yes," Chester agreed, and stepped toward Humfrey.

"No, please—let me do it," Bink said quickly, confident that his talent could handle the situation best. He approached Humfrey. "Excuse me, sir." He lifted the chunk gently from the Magician's grasp.

"Why doesn't it affect you?" Chester asked. "Or me?"

"It affects you, centaur," Humfrey said. "But since

you don't know your talent, you don't see how it is reversed. As for Bink—he is a special case."

So the Good Magician was back in form. "Then this wood . . . reverses spells?" Bink asked.

"More or less. At least it changes the thrust of active magic. I doubt it would restore the griffin cow or the stone men, if that's what you're contemplating. Those spells are now passive. Only a complete interruption of magic itself would nullify them."

"Uh, yes," Bink said uncertainly.

"What kind of a special case are you?" Chester demanded of Bink. "You don't do any magic."

"You might say I'm immune," Bink said cautiously, wondering why his talent was no longer protecting itself from discovery. Then he looked down at the wood in his hand. *Was* he immune?

He dropped the wood. "Squawk!" Crombie said. "So that's why my talent missed! That wood made me . . . *pumf squawk screech—*"

The golem had wandered near the wood, and his translation had disintegrated. Bink gently lifted Grundy away from it.

". . . of what I meant to," the golem continued, blithely unaware of the change. "It's dangerous!"

"It certainly is," Bink agreed. He kicked the wood away.

Chester was not reassured. "That means this was an incidental foul-up. We have yet to face the madness."

Crombie located the nearest safe food, successfully this time. It was a lovely cookie bush growing from the rich soil beside the bones. They feasted on chocolate-chip cookies. A handy water-chestnut tree provided ample drink: all they had to do was pluck the fresh chestnuts and puncture them to extract the water.

As Bink chewed and drank, his eye fell on another earth mound. This time he scraped it away carefully with a stick, but could find nothing except loose earth. "I think these things are following me," he said. "But what is the point? They don't do anything, they just sit there."

"I'll take a look at one in the morning," the Magician said, his curiosity moderately aroused.

They set up house within the gaunt cage of bones as

darkness closed in. Bink lay back on the cushion of sponge moss beneath the skeleton—he had checked this out carefully to make sure it was harmless—and watched the stars emerge. Camping out was not so terrible!

At first the stars were mere points of light peeking between the bars of the bone-enclosure. But soon Bink perceived patterns in them: the constellations. He was not conversant with the stars, because Xanth was not safe at night; he had stayed inside, and when caught outside had hurried to shelter. Thus he found the landscape of the night sky intriguing. He had somehow thought, for no good reason, that the stars were of equivalent brightness, evenly dispersed. Instead, they were highly varied in both respects, ranging from piercing-bright to look-again dim, and from solitary splendor to clustered confusion. In fact they seemed to form patterns. In his mind he could draw lines between them, fashioning pictures. There was the head of a man, and a curving line like a snake, and a blob with tentacles like a tangle tree. As he concentrated, these things became more definite. The figures assumed greater definition and conviction, seeming almost real.

"Say, there's a centaur!" Bink exclaimed.

"Naturally," Chester said. "That's one of the established constellations. Been there for centuries."

"But it looks alive! I thought I saw it move."

"No, the constellations don't move. Not that way. They—" Chester broke off.

"He *did* move!" Bink cried. "His arm, fetching an arrow from his bag—"

"His quiver," Chester corrected him. "Something strange here. Must be atmospherics."

"Or maybe the air moving," Bink said.

Chester snorted. They watched the centaur in the sky take out his arrow, fit it to his bow, and cast about for some target. There was a swan in view, but it was a very large, tame bird, not suitable for hunting. There was a fox, but it slid out of sight behind some herdsmen before the centaur could take proper aim. Then a great bear showed up. It was trying to catch a lion cub, but the adult lion was nearby, almost as large as the bear and in an ornery mood. The two big predators circled each other, while the pointing arrowhead of the centaur traced their movements; which one should be taken first?

"Take the lion, stupid," Chester muttered. "Then the bear will take the cub, and leave you alone."

Bink was fascinated, both by this animation of the constellations, and by the strength and grace of the weird beasts. The centaur was a regular creature, of course—but only in mythology relating to Mundania did animals like bears and lions and swans exist. Parts of them showed up in the form of sphinxes, chimerae, griffins, and such, but that didn't really count. A Mundane lion could also be reckoned as the body of a griffin with the head of an ant lion, a composite deriving from the Xanth originals. Now with the shield down, animals could cross the boundary freely, and probably at the fringe all types mixed. Bink regretted, in retrospect, that he had not had the chance to see such creatures as bears in the flesh, when he had visited Mundania. But he had been glad enough to return to Xanth, then!

Almost under the centaur's tail, another strange Mundane creature appeared: a wolf. It resembled a one-headed dog. Bink had seen werewolves in the flesh, but that might not count. What a horror it must be in Mundania, where wolves were locked permanently in their animal form, unable to revert to men!

The sky-centaur whirled on the wolf, aiming his bow. But the wolf was already moving on, because a huge scorpion was following him. The scorpion was being chased by a man—no, it only thought the man was after it. The man, a hugely muscled brute, was actually pursuing a serpent, trying to smash in its head with a club. Yet a dragon was hot after the man, and a really strange long-necked animal followed the dragon. In fact the whole sky was alive with oddities, making it seem like a much more interesting place than the Land of Xanth.

"What is that thing with the neck?" Bink asked.

"Mythological zoology is not my specialty," Chester said. "But I believe it is a Mundane monster called a gaffe." He paused. "No, that's not quite it. A grraff. No. A—a giraffe! That's it. The long neck is to keep it

159

clear of hostile ground magic, or something. Its strangest feature, as I understand it, is that despite that long neck it has no voice."

"Strange magic indeed!" Bink agreed.

"Strange *un*magic, technically. The Land of Mundania could use a good, sensible shot of magic."

The sky was now densely crowded with animals, as the remaining stars emerged. Farther along was a crab, and a wingless bull, and a genuine single-headed dog. Birds abounded—half-familiar ones like the phoenix and bird of paradise, and a host of strange ones, like the crane, toucan, eagle, peacock, dove, and crow. There were people too—men, children, and several fetching young women.

That reminded Bink again of Chameleon. The longer he was away from her, the more he missed her. So what if she had her ugly phase? She also had her lovely phase—

"Look—there is the River Eridanus," Chester cried.

Bink found it. The river flowed half across the sky, meandering from the feet of a giant all the way to— Bink couldn't see where it finished. Where could a river in the sky go? All manner of fish were associated with it, and one— "What is that?" Bink cried.

"The fabulous Mundane whale," Chester said. "I'm glad no such monster as that exists in our land!"

Bink agreed emphatically. He traced the river again, seeking its termination. It spread and thinned, becoming vague, eluding him. Then he spied a small lizard. "A chameleon!" he exclaimed.

As he spoke its name, the lizard changed, becoming the human Chameleon he knew and loved: his wife. She looked out at him from the deepest depths of the sky, and her mouth opened. *Bink, Bink,* she seemed to say. *Come to me . . .*

Bink was on his feet, nearly banging his head against a bone. "I'm coming!" he cried joyfully. Why had he ever left her?

But there was no way to reach her. He could not climb the air, or fly up there, and in any event he knew she was just a picture, not real. Just a transformed lizard, itself imaginary. Still, he wished—

Now the constellation centaur shot his arrow. The

missile blazed as it flew, forming a brilliant streak across the sky, growing brighter and yet brighter as it drew near. Suddenly it loomed frighteningly large and close, as if flying right out of the sky—and cracked into a nearby tree. It was a dogwood; it yelped with pain, then growled and bared its teethlike inner branches in canine fury, seeking its enemy. In a moment it had torn the arrow to shreds.

Bink looked across at Chester, but could not make out the centaur's expression in the dark. That constellation arrow, no more than a shooting star, had struck a real tree close by! "Was that centaur shooting at *us?*"

"If he wasn't, he was criminally careless," Chester replied grimly. "If he was, he made a damn poor shot. That's a bad example that reflects on the merits of all centaurs. I will forward him a reminder." Now, visible against the sparkling night sky in silhouette, Chester stood tall and magnificent, a fine stallion of a man, and nocked one of his own arrows. He drew on the bow with all his formidable power and loosed the shaft upward.

Up, up it flew, somehow visible despite the night. Up, impossibly high, right to the verge of the nocturnal dome, right toward the centaur constellation.

Bink knew no physical arrow could strike a star or pattern of stars. After all, the constellations were merely imaginary lines drawn between those stars. Yet—

Chester's arrow plunked into the flank of the constellation centaur. The creature leaped with pain. From his mouth issued two comets and a shooting star: a powerful exclamation!

"Yeah? Same to you, vacuumhead!" Chester retorted.

The constellation reached back and yanked at Chester's arrow. A nova exploded from his mouth as he contemplated the damage. Several dim stars pulsed there, suggestive of the wound. He grabbed a handful of soft down feathers from the swan and rubbed them against the injury. Now it was the defeathered swan who cussed a bright streak of shooting stars, but the bird did not dare attack the centaur.

The sky-centaur snatched the extensible tube called

the telescope and put it to his eye. The magic of this tube enabled him to see much farther than otherwise. "****!!" he exclaimed with really foul invective, looking for the originator of the objectionable arrow.

"Right here, hoofhead!" Chester bawled, and lofted another arrow into the sky. "Come down and fight like a centaur!"

"Uh, I wouldn't—" Bink cautioned.

The constellation seemed to hear the challenge. He swung his telescope around and oriented on the bone-camp. A vile ringed planet shot from his mouth.

"That's right, dope!" Chester cried. "Come prove you're worthy of the name!"

Worthy of the name "dope"? Bink didn't like this at all, but was unable to stop it.

The constellation nocked another arrow. So did Chester. For a time the two faced each other, bows drawn, as it were, daring each other to shoot first. Then, almost together, their arrows leaped forth.

Both shots were uncomfortably accurate. Bink saw the two arrows cross midway in the heavens and home in on their targets as if magically guided. Neither centaur moved: this was evidently a point of honor in such duels. The one who jumped clear would show weakness of nerve, and few centaurs were weak in that department.

Both arrows missed—but not by much. Chester's shot almost grazed the constellation's forehead while the sky-centaur's arrow thunked into the ground beside Chester's left forehoof, which happened to be quite close to the Good Magician's head.

Humfrey woke with a start. "You equine menace!" he cried grumpily. "Watch what you're doing!"

"I am watching," Chester said. "That's not my arrow. See, it has stardust on it."

Humfrey drew the arrow from the dirt. "Why, so it does." He squinted up into the sky. "But stardust is not supposed to be down here. What's going on?"

Now Crombie stirred. "Squawk!" "You're the Magician," the golem said. "You're supposed to know about things."

"About stellar constellations coming to life? It's been a long time since I reviewed that particular magic."

162

Humfrey stared up into the sky. "However, it would be a worthwhile study. Crombie, where's the most convenient access to that realm?"

Crombie pointed. Now Bink saw a pattern of stars resembling steps coming down to the horizon. They looked increasingly solid, and they seemed closer as he looked, descending almost to the rim of bones. Maybe it was possible after all to ascend!

He looked up into the stars again. They were even more brilliant than before, and the lines between them were stronger. The stick figures had assumed shadings that made them quite realistic. He saw Chameleon again, beckoning him. "I'm going up!"

"Squawk!" Crombie agreed. "I'm always ready for a good fight, and that comet-mouthed centaur needs a lesson."

Chester was already on his way to the steps, but at this he paused.

"Don't be a fool," the Magician snapped, running after them. "Crombie refers to the centaur in the sky, not you. You are loudmouthed, not comet-mouthed."

"Um, of course," Chester agreed without complete enthusiasm. He made a visible effort to shake off the annoyance. "Charge!"

They charged for the steps.

"Are you fools crazy?" Grundy yelled. "There's nothing up there for you!"

Chester glanced at him; Bink saw the change in the shape of the centaur's head outlined against the massed constellations. "I didn't hear Crombie squawk."

"He didn't squawk!" the golem yelled. "I'm speaking for myself this time. Don't go into the sky! It's madness!"

"It's fascinating," Humfrey said. "Firsthand study of animated constellations! There may never be a better opportunity."

"I have to teach that centaur a lesson," Chester said.

Bink's eyes had returned to Chameleon. His need for her became as big as the sky. He continued forward.

"It's the madness," Grundy cried, yanking at the feathers of Crombie's neck. "It doesn't affect me. I see

163

only the facts, because I'm not real. This is hostile magic. Don't go!"

"You're probably right, twerp," Humfrey agreed. "But this offering is too compelling to be denied."

"So was the siren! Don't do it!" Grundy repeated. "Where is your quest, if you let the madness take you now?"

"What do you care?" Chester demanded. "You have no feelings." He put his forehooves on the first step. It was firm, anchored at every corner by a pinpoint star. The lines were like threads, and the panels between them like glass. A translucent staircase, not quite invisible, going up into the sky.

Bink knew it was magic, and not to be trusted. But Chameleon was up there, waiting for him, and he had to go. His talent would not permit it if it were not safe, after all.

"Well, I'm not going!" Grundy screamed. He jumped from the griffin's back, fell into the foliage of a flower-bug bush, and scared up a swarm of flowerbugs. In a moment he was lost in the night.

"Good riddance," Chester muttered, mounting the steps. The surfaces bowed slightly under his weight, drawing the anchoring stars inward, but held. Crombie, impatient with this, spread his wings and flew around the centaur and came to rest higher on the stairway. Apparently the ascent was too steep for comfortable flying by a creature of this size, so he preferred to mount by foot. The Good Magician was third, and Bink last.

In a line they ascended. The stairway spiraled, so that soon Crombie was climbing directly above Bink. It was an interesting effect, but Bink was more intrigued by the view below. As he climbed above the level of the trees, the nocturnal landscape of the Xanth wilderness opened out below, impressive because of its special nature. Bink had once been transformed into a bird, and once had ridden a magic carpet, and once had flown in human form; magic had given him quite a varied experience. But this slow ascent up through the levels of the forest, with firm footing beneath him —this was different from the various forms of flight, and in a certain respect unique. He was highly aware than he could fall; the steps had no railing to hold him in, no barrier at the fringes of the steps. This seemed to put him right into the situation in a way that flight did not. To be above the ground, yet tied to it . . .

The night forest was beautiful. A number of trees glowed. Some reached bone-white tentacles up; others were balls of pastel hues. Some had giant flowers that resembled eyes, and these eyes seemed to be focusing on Bink. Other treetops formed into mazes of interlocking branches. As he watched, the whole forest assumed the shape of a single human face. DON'T GO! it mouthed.

Bink paused, momentarily disgruntled. Was the wilderness really trying to speak to him? Whose interest did it represent? It could be jealous of his escape to the sky. Hungry for his body. Or just mischievous.

Crombie had balked at the tangle tree. Chester had been fortuitously deafened in time to save them from the siren's call. His talent had been operating then. Why was it quiescent now?

He looked upward. The enormous panorama of the sky awaited him—animals, monsters, and people. They were all frozen in place at the moment, awaiting the arrival of Bink's party. Up there lay adventure.

He resumed his climb. He had to hurry, because the others had continued moving, and were now several spirals ahead of him. He didn't want to be late for the action!

As he caught up to the Magician, who was lagging behind the stout four-legged entities, something buzzed in from the darkness to the side. It sounded like a very large insect, one of the exotic bugs. Not another gold bug, he hoped! He waved his arms, hoping to scare it off.

"Bink!" a small voice cried.

What now? He was getting winded from his rapid climb, and had to watch carefully to be sure he didn't make a misstep while absorbing the splendors of the immense canopy above and the broad disk below. He was in the very center of a phenomenal scene, and he wanted to experience every aspect of it with full intensity, and he didn't need any bugs distracting him. "Go away!"

The bug flew near. There was light associated with it. It was a flying fish, propelling itself by a jet of bubbles from its fuselage, so that its rigid wings could provide sufficient lift. The gills were air-intakes, and assorted little fins provided stability and spot maneuverability. Flying fish were swift, Bink knew; they had to be, or they dropped to the ground. This one carried a light on its back like a miniature lantern, and—

"Bink! It's Grundy!" And lo, it was indeed the golem, braced on the back of the fish, guiding it with little reins and a bit set in its mouth. Grundy's free hand held the lamp, which seemed to be a tiny star, captive in a little net. "I caught this fish by luring it with fish-talk; now it understands and is helping. I have the spell-reversal wood along." He tapped his saddle with his rein-hand. It was the gnarly fragment that Bink had discarded.

"But how can the fish fly?" Bink demanded. "How can you translate? The reversal—"

"It doesn't affect the fish because the fish has no talent; the fish *is* magical," Grundy explained with limited patience. "The wood only reverses exterior magic, not inherent magic."

"That doesn't make much sense to me," Bink said.

"The wood reversed birdbeak's talent, but did not change him back into a man," the golem continued. "It fouled up the gnome's information, but did not make him a regular man either. It didn't affect you, because—"

The golem was not aware of Bink's talent, but this remained a pertinent question: had Bink's talent conquered the wood—or been reversed by it? The answer could be a matter of life and death! "What about you?" Bink demanded. "You're still translating!"

"I'm not real," Grundy said shortly. "Take away my magic and I'm nothing but string and mud. The wood is just wood, to me."

"But the wood was affecting you before! You were speaking gibberish, until I got you away from it."

"Was I?" Grundy asked, startled. "I never realized. I guess translation *is* my talent, so . . ." He faded out, considering. "I know! I'm not translating now. I'm speaking for myself!"

And there was the answer. "Well, keep that wood away from me," Bink said. "I don't trust it."

"No. I have to bring it close to you. Put your hand on it, Bink."

"I will not!" Bink exclaimed.

Grundy jerked the reins to one side, kicked the flanks of the fish, and leaned forward. The fish swerved, reared, and accelerated right at Bink. "Hey!" he protested as it grazed his hand.

But at that moment his outlook changed. Abruptly the stars were mere stars, and the stairs—were the branches of a latticework tree. Above him the others were near its summit, about to step onto the thinning twigs that could not support their weight. Crombie was already supporting much of his mass by flapping his wings, and Chester—

Bink shook his head in amazement. A centaur climbing a tree!

Then the fish buzzed out of range, and the madness returned. Bink was on the translucent stairway again, climbing toward the glowing constellations. "It's crazy, I know!" he cried. "But I can't help myself. I have to go on up!"

The golem guided his fish in close again. "You can't throw it off even when you *know* it's doom?"

"It's mad!" Bink agreed, suffering a measure of sanity as the wood passed near again. "But true! But don't worry about me—I'll survive. Go get Chester off that branch before he kills himself!"

"Right!" Grundy agreed. He spurred his mount and buzzed upward. Bink resumed his climb, cursing himself for his foolishness.

The fish disappeared in the night. Only the caged star—that Bink now knew was nothing more than a glowberry—showed Grundy's location. That light moved up near the centaur.

"Good grief, golem!" Chester exclaimed. "What the horsefeathers am I doing in a tree?"

Bink could not hear Grundy's side of the conversation, but could guess its nature. After a moment Chester started backing down the stairway steps.

167

"Hey, oaf!" the Magician cried. "Get your ass's rear out of my face!"

"Go down," the centaur cried. "This is no stair, it's a tree. We're climbing to our doom."

"It's information. Let me by!"

"It's madness! Grundy, take your wood to him."

The light descended. "Great galloping gizzards!" Humfrey cried. "It *is* a tree! We've got to get down!"

But now the centaur was climbing again. "I haven't finished my business with that constellation centaur," he said.

"You equine fool!" Humfrey exclaimed. "Desist!"

The fish zoomed down toward Bink. "I can't handle them both," Grundy cried. "I've only got the single piece of wood, and there are four of you."

"The griffin can fly; he'll be all right for now," Bink said. "The stair—I mean the tree—is narrow. Give Chester the wood; no one can pass him. Then you search for more wood."

"I had already thought of that," the golem said. The fish zoomed off. In a moment Chester reversed his course again. The Good Magician cursed in most un-Magicianlike vernacular, but was forced to retreat in the face of the centaur's rear. Soon they were right above Bink—and he too cursed as his ascent was balked.

The constellations, seeing the retreat, exploded in rage. "***!!" the sky centaur cried silently. At his summons, the other monsters of the heavens gathered: the dragon, the hydra, the serpent, the winged horse, the giant, and in the river the whale.

The madness remained upon him, but Bink no longer wanted to climb the stairway. The monsters were converging, clustering about the top of the stair-spiral. The serpent was starting down, its sinuous body coiling along the spiral, while the winged ones flew down. Bink was not certain whether they were real or illusion or something in between—but remembering the arrow-strike at the dogwood tree, he was disinclined to gamble. "We've got to get under cover!" he cried.

But Crombie, highest on the stair and unaffected by the spell-wood, flew up to do battle with the winged horse. "Squawk!" he cried. "Neigh!" the horse replied.

Grundy buzzed by on his steed. "Oooh, what they said!"

Wings spread, griffin and horse faced off, claws swiping, hooves striking. Contact was made, but Bink couldn't tell from the whirling, flapping silhouettes which creature was prevailing.

Then the serpent arrived. Chester could not use his bow effectively, since no arrow would travel a spiral path, so waited with his sword. Bink wondered what the centaur saw, since he had the wood and so perceived reality—or something. Probably it was not a serpent, but an equivalent threat. Meanwhile Bink had to interpret it as he saw it.

As the huge snake-head came close, the centaur bellowed a warning and struck it across the nose. Blade met fang. The serpent's teeth were large, reflecting starlight, and they gleamed with what might be poison. There were two projecting ones, and they moved with the precision of a fencer. Chester was compelled to retreat, since he had only one sword.

Then Chester took a cue from the winged horse, and used his front hooves. He bashed the serpent on the nose, one-two, one-two, while dazzling it with the sword. His front feet did not have the power of his rear ones, but his hooves had sharp fighting edges and a cumulative impact that could splinter bark from a tree, or scales from a serpent.

What would happen, Bink wondered, if the wood were to touch the serpent? Would it give the serpent a different view of reality? Would the centaur then seem to be something else? How could anyone be sure what magic was real, and what false?

The serpent hissed and gaped its jaws so widely that its mouth became as tall as the centaur. Its sinuous tongue snaked out to wrap around Chester's sword arm, immobilizing it, but Chester shifted his weapon to his other hand, and efficiently lopped off the tongue. The serpent made a hissing howl of agony and snapped its mouth closed, the tusks clanging against each other. Chester took a moment to unwrap the segment of tongue from his arm, then resumed slashing at the nose. He was holding his own.

The dragon arrived. It zoomed in at the Good

Magician. Humfrey might be captive to the madness, but he was not a fool. His hand dived into his jacket and came out with a vial. But so swift was the dragon's onslaught that there was no time to open the container. Instead, Humfrey flipped it into the opening mouth. The dragon snapped at it automatically. The vial crunched under its bite. Vapor exploded, expanding into a cloud that jetted out between the dragon's teeth and coalesced about its head. But it did not form into anything else—no demon, no smoke screen, not even a sandwich. It just clung there in hardening gobs.

"What is it?" Bink cried. "Did the vial misfire?"

"I had to grab randomly," Humfrey replied. "It's —I believe it is foaming insulation."

"Slavering what?"

"Foaming insulation. It foams up, then hardens in place to keep things warm—or cold."

Bink shook his head. The Magician was mad all right.

How could anything act to keep things hot *or* cold? It either had to be like fire, heating, or like ice, cooling. And why would anyone bother with such magic?

The dragon, however, was not taking it with equanimity. It flexed in midair, and shook its head violently from side to side, trying to rid itself of the clinging stuff. It chewed and gulped, seeking to eliminate the foam. "I wouldn't do that, if I were you," Humfrey told it.

The dragon ignored him. It roared. Then it huffed and puffed, working up a head of fire in its belly. It looped about, its flapping wings throwing off chunks of hardened foam. Then it oriented on the Magician and blasted out its terrible fire.

Only a thin jet of flame emerged. Then, surprisingly, the dragon's body began inflating. It swelled up like a balloon, until only the legs, tail, wing tips and snout projected from the ball.

"What—?" Bink asked, amazed.

"The insulation hardens in place immediately in the presence of heat," Humfrey explained. "Thus the dragon's own fire had solidified it. Unfortunately that particular type of insulation is also——"

The dragon exploded. Stars shot out in every direction, scorching the jungle foliage below, zooming by Bink to the side, and making a fine display above.

"——explosively flammable when ignited," Humfrey finished.

They watched the upward-flying stars rise to their heights, then explode in multicolored displays of sparks. The whole night sky became briefly brighter.

"I tried to warn that dragon," Humfrey said without sympathy. "One simply does not apply open flame to flammable insulation."

Bink, privately, hardly blamed the dragon for misunderstanding that caution. He would have made the same mistake as the dragon had. If his talent permitted it. But this did impress on him one thing: should he (perish the thought!) ever have a serious disagreement with the Good Magician, he would have to watch out for those magic bottles! There was no telling what might come out of them.

Now a monster found Bink. It was the hydra. It had no wings, and could not have used the stairs because they were blocked by the serpent. The hydra seemed to have descended by hanging from a thread—but no such thread was visible.

Bink swung at the monster with his sword. He was in excellent form; he caught the nearest of the seven heads cleanly, just behind the horns, and it flew off. Gore spouted out of the neck with such force that the jet separated into two channels. If this was all it took to beat this monster, Bink would have no trouble!

The two jets coagulated in midair, forming into twin lumps still attached to the neck. As more gore emerged, it splashed over these lumps, hardening, enlarging them. Excrescences developed, and the color darkened, until—

The lumps became two new heads! Each was smaller than the original, but just as vicious. Bink had only succeeded in doubling the menace he faced.

This was a problem. If each head he cut off converted into two, the longer and better he fought, the worse off he would be!! Yet if he did not fight well, he would soon be consumed in seven—no, eight chunks.

"Catch, Bink!" Chester called, throwing something. Bink didn't appreciate the interruption to his concentration, but grabbed for it anyway. In the dark his sweeping fingers merely batted it aside. In the moment it touched him, his sanity returned. He saw himself on a branch of the tree, pointing his sword at—

But then the reverse-spell wood bounced out of range, and the madness resumed its grip on him. He saw the chunk fly toward the hydra—and one of the heads reached out to gulp it down.

In that instant Bink suffered a rapid continuation of his prior line of thought. What would spell-reversal do *inside* an imaginary monster? If the hydra form were wholly a product of Bink's distorted perception—his madness, which he shared with his friends—it should be nullified—no, the wood had to be near him, to nullify the monsters he perceived. But since his friends saw the monsters too, and the wood could not be near them all at once—it had to be that the wood would *not* affect the monster, unless that monster had objective reality. Even then, the wood would not affect the form of the hydra, but only its talent—if the hydra had a talent. Most magical creatures did not have magic talents; their magic consisted of their very existence. So—nothing should happen.

The hydra screamed from all its eight mouths. Abruptly it dropped to the ground. It landed heavily and lay still, its stars fading out.

Bink watched it, openmouthed. The hydra had not changed form—it had suffered destruction. What had happened?

Then he worked it out. The hydra had a magic talent after all: that of hanging by an invisible thread. The spell-reversal wood had nullified that magic, causing the monster to plummet forcefully down to its death. Its invisible thread had not disappeared; it had acted to draw the creature *down* as powerfully as it had drawn it *up* before. Disaster!

But now the wood was gone. How were they to escape the madness?

Bink looked up. The Good Magician's foaming agent had destroyed the dragon, and Chester's hooves

172

and sword had beaten back the serpent. Crombie's fighting spirit had proved to be too much for the winged horse. So the individual battles had been won. But the war remained unpromising.

A number of constellations had remained in the sky. The centaur, giant, and whale had not been able to descend, because they lacked wings or flying magic, and the stairway had been pre-empted by the serpent. Now, seeing the fate of their companions, these three bellowed their rage from the safety of the nocturnal welkin. Novas and ringed planets and miniature lightning bolts and curly-tailed comets radiated from their mouths in confusing profusion and wonderful foulness, with the whale spouting obscene curlicues.

"Oh, yeah?" Chester bawled. "We'll come up there and do the same to you! You're the cowards who started it all!" And Crombie and Humfrey and Bink closed in about him as well as they were able.

"No, stop!" Grundy screamed from his flying fish, zooming in a circular holding pattern. "You've all seen the nature of your madness. Don't yield to it again! Pass the wood around, restore your perspectives, get your feet on the ground again! Don't let the spooks lure you to destruction!"

"He's right, you know," Humfrey muttered.

"But I dropped the wood!" Bink cried, "I dropped our sanity!"

"Then go down and fetch it!" the golem cried. "And you, horserear—you threw it to him. You go down and help him."

"Squawk!" Crombie exclaimed. "And birdbeak says he's going up alone to grab all the glory for himself."

"Oh no he doesn't!" Chester roared.

"Right!" the golem agreed. "You have to go together, to be fair about it. You real creatures place great store by fairness, don't you? Or is honor a foreign concept to you, birdbeak? You don't want horserear's competition, because you know he'd show you up if you didn't have a head start?"

"Squawk! Squawk!" Bink almost thought he saw a comet spew from Crombie's mouth.

"Right! So you prove you can match him anywhere, anytime—by getting down there and finding that wood before he does. And take the gnome with you. Horse-rear can take the washout with him."

Washout? That was what the golem had decided to call Bink? Bink's blood pressure started building. Just because his talent wasn't visible—

"All right, and may dung fall on you!" Chester said. "I'll fetch the stupid wood. Then on to glorious battle!"

Thus, ingloriously, they descended the glassy stair.

The monsters above exploded with derision. The sky lit up with their exclamations: exploding cherry bombs in many silent colors, glowing tornadoes, forest fires. The whale diverted the River Eridanus so that its water poured down in a scintillating cataract. The giant swung his huge club, bashing stars out of their sockets and sending them flying down. The centaur fired glowing arrows.

"Keep moving, slowpokes!" the golem yelled. "Keep walking away from their challenges. That makes them madder than anything else you can do!"

"Hey, yeah," Chester agreed. "You're pretty smart for a tangle of string and tar."

"I'm sane—because I have none of the foolish emotions of reality to interfere with my thought processes," Grundy said. "Sane—*because* I am string and tar."

"Therefore you are the only one qualified to lead us out of madness," the Magician said. "You are the only one who can perceive objective reality—because you have no subjective aspect."

"Yes, isn't it great?" But the golem hardly looked happy.

Bink understood, suddenly, that Grundy would gladly join them in madness, though he knew it led to disaster, if this could be the proof of his reality. Only the golem's unreality enabled him to hang on to what life he had. What a paradoxical fate!

An arrow struck a catnip bush right beside him. The plant yowled and spat, nipping at the shaft, then batting it back and forth with its paw-buds.

"Oh, I want to stick an arrow right up under his tail!" Chester muttered. "That centaur's a disgrace to the species."

"First find the wood," Grundy cried.

One of the giant's batted stars whizzed over Bink's

head and ignited a rubber tree. The plant stretched enormously, trying to get away from its own burning substance. The smell was horrible.

"We can't find anything here in the smoke," Chester complained, coughing.

"Then follow me!" Grundy cried, showing the way on his fish.

Choking, they followed the golem. The constellations raged above them, firing volleys of missiles, but could not score directly. Madness had no power over sane leadership.

Yet the madness tried! The whale took hold of the river again and yanked it brutally from its new channel. The water spilled across the starry field in a thinning, milky wash, forming a flood. Then it found a new channel, coursed along it, ripped out several stars growing there, and poured down toward the ground.

"Look out!" Bink cried. "We're at the foot of that waterfall!"

Indeed they were. The mass of water was descending at them like a globulous avalanche. They scrambled desperately—but it caught them, drenching them instantly in its milky fluid, crashing about them with a sound like thunder and foaming waist high. Crombie hunched, bedraggled, his feathers losing their luster; Chester wrapped his arms about his human torso as if to fend the liquid off; and the Magician—

The Good Magician was wrapped in a big, bright, once-fluffy beach towel. Soaked, it was worse than nothing. "Wrong vial," he explained sheepishly. "I wanted a raincoat."

They slogged out of the immediate waterfall and through the runoff. Bink found himself shivering; the water of the sky river was chill. The madness had been intriguing when the constellations first took on life, but now he wished he were home, warm and dry, with Chameleon.

Ah, Chameleon! He liked her especially in her "normal" stage, neither beautiful nor smart, but a pleasant middle range. It always seemed so fresh, that brief period when she was average, since she was always changing. But he loved her in any form and intellect

175

—especially at times like now, when he was wet and cold and tired and afraid.

He swiped at a floating star, taking out some of his discomfort on it. The bright mote was probably as miserable as he, washed out of its place in the sky and become mere flotsam on earth.

The water here was too shallow for the whale, the only sky monster that might have been a real threat at this stage. The party wandered out of the slush. "In real life this must be a thunderstorm," Chester commented.

The walk became interminable. The golem kept urging them through the night. The wrath of the constellations pursued them some distance, then was lost as they plunged under the jungle canopy. The madness remained with them, however. The ground seemed to become a mass of peanut butter, roiling under their steps. The trees, dangerous in their own right, seemed to develop an alien menace: they turned purple, and hummed in chorus, and proffered sinister, oblong fruits.

Bink knew that the madness, whether it seemed benign or malign, would destroy them all in moments if they yielded to it. His sense of self-preservation encouraged him to resist it, and his resistance became stronger with practice—but still he could not penetrate all the way to reality. In a way this resembled the Queen's illusion—but this affected emotion as well as perception, so was more treacherous.

He heard the golem squawking at Crombie in griffin-talk, then saw Grundy rest his flying-fish steed on Crombie's head. Apparently the fish was tired, and had to be relieved. "It deserves a reward," Bink said. "For its timely service."

"It does? Why?" Grundy asked.

Bink started to answer, then realized the futility of it. The golem was not real; he did not *care*. Grundy did what he had to do, but human conscience and compassion were not part of his makeup. "Just take my word: the fish must be rewarded. What would it like?"

"This is a lot of trouble," Grundy muttered. But he swished and gurgled at the fish. "It wants a family."

"All he needs is a lady of his species," Bink pointed

176

out. "Or a man, if he happens to be female. She. Whatever."

More fish-talk. "In the mad region he can't locate one," the golem explained.

"A little of that spell-reversal wood would solve that problem," Bink said. "In fact, we could all use some. We got mixed up by the madness and water and never thought of the obvious. Let's see if Crombie's talent can locate some more of that wood."

Crombie squawked with dismayed realization. He whirled and pointed—right at a quivering mound of jelly. "That's a bloodsucker tree," Grundy said. "We can't go there!"

"Why not?" Chester asked facetiously. "You don't have any blood."

"The wood must be beyond it," Bink said. "Crombie's talent is still working but we have to watch out for the incidental hazards along the way, now more than ever. In the night, and with the madness—only you can do it, Grundy."

"I've *been* doing it!" the golem said, aggrieved.

"We need light," Chester said. "Birdbe—uh, Crombie, where can we get safe light?"

The griffin pointed. There was a flock of long-legged, bubbly things with horrendously glowing eyes. Bink walked over cautiously, and discovered that these were plants, not animals; what had seemed like legs were actually stems. He picked one, and its eye emitted a beam that illuminated everything it touched. "What is it, really?" Bink asked.

"A torch-flower," Grundy said. "Watch you don't set fire to the forest."

The rain had stopped, but the foliage still dripped. "Not too much danger of that at the moment," Bink said.

Armed with their lights, they moved in the direction Crombie had pointed for the wood, meandering circuitously to avoid the hazards the golem perceived. It was obvious that they could not have survived the natural traps of the jungle without the guidance of the golem. It would have been bad enough in ordinary circumstances; the madness made it impossible.

Suddenly they arrived. A monstrous stump loomed

out of the ground. It was as thick at the base as a man could span, but broke off at head-height in jagged ruin.

"What a tree that must have been!" Bink exclaimed. "I wonder how it died?"

They closed about the stump—and suddenly were sane. The glowing eyes they held were revealed as the torch-flowers the golem had said they were, and the deep jungle showed its true magic instead of its mad-magic. In fact, Bink felt clearer-headed than ever before in his life. "The madness spell—it has been reversed to make us absolutely sane!" he exclaimed. "Like the golem!"

"Look at the path we came by!" Chester said. "We skirted poison thorns, carnivorous grass, oil-barrel trees—our torches could have exploded this whole region!"

"Don't I know it," Grundy agreed. "Why do you think I kept yelling at you? If I had nerves, they'd be frayed to the bone. Every time you wandered from the course I set—"

More things were coming clear to Bink. "Grundy, why did you bother to help us, instead of riding away on your fish? You went to extraordinary trouble—"

"The fish!" Grundy exclaimed. "I have to pay him off!" He pried a sliver of wood from the massive stump and affixed it to the fish's dorsal fin with a bit of his own string. "There you go, bubble-eye," he said with something that sounded suspiciously like affection. "As long as you carry that, you'll see everything as it is, in the madness region. So you can spot your lady fish. Once you have succeeded, ditch the wood; I under-stand it is not good to see a female too realistically."

Crombie made an emphatic squawk of agreement that needed no translation.

The fish took off, zooming into the sky with a power-ful thrust of bubbles, banking neatly around branches. Relieved of the golem's weight, and spurred by the hope of mad romance, it was a speedy creature.

"Why did you do that?" Bink asked the golem.

"You short of memory? You told me to, nitnoggin!"

"I mean, why did you do it with such grace? You showed genuine feeling for that fish."

"I couldn't have," Grundy snapped.

"And why did you guide us all around the hazards? If we had perished, your service to the Good Magician would have been finished."

"What use would that have been to me?" Grundy demanded, kicking angrily at a tuft of grass with one motley foot.

"It would have freed you," Bink said. "Instead, you went to a great deal of trouble to herd us off that stair and to safety. You really didn't have to; your job is translation, not leadership."

"Listen, washout—I don't have to take this crap from you!"

"Think about it," Bink said evenly. "Why help a washout?"

Grundy thought about it. "I must have been mad after all," he admitted.

"How could you be mad—when you weren't affected by the madness?"

"What are you up to?" Chester demanded. "Why hassle the golem? He did good work."

"Because the golem is a hypocrite," Bink said. "There was only one reason he helped us."

"Because I *cared,* you nitwit!" Grundy yelled. "Why do I have to justify saving your life?"

Bink was silent. Crombie and Chester and the Good Magician turned mutely to face the golem.

"What did I say?" Grundy demanded angrily. "Why are you freeloaders staring at me?"

Crombie squawked. "Birdbeak says—" The golem paused. "He says—I can't make out what he says! What's the matter with me?"

"The wood of this tree reverses spells," Humfrey said. "It has canceled out your talent."

"I'm not touching that wood!"

"Neither are we," Bink said. "But we are all quite sane at the moment, because the ambience of the stump is stronger than that of a single chip. That is why we are now able to perceive you as you are. Do you realize what you said?"

"So the wood messes up my talent, same as it does yours. We knew that already!"

179

"Because it changes our magic without changing *us*," Bink continued. "Because what is *us* is real."

"But that would mean *I'm* halfway real!"

"And you halfway care," Chester said.

"That was just a figure of speech! I have no emotion!"

"Move away from the tree," Bink said. "Get out of the range of the stump. Tell us what you see out there."

Grundy paced away and looked about. "The jungle!" he cried! "It's changed! It's mad!"

"Care," Bink said. "The Good Magician's Answer. In your effort to save us, you brought yourself halfway to your own destination. You have begun to assume the liabilities of being real. You feel compassion, you feel anger, you suffer pleasure and frustration and uncertainty. You did what you did because conscience extends beyond logic. Is it worth it?"

Grundy looked at the distortions beyond the stump. "It's madness!" he exclaimed, and they all laughed.

Chapter 9. Vortex Fiends

At dawn they emerged from the madness region, each holding a piece of spell-reversal wood. They had traveled tediously, separating Crombie at intervals from his piece of wood, getting his indication of the best immediate route, then returning his chunk to him so that he could perceive threats accurately until the next orientation.

Once they were out, they located a reasonably secure roost in a stork-leg tree, setting their pieces of wood in a circle about its spindly trunks so that no hostile magic could approach them without getting reversed. That was not a perfect defense, but they were so tired they had to make do.

Several hours later Bink woke, stretched, and descended. The centaur remained lodged on a broad branch, his four hooves dangling down on either side; it seemed the tree-climbing experience during the madness had added a nonmagical talent to his repertoire. The Magician lay curled in a ball within a large nest he had conjured from one of his vials. Crombie, ever the good soldier, was already up, scouting the area, and the golem was with him.

"One thing I want to know . . ." Bink started, as he munched on slices of raisin bread from a loaf Crombie had plucked from a local breadfruit tree. It was a trifle overripe, but otherwise excellent.

Crombie squawked. ". . . is who destroyed that reverse-spell tree," Grundy finished.

"You're translating again!"

"I'm not touching any wood at the moment." The golem fidgeted. "But I don't think I'm as real as I was last night, during the madness."

"Still, there must be some feeling remaining," Bink said. "It can be like that, approaching a goal. Two steps forward, one back—but you must never give up."

Grundy showed more animation. "Say, that's a positive way of looking at it, mushmind!"

Bink was glad to have given encouragement, though the golem's unendearing little mannerisms remained evident. "How did you know what I was about to ask? About the destruction of—"

"You always come up with questions, Bink," the golem said. "So we pointed out the location of the subject of your next question, and it matched up with the tree stump. So we researched it. It was a challenge."

That was an intriguing ramification of Crombie's talent! Anticipating the answers to future questions! Magic kept coming up with surprises. "Only a real creature likes challenges," Bink said.

"I guess so. It's sort of fun, the challenge of becoming real. Now that I know that maybe it's possible. But I still have this ragtag body; no amount of caring can change that. It just means that now I fear the death that will surely come." He shrugged, dismissing it. "Anyway, the tree was blasted by a curse from that direction." He pointed.

Bink looked. "All I see is a lake." Then, startled: "Didn't the ogre say something about—?"

"Fiends of the lake, who hurled a curse that blasted the whole forest," Grundy said. "We checked: that is the lake."

Humfrey descended from the tree. "I'd better bottle some of this wood, if I can get my magic to work on it," he said. "Never can tell when it might be useful."

"Cast a spell hurling it away from your bottle," Chester suggested from the tree. He, too, dropped to the ground, after some awkward maneuvering that put his handsome posterior in jeopardy. Centaurs really did not belong in trees.

The Magician set up his vial and wood and uttered an incantation. There was a flash, a puff of smoke, and a gradual clearing of the air.

There sat the vial, corked. There sat the wood. The Good Magician was gone.

"Where did he go?" Bink demanded.

Crombie whirled and pointed his wing. Directly toward the bottle.

"Oh, *no!*" Bink cried, horrified. "His spell reversed, all right! It banished *him* to the bottle!" He dashed over and picked it up, jerking out the cork. Vapor issued forth, expanding and swirling and coalescing and forming in due course into the Good Magician. There was a fried egg perched on his head. "I forgot I was keeping breakfast in that one," he said ruefully.

Grundy could hold back his newfound emotion no longer. He burst out laughing. He fell to the ground and rolled about, guffawing. "Oh, nobody gnomes the trouble he's seen!" the golem gasped, going into a further paroxysm.

"A sense of humor is part of being real," Chester said solemnly.

"Just so," Humfrey agreed somewhat shortly. "Good thing an enemy did not get hold of the bottle. The holder has power over the content."

The Magician tried again—and again. Eventually he found the proper aspect of reversal and managed to conjure the wood into the vial. Bink hoped the effort was worth it. At least he knew, now, how the Good Magician had assembled such an assortment of items. He simply bottled anything he thought he might need.

Then Bink encountered another pile of earth. "Hey, Magician!" he cried. "Time to investigate this thing. What is making these mounds? Are they all over Xanth, or just where we happen to be?"

Humfrey came over to contemplate the pile. "I suppose I'd better," he grumped. "There was one on the siren's isle, and another at our bone-camp." He brought out his magic mirror. "What thing is this?" he snapped at it.

The mirror clouded thoughtfully, then cleared. It produced the image of a wormlike creature.

"That's a wiggle!" Bink exclaimed, horrified. "Are the wiggles swarming again?"

"That's not a wiggle," Chester said. "Look at the

scale. It's ten times too large." And in the mirror a measuring stick appeared beside the worm, showing it to be ten times the length of a wiggle. "Don't you know your taxonomy? That's a squiggle."

"A squiggle?" Bink asked blankly. He did not want to admit that he had never heard of that species. "It looks like an overgrown wiggle to me."

"They are cousins," Chester explained. "The squiggles are larger, slower, and do not swarm. They are solitary creatures, traveling under the ground. They are harmless."

"But the piles of dirt—"

"I had forgotten about that," Chester said. "I should have recognized the castings before. They eject the dirt from their tunnels behind them, and where they touch the surface it forms into a pile. As they tunnel on, the further castings plug up the hole, so there is nothing left except the pile."

"But what do they *do?*"

"They move about, make piles of earth. That's all."

"But why are they following me? I have nothing to do with squiggles."

"Could be coincidence," Humfrey said. He addressed the mirror. "Is it?"

The mirror's unhappy baby face showed.

"Someone or something is setting the squiggle to spy on us, then," Humfrey said, and the mirror smiled. "The question is, who?"

The mirror turned dark. "The same as the source of magic?" Humfrey demanded. The mirror denied it. "Bink's enemy, then?" And the smiling baby returned.

"Not the same as the fiends of the lake?" Bink asked.

The baby smiled.

"You mean it *is* the same?"

"Don't confuse the mirror with your illogic," the Magician snapped. "It agreed it was *not* the same!"

"Uh, yes," Bink said. "Still, if our route takes us past the fiends, we have a problem. With the enemy spying on us all the way, and throwing obstacles in our way, he's sure to excite the fiends into something dire."

"I believe you are correct," Humfrey said. "It may be time for me to expend some more of my magic."

"Glory be!" Chester exclaimed ironically.

"Quiet, horserear!" Humfrey snapped. "Now let me see. *Do* we have to pass the fiends of the lake to reach our destination?"

The mirror smiled.

"And the fiends have curse-magic sufficient to blast forests?"

The mirror agreed.

"What's the most convenient way to pass without trouble?"

The mirror showed a picture of Bink watching a play.

Humfrey looked up. "Can any of you make sense of this?"

Crombie squawked. "Where am I?" Grundy translated.

"Let me rephrase that question," Humfrey said quickly. "Where is Crombie while Bink is watching the play?"

The mirror showed one of the Magician's vials.

The griffin went into an angry medley of squawks. "Oh come off it, beakbrain!" the golem said. "You know I can't repeat words like that in public. Not if I want to become real."

"Beakbrain's concern is understandable," Chester said. "Why should he be banished to a bottle? He might never get out."

"*I'm* supposed to do the translations!" Grundy complained, forgetting his prior reluctance.

Humfrey put away the mirror. "If you won't pay attention to my advice," he informed Crombie, "then do it your own way."

"You temperamental real people are at it again," Grundy said. "The rational thing to do is listen to the advice, consider the alternatives, discuss them, and form a consensus."

"The little imp is making uncommon sense," Chester said.

"*Which* little imp?" Grundy demanded.

"I suspect," the Magician said grimly, "that the garrulous golem would be best off in a bottle."

185

"We're fighting again," Bink said. "If the mirror says we can pass the fiends most conveniently by traveling in bottles, I'd rather gamble on that than on the sort of thing we've just been through."

"You don't have to gamble," Grundy pointed out. "You have to go watch a dumb play."

"I have faith in my mirror," Humfrey said, and the mirror blushed so brightly there was a faint glow through his jacket. "To prove it, I will submit to bottling myself. I believe the one Beauregard used is pleasantly upholstered and large enough for two. Suppose Crombie and Grundy and I enter that bottle and give it to Bink to carry? Then he can ride Chester to the play."

"I'm willing," Bink said. He wondered privately whether the Good Magician would take all his other bottles with him into the bottle. That seemed a bit paradoxical, but no doubt was possible. "But I don't know exactly where the fiends are, and I'd rather not barge in on them unexpectedly. If we approach carefully, circumspectly, they may be less fiendish."

Crombie pointed to the lake.

"Yes, I know. But *where* at the lake? At the edge? On an island? I mean, before I innocently walk into a tree-blasting curse—"

Crombie squawked and spread his wings. His proud colors flashed as he flew up and made for the lake.

"Wait, featherbrain!" Chester cried. "They'll see you by air! That will give us all away!" But the griffin ignored him.

They watched Crombie wing handsomely out over the water, his plumage flexing red, blue, and white. "I have to admit the ornery cuss is a beautiful animal," Chester murmured.

Then the griffin folded his wings and plummeted toward the surface of the lake, spinning in the air. "A curse!" Bink cried. "They shot him down with a curse!"

But then the figure straightened out, regained altitude, and winged back. Crombie seemed to be all right.

"What happened?" Bink demanded as the griffin landed. "Was it a curse?"

"Squawk!" Crombie replied. Grundy translated: "What curse? I merely did my turnabout to get a closer fix on the fiends. They reside under the water."

"Under the water!" Bink cried. "How can we go there?"

Humfrey brought out another vial and handed it to Bink. "These pills will do the trick. Take one every two hours while submerged. It will—"

"There's a mound starting!" Chester cried. "A spy!"

Humfrey whipped out yet another vial, uncorked it, and aimed it at the upwelling dirt. A jet of vapor shot out, striking the mound. Crystals of ice formed. The mound froze.

"Fire extinguisher," the Magician explained. "Very cold. That squiggle is frozen stiff in its tunnel."

"Let me kill it while I can catch it!" Chester said eagerly.

"Wait!" Bink said. "How long will the freeze last?"

"Only a couple of minutes," Humfrey said. "Then the squiggle will resume activity with no impairment."

"And no memory of the missing minutes?" Bink asked.

"It should not be aware of the lapse. Squiggles aren't very smart."

"Then don't kill it! Get out of its observation. It will be convinced this was a false alarm, that we were never here. It will so report to its master, throwing the enemy off the track."

The Magician's brow lifted. "Very intelligent, Bink. You are thinking more like a leader now. We shall hide in the bottle, and you and Chester can carry it with you. Quickly, before the freeze abates."

The griffin remained uncertain, but acquiesced. The Magician set the vial, performed his incantation, and man, griffin, and golem vanished.

"Grab the bottle, get on my back, hang on!" Chester cried. "Time's almost up!"

Bink snatched up the lone vial remaining, jumped on Chester's back, and hung on. The centaur took off. In a moment his hooves were splashing through the shallow water. "Gimme a pill!" Chester cried.

Bink fumbled out a pill from the bottle, praying he would not spill the works as he bounced around. He

187

popped one into his mouth and handed the other forward to Chester's raised hand. "I hope these work!" he cried.

"That's all we need—another wrong bottle!" Chester exclaimed. "Gobble a foaming insulation pill . . ."

Bink wished the centaur hadn't thought of that. Insulation, or freezing extinguisher—ouch!

He glanced back. Was it his imagination, or was the dirt mound growing again? Had they gotten away in time? Suppose the squiggle saw their footprints?

Then Chester hit a dropoff, and they plunged underwater. Bink choked involuntarily as the liquid covered his mouth—but the water was just like air to his breathing. In fact, it was like air to his whole body, except for its color. They could breathe!

This experience reminded him of something. In a moment he had it: the Queen's anniversary party! That had been illusory underwater scenery, while this was genuine. Unfortunately, the Queen's version had been prettier. Here things were murky and dull.

Chester plodded on, picking his way carefully through the unfamiliar aquatic environment. Dusky clouds of sediment stirred up around his legs. Curious fish looked the pair over. Chester now held his bow in his hands, in case they should encounter a sea monster. Apart from the tension, it was soon rather dull going.

Bink drew out the bottle that held the Magician and put his eye to the side. Vaguely he made out the shapes of a tiny griffin and tinier man. They were in a carpeted room like that of a palace, and were looking at moving pictures in the magic mirror. It seemed very comfortable. Much nicer, in fact, than forging through the murk toward fiends.

Another ugly thought came. Suppose he had grabbed the wrong bottle himself, and popped the Magician into his mouth in lieu of a water-breathing pill? Such things were very scary right now.

Bink put the vial in his pocket, reassured that his friends were secure. He wondered what would happen if he shook the bottle violently, but resisted the urge to experiment. "Let's go visit the fiends," he said with false cheer.

Shortly they approached a splendid marine castle. It was formed from seashells—which meant it was probably magical, since few seashells formed in lakes without the aid of magic. Little whirlpools ascended from its turrets, apparently bringing air down to the inhabitants. Instead of a moat, the castle had a thick wall of seaweed, patrolled by vigilant swordfish.

"Well, let's hope the fiends are kind to travelers," Bink said. There were no bubbles as he spoke; the pill had fully acclimatized him.

"Let's hope the Magician's mirror knew its business," the centaur responded grimly. "And that the fiends don't connect the fool griffin with us, if they saw him."

They marched up to the main gate. A behemoth rose out of the muck, mostly mouth.

"Hooold!" the behemoth bellowed. "Whoo goooes there?" It was very proficient and resonant on the long O's; the sound reverberated across the reaches of the cavernous maw.

"Chester and Bink, travelers," Bink said with some trepidation. "We'd like lodging for the night."

"Soooo?" the monster inquired. "Then goooo!" Its mouth gaped even more horrendously.

"Go?" the centaur repeated aggressively. "We just came!"

"Soo gooo!" the behemoth reverberated, its orifice gaping so widely that the centaur could have ridden right into it without ducking his head.

Chester reached for his sword. "Uh, hooold—I mean hold," Bink murmured. "I remember—the gargoyle—I think it means to go inside. Inside the mouth."

The centaur peered into the monster's tunnel-like throat. "Damned if I'll cooperate in my own consumption!"

"But that's the entrance to the castle!" Bink explained. "The behemoth itself."

Chester stared. "Well I'll be gelded!" And without further hesitation he galloped in.

Sure enough, the throat continued on into the castle. Lights appeared at the end of the tunnel, and soon they emerged into a palatial receiving hall. Intricately

189

woven tapestries covered the walls, and the floor was done in fancy wooden squares.

A handsome, almost pretty young man walked up to greet them. He had ornate curls about his ears and a neat mustache. His costume was a princely robe embroidered with brightly colored threads, and he wore soft slippers with pointed toes. "Welcome to Gateway Castle," he said. "May I inquire your identities and the purpose of this visit?"

"You may," Chester said.

There was a pause. "Well?" the man said, a bit nettled.

"Well, why don't you inquire?" Chester said. "I gave you permission."

Small muscles quirked about the man's mouth, making him less pretty. "I so inquire."

"I am Chester Centaur, and this is my companion Bink. He's human."

"So I noted. And your purpose?"

"We seek the source of magic," Bink said.

"You have lost your way. It is at the amazon village, some distance north. But the direct route is hazardous to your sanity."

"We have been there," Bink said. "That is not the ultimate source, but merely the upwelling of magic dust. What we seek lies below. According to our information, a more convenient route passes through this castle."

The man almost smiled. "Oh, you would not care for that route!"

"Try us and see."

"This is beyond my cognizance. You will have to talk with the lord of the manor."

"Good enough," Bink said. He wondered what sort of a fiend this lord would be, who had such a docile human servant.

"If you would be good enough to come this way."

"We're good enough," Chester said.

"But first we must do something about your hooves. The floor is teak parquet; we do not wish it scratched or dented."

"Why put it on the floor, then?" Chester demanded.

"We do not apply it to the floor of our stable," the

190

man said. He produced several disks of furry material. "Apply these to your hooves; they will adhere, and muffle the impact."

"How about wearing one of these on your mouth?" Chester demanded.

"It's a small concession," Bink murmured. Chester's hooves were sound, since the healing elixir had eliminated all damage to the centaur's hind end, but they were hard enough to leave an imprint. "Humor the poor man. The fiends are probably very strict about such things, and punish their servants for violations."

With imperfect grace, Chester pressed his hooves one at a time onto the felt disks. The material clung to them, and it made the centaur's footfalls silent.

They moved through an elegant hall, descended carpeted steps, and entered a small chamber. There was barely room for Chester to stand. "If this is your main hall—" he began.

The man touched a button. The door slid closed. Then, abruptly, the room moved.

Bink flung out his hands, startled, and Chester kicked a hole in the rear wall.

"Easy, visitors," the man said with a small frown. "Haven't you ridden an elevator before? It is inanimate magic, a chamber that rises or sinks when occupied. Saves wear on stairs."

"Oh," Bink said, abashed. He preferred more conventional magic.

The magic lift stopped. The door slid open. They stepped out into another hall, and in due course came to the chambers of the lord of the manor.

He was, to Bink's surprise, a man, garbed richly in silver cloth and diamonds, but with the same foolish slippers his servant wore. "So you proffer service for a night's lodging," he said briskly.

"This is our custom," Bink said.

"And ours too!" the lord agreed heartily. "Have you any special talents?"

Bink couldn't tell his own, and didn't know Chester's. "Uh, not exactly. But we're strong, and can do work."

"Work? Oh my heavens no!" the lord exclaimed. "People do not work here!"

Oh? "How do you live, then?" Bink asked.

"We organize, we direct—and we entertain," the lord said. "Have you any entertainment abilities?"

Bink spread his hands. "I'm afraid not."

"Excellent! You will make an ideal audience."

"Audience?" Bink knew that Chester was as perplexed as he. The mirror had shown him watching a play—yet that could hardly be a service!

"We send our troupes out to entertain the masses, accepting payment in materials and services. It is a rewarding profession, esthetically and practically. But it is necessary to obtain advance audience ratings, so that we can gauge our reception precisely."

This innocuous employment hardly jibed with the local reputation! "To be an audience—to watch your shows—that's all you require? It hardly seems equitable! I'm afraid we would not be able to present an informed critical report—"

"No necessity! Our magic monitors will gauge your reactions, and point up our rough edges. You will have nothing to do but react, honestly."

"I suppose we could do that," Bink said dubiously. "If you really are satisfied."

"Something funny here," Chester said. "How come you have a reputation as fiends?"

"Uh, that's not diplomatic," Bink murmured, embarrassed.

"Fiends? Who called us fiends?" the lord demanded.

"The ogre," Chester replied. "He said you blasted a whole forest with a curse."

The lord stroked his goatee. "The ogre survives?"

"Chester, shut up!" Bink hissed.

But the centaur's unruly nature had taken control. "All he was doing was rescuing his lady ogre, and you couldn't stand to have him happy, so—"

"Ah, yes, that ogre. I suppose to an ogre's way of thinking, we would be fiends. To us, crunching human bones is fiendish. It is all in one's perspective."

Apparently the centaur had not antagonized the lord, though Bink judged that to be sheer luck. Unless the lord, like his troupe, was an actor—in which case there could be serious and subtle trouble. "This one is now a vegetarian," Bink said. "But I'm curious: do you really have such devastating curses, and why should you care what an ogre does? You really don't have cause to worry about ogres, here under the lake; they can't swim."

"We do really have such curses," the lord said. "They constitute group effort, the massing of all our magic. We have no individual talents, only individual contributions toward the whole."

Bink was amazed. Here was a whole society with duplicating talents! Magic *did* repeat itself!

"We do not employ our curses haphazardly, however. We went after the ogre as a professional matter. He was interfering with our monopoly."

Both Bink and Chester were blank. "Your what?"

"We handle all formal entertainments in southern Xanth. That bad actor blundered into one of our sets and kidnapped our leading lady. We do not tolerate such interference or competition."

"You used an ogress for a leading lady?" Bink asked.

"We used a transformed nymph—a consummate actress. *All* our players are consummate, as you shall see. In that role she resembled the most ogrelike ogress imaginable, absolutely horrible." He paused, considering. "In fact, with her artistic temperament, she was getting pretty ogrelike in life. Prima donna . . ."

"Then the ogre's error was understandable."

"Perhaps. But not tolerable. He had no business on that set. We had to scrub the whole production. It ruined our season."

Bink wondered what reception the ogre would encounter, as he rescued his ideal female. An actress in ogress guise, actually from the castle of the fiends!

"What about the reverse-spell tree?" Chester asked.

"People were taking its fruit and being entertained by the reversal effects. We did not appreciate the competition. So we eliminated it."

Chester glanced at Bink, but did not speak. Perhaps these people really were somewhat fiendish. To abolish all rival forms of entertainment—

"And where did you say you were traveling to?" the lord inquired.

"To the source of magic," Bink said. "We understand it is underground, and that the best route leads through this castle."

"I do not appreciate humor at my expense," the lord said, frowning. "If you do not wish to inform me of your mission, that is certainly your privilege. But do not taunt me with an obvious fabrication." Bink had the impression that obviousness was a worse affront than fabrication, to this person.

"Listen, fiend!" Chester said, bridling in most obvious fashion. "Centaurs do not lie!"

"Uh, let me handle this," Bink said quickly. "There is surely some misunderstanding. We are on quest for the source of magic—but perhaps we have been misinformed as to its access."

The lord mellowed. "That must be the case. Below this castle lies only the vortex. Nothing that goes that route ever returns. We are the Gateway; we straddle the vortex, protecting innocent creatures from being drawn unwittingly into that horrible fate. Who informed you that the object of your quest lay in such a direction?"

"Well, a Magician—"

"Never trust a Magician! They are all up to mischief!"

"Uh, maybe so," Bink said uneasily, and Chester nodded thoughtfully. "He was very convincing."

"They tend to be," the lord said darkly. Abruptly he shifted the subject. "I will show you the vortex. This way, if you please." He led the way to an interior panel. It slid aside at his touch. There was a glistening wall of glassy substance. No, not glass; it was moving. Fleeting irregularities showed horizontally. Now Bink could see through it somewhat vaguely, making out the three-dimensional shape. It was a column, perhaps twice his armspan in diameter, with a hollow center. In fact it was water, coursing around in circles at high speed. Or in spirals, going down—

"A whirlpool!" Chester exclaimed. "We are looking at the nether column of a whirlpool!"

"Correct," the lord said with pride. "We have constructed our castle around it, containing it by magic. Substances may pass into it, but not out of it. Criminals and other untoward persons are fed into its maw, to disappear forever. This is a most salutary deterrent."

Surely so! The mass of moving fluid was awesome in its smooth power, and frightening. Yet it was also in its fashion luring, like the song of the siren, or the madness.

Bink yanked his gaze away. "But where does it go?"

"Who would presume to know?" the lord inquired in return, quirking an eyebrow expressively. He slid the panel across and the vision of the vortex was gone.

"Enough of this," the lord decided. "We shall wine and dine you fittingly, and then you will audience our play."

The meal was excellent, served by fetching young women in scant green outfits who paid flattering attention to the travelers, especially Chester. They seemed to admire both his muscular man-portion and his handsome equine portion. Bink wondered, as he had before, what it was girls saw in horses. The siren had been so eager to ride!

At last, stuffed, Bink and Chester were ushered to the theater. The stage was several times the size of the chamber for the audience. Apparently these people did not like to watch as much as they liked to perform.

The curtain lifted and it was on: a gaudily costumed affair replete with bold swordsmen and buxom women and funny jokers. The staged duels were impressive, but Bink wondered how proficient those men would be with their weapons in a real battle. There was a considerable difference between technical skill and combat nerve! The women were marvelously seductive—but would they be as shapely without the support of their special clothes, or as wittily suggestive minus the memorized lines?

"You do not find our production entertaining?" the lord inquired.

"I prefer life," Bink replied.

The lord made a note on his pad: MORE REALISM.

Then the play shifted to a scene of music. The heroine sang a lovely song of loss and longing, meditating on her faithless lover, and it was difficult to imagine how any lout, no matter how louty, could be faithless to such a desirable creature. Bink thought of Chameleon again, and longed for her again. Chester was standing raptly beside him, probably thinking of horsing around with Cherie Centaur, who was indeed a fetching filly.

Then the song was augmented by a hauntingly lovely accompaniment. A flute was playing, its notes of such absolute quality and clarity that the lady's voice was shamed. Bink looked toward that sound—and there it was, a gleaming silver flute hanging in the air beside the heroine, playing by itself. A magic flute!

The lady ceased singing, surprised, but the flute played on. Indeed, freed of the limitations of her voice, it trilled on into an aria of phenomenal expertise and beauty. Now the entire cast of players stood listening, seeming to find it as novel as Bink did.

The lord jumped to his feet. "Who is performing that magic?" he demanded.

No one answered. All were absorbed in the presentation.

"Clear that set!" the lord cried, red-faced. "Everybody out. Out, out!"

Slowly they cleared, fading into the wings, looking back at the solo instrument. The stage was empty—but still the flute played, performing a medley of melodies, each more lovely than the one preceding.

The lord grabbed Bink by the shoulders. "Are you doing it?" he demanded, seeming about ready to choke.

Bink tore his attention from the flute. "I have no magic like that!" he said.

The lord hauled on Chester's muscular arm. "You—it must be yours, then!"

Chester's head turned to face him. "What?" he asked, as if coming out of a reverie. In that instant, flute and music faded.

"Chester!" Bink exclaimed. "Your talent! All the beauty in your nature, suppressed because it was linked to your magic, and as a centaur you couldn't—"

"My talent!" Chester repeated, amazed. "It must be me! I never did dare to—who would have believed—"

"Play it again!" Bink urged. "Make beautiful music! Prove you have magic, just as your hero-uncle Herman the Hermit did!"

"Yes," Chester agreed. He concentrated. The flute

196

reappeared. It began to play, haltingly at first, then with greater conviction and beauty. And strangely, the centaur's rather homely face began to seem less so. Not so strange, Bink realized: much of Chester's brutality of expression stemmed from his habitual snarl. That snarl had abated; he had no need of it any more.

"Now you don't owe the Magician any service," Bink pointed out. "You found your talent yourself."

"What abominable mischief!" the lord cried. "You accepted our hospitality on the agreement that you would render service as an audience. You are not an audience—you are a performer. You have reneged on your agreement with us!"

Now a portion of Chester's familiar arrogance reasserted itself. The flute blew a flat note. "Manfeathers!" the centaur snapped. "I was only playing along with your heroine's song. Bring your play back; I'll watch it, and accompany it."

"Hardly," the lord said grimly. "We tolerate no non-guild performances in our midst. We maintain a monopoly."

"What are you going to do?" Chester demanded. "Throw a fit? I mean, a curse?"

"Uh, I wouldn't—" Bink cautioned his friend.

"I'll not tolerate such arrogance from a mere halfman!" the lord said.

"Oh, yeah?" Chester retorted. With an easy and insulting gesture he caught the man's shirtfront with one hand and lifted him off the floor.

"Chester, we're their guests!" Bink protested.

"Not any more!" the lord gasped. "Get out of this castle before we destroy you for your insolence!"

"My insolence—for playing a magic flute?" Chester demanded incredulously. "How would you like that flute up your—"

"Chester!" Bink cried warningly, though he had considerable sympathy for the centaur's position. He invoked the one name that had power to restrain Chester's wrath: "Cherie wouldn't like it if you—"

"Oh, I wouldn't do it to *her!*" Chester said. Then he reconsidered. "Not with a flute—"

All this time the centaur had been holding the lord suspended in air. Suddenly the man's shirt ripped, and he fell ignominiously to the floor. More than ignominiously: he landed in a fresh pile of dirt.

Actually, this cushioned his impact, saving him from possible injury. But it multiplied his rage. "Dirt!" the lord cried. "This animal dumped me in dirt!"

"Well, that's where you belong," Chester said. "I really wouldn't want to dirty my clean silver flute on you." He glanced at Bink. "I'm glad it's silver, and not some cheap metal. Shows quality, that flute."

"Yes," Bink agreed hastily. "Now if we can leave——"

"What's dirt doing on my teak parquet?" the lord demanded. There was now a crowd of actors and servants about him, helping him up, brushing him off, fawning.

"The squiggle," Bink said, dismayed. "It found us again."

"Oh, so it's a friend of yours!" the lord cried, proceeding dramatically from rage to rage. "I should have known! It shall be the first to be cursed!" And he pointed one finger, shaking with emotion, at the pile. "All together now. A-one, a-two, a-three!"

Everyone linked hands and concentrated. At the count of three the curse came forth, like a bolt of lightning from the lord's finger. Ball lightning: it formed into a glowing mass the size of a fist, and drifted down to touch the dirt. At contact it exploded—or imploded. There was a flash of darkness and a momentary acrid odor; then the air cleared and there was nothing. No dirt, no squiggle, no flooring, in that region.

The lord glanced at the hole with satisfaction. "That's one squiggle that will never bother us again," he said. "Now for you, half-man." He raised his terrible finger to point at Chester. "A-one, a-two——"

Bink dived across, knocking the man's arm aside. The curse spun off and smashed into a column. There was another implosion of darkness, and a chunk of the column dissolved into nothingness.

"Now see what you've done!" the lord cried, becoming if possible even more angry than before. Bink could not protest; probably his talent had been responsible for the seemingly random shot. The curse had to destroy something, after all.

Bink himself would be immune—but not Chester.

198

"Let's get out of here!" Bink said. "Give me a ride out of range of those curses!"

Chester, about to draw his sword, reconsidered in mid-motion. "That's right—I can take care of myself, but you're just a man. Come on!"

Bink scrambled to straddle the centaur's back, and they leaped away just as the lord was leveling another curse. Chester galloped down the hall, his feet oddly silent because of the hoofpads. The fiends set up a howl of pursuit.

"Which way is out?" Bink cried.

"How should I know? That's birdbeak's department. I'm only a former guest of the fiends."

Good old Chester! All prickle and performance.

"We're somewhere upstairs," Bink said. "Except they don't use stairs. We could break out a window and swim—" He reached into his pocket, feeling the bottle that contained Crombie, Grundy, and the Magician. He fumbled until he found the one containing the water-breathing-spell pills; couldn't afford a mistake now! "We'd better take new pills; it's been over two hours."

They gulped their pills on the run. Now they were ready for the water—if they could find it. They had left the pursuit behind for the moment; no man on foot could match the speed of a centaur.

Bink had a second thought. "We don't want to go out—we want to go down. Into the nether region, to the source of magic."

"Where they tried to scare us away from," Chester agreed. He spun about as neatly as he had when dodging exploding pineapples, his two front feet down so that fore and hind sections rotated about the axis. Then he cantered back the way they had come.

"Hold up!" Bink screamed. "This is suicidal! We don't even know where the entrance to the vortex is!"

"The vortex has to be in the center of the castle; matter of architectural stability," Chester said. "Besides which, I have a fair directional sense of my own; I know roughly where it is from here. I am prepared to make my own entrance." Bink tended to forget that behind the brutal façade lay a fine centaur mind. Chester knew what he was doing.

They rounded a corner—and plowed into the charging fiends. People went tumbling every which way—but a massive curse rose up from the jumble and sailed after Chester.

Bink, glancing nervously back, spied it. "Chester—run!" he cried. "There's a curse on your tail!"

"On my tail!" Chester cried indignantly, and leaped forward. He didn't mind threats to his homely face, but his beautiful behind was sacred.

The curse, oriented on its target, pursued with determination. "This one we can't avoid," Bink said. "It's locked onto us, as the other was locked onto the ogre."

"Should we swear off crunching bones?"

"I never was much for human bones anyway!"

"I think the vortex is ahead," Chester said. "Hang on—I'm going in!"

He leaped—directly at a blank wooden panel. The wood shattered under the impact of his forehooves, and the two of them crashed directly into the vortex.

Bink's last thought as the awful swirl engulfed him, hauling him brutally around and around and down and down, providing one terrifying glimpse of its dark center shaft, was: what would happen to the curse that followed them? Then he spiraled into oblivion.

Chapter 10. Precious Nymph

Bink woke naked and battered, but not cold. He lay strewn on the edge of a warm, glowing lake. Hastily he dragged his feet out of the water, fearful of predators.

He heard a groan. A little farther along lay the centaur, limbs projecting in six directions. It had been an extremely violent descent; had they not had that water-breathing magic, they would surely have drowned. Bink scrambled to his feet and lumbered toward his friend. "Chester! Are you—?"

He paused. Midway between them he spied the sparkle of a star or jewel. Foolishly he paused to pick it up; he had no use for such a bauble. But it turned out to be only a shard of glass.

Chester groaned again, and lifted his head. "Takes more than a mere vortex to put away a centaur," he said. "But maybe not *much* more . . ."

Bink completed the distance between them, and tried to help his friend rise. "Hey, are you trying to cut me?" Chester demanded.

"Oops, sorry. I picked up this fragment of—" Bink paused again, looking at it. "There's something in it! That is—"

Chester got to his feet. "Let me see that." He reached down to take the fragment. His eyes rounded in surprise. "That's Humfrey!"

"What?" Bink thought he had misheard.

"It's hard to see in this dim glow, but it's him, all right. This must be a piece of the magic mirror, thrown ashore by coincidence. What happened to the Good Magician?"

"I lost the bottle!" Bink exclaimed with horror. "It was in my pocket——" His hand slapped his flesh where his pocket had been.

"He had the mirror with him. How did even one fragment of it get out of the bottle, unless——"

"Unless the bottle was smashed," Bink finished. "In which case——"

"In which case they were released. But where—and in what condition? They didn't have the water-breathing pills."

"If they got out just when that curse caught up——"

Chester looked closely at the fragment of glass. "Humfrey seems to be well—and I see the griffin behind him. I think they're still inside the bottle, though."

Bink looked. "They are! I see the curving glass walls, and the upholstery. It has been shaken up some, but the bottle never broke." He was relieved. A broken bottle might well have meant the end of his friends. "And they have another fragment of glass!" He raised his hand in a wave. "Hi, folks!"

Silently, Humfrey waved back. "He sees us in his fragment!" Chester exclaimed. "But that's impossible, because the broken mirror is out here."

"Anything is possible, with magic," Bink said. It was a cliché truism, but right now he had his doubts.

"Look at the shambles in there," Chester said. "That bottle must have been bounced against a wall."

"And the mirror broke, and a piece of it flew out here," Bink said uncertainly. "Right where we could find it. That's quite a coincidence, even if we can believe the possibility."

"What else can we believe?" Chester demanded.

Bink could not argue. His talent operated through seeming coincidence; it must have had a part in this. But wouldn't it have been easier to have the Magician's bottle itself float to shore here, instead of one piece of glass? "We can see them, but not hear them. Maybe if we print a message——" But they had nothing to do that with.

"If we can find the bottle, we can let them out," Chester pointed out. He seemed to be feeling better, physically.

"Yes." Bink held the fragment close to his face and mouthed elaborately *"Where are you?"*

Humfrey spread his hands. He pointed to the bottle wall. Outside it, turbulent water swirled, its phosphorescence making streaky line-patterns. The bottle was somewhere in a river, being carried along by the current—where?

"I guess that mirror isn't much use," Chester said. "Crombie could locate us—but can't get to us. We might get to the bottle—but can't find it."

"We'll have to follow the river down," Bink said. "It must start at the vortex pool here in this lake, and dribble on to wherever it goes. Yet if we follow it—"

"We delay our quest for the source of magic," Chester finished.

That made Bink pause. "The quest will have to wait," he decided. "We have to save our friends."

"I suppose so," the centaur agreed. "Even that arrogant griffin."

"Do you really dislike Crombie?"

"Well . . . he's a scrapper, like me. Can't blame him for that, I suppose. But I'd like to try his strength, once, just for the record."

Male competition. Well, Bink understood that, for he experienced it himself at times.

But there were more important matters now. "I'm thirsty," Bink said. He walked back to the lake shore.

"Have you noticed," Chester remarked, "that there is no life in this lake? No fish, no monsters, no plants, no beach creatures . . ."

"No life," Bink repeated. "But we're all right, so—"

"We haven't drunk from it yet. Or if we did, it was from the fresh water of the vortex, when we were on the pill."

"That's true," Bink said uncomfortably.

"I wonder whether the cork loosened in Humfrey's bottle, and he got a sample of this water, and hauled the cork back in place right after the mirror broke."

"Could be," Bink agreed. "We'd best not gamble. We'll need food soon, too. We'd better check around. We can't rescue the Magician if we don't take care of ourselves."

"Right," Chester agreed. "And the first thing to do is—"

"Is to find my clothes," Bink finished.

They were farther along the shore, complete with Bink's sword, as luck would have it. But as luck would also have it, the bottle was not with them. Chester had retained his weapons and rope, so was in good shape.

They moved on through the cavern passages, leaving the suspicious river behind, their eyes acclimatizing to the dimming subterranean reaches. Bink hoped they would not encounter nickelpedes here, but was careful not to voice this wish. No sense alarming Chester. They tried to mark their way by scratching X's in the floor every so often, but Bink wasn't sure how effective this would be. Time passed, and the way was interminable—especially since they did not know where they were going.

Bink's thirst had been casual, at first, but now that he knew there was no water it became more pressing. How long could they go on, before—?

Abruptly they saw light—real light, not the mere passage glow. They hurried cautiously up to it—and discovered a magic lantern suspended from a jag of stone. Its soft effulgence was a welcome sight—but there was nothing else.

"People—or goblins?" Bink asked, nervous and hopeful.

Chester took it down and studied it. "Looks like fairy-work to me," he said. "Goblins don't really need light, and in any event this is too delicately wrought."

"Even fairies aren't necessarily friendly," Bink said. "Still, it seems a better risk than starving here alone."

They took the lamp and went on with slightly improved prospects. But nothing further developed. Apparently someone or something had lit a lamp, left it, and departed. Strange.

Weary, dirty, hungry, and unpleasantly thirsty, they parked at last on a boulder. "We have to find food, or at least water," Bink said, trying to make it seem casual. "There doesn't seem to be any on this main passage, but—" He paused, listening. "Is that—?"

Chester cocked his head. "Yes, I think it is. Water dripping. You know, I haven't wanted to say anything,

204

but my tongue has been drying up in my mouth. If we could—"

"Behind this wall, I think. Maybe if we—"

"Stand clear." The centaur faced about so that his better half addressed the wall in question. Then he kicked.

A section of the wall collapsed. Now the sound was louder: water flowing over stone. "Let me climb in there," Bink said. "If I can collect a cupful—"

"Just in case," Chester said, taking his coil of rope and looping it about Bink's waist. "We don't know what to expect in these dark chambers. If you fall in a hole, I'll haul you out."

"Yes," Bink agreed. "Let me take the magic lantern."

He scrambled into the hole. Once he got by the rubble, he found himself in a larger, irregular cavern whose floor slanted down into darkness. The sound of water was coming from that darkness.

He moved forward, careful of his footing, trailing the line behind him. The water sound became temptingly loud. Bink traced it to a crevice in the floor. He held his lantern over it. Now at last he saw the glint of a streamlet. He reached down with his fingers, and just as his shoulder nudged the crevice lip his fingers touched the water.

How could he draw any up? After a moment's thought he ripped a piece of cloth from his already tattered sleeve, and dangled that down into the water. He let it soak up what liquid it cared to, then brought it to the surface.

While he was doing this, he heard a distant singing. He stiffened with alarm. Were the lake fiends coming here? No, that seemed highly unlikely; they were water dwellers, not rock dwellers, and by the lord of the manor's own admission they knew nothing of this nether region. This had to be some creature of the caves. Perhaps the owner of the magic lantern.

By the time he brought the dripping rag to his mouth, the singing was quite close. There was the scent of fresh flowers. Bink put the dangling end of the rag in his mouth and squeezed. Cool, clear liquid dripped down. It was the best water he had ever tasted!

Then something strange happened. Bink experienced a surge of dizziness—not sickening, but wonderfully pleasant. He felt alive, vibrant, and full of the warmth of human spirit. That was good water indeed!

He dipped his rag into the crevice again, soaking it for Chester. This was an inefficient way to drink, but a great deal better than nothing. While he lay there he heard the singing again. It was a nymph, of imperfect voice but sounding young and sweet and joyful. A pleasant shiver went through him.

Bink brought up the rag and laid it on the cave floor. He took up the light and moved toward the voice. It came from a section beyond the water, and soon Bink came to the end of his tether. He untied the rope, let it drop from his waist, and went on.

Now he spied a beam of light emanating from another crack. The singer was in the chamber beyond. Bink knelt and put his eye to the crack, silently.

She was sitting on a stool fashioned of silver, sorting through a barrel filled with precious stones. Their colors reflected brilliantly, decorating all the walls of the room. She was a typical nymph, long and bare of leg with a tiny skirt just about covering a pert derrière, slender of waist, full of bosom, and innocent and large-eyed of face. Her hair sparkled like the keg of jewels. He had seen nymphs like this many times; each had her association with tree or rock or stream or lake or mountain, yet they were all so uniform in face and feature that their beauty became commonplace. It was as if some Magician had established the ideal female-human aspect and scattered it about the Land of Xanth for decoration, attaching individual units to particular locales so that the distribution would be uniform. So she was nothing special. The precious stones, in contrast, were a phenomenal treasure.

Yet Bink glanced only passingly at the stones. His gaze became fixed on the nymph. She—he felt—it was rapt adoration.

What am I doing? he demanded of himself. With Chester waiting for a drink, Bink had no business here! And for answer, he only sighed longingly.

The nymph overheard. She glanced up alertly, breaking off her innocent melody, but could not see him. Perplexed, she shook her maiden tresses and returned to her work, evidently deciding that she had imagined it.

"No, I am here!" Bink cried, surprising himself. "Behind the wall!"

She screamed a cute little scream, jumped up, and fled. The keg overturned, dumping jewels across the floor.

"Wait! Don't run!" Bink cried. He smashed his fist into the wall with such force the stone cracked. He wrenched out more fragments, widening the hole, then jumped down into the room. He almost slipped on some pearls, but did a little dance and got his balance.

Now he stood still and listened. There was a strange smell, reminiscent of the breath of an attacking dragon, one just behind a person and gaining. Bink looked about nervously, but there was no dragon. All was silent. Why didn't he hear her still running?

In a moment he had it figured. She might flee in alarm, but she would hardly leave her treasure unguarded. Obviously she had dodged around a corner and now was watching him from hiding.

"Please, miss," Bink called. "I mean no harm to you. I only want to——"

To hug you, to kiss you, to——

Shocked, he halted his thoughts in mid-train. He was a married man! What was he doing chasing a strange nymph? He should get back to Chester, take the centaur his ragful of water——

Again he paused in his thoughts. *Oh, no!*

Yet he could hardly doubt his sudden emotion. He had imbibed from a spring, and become enamored of the first maiden he had seen thereafter. It must have been a love spring!

But why had his talent let him drink it?

The answer was distressingly obvious. He wished he hadn't thought of the question. His talent had no regard for his feelings, or those of others. It protected only his physical, personal welfare. It must have decided that his wife Chameleon represented some kind of threat to his welfare, so it was finding him another love. It had not been satisfied with separating him from Chameleon temporarily; now it intended to make that separation permanent.

"I will not have it!" he cried aloud. "I love Chameleon!"

And that was true. Love potions did not undo existing relations. But now he also loved this nymph—and she was a great deal more accessible.

Was he at war with his own talent? He had ethics it evidently did not; he was civilized while it was primitive. Who was to be the master, here?

He fought, but could not undo the effect of the love spring. Had he anticipated what his talent was leading him into, he might have balked it before he drank, but now he was the victim of a *fait accompli*. Well, he would settle with his talent when he found a better occasion.

All was fair in magic. "Nymph, come here and tell me your name, or I'll steal all your treasure!" he yelled.

When she did not respond, he righted the keg and began scooping up gems. There was an amazing assortment: diamonds, pearls, opals, emeralds, sapphires, and too many others to classify. How had the nymph come by such a fortune?

Now the nymph appeared, peeking around a curve in the tunnel. Coincidentally, Bink smelled the fleeting scent of woodland flowers. "But I *need* that treasure!" she protested.

Bink continued his work. The stones sailed into the barrel. "What is your name?" he demanded.

"What's yours?" There was an odor like that of a hesitant deerfly at the edge of a glade.

"I asked you first." All he wanted to do was keep her in conversation until he could catch her.

"But you're the stranger!" she pointed out with female logic.

Ah, well. He liked her logic. He knew it was the effect of the potion, but he was captive to her mannerisms. "My name is Bink."

"I am Jewel," she said. "The Nymph of Jewels, if you insist on the whole definition. Now give me back my stones."

"I'll be glad to, Jewel. For a kiss."

"What kind of a nymph do you think I am?" she protested in typical nymphly fashion. Now there was the odor of pine-oil disinfectant.

"I hope to find out. Tell me about yourself."

She edged farther into the room, distrusting him. "I'm just a rock nymph. I see that all the precious stones get properly planted in the ground, so that goblins, dragons, men, and other voracious creatures can mine them." Bink smelled the mixed fumes of hard-laboring men and goblins. "It's all very important, because otherwise those creatures would be even wilder than they are. The mining gives them something to do."

So that was how the jewels got planted. Bink had always wondered about that, or would have wondered had he thought about it. "But where do you get them to start with?"

"Oh, they just appear by magic, of course. The keg never empties."

"It doesn't?"

"See, it is already overflowing with the gems you are trying to put back. You aren't supposed to put them back."

Bink looked, surprised. It was so. He had assumed the keg was empty without really checking it, because his main attention had been on the nymph.

"How am I ever going to process all those extra stones?" she demanded with cute petulance. "Usually it takes an hour to place each one, and you have spilled hundreds." She stamped her sweet little foot, not knowing how to express her annoyance effectively. Nymphs had been designed for appearance, not emotion.

"Me? *You* spilled them when you ran!" Bink retorted. "I'm trying to pick them up."

"Well, it's your fault because you scared me. What were you doing behind the wall? No one's supposed to go there. That's why it's walled off. The water—" She paused with new alarm. "You didn't—?"

"I did," Bink said. "I was thirsty, and—"

She screamed again, and fled again. Nymphs by nature were flighty. Bink continued his gathering, ar-

209

ranging the surplus jewels in a pile beside the keg, knowing she would be back. He hated himself somewhat, knowing he should leave her alone, but found himself unable to stop himself. And he did owe it to her to clean up this mess as well as he could, though the pile was getting unwieldy.

Jewel peeked back around the corner. "If you'd just go away and let me catch up—"

"Not until I've finished cleaning up this overflow," Bink said. "As you pointed out, it is my fault." He placed a huge egg-shaped opal on top of his mound—and watched the whole thing subside, squirting out diamonds and things. He was getting nowhere.

She edged in closer. "No, you're right. I spilled it. I'll catch up somehow. You just—just leave. Please." The sneezy tang of dust tickled his nose, as if a herd of centaurs had just charged along a dry road in midsummer.

"Your magic talent!" Bink exclaimed. "Smells!"

"Well, I never," she said, modestly affronted. Now the dust-odor was tinged by the fumes of burning oil.

"I mean you can make—you smell like what you feel."

"Oh, that." The oil merged into perfume. "Yes. What's your talent?"

"I can't tell you."

"But I just told you mine! It's only fair—"

She edged within range. Bink grabbed her. She screamed again most fetchingly, and struggled without much strength. That, too, was the way nymphs were: delightfully and ineffectively difficult. He drew her in for a firm kiss on the lips. She was a most pleasant armful, and her lips tasted like honey. At least they smelled like it.

"That wasn't very nice," she rebuked him when he ended the kiss, but she didn't seem very angry. Her odor was of freshly overturned earth.

"I love you," Bink said. "Come with me—"

"I can't go with you," she said, smelling of freshly cut grass. "I have my job to do."

"And I have mine," Bink said.

"What's your job?"

"I'm on a quest for the source of magic."

"But that's way down in the center of the world, or somewhere," she said. "You can't travel that way. There are dragons and goblins and rats—"

"We're used to them," Bink said.

"I'm not used to them! I'm afraid of the dark! I couldn't go there, even if—"

Even if she wanted to. Because of course she did not love him. She had not drunk the love-water.

Bink had a naughty idea. "Come and take a drink with me! Then we can—"

She struggled to disengage, and he let her go. The last thing he wanted to do was hurt her! "No, I couldn't afford love. I must plant all these jewels."

"But what am I to do? From the moment I saw you—"

"You'll just have to take the antidote," she said, smelling of a newly lit candle. Bink recognized the connection: the candle symbolized her bright idea.

"There is an antidote?" He hadn't thought of that.

"There must be. For every spell there's an equal and opposite counterspell. Somewhere. All you have to do is find it."

"I know who can find it," Bink said. "My friend Crombie."

"You have friends?" she asked, surprised, smelling of startled birds.

"Of course I have friends!"

"Down here, I meant. I thought you were alone."

"No. I was looking for water for me and Chester. We—"

"Chester? I thought your friend was Crombie."

"Chester Centaur. Crombie is a griffin. And there's Magician Humfrey, and—"

"A Magician!" she exclaimed, impressed. "All to look for the source of magic?"

"Yes. The King wants to know."

"There's a King along too?"

"No," Bink said, momentarily exasperated. "The King assigned me to make the quest. But we had some trouble, and got separated, and—"

"I suppose I'd better show you where there's water," she decided. "And food—you must be hungry too."

"Yes," he said, reaching for her. "We'll be glad to do some service in return—"

"Oh, no!" she cried, skipping away with an enticing bounce of anatomy and the scent of hickory smoke. "Not until you drink the antidote!"

Just so. "I really must get back to Chester," Bink said. "He'll be worried."

She considered for a moment. "Bink, I'm sorry about what happened. Fetch your friends, and I'll see they get fed. Then you really must go."

"Yes." Bink walked slowly to the hole in the wall.

"Not that way!" she cried. "Go round by the regular passages!"

"But I don't know the way! I have no light. I have to follow the rope back."

"Definitely not!" She took her own magic lantern, a twin of the one Bink had found before, from the wall and grasped Bink's arm firmly. "I know all the halls around here. I'll find him for you."

Bink willingly suffered himself to be led. Even apart from the potion, he was discerning commendable traits in her. She was not one of the empty-headed nymphs like those associated with ocean foam or wild oats; she had a sense of purpose and fitness and decency. No doubt her responsible job of jewel-placing had matured her. Still, potion or not, he had no business with this creature! Once his friends were fed, he would have to leave her. He wondered how long it would take the potion to wear off. Some spells were temporary, but others were lifelong.

They circled through intersecting passages. In a moment they came upon Chester, still waiting by the hole. "Here we are!" Bink called.

Chester jumped so that all four hooves were off the floor. "Bink!" he exclaimed as he landed. "What happened? Who is that nymph?"

"Chester, this is Jewel. Jewel—Chester," Bink introduced. "I—" He hesitated.

"He drank a love potion," Jewel said brightly.

The centaur made a motion as of tearing out two fistfuls of mane. "The secret enemy strikes again!"

Bink hadn't thought of that. Of course that was the most reasonable explanation! His talent hadn't betrayed him, but it hadn't protected him from this non-physical threat either. Thus his enemy had scored. How could he pursue the source of magic, when his heart was tied up here?

But his heart was also tied up back home, with Chameleon. That was part of the reason he was on this quest. So—he had better just get on with it. "If we can get back together with Crombie and the Magician, maybe Crombie can point out the location of the antidote," Bink said.

"Where are your friends?" Jewel asked.

"They're in a bottle," Bink explained. "But we can communicate with them through a fragment of magic mirror. Here, I'll introduce you to them." He fumbled in his pocket for the bit of glass.

His fingers found nothing. "Oh, no—I've lost the fragment!" He turned the pocket inside out. There was a hole in it, where the sharp edge of glass had sawed its way out.

"Well, we'll find them somehow," Bink said numbly. "We won't give up until we do."

"That would seem best," Chester agreed gravely. "However, we'll have to take the nymph along with us."

"Why?" Bink had mixed emotions.

"The object of the counterspell has to be present; that's the way these things work. You loved the first female you encountered after imbibing the potion; you must *un*love her in the same fashion."

"I can't come with you!" Jewel protested, though she looked at Chester as if wishing for a ride on his back. "I have a lot of work to do!"

"How much will you get done if Bink stays here?" Chester inquired.

She threw up her hands in feminine exasperation. "Come to my apartment, both of you. We'll discuss it later."

Jewel's apartment was as attractive as herself. She had a cluster of caves completely carpeted; the carpet-moss ran across the floor, up over the walls, and across the ceiling without a break except for the round doors. It was extremely cosy. She had no chairs, table, or bed; it seemed she sat or lay down anywhere, anytime, in perfect comfort.

"We'll have to do something about those clothes," she said to Bink.

Bink looked down at himself. His clothing had more or less dried on him, after its soaking in the vortex and lake; it glowed in uneven patches. "But these are all I have," he said regretfully.

"You can dry-clean them," she said. "Go into the lavatory and put them in the cleaner. It only takes a moment."

Bink entered the room she indicated and closed the curtain. He located the cleaner: an ovenlike alcove through which a warm current of air passed his tunic and shorts. He set them within this, then moved over to the basin where a rivulet of water ran through. Above it was a polished rock surface: a mirror. The vanity of the distaff always required a mirror!

Seeing himself reflected was a shock: he was more bedraggled than his clothes. His hair was tangled and plastered over his forehead, and he had a beard just at the ugly starting stage. Cave-dirt was smeared over portions of his face and body, from his crawl through the wall. He looked like a juvenile ogre. No wonder the nymph had been afraid of him at first!

He used the keen blade of his sword to shave his face, since there was no magic shaving brush here to brush his whiskers away conveniently. Then he rinsed and combed his hair. He found his clothing dry and clean and pressed: obviously more than hot air was at work. His torn sleeve had been neatly hemmed so that the absence of cloth looked intentional. He wondered if some magic dust circulated in these caves, augmenting the function of such things as dry cleaners. The nymph seemed to have many magical conveniences, and quite a comfortable life-style. It would not be hard to adapt to such a style—

He shook his head. That was the love potion speaking, not his common sense! He had to be on guard against rationalization. He did not belong down here, and he would have to leave when his mission was done, though he leave part of his heart behind.

Nevertheless, he dressed himself neatly, even giving his boots a turn at the cleaner. Too bad the Magician's bottle couldn't have washed ashore instead of his footwear!

When he emerged from the lavatory, Jewel looked him over with surprised admiration. "You are a handsome man!"

Chester smiled wryly. "I suppose it was hard to tell, before. Would that I could wash my face and suffer a similar transformation!" They all laughed, somewhat ill at ease.

"We must pay for your hospitality—and for your help," Chester said when the laugh subsided fitfully.

"My hospitality I give freely; pay would demean it," Jewel said. "My help you seem to be co-opting. There is no pay for slave labor."

"No, Jewel!" Bink cried, cut to the heart of his emotion. "I would not force anything on you, or cause you grief!"

She softened. "I know it, Bink. You drank of the love-water; you would not hurt me. Yet since I must help you find your friends, so they can find the counterspell, and this takes me away from my work—"

"Then we must help you do your work!" Bink said.

"You can't. You don't know the first thing about sorting precious stones, or where they should be set. And if you did, the borer would not work for you."

"The borer?"

"My steed beast. He phases through the rock to reach where I must set the stones. I alone can control him—and then only when I sing. He works for a song, nothing else."

Bink exchanged glances with Chester. "After we eat, we will show you our music," Chester said.

Jewel's meal was strange but excellent. She served an assortment of mushrooms and fungus—things that grew magically, she explained, without the need of light. Some tasted like dragon steak, and some like potato chips chipped from a hot potato tree, and dessert was very like chocolate pie fresh from the brown cow, so round and soft and pungent it practically flowed off the plate. She also had a kind of chalky powder she mixed with the water to produce excellent milk.

"You know," Chester murmured aside to Bink, "you could have found a worse nymph to encounter after your draught."

Bink didn't answer. After the magic drink, he would have loved a harpy; it wouldn't have mattered how foul she was. The love potion was absolutely heedless of its consequence. Magic without conscience. Indeed, as he had learned to his horror, the history of Xanth had been influenced by just such love springs. The original, mundane species had intermated, producing crossbreeds like the chimerae, harpies, griffins —and centaurs. Who was to say this was wrong? Where would the Land of Xanth be now, without the noble centaurs? Yet Bink's own drink of this water was supremely inconvenient in a personal way. Rationally, he had to stay with his wife, Chameleon; but emotionally—

Chester finished his repast. He concentrated, and the silver flute appeared. It played rapturously. Jewel sat frozen, listening to the silvery melody. Then she began to sing in harmony with it. Her voice could not approach the purity of the flute, but it complemented the instrument nicely. Bink was entranced—and would have been, he told himself, regardless of the potion.

Something grotesque poked into the room. Chester's flute cut off in midnote, and his sword appeared in his hand.

"Stay your hand, centaur!" Jewel cried. "That is my borer!"

Chester did not attack, but his sword remained ready. "It looks like a giant worm!"

"Yes," she agreed. "He's related to the wiggles and squiggles, but he's much larger and slower. He's a diggle—not very bright, but invaluable for my work."

Chester decided it was all right. "I thought I had seen everything in the lexicon, but I missed this one. Let's see whether we can help you work. If he likes my music, and you have any stones to place near the river—"

"Are you kidding?" Jewel asked in her nymphly idiom. "With half the keg spilled, I have dozens of stones for the river. Might as well start there."

Under her direction, they boarded the diggle. Jewel

216

bestrode the monster worm near its front end, a basket of precious stones held before her. Bink sat next, and Chester last, his four feet somewhat awkward in this situation. He was used to being ridden, not to riding, though he had done it before with the dragon.

"Now we make music," Jewel said. "He will work as long as he likes the sound, and he doesn't require much variation. After a few hours I get tired and have to stop, but if the centaur's flute——"

The flute appeared. It played. The great worm crawled forward, carrying them along as if they were mere flies. It did not scramble or flex, as the dragon did; it elongated and contracted its body in stages, so that the sections they rode were constantly changing in diameter. It was a strange mode of travel, but an effective one. This was a very large worm, and it traveled swiftly.

A flange flexed out from the diggle's front segment, and as he tunneled into the rock, the flange extended the diameter of the phase-tunnel so that the riders could fit through also. It occurred to Bink that this was a variant of the type of magic in the Good Magician's water-breathing pills. The rock, like the water, was not being tunneled through so much as it was being temporarily changed so that they could pass through it without making a hole. Chester had to duck his head to stay within the phase, and his flute was crowded, but it kept playing its captivating melodies. Bink was sure Chester was more than happy to have this pretext to practice his newly discovered talent, after a lifetime of suppression.

"I have to admit, this is a worthwhile service," the nymph said. "I always thought centaurs had no magic."

"The centaurs thought so too," Bink said, covertly admiring her form from behind. To hell with the love potion; she had a shape to conjure with.

Then the worm lurched, striking a different type of rock, and Bink was thrown forward against the nymph. "Uh, sorry," he said, righting himself, though indeed he was not very sorry. "I, uh——"

"Yes, I know," Jewel said. "Maybe you'd better put your arms about my waist, to steady yourself. It does get bumpy on occasion."

"I . . . think I'd better not," Bink said.

"You're sort of noble, in your fashion," she observed. "A girl could get to like you."

"I—I'm married," Bink said miserably. "I—I need that antidote."

"Yes, of course," she agreed.

Suddenly the diggle emerged through a wall into a large chamber. "The river," Chester observed. When he spoke, his flute ceased its playing. The worm turned, his snout questing for the vanished music.

"Don't stop!" Jewel cried. "He quits when—"

The flute resumed. "We want to follow the river down," Bink said. "If we see a bottle floating in it—"

"First, I have to place some stones," he said firmly. She guided the worm to a projecting formation, halted him, and held out a fat diamond. "Right inside there," she said. "It'll take a million years for the water to wash that into sight."

The diggle took the stone in his orifice and carried it into the rock. His head tapered into a virtual point, with a mouth smaller than a man's, so holding the jewel was no problem. When his snout emerged, the diamond was gone and the formation was whole. Bink was startled, then realized he shouldn't be; they had not left any tunnel behind them, either.

"One down," Jewel said briskly. "Nine hundred and ninety-nine to go."

But Bink's eyes were on the glowing river, looking for the bottle. Such as the power of the potion, he half-hoped he wouldn't find it. Once they found the magician, and then located the antidote, he would be out of love with Jewel—and that was difficult to contemplate. He knew what was right, but his heart wasn't in it.

Time passed. Jewel placed diamonds, opals, emeralds, sapphires, amethysts, jades, and many garnets in the rocks along the river, and sprinkled pearls in the water for the oysters to find. "Oysters just love pearls," she explained. "They just gobble them up." She sang as she worked, alternating with Chester's flute, while Bink's attention roved from her to the water and back again. He could, indeed, have encountered a worse subject for the potion to fix on!

Then the river opened out into another lake. "This is the abode of the demons, who are able to drink and use the tainted water," Jewel cautioned them. "The demons know me, but the two of you will have to obtain a permit to pass through their territory. They don't like trespassers."

Bink felt Chester's motion behind him, as of hand touching bow and sword. They had had trouble with fiends; they didn't need trouble with demons!

The cavern walls became carved to resemble stone buildings, with squared-off corners and alleys between: very like a city. Bink had never actually seen a city, except in pictures; the early settlers of Xanth had made cities, but with the decline in population these had disappeared.

Bink and Chester dismounted and walked beside the worm, here on the street. Soon a magic wagon rolled up. It resembled a monster-drawn coach, but lacked the monster. The wheels were fat bouncy donuts of rubber, and the body seemed to be metal. A purring emanated from the interior. There was probably a little monster inside, pedaling the wheels.

"Where's the fire?" the demon demanded from the coach. He was blue, and the top of his head was round and flat like a saucer.

"Right here, Blue Steel," Jewel said, clapping one hand to her bosom. "Will you issue a ticket for my friends? They're looking for the source of magic."

"The source of magic!" another voice exclaimed. There were, Bink now saw, two demons in the vehicle; the second was of coppery hue. "That's a matter for the Chief!"

"All right, Copper," Jewel agreed. She evidently knew these demons well enough to banter with them. Bink suffered a sharp green pang of jealousy.

Jewel guided them to a building marked PRECINCT STATION and parked the worm. "I must remain with the diggle to sing him a song," she said. "You go in and see the Chief; I will wait."

Now Bink was afraid she would not wait, that she would take this opportunity to leave them, to betray them to the demons. That way she would be safe from pursuit, either vengeful or romantic. But he had to trust her. After all, he loved her.

The demon inside sat at a broad desk, poring over a book. He glanced up as they entered. "Ah, yes—we were fated to meet again," he said.

"Beauregard!" Bink exclaimed, amazed.

"I'll issue the permits, of course," the demon said. "You were the specific instrument of my release, according to the rules of the game, and I feel an undemonly obligation. But allow me to entertain you properly, as you entertained me at the ogre's domicile. There is much you must be advised of before you pursue your quest further."

"Uh, there's a nymph waiting outside—" Bink said.

Beauregard shook his head. "You do seem to be jinxed, Bink. First you lose the bottle, then your heart. But never fear; we'll include the nymph in the party. We shall entertain the diggle at our motor pool; he will enjoy the swim. We know Jewel well; in fact, you could hardly have been more fortunate in your misfortune."

In due course Jewel joined them for supper. It was hard to believe that dawn had been at the fringe of the Region of Madness, in a tree, and breakfast had been at the lake castle of the fiends, lunch with the nymph, and supper here—all in the same day. Down here under the ground day had less meaning; still, it had been an eventful period.

The demon's meal was similar to the nymph's, only it was fashioned from minute magic creatures called yeast and bacteria. Bink wondered whether there were front-teria too, but didn't ask. Some of the food was like squash, which had been squashed only minutes before; some resembled roast haunch of medium-long pig. Dessert was the frozen eye of a scream bird. Genuine eye scream was a rare delicacy, and so was this yellow flavored imitation.

"I sampled the eye of a smilk once," Chester said. "But it was not as good as this."

"You have good taste," Beauregard said.

"On, no! Centaur eyes have inferior flavor," Chester said quickly.

"You are too modest." But the demon smiled reassuringly. "Screams have more fat than smilks, so their eyes provide more flavor, as you recognized."

After the repast they retired to Beauregard's den, where a tame firedrake blazed merrily. "Now we shall provide you excellent accommodations for the night," the demon said. "We shall not interfere in any way with your quest. However—"

"What is it you know, that we don't?" Bink asked anxiously.

"I know the nature of demons," Beauregard said.

"Oh, we don't plan to bother you here! We're going on to—"

"Bear with me, Bink." Beauregard brought out a fancy little bottle, uttered an obscure word, and made a mystic gesture. The cork popped out, vapor issued forth, and formed into—Good Magician Humfrey.

Amazed, Bink could only ask: "But where is Crombie?"

"Back in the bottle," Humfrey said shortly. "It would help if you recovered your fumble promptly."

"But if Beauregard can rescue you—"

"I have not rescued him," the demon said. "I have conjured him. He must now do my bidding."

"Just as you once did *his* bidding!" Bink said.

"Correct. It all depends on who is confined, and who possesses the controlling magic. The Magician has dabbled in demonology; he is now subject to our humanology."

"But does that mean—"

"No, I shall not abuse the situation. My interest is in research, not ironies. I merely make this demonstration to convince you that there is more to magic than you may have supposed, and that the possible consequences of your quest may be more extensive than you would care to risk."

"I already know something is trying to stop me," Bink said.

"Yes. It is some kind of demon—and that is the problem. Most demons have no more magic than most humans do, but the demons of the depths are something else. They are to ordinary demons like me as Magicians are to ordinary people like you. It is not wise to venture into their demesnes."

"You're a demon," Chester said suspiciously. "Why are you telling us this?"

"Because he's a good demon," Jewel said. "He helps people."

"Because I care about the welfare of Xanth," Beauregard said. "If I were convinced Xanth would be better off without people, I would work toward that end. But though I have had doubt on occasion, so far I believe the species of man is a net benefit." He looked at the Magician. "Even gnomes like him."

Humfrey merely stood there. "Why don't you set him free, then?" Bink asked, not wholly trusting the demon.

"I can not free him. Only the holder of his container can do that."

"But here he is! You summoned him from your bottle!"

"My magic has granted me a temporary lease on his service. I can only evoke him briefly, and can not keep him. If I had *his* bottle, then I could control him, since he was so foolish as to confine himself in that manner. That is why you must recover that bottle, before—"

"Before it breaks!" Bink said.

"It will never break. It is an enchanted bottle; I know, for I occupied it, and made sure it was secure. No, the danger is that your enemy will recover it first."

Bink was appalled. "The enemy!"

"For then that enemy would control the Magician, and all Humfrey's power would be at the enemy's service. In that event, Humfrey's chances of surviving would be poor—almost as poor as yours."

"I must get that bottle!" Bink cried. "If only I knew where it is!"

"That is the service I require," Beauregard said. "Magician, inform Bink of your precise location, so he can rescue you."

"Latitude twenty-eight degrees northwest, longitude one hundred and—"

"Not that way, simpleton!" Beauregard interrupted. "Tell it so he can use it!"

"Er, yes," Humfrey agreed. "Perhaps we'd better put Crombie on."

222

"Do it," the demon snapped.

The griffin appeared beside the Magician. "Say, yes," Bink said eagerly. "If we have him point out your direction from here, I mean our direction from there, we can reverse it to reach you."

"Won't work," Beauregard said. But Crombie was already whirling. His wing came to rest pointing directly at Bink.

"Fine," Bink said. "We'll go that way."

"Try walking across the den," Beauregard said. "Griffin, hold that point."

Perplexed, Bink walked. Crombie didn't move, but his pointing wing continued aiming at Bink. "It's just a picture!" Bink explained. "No matter how you look at it, it looks right at you."

"Precisely," the demon agreed. "This conjuration is in a certain respect an image. The same aspect appears regardless of the orientation of the viewer. To orient on the conjuration is useless; it is the original we require."

"Easily solved, demon," Humfrey snapped. "Crombie, point out the direction of our bottle as viewed from the locale of the conjuration."

How simple! The conjuration was *here,* so this would give the proper direction to *there.* But would it work?

The griffin whirled and pointed again. This time the wing aimed away from Bink, and downward.

"That is the way you must go," Beauregard said gravely. "Now before I banish the image, have you any other questions?"

"I do," Chester said. "About my talent—"

Beauregard smiled. "Very clever, centaur. I think you have the mind of a demon! It is indeed possible, in this situation, for you to obtain the information you seek without incurring the Magician's normal fee, if your ethics permit such exploitation."

"No," Chester said. "I'm not trying to cheat! Magician, I know my talent now. But I've already served part of the fee, and am stuck for the rest."

Humfrey smiled. "I never specified the Question I would Answer. Pick another Question for the fee. That was part of the agreement."

"Say, good," Chester said, like a colt with sudden access to the farthest and greenest pasture. He pondered briefly. "Cherie—I'd sure like to know *her* talent, if she has one. A magical one, I mean. Her and her less-magical-than-thou attitude—"

"She has a talent," Humfrey said. "Do you wish the Answer now?"

"No. I might figure it out myself, again."

The Magician spread his hands. "As you prefer. However, we are not insured against accidents of fate. If you don't solve it, and Bink doesn't find my bottle before the enemy does, I may be forced to renege. Do you care to take that risk?"

"What do you mean, before the enemy does?" Bink demanded. "How close is the enemy to—"

"That is what we were discussing before," Beauregard said. "It seems the Magician can not be protected from his own information-talent. He is correct: that bottle has been carried very close to the region your enemy inhabits, and it is very likely that the enemy is aware of that. Thus this is not a routine search for the bottle, but a race against active opposition."

"But what is the nature of the enemy?" Bink demanded.

"Begone, Magician," Beauregard said. Humfrey and Crombie converted into smoke and swirled into the bottle. "I can not answer that Question directly, other than to remind you that the enemy must be some sort of demon. Therefore I spare myself the embarrassment of confessing my ignorance in the presence of my human counterpart in research. Professional rivalry, you might say."

"I don't care about professional rivalry!" Bink retorted. "The Good Magician and Crombie are my friends. I've got to save them!"

"You're loyal," Jewel said admiringly.

"The thing you must understand," Beauregard continued, "is that as you approach the source of magic, the magic of the immediate environment becomes stronger, in a function resembling a logarithmic progression. Therefore—"

"I don't understand that," Bink said. "What have logs to do with it? Is the enemy a tree?"

"He means the magic gets stronger faster as you get closer," Chester explained. Centaurs had excellent mathematical comprehension.

"Precisely," the demon agreed. "Thus we demons, being more proximate to the source, tend to be more magical than you creatures at the fringe. But in the immediate vicinity of the source, the magic is far stronger than we can fathom. Therefore I can not identify your specific enemy or describe his magic— but it is likely that it is stronger magic than you have encountered before."

"I've met pretty strong magic," Bink said dubiously.

"Yes, I know. And you have extremely strong magic yourself. But this—well, though I have never been able to fathom the precise nature of your talent, therefore my prior remark about you being an ordinary individual, empirical data suggest that it relates to your personal welfare. But at the source—"

"Suddenly I understand," Bink said. "Where I'm going, the magic is stronger than mine."

"Just so. Thus you will be vulnerable in a manner you have not been before. Your own magic suffers enhancement as you proceed, but only in a geometric ratio. Therefore it can not—"

"He means the enemy magic gets stronger faster than our magic," Chester said. "So we're losing power proportionately."

"Precisely," the demon agreed. "The nature of the curves suggests that the differential will not become gross until you are extremely close to the source, so you may not be much inconvenienced by it, or even aware of it. Still—"

"So if I continue," Bink said slowly, "I'll come up against an enemy who is stronger than I am."

"Correct. Because the strength of the magic field of Xanth varies inversely with distance, on both an individual and environmental basis—"

"What about the magic dust?" Chester demanded.

"That does indeed enhance magic in its vicinity," Beauregard agreed. "But it is not the major avenue for the distribution of magic. The dust is basically convective, while most magic is conductive. Were that village to close down its operations, the magic of Xanth would continue only slightly abated."

"So they might as well relax," Bink said.

"To continue: because of the inverse ratio, the enemy was not able to harm you on the surface, though he tried with demonic persistence and cunning. (I distinguish between the terms 'demonic' and 'demoniac'; the latter has a pejorative connotation that is unwarranted.) Which is why I am convinced it is in fact a demon you face. But here in the nether region, the enemy can and will bring to bear overwhelming magic. Therefore it is foolish to pursue your quest further."

"I'm human," Bink said.

"Yes, unfortunately. A demon would be more rational. Since you *are* a foolish human of exactly the type my research paper describes, you will continue inevitably to your doom—for the sake of your ideals and friendships."

"I must be more human than demon," Jewel said. "I think he's noble."

"Don't flatter me," Bink warned her. "It only exaggerates the effect of the potion."

She looked startled, then prettily resolute. "I'm sorry the potion had to—I mean, you're such a nice, handsome, courageous, decent man, I—I can't say I'm sorry it happened. When we get back maybe I *will* take a drink myself."

"But one reason I need the Magician is to find the antidote," Bink pointed out. "Apart from my friendship for him, I mean. In fact, we should have asked Crombie to point out the locale of the antidote, so—"

"I could summon them again," Beauregard said. "But I would not advise it."

"Why not?" Bink asked.

"Because in the event the enemy is not yet aware of the precise location of their bottle, we do not wish to call further attention to it. We do not know what mechanisms the enemy has to observe you, now that its squiggle is gone, but we can not afford to assume they are negligible. It would be better to rescue your friends first, then attend to your more personal business."

"Yes, that is true," Bink said. He turned to the

nymph. "Jewel, I regret having to inconvenience you further, but my loyalty to my friends comes first. I promise, as soon as we rescue them——"

"That's all right," she said, seeming not at all displeased.

"She could wait here," Chester said. "Or go about her normal business. Once we obtain the antidote, we can bring it back and——"

"No, only the diggle can take you there fast enough," Jewel said. "And only I can guide the diggle. There's lots of bad magic in the river channel, and very little in the solid rock. I'm coming along."

"I hoped you would say that," Bink said. "Of course my feeling doesn't count, since——"

Jewel stepped up and kissed him on the mouth. "I like your honesty, too," she said. "Let's get going."

Bink, momentarily stunned by the potency of this first voluntary kiss, forced his mind to focus on the mission. "Yes—we must hurry."

"The goblins are very bad in the deeper reaches," Beauregard said. "In recent years they have lost their savagery on the surface, but below they retain it. You have not encountered goblins like these."

"It is not a matter of choice," Bink said. "We have to go there."

"Then stay on well-lighted routes, when you're not phasing through actual rock. Like nickelpedes, they don't like light. They will face it if they have to, but generally they avoid it."

Bink turned to the nymph. "Is that why you're afraid of the dark? Can you keep us in the light?"

She nodded. "Yes . . . yes," she agreed to each question. Bink somehow had the impression that he could have asked somewhat more personal questions and had the same response. Or was that a flight of romantic fancy spawned by the potion?

"At least get a good night's rest," Beauregard urged. "We demons don't need sleep, as such, but you humans can get very irritable if——"

"No, we'd better move right along," Bink said. "A few hours could make the difference."

"So could fatigue," Beauregard pointed out. "You

will need all your faculties about you, when you face the big magic."

"Seems to me one demon's stalling," Chester said.

Beauregard spread his hands. "Perhaps I am, centaur. There is one thing I have not told you."

"If you plan to tell it, tell it now," Bink said. "Because we're leaving now."

"It is this," the demon said reluctantly. "I am not at all certain that your quest is proper."

"Not proper!" Bink exploded. "To rescue my friends?"

"To seek the source of the magic of Xanth."

"All I want is information! You, of all demons, should understand that!"

"Too well," Beauregard said. "Information can be the most dangerous thing there is. Consider the power of your Magician, who specializes in information. Suppose he were armed with full knowledge about the ultimate nature of magic? Where would be the limits of his power then?"

"Humfrey wouldn't hurt Xanth," Bink protested. "He's a *good* Magician!"

"But once knowledge of the nature of the source of magic were known, what would stop an evil Magician from obtaining it? With the strongest magic of all, he could rule Xanth—or destroy it."

Bink considered. He remembered how an Evil Magician *had* taken over the crown of Xanth—and had turned out not to be evil at all. But that had been a special situation. Suppose a truly evil man—or woman —obtained unconscionable power? "I see your point. I'll think about it. Maybe I won't go all the way to the source. But I must rescue the Magician, regardless."

"Yes of course," Beauregard agreed, seeming ill at ease for a demon.

They boarded the diggle and moved out, following the direction Crombie had indicated. "I don't know the deeper depths so well," Jewel said. "But there's a whole lot of solid rock here, since we're not following so close to the river. I'll tell the diggle to stay within the rock until we get there, and only to come out where there is light. I think you could sleep some while we travel, while I sing the worm along."

"You are beautiful," Bink said gratefully. He leaned his head against her back and was lulled to sleep by her singing, amplified and sweetened by his contact with her. And the worm ground on.

Chapter 11. Brain Coral

Bink woke with a start as the diggle halted. "I think we're here," Jewel murmured. Her voice was hoarse from hours of singing.

"You should have waked me before!" Bink said. "To take my turn singing the worm along. You've sung yourself out."

"Your head was so nice on my shoulder, I couldn't disturb you," she rasped. "Besides, you'll need all your strength. I can feel the magic intensifying as we move along."

Bink felt it too: a subtle prickle on his skin like that of the magic dust. For all he knew, the rock through which they traveled might be the magic-dust rock, before it welled to the surface. But the mystery remained: what was it that imbued that rock with magic? "Uh, thanks," he said awkwardly. "You're a sweet nymph."

"Well—" She turned her head, making it easy to kiss. She smelled of especially fine roses: this magic, too, was enhanced by the environment. Bink leaned forward, inhaling the delicious fragrance, bringing his lips close to—

They were interrupted by the sight of the bottle. It bobbled on the glowing surface of another lake. Something was attached to it, a bit of string or tar—

"Grundy!" Bink cried.

The golem looked up. "About time you got here! Fetch in this bottle, before—"

"Is it safe to swim in this lake?" Bink asked, wary of the glow. It might keep the goblins away, but that didn't make it safe for people.

"No," Jewel said. "The water is slowly poisonous to most forms of life. One drink won't hurt much, if you get out of it soon, up at the headwaters where it is diluted by the fresh flow from the surface. But down here, where it has absorbed much more horrible magic—"

"Right. No swimming," Bink said. "Chester, can you lasso it?"

"Out of range," the centaur said. "If the eddy currents carry it closer to shore I can snag it readily enough."

"Better hurry," Grundy called. "There's something under the lake, and it—"

"The fiends lived under a lake," Chester said. "Do you think the enemy—?"

Bink started stripping off his clothing. "I think I'd better swim out and get that bottle right now. If the lake harms me, the Magician can give me a drop of his healing elixir. That should be more potent, too, here."

"Don't do that!" Jewel cried. "That lake—I don't think you'd ever reach the bottle. Here, I'll have the diggle phase through the water. Nothing hurts him when he's in phase."

At her direction, and hoarse singing, the worm slid into the water, erecting its circular flange to form a temporary tunnel through the liquid, as through rock. He moved very slowly, until Chester's flute appeared and played a brisk, beautiful marching tune. The flute seemed larger and brighter than it had before, and its sound was louder: more magical enhancement. The diggle speeded up, expanding and contracting in time to the music. He advanced purposefully toward the bottle. "Oh, thank you, centaur," Jewel whispered.

"Hurry! Hurry!" the golem called. "The coral is aware of the—is trying to—is—HELP! IT'S COMING UP TO GET ME!"

Then Grundy screamed horribly, as if in human pain. "I'm not real enough, yet," he gasped after the scream had torn its way out of his system. "I'm still just a golem, just a thing, string and gum. I can be controlled. I—"

He broke off, then screamed again, then resumed more quietly. "I'm gone."

Bink understood none of this, yet had the sinking feeling that he should somehow have tried to help the golem to fight off—what? Some encouragement, some reminder of the feelings Grundy evidently did have. Maybe the golem could have fought off his private personal horror, if—

Now the worm was almost at the bottle. Quickly Grundy wrapped his string-arms about the cork, braced his feet against the neck of the bottle, and heaved. "By the power of the brain coral, emerge!" he gasped.

The cork flew out. Smoke poured from the bottle, swirled into a whirlwind, ballooned, then coalesced into the figures of the Good Magician and the griffin. "Grundy rescued them!" Chester exclaimed as his flute faded out.

"Fly to shore!" Bink cried. "Don't touch the water!"

Humfrey caught hold of Crombie, who spread his wings and bore them both up. For a moment they tilted unsteadily, then righted and moved smoothly forward.

Bink ran up as they landed at the shore. "We were so worried about you, afraid the enemy would get you first!"

"The enemy did," Humfrey said, reaching for a vial as he let go of the griffin. "Turn about, Bink; desist your quest, and you will not be harmed."

"Desist my quest!" Bink cried, amazed. "Right when I'm so close to accomplishing it? You know I won't do that!"

"I serve a new master, but my scruples remain," Humfrey said. There was something sinister about him now; he remained a small, gnomish man, but now there was no humor in that characterization. His gaze was more like that of a basilisk than that of a man: a cold, deadly stare. "It is necessary that you understand. The bottle was opened by the agency of the entity that lies beneath this lake, a creature of tremendous intelligence and magic and conscience, but lacking the ability to move. This is the brain coral, who has to operate through other agencies to accomplish its noble purpose."

"The—enemy?" Bink asked, dismayed. "The one

who sent the magic sword, and the dragon, and the squiggle—"

"And countless other obstructions, most of which your own magic foiled before they manifested. The coral can not control a conscious, intelligent, living entity; it must operate through thought suggestions that seem like the creature's own notions. That was why the dragon chased you, and the squiggle spied on you, and why the other seemingly coincidental complications occurred. But your talent brought you through almost unscathed. The siren lured you, but the gorgon did not enchant you into stone; the midas fly was diverted to another target, the curse of the fiends missed you. Now, at the heart of the coral's magic, you are finally balked. You must turn back, because—"

"But it can not control *you!*" Bink protested. "You are a man, an intelligent man, a Magician!"

"It assumed control of the golem, possible only because Grundy's reality was not complete and this is the region of the coral's greatest power. It caused the golem to open the bottle. Crombie and I are subject to the holder of the bottle. It does not matter that the bottle is now floating on the surface of the coral lake; the conjuration was done in the name of the brain coral, and it is binding."

"But—" Bink protested, unable to continue because he could not formulate his thought.

"That was the most savage engagement of this campaign," Humfrey continued. "The struggle for possession of the bottle. The coral managed to dislodge it from your clothing, but your magic caused the cork to work loose, and we started to emerge. That was the impact of the fiends' curse, aiding you by what seemed like an incredible coincidence. It shook the bottle within the vortex. But the coral used a strong eddy current to jam the stopper back, trapping Grundy outside. But your magic made the magic mirror get caught halfway, shattering it, with fragments inside and out, enabling us to establish communication of a sort. Then the coral's magic caused you to lose your fragment of glass. But your magic guided you to Beauregard, who re-established communication. You very nearly reached the bottle in time, by turning the

233

liability of your infatuation for the nymph into an asset—your talent outmaneuvered the coral neatly there!—but here the coral's magic is stronger than yours, and so it got the bottle first. Barely. In effect, your two talents have canceled out. But now the coral, through the power of the bottle, controls Crombie and me. All our powers are at its service, and you have lost."

Chester stood beside Bink. "So you have become the enemy," he said slowly.

"Not really. Now that we have access to the coral's perspective, we know that it is on the side of reason. Bink, your quest is dangerous, not merely for you, but for all the land of Xanth. You *must* desist, believe me!"

"I do not believe you," Bink said grimly. "Not now. Not now that you've changed sides."

"Same here," Chester said. "Conjure yourself back into the bottle, and let us rescue the bottle and release you in our power. Then if you can repeat that statement, I'll listen."

"No."

"That is what I thought," Chester said. "I undertook this mission as a service to you, Magician, but I have never collected my Answer from you. I can quit your service anytime I want. But I shall not renounce this quest merely because some hidden monster has scared you into changing your mind."

"Your position is comprehensible," Humfrey said with surprising mildness. "I do not, as you point out, have any present call on your service. But I am obliged to advise you both that if we can not prevail upon your reason, we must oppose you materially."

"You mean you would actually fight us?" Bink asked incredulously.

"We do not wish to resort to force," Humfrey said. "But it is imperative that you desist. Go now, give up your quest, and all will be well."

"And if we don't quit?" Chester demanded belligerently, eyeing Crombie. Obviously the centaur would not be entirely loath to match his prowess against that of the griffin. There had been a kind of rivalry between them all along.

"In that case we should have to nullify you," Humfrey said gravely. Small he was, but he remained a Magician, and his statement sent an ugly chill through Bink. Nobody could afford to take lightly the threat of a Magician.

Bink was torn between unkind alternatives. How could he fight his friends, the very ones he had struggled so hard to rescue? Yet if they were under the spell of the enemy, how could he afford to yield to their demand? If only he could get at the brain coral, the enemy, and destroy it, then his friends would be freed from its baleful influence. But the coral was deep under the poison water, unreachable. Unless—

"Jewel!" he cried. "Send the diggle down to make holes through the coral!"

"I can't, Bink," she said sadly. "The diggle never came back after we sent it after the bottle. I'm stuck here with my bucket of gems." She flipped a diamond angrily into the water. "I can't even plant them properly, now."

"The worm has been sent away," Humfrey said. "Only the completion of your quest can destroy the coral—along with all the Land of Xanth. Depart now, or suffer the consequence."

Bink glanced at Chester. "I don't want to hurt him. Maybe if I can knock him out, get him out of range of the coral—"

"While I take care of birdbeak," Chester said, nominally regretful.

"I don't want bloodshed!" Bink cried. "These are our friends, whom we must rescue."

"I suppose so," Chester agreed reluctantly. "I'll try to immobilize the griffin without hurting him too much. Maybe I'll just pull out a few of his feathers."

Bink realized that this was as much of a compromise as Chester was prepared to make. "Very well. But stop the moment he yields."

Now he faced Humfrey again. "I intend to pursue my quest. I ask you to depart, and to refrain from trying to interfere. It grieves me even to contemplate strife between us, but—"

Humfrey rummaged in his belt of vials. He brought one out. "Huh-*uh!*" Bink cried, striding across. Yet his horror at practicing any kind of violence against his friends held him back, and he got there too late. The cork came out and the vapor issued. It formed into . . . a green poncho, which flapped about in the air before settling to the floor.

"Wrong bottle," the Magician muttered, and uncorked another.

Bink, momentarily frozen, realized that he could not subdue the Magician until he separated the man from his arsenal of vials. Bink's talent might have helped Humfrey to confuse the bottles, but that sort of error could not be counted on after the first time. Bink drew his sword, intending to slice the belt from the Good Magician's waist—but realized that this seemed like a murderous attack. Again he hesitated—and was brought up short by the coalescing vapor. Suddenly thirteen black cats faced him, spitting viciously.

Bink had never seen a pure cat before, in the flesh. He regarded the cat as an extinct species. He just stood there and stared at this abrupt de-extinction, unable to formulate a durable opinion. If he killed these animals, would he be re-extincting the species?

Meanwhile, the centaur joined battle with the griffin. Their encounter was savage from the outset, despite Chester's promises. His bow was in his hands, and an arrow sizzled through the air. But Crombie, an experienced soldier, did not wait for it to arrive. He leaped and spread his wings, then closed them with a great backblast of air. He shot upward at an angle, the arrow passing beneath his tail feathers. Then he banked near the cavern ceiling and plummeted toward the centaur, screaming, claws outstretched.

Chester's bow was instantly replaced by his rope. He swung up a loop that closed about the griffin's torso, drawing the wings closed. He jerked, and Crombie was swung about in a quarter-circle. The centaur was about three times as massive as his opponent, so was able to control him this way.

A black cat leaped at Bink's face, forcing him to pay attention to his own battle. Reflexively he brought his sword around—and sliced the animal cleanly in half.

Bink froze again in horror. He had not meant to kill

it! A rare creature like this—maybe these cats were all that remained in the whole Land of Xanth, being preserved only by the Magician's magic.

Then two things changed his attitude. First, the severed halves of the cat he had struck did not die; they metamorphosed into smaller cats. This was not a real cat, but a pseudo-cat, shaped from life-clay and given a feline imperative. Any part of it became another cat. Had a dog been shaped from the same material, it would have fractured into more dogs. So Bink hardly needed to worry about preservation of that species. Second, another cat was biting him on the ankle.

In a sudden fury of relief and ire, Bink laid about him with his blade. He sliced cats in halves, quarters, and eighths—and every segment became a smaller feline, attacking him with renewed ferocity. This was like fighting the hydra—only this time he had no spell-reversal wood to feed it, and there was no thread to make it drop. Soon he had a hundred tiny cats pouncing on him like rats, and then a thousand attacking like nickelpedes. The more he fought, the worse it got.

Was this magic related to that of the hydra? That monster had been typified by seven, while the cats were thirteen, but each doubled with each strike against a member. If there were some key, some counterspell to abolish doubling magic—

"Get smart, Bink!" Chester called, stomping on several cats that had wandered into his territory. "Sweep them all into the drink."

Of course! Bink stooped low and swung the flat of his sword sidewise, sweeping dozens of thumbnail-sized cats into the lake. They hissed as they splashed, like so many hot pebbles, and then thrashed to the bottom. Whether they were drowning or being poisoned he could not tell, but none emerged.

While he swept his way to victory, Bink absorbed the continuing centaur-griffin engagement. He could not observe everything, but was able to bridge the gaps well enough. He had to keep track, because if anything happened to Chester, Bink would have another enemy to face.

Crombie, initially incapacitated by the rope, bent his head down and sheared his bond cleanly with one crunch of his sharp beak. He spread his wings explosively, made a defiant squawk, and launched a three-point charge at Chester's head: beak, claw, and talon.

The centaur, thrown off balance by the abrupt slackening of the rope, staggered. He had better stability than a man, but he had been hauling hard. His equine shoulder thudded against a stalagmite and broke it off as the griffin made contact. Bink winced—but as it turned out, the stalagmite was more of a problem to Crombie than to Chester. The pointed top fell across the griffin's left wing, weighing it down, forcing Crombie to flap his other wing vigorously to right himself.

Chester rose up, one talon slash down the side of his face where the griffin's strike had missed his eye. But his two great hands now grasped the griffin's two front legs. "Got you now, birdie!" he cried. But in this position he could not use his sword, so he tried to bash the griffin against the broken base of the stalagmite.

Crombie squawked and brought his hind legs up for a double slash that would have disemboweled the centaur's human portion had it scored. Chester hastily let go, throwing Crombie violently away from him. Then he grabbed for his bow and arrow again. The griffin, however, spread his wings to brake his flight, looped about, and closed in again before the arrow could be brought to bear. Now it was hand-to-claw.

Bink had cleared his area of little cats—but the Good Magician had had time to organize his vials and open the next. This coalesced into a mound of bright-red cherry bombs. Oh, no! Bink had had experience with these violent little fruits before, as there was a tree of them on the palace grounds. In fact, these were probably from that same tree. If any of them scored on him—

He dived for Humfrey, catching the Magician's arm before he could throw. Humfrey struggled desperately against Bink's superior strength. Bink still held back, hating this violence though he saw no alternative to it. Both of them fell to the floor. The Magician's belt tore loose, and a collection of vials tumbled across the stone. Some of their corks popped out. The cherry bombs were dislodged; they rolled away and dunked into the lake, where they detonated with harmless thuds and clouds of steam. One rolled into Jewel's bucket of gems.

The explosion sent precious stones flying all over the cavern. Diamonds shot by Bink's ears; a huge pearl thunked into the Magician's chest; opals got under Chester's hooves. "Oh, no!" Jewel cried, horrified. "That's not the way it's supposed to be done! Each has to be planted in exactly the right place!"

Bink was sorry about the gems, but he had more pressing problems. The new bottles were spewing forth a bewildering variety of things.

The first was a pair of winged shoes. "So that's where I left them!" Humfrey exclaimed. But they flew out of reach before he could grab them. The second vial loosed a giant hour-glass whose sands were running out—also harmless in this instance. The next was a collection of exotic-looking seeds, some like huge flat fish eyes, others like salt-and-pepper mix, others like one-winged flies. They fluttered out and littered a wide patch, crunching underfoot, rolling like marbles, squishing and adhering like burrs. But they did not seem to be any direct threat.

Unfortunately, the other vials were also pouring out vapors. These produced a bucket of garbage (so that was how the Magician cleaned his castle: he swept it all into a vial!), a bag of supergrow fertilizer, a miniature thunderstorm, and a small nova star. Now the seeds had food, water, and light. Suddenly they were sprouting. Tendrils poked out, bodies swelled, pods popped, leaves burst forth. Roots gripped the rock and clasped items of garbage; stems shot up to form a dense and variegated carpet. Diverse species fought their own miniature battles over the best fertilizer territory. In moments Bink and the Magician were surrounded by an expanding little jungle. Vines clung to feet, branches poked at bodies, and leaves obscured vision.

Soon the plants were flowering. Now their species were identifiable. Lady slippers produced footwear of a most delicate nature, causing Jewel to exclaim in delight and snatch off a pair for herself. Knotweeds formed the most intricate specialized knots: bow, granny, lanyard, clinch, hangman, and half-hitch. Bink

239

had to step quickly to avoid getting tied up. That would cost him the victory right there!

Meanwhile, the Magician was trying to avoid the snapping jaws of dog-tooth violets and dandelions, while a hawkweed made little swoops at his head. Bink would have laughed—but had too many problems of his own. A goldenrod was trying to impale him on its metallic spire, and a sunflower was blinding him with its effulgence. The nova star was no longer needed; the cave was now as bright as day, and would remain so until the sunflower went to seed.

Bink ducked just in time to avoid a flight of glinting arrowheads—but his foot slipped on a buttercup, squirting butter out and making him sit down hard—ooomph —on the squishy head of a skunk cabbage. Suddenly he was steamed in the nauseating fragrance.

Well, what had he expected? He had very little protective talent now; the enemy brain coral had canceled out his magic. Bink was on his own, and had to make his own breaks. At least Humfrey was no better off; at the moment he was being given a hotfoot by a patch of fireweed. He snatched up a flower from a water lily and poured its water out to douse the fire. Meanwhile, several paintbrushes were decorating him with stripes of red, green, and blue. Stray diamonds from the nymph's collection were sticking to his clothes.

This was getting nowhere! Bink tore his way out of the miniature jungle, holding his breath and closing his eyes as a parcel of poppies popped loudly about his head. He felt something enclosing his hands, and had to look: it was a pair of foxgloves. A bluebell rang in his ear; then he was out of it. And there was the Magician's belt with its remaining vials. Suddenly he realized: if he controlled this, Humfrey would be helpless. All his magic was contained in these vials!

Bink stepped toward it—but at that moment the Magician emerged from the foliage, plastered with crowfeet. Humfrey brushed them off, and the feet scampered away. A lone primrose turned its flower away from this gaucherie. Humfrey dived for his magic belt, arriving just as Bink did.

Bink laid his hands on it. There was a tug-of-war. More vials spilled out. One puffed into a kettle of barley soup that spilled across the floor and was eagerly lapped up by the questing rootlets of the jungle. Another developed into a package of mixed nuts and bolts. Then Bink found a steaming rice pudding and heaved it at the Magician—but Humfrey scored first with a big mince pie. Minces flew out explosively, twenty-four of them, littering a yet wider area. Bink caught the brunt of it in his face. Minces were wriggling in his hair and down his neck and partially obscuring his vision. Bink fanned the air with his sword, trying to keep the Magician back while he cleared his vision. Oddly, he could perceive the neighboring battle of centaur and griffin better than his own, at this moment.

Chester's human torso was now streaked with blood from the vicious raking of the griffin's talons. But one of Crombie's forelegs was broken, and one of his wings half-stripped of feathers. That hand-to-claw combat had been savage!

Now the centaur was stalking his opponent with sword in hand, and the griffin was flying in ragged circles just out of reach, seeking an opening. Despite Bink's cautions, these two were deadly serious; they were out to kill each other. Yet how could Bink stop them?

The Magician found a vial and opened it. Bink advanced alertly—but it was another miscue. A huge bowl of yogurt manifested. It had, by the look and smell of it, been in the bottle too long; it had spoiled. It floated gently toward the lake; let the brain coral try a taste of *that!* But Humfrey already had another vial. These mistakes were not the result of Bink's talent so much as sheer, honest chance; Humfrey seemed to have a hundred things in his vials (he was reputed to have a hundred spells, after all), and few were readily adaptable to combat, and now they were all mixed up. The odds were against anything really dangerous appearing from any randomly chosen vial.

Yet the odds could be beaten. The vial produced a writhing vine from a kraken, which undulated aggressively toward Bink. But he sliced it into fragments with his sword, and advanced on the Magician again. Bink knew he could control the situation now; nothing in Humfrey's bottles could match the devastating presence of a capable sword.

Desperately Humfrey opened bottles, searching for something to further his cause. Three dancing fairies materialized, hovering on translucent, pastel-hued wings, but they were harmless and soon drifted over to consult with Jewel, who put them to work picking up stray gems. A package of cough drops formed and burst —but too close to the Magician, who went into paroxysms of coughing. But then a wyvern appeared.

Wyverns were basically small dragons—but even the tiniest of dragons were dangerous. Bink leaped at it, aiming for the monster's neck. He scored—but the wyvern's tough scales deflected the blade. It opened its mouth and fired a jet of hot steam at Bink's face. Bink danced back—then abruptly rammed his point directly into the cloud of vapor with all his force. The sword plunged into the creature's open mouth, through its palate, and out the top of its head. The wyvern gave a single cry of agony and expired as Bink yanked back his weapon.

Bink knew he had been lucky—and that this was genuine luck, not his talent at work. But the problem with such luck was that it played no favorites; the next break could go against him. He had to wrap this up before such a break occurred.

But the Magician had had time to rummage among more vials. He was looking for something, having trouble locating it amid the jumble. But each failure left him fewer vials to choose from, and a correspondingly greater chance of success. As Bink turned on him again, a set of long winter underwear formed, and several tattered comic books, and a wooden stepladder, a stink bomb, and a gross of magic writing quills. Bink had to laugh.

"Bink—watch out!" Chester cried.

"It's only a lady's evening gown," Bink said, glancing at the next offering. "No harm in it."

"Behind it is an evil eye!" Chester cried.

Trouble! *That* was what Humfrey had been searching for! Bink grabbed the gown, using it as a shield against the nemesis beyond.

A beam of light shot out, passed him—and scored

on the centaur. Half-stunned, Chester reeled—and the griffin dived in for the kill. His beak stabbed at Chester's blinded eyes, forcing the centaur to prance backward.

"No!" Bink screamed.

Again, too late. Bink realized that he must have leaned on his talent a long time, so that his reactions to chance happenings were slow. Chester's rear hooves stepped off the ledge. The centaur gave a great neighing cry of dismay and tumbled rear first into the evil water of the lake.

The water closed murkily over Chester's head. Without further sound or struggle, the centaur disappeared below. Bink's friend and ally was gone.

There was no time for remorse. Humfrey had found another vial. "I have you now, Bink! This one contains sleeping potion!" he cried, holding it up.

Bink did not dare charge him, because the evil eye still hovered between them, balked only by the evening gown Bink held as a feeble shield. He could see the eye's outline vaguely through the filmy cloth, and had to maneuver constantly to avoid any direct visual contact with it. Yet that sleeping potion would not be stopped by mere cloth!

"Yield, Bink!" Humfrey cried. "Your ally is gone, my ally hovers behind you, the eye holds you in check, and the sleeping potion can reach you where you stand. Yield, and the coral grants you your life!"

Bink hesitated—and felt the swish of air as the griffin flew at him from behind. Bink whirled, seeing the nymph standing nearby, petrified with terror, and he knew that even as the brain coral made the offer of clemency with one mouth, it was betraying that offer with action.

Until this point Bink had been fighting a necessary if undesired battle. Now, abruptly, he was angry. His friend gone, himself betrayed—what reason had he now to stay his hand? "Look, then, at the evil eye!" Bink cried at Crombie, whipping away the gown as he faced away from the menace. Instantly Crombie turned his head away, refusing to look. Bink, still in his rage, charged the griffin with his sword.

Now it was claw and beak against sword—with neither party daring to glance toward the Magician. Bink waved the bright gown as a distraction while he sliced at the griffin's head, then wrapped the material about his left arm as a protection against the claws. Crombie could attack only with his left front leg; his tattered wings did not provide sufficient leverage for close maneuvering, so he had to stand on his hind legs. Still, he had the deadly body of a griffin, and the combat-trained mind of a soldier, and he was as clever and ferocious an enemy as Bink had ever faced. Crombie knew Bink, was long familiar with his mannerisms, and was himself a more competent swordsman than Bink. In fact, Crombie had been Bink's instructor. Though as a griffin he carried no sword, there was no maneuver Bink could make that Crombie did not know and could not counter. In short, Bink found himself overmatched.

But his anger sustained him. He attacked the griffin determinedly, slicing at legs and head, stabbing at the body, forcing his opponent to face the evil eye. He swung the gown to entangle Crombie's good wing, then screamed terribly and launched his shoulder into Crombie's bright breast. Bink was as massive as the griffin; his crudely hurtling weight bore Crombie back toward the deadly water. But it was useless; just as Bink thought he had gained the advantage, Crombie slid sidewise and let Bink stumble toward the water alone.

Bink tried to brake, and almost succeeded. He teetered on the brink. And saw—the golem Grundy, astride the still-floating bottle, now quite near the shore. "Fish me out, Bink!" the golem cried. "The poison can't hurt me, but I'm beginning to dissolve. Look out!"

At the warning, Bink dropped flat, his face landing bare inches from the water. Crombie passed over him, having missed his push, spreading his wings to sail out over the dark lake. Grundy scooped one tiny hand through the water, splashing a few drops up to splatter the griffin's tail—and immediately that tail drooped. The water was deadly, all right!

Crombie made a valiant effort, flapping so vigorously that he rose up out of range of the splashing.

Then he glided to the far side of the lake and crash-landed, unable to control his flight well because of the defeathered wing and stunned tail. Bink used the respite to extend his sword to the golem, who grabbed the point and let himself be towed to shore.

Then Bink remembered: Grundy had freed Humfrey and Crombie—in the name of the enemy. The golem was also a creature of the brain coral. Why was he siding with Bink, now?

Two possibilities: first, the coral might have only borrowed the golem, then released him, so that Grundy had reverted to Bink's camp. Yet in that case, the coral could take over the golem again at any time, and Grundy was not to be trusted. In the heat of battle the coral might have forgotten Grundy, but as that battle simplified, that would change. Second, Grundy might remain an agent of the enemy right now. In that case—

But why should the coral try to fool Bink this way? Why not just finish him off without respite? Bink didn't know, but it occurred to him it might be his smartest course to play along, to pretend to be fooled. The enemy might have some weakness Bink hadn't fathomed, and if he could figure it out, using the golem as a clue—

The soldier had not given up. Unable to turn in air because of his disabled guidance system, Crombie oriented himself on land, got up speed, and took off across the lake again.

"Don't touch me—I'm steeped in poison!" Grundy cried. "I'll spot the eye for you, Bink. You concentrate on—"

Glad for the little ally despite his doubts, Bink did. As the griffin sailed at him, Bink leaped up, making a two-handed strike directly overhead with his sword. Crombie, unable to swerve, took the slash on his good wing. The blade cut through the feathers and muscle and tendon and bone, half-severing the wing.

Crombie fell to the ground—but he was not defeated. He squawked and bounced to his feet, whirling and leaping at Bink, front claw extended. Surprised at the soldier's sheer tenacity, Bink fell away, tripped over an irregularity in the rock, and landed on his back. As the griffin landed on him, beak plunging for his face, Bink shoved his sword violently upward.

This time it was no wing he scored on, but the neck. Blood spurted out, soaking him, burning hot. This had to be a mortal wound—yet still the griffin fought, slashing with three feet, going for Bink's gut.

Bink rolled from under, dragging his sword with him. But it snagged on a bone and was wrenched out of his hand. Instead he threw himself on Crombie's neck from behind, wrapping both arms about the spilling neck, choking it, trying to break it. Until this moment Bink could not have imagined himself killing his friend—but the vision of Chester's demise was burning in his mind, and he had become an almost mindless killer.

Crombie gave a tremendous heave and threw him off. Bink dived in again, grabbing for the legs as Chester had, catching a hind one. Such a tactic could never have worked on the soldier in his human form, for Crombie was an expert hand-to-hand fighter; but he was in animal form, unable to use much of his highly specialized human expertise. To prevent the griffin from reorienting, Bink hauled hard on that leg, putting his head down and dragging the form across the rock.

"Don't look!" Grundy cried. "The eye is ahead of you!"

Could he trust the golem? Surely not—yet it would be foolish to risk looking where the eye might be. Bink closed his eyes, took a new grasp, and with his greatest exertion yet, heaved the griffin over his head and forward. Crombie flew through the air—and didn't land. He was flying again, or trying to! Bink had only helped launch him; no wonder the griffin had not resisted that effort!

"The eye is circling, coming in toward your face!" Grundy cried.

To believe, or not to believe? The first demonstrably false statement the golem made would betray his affiliation. So probably Grundy would stick to the truth as long as he could. Bink could trust him *because* he was an enemy agent, ironic as that seemed. He kept his eyes closed and shook out his robe. "Where?"

"Arm's length in front of you!"

Bink spread the gown, held it in both hands, and leaped. He carried the material across and down. "You got it!" the golem cried. "Wrap it up, throw it in the lake!" And Bink did. He felt the tugging within the gown, and felt the slight mass of the captive eye; the golem had spoken truly. He heard the splash, and cautiously opened one eye. The gown was floating, but it was soaked through; anything caught in it would be finished.

Now he could look about. Crombie had flown only a short distance, and had fallen into a small crevasse; he was now wedged in its base, prevented by his wounds and weakness from rising. But the Magician had remained active. "One step, and I loose the sleeping potion!" he cried.

Bink had had enough. "If you loose it, you will be the first affected!" he said, striding toward Humfrey. "I can hold my breath as long as you can!" His sword was on the floor, where it had dropped from the griffin's wounds. Bink paused to pick it up, wiping some of the blood off against his own clothing, and held it ready. "In any event I doubt it takes effect before I reach you. And if it does, the golem will not be affected. What side will he be on then? He's part real, you know; the coral can never be certain of its control."

The Magician jerked the cork out, refusing to be bluffed. The vapor issued. Bink leaped forward, swinging his sword as the substance coalesced—and struck a small bottle.

A bottle materializing from a bottle?

"Oh, no!" Humfrey cried. "That was my supply of smart-pills, lost for this past decade!"

What irony! The Magician had absentmindedly filed his smart-pills inside another bottle, and without them had been unable to figure out where he had put them. Now, by a permutation of the war of talents, they had shown up—at the wrong time.

Bink touched the Magician's chest with the point of his sword. "You don't need any smart-pill to know what will happen if you do not yield to me now."

Humfrey sighed. "It seems I underestimated you, Bink. I never supposed you could beat the griffin."

Bink hoped never to have to try it again! If Crombie hadn't already been tired and wounded—but no sense worrying about what might have been. "You serve an enemy master. I can not trust you. Yield, and I will require one service of you, then force you back into the bottle until my quest is complete. Otherwise I must slay you, so as to render your brain coral helpless." Was this a bluff? He did not want to kill the Magician, but if the battle renewed . . . "Choose!"

Humfrey paused, evidently in communion with some other mind. "Goblins can't come; too bright, and besides, they hate the coral. No other resources in range. Can't counter your check." He paused again. Bink realized the term "check" related to the Mundane game King Trent sometimes played, called chess; a check was a direct personal threat. An apt term.

"The coral is without honor," Humfrey continued. "But I am not. I thought my prior offer to you was valid; I did not know the griffin would attack you then."

"I would like to believe you," Bink said, his anger abating but not his caution. "I dare not. I can only give you my word about my intent."

"Your word is better than mine, in this circumstance. I accept your terms."

Bink lowered the sword, but did not put it away. "And what of the golem?" he demanded. "Whose side is he on?"

"He—is one of us, as you surmised. You tricked me into acknowledging that by my reaction a moment ago. You are very clever in the clutch, Bink."

"Forget the flattery! Why was Grundy helping me?"

"The coral told me to," the golem answered.

"It doesn't make sense for the coral to fight itself! If you'd fought on Crombie's side, he might have beaten me!"

"And he might still have lost," Humfrey said. "The coral, too, had seriously underestimated you, Bink. It thought that once it canceled out your talent—which remains horribly strong and devious, forcing constant attention—you could readily be overcome by physical means. Instead you fought with increasing savagery and skill as the pressure mounted. What had seemed a near-certainty became dubious. Thus the chance of the coral prevailing by force diminished, while the chance of prevailing by reason increased."

"Reason!" Bink exclaimed incredulously.

"Accordingly, the coral delegated the golem to be your friend—the coral's agent in your camp. Then if you won the physical battle, and I were dead, you would be prepared to listen to this friend."

"Well, I'm not prepared," Bink said. "I never trusted Grundy's change of sides, and would have thrown him back into the lake the moment he betrayed me. At the moment I have more important business. Find the vial containing the healing elixir. I know that has not yet been opened."

The Magician squatted, picking through the remaining vials. "This one."

"Jewel!" Bink snapped.

Timidly the nymph stepped toward him. "I'm afraid of you when you're like this, Bink."

And she had been afraid during the battle. He could have used her help when the evil eye was stalking him, instead of having to rely on the extremely questionable aid of the golem. She was an all-too-typical nymph in this respect, incapable of decisive action in a crisis. Chameleon had been otherwise, even in her stupidest phase; she had acted to save him from harm, even sacrificing herself. He loved them both—but he would stay with Chameleon.

"Take this vial and sprinkle a drop on the griffin," he directed her.

She was startled. "But—"

"Crombie may be controlled by the enemy, and because of that he did a horrible thing, but he is my friend. I'm going to cure him, and have the Magician put him back in the bottle, along with himself, until this is over."

"Oh." She took the vial and headed for the broken griffin. Bink nudged the Magician forward with the point of his sword, and they followed Jewel more slowly. Humfrey had told Bink he had won, but Bink knew it was not over yet. Not until the Magician and griffin and golem were back in the bottle, and Bink had control of that bottle. And the coral would do its best to keep them out of that bottle.

Jewel paused at the brink of the crevice, looking down. Her free hand went to her mouth in a very feminine gesture that Bink found oddly touching. No, not oddly; he loved her, therefore he reacted in a special manner even to her minor mannerisms. But intellectually he knew better. "He's all blood!" she protested.

"I can't take my attention from the Magician," Bink said, and added mentally: or the golem. "If that vial does not contain the healing elixir, I shall slay him instantly." Bold words, bolstering his waning drive. "You have to apply it. We need that griffin to point out the location of the antidote to the love potion."

"I—yes, of course," she said faintly. She fumbled at the cork. "He's—there's so much gore—where do I—?"

Crombie roused himself partially. His eagle head rotated weakly on the slashed neck, causing another gout of blood to escape. "Squawk!"

"He says don't do it," Grundy translated. "He'll only have to kill you."

Bink angled his sword so that the blade reflected a glint of nova-starlight into the griffin's glazing eyes. The sunflower had been brighter, but now was fading; its harvest time was approaching. "I don't expect honor in a creature of the enemy, or gratitude for a favor rendered," he said grimly. "I have made a truce of sorts with the brain coral, and I enforce it with this sword. Crombie will obey me implicitly—or the Magician dies. Doubt me if you will."

How could they fail to doubt him, when he doubted himself? Yet if violence broke out again, he would not simply let the coral take over.

Crombie turned his tortured gaze on Humfrey. "What Bink says is true," the Magician said. "He has defeated us, and now requires service in exchange for our lives. The coral accedes. Perform his service, and suffer confinement in the bottle—or I will die and you will have to fight him again."

The griffin squawked once more, weakly. "What is the service?" Grundy translated.

"You know what it is!" Bink said. "To point out the nearest, safest love-reversal magic." Were they stalling, waiting for the sunflower to fade all the way so the goblins could come?

Another squawk. Then the noble head fell to the floor. "He agrees, but he's too weak to point," Grundy said.

"We don't really need the antidote. . . ." Jewel said.

"Get on with it," Bink grated. He had deep cuts where the griffin's claws had raked his body, and he was desperately tired, now that the violent part of the action had abated. He had to wrap this up before he collapsed. "Sprinkle him!"

Jewel finally got the bottle open. Precious fluid sprayed out, splattering her, the rocks, and the griffin. One drop struck the golem, who was suddenly cured of his partially dissolved state. But none of it landed on Bink, with what irony only the coral knew for sure.

Crombie lifted his body free of the crevice. Bright and beautiful again, he spread his wings, turning to orient on Bink. Bink's muscles tensed painfully; he held the Magician hostage, but if the griffin attacked now—

Jewel jumped between Bink and Crombie. "Don't you dare!" she cried at the griffin. There was the odor of burning paper.

For a long moment Crombie looked at her, his colorful wings partially extended, beating slowly back and forth. She was such a slip of a girl, armed only with the bottle of elixir; there was no way she could balk the magnificent animal. Indeed, her body trembled with her nervousness; one squawk and she would collapse in tears.

Yet she had made the gesture, Bink realized. This was an extraordinary act for a true nymph. She had tried to stand up for what she believed in. Could he condemn her because her courage was no greater than her strength?

Then Crombie rotated, extended one wing fully, and pointed. Toward the lake.

Bink sighed. "Conjure him into the bottle," he told the Magician. "Do it right the first time. If you try to conjure *me,* you're dead."

251

There was a delay while Jewel fetched the bottle from the edge of the lake, where it still floated. She had to scoop it up carefully, not letting the moisture touch her skin, then dry it off and set it within range of the Magician.

Humfrey performed his incantation. The griffin dissolved into vapor and siphoned into the bottle. Belatedly it occurred to Bink that Humfrey could have done the same to Bink, anytime during their battle—had he thought of it. The loss of those smart-pills must really have hurt! Yet it was hard to think of the obvious, when being stalked by a sword. And—the best bottle, the demon's residential one, had not been available, then.

"Now your turn," Bink told the Magician. "Into the same bottle—you and the golem."

"The coral is reconsidering," Humfrey said. "It believes that if you knew the full story, you would agree with the coral's viewpoint. Will you listen?"

"More likely the coral is stalling until more of its minions can arrive," Bink said, thinking again of the goblins. They might not get along well with the brain coral, but if some kind of deal were made . . .

"But it knows the location and nature of the source of magic!" Humfrey said. "Listen, and it will guide you there."

"Guide me there first, then I will listen!"

"Agreed."

"Agreed?"

"We trust you, Bink."

"I don't trust *you*. But all right—I'll make the deal. I hope I'm not making a fatal mistake. Show me the source of magic—and not with any one-word riddle I can't understand—then tell me why the brain coral has tried so hard to stop me from getting there."

"First, I suggest you imbibe a drop of the healing elixir yourself," the Magician said.

Startled, Jewel turned. "Oh, Bink—you should have been the first to have it!"

"No," Bink said. "It might have been the sleeping potion."

Humfrey nodded. "Had I attempted to betray you, it would have shown when the griffin was treated," he said. "You maneuvered to guard against betrayal most efficiently. I must say, even with your talent canceled out, you have managed very well. You are far removed from the stripling you once were."

"Aren't we all," Bink growled, hand still on sword.

Jewel sprinkled a drop of elixir on him. Instantly his wounds healed, and he was strong again. But his suspicion of the Good Magician did not ease.

Chapter 12. Demon Xanth

"This way," Humfrey said. Bink kept his sword drawn as he followed the Magician. Jewel walked silently behind him, carrying the golem.

"Incidentally," Humfrey said. "Crombie was not deceiving you. The antidote you seek does lie in the direction of the lake—but beyond it. The coral could enable you to obtain it—if things work out."

"I have no interest in bribes from the enemy," Bink said curtly.

"You don't?" Jewel asked. "You don't want the antidote?"

"Sorry—I didn't mean I intended to renege," Bink told her. "It's a matter of principle. I can't let the enemy subvert me, even though I do not wish to burden you with my love any longer than—"

"It's no burden, Bink," she said. "I never saw anything so brave as—"

"But since the antidote is evidently out of reach, there is no point in keeping you. I'm sorry I inconvenienced you for nothing. You are free to go, now."

She caught at his arm. Bink automatically moved his sword out of the way. "Bink, I—"

Bink yielded to his desire at last and kissed her. To his surprise, she returned the kiss emphatically. The scent of yellow roses surrounded them. Then he pushed her gently away. "Take good care of yourself, nymph. This sort of adventure is not for you. I would like to believe that you are safe and happy with your gems and your job, always."

"Bink, I can't go."

"You have to go! Here there is only horror and danger, and I have no right to subject you to it. You must depart without discovering the source of magic, so that you will have no enemy."

Now she smelled of pine trees on a hot day, all pungent and fresh and mildly intoxicating. The elixir had cured her hoarseness, too, and had erased the no-sleep shadows under her eyes. She was as lovely as she had been the moment he first saw her. "You have no right to send me away, either," she said.

Humfrey moved. Bink's sword leaped up warningly. Jewel backed off, frightened again.

"Have no concern," the Magician said. "We approach the source of magic."

Bink, wary, hardly dared believe it. "I see nothing special."

"See this rock?" Humfrey asked, pointing. "It is the magic rock, slowly moving up, leaking through to the surface after hundreds of years, squeezing through a fault in the regular strata. Above, it becomes magic dust. Part of the natural or magical conversion of the land's crust." He pointed down. "Below—is where it becomes charged. The source of magic."

"Yes—but *how* is it charged with magic?" Bink demanded. "Why has the coral so adamantly opposed my approach?"

"You will soon know." The Magician showed the way to a natural, curving tunnel-ramp that led down. "Feel the intensifying strength of magic, here? The most minor talent looms like that of a Magician—but all talents are largely nullified by the ambience. It is as if magic does not exist, paradoxically, because it can not be differentiated properly."

Bink could not make much sense of that. He continued on down, alert for further betrayal, conscious of the pressure of magic all about him. If a lightning bug made its little spark here, there would be a blast sufficient to blow the top off a mountain! They were certainly approaching the source—but was this also a trap?

The ramp debouched into an enormous cave, whose far wall was carved into the shape of a giant demon face. "The Demon Xanth, the source of magic," Humfrey said simply.

"This statue, this mere mask?" Bink asked incredulously. "What joke is this?"

"Hardly a joke, Bink. Without this Demon, our land would be just like Mundania. A land without magic."

"And this is all you have to show me? How do you expect me to believe it?"

"I don't expect that. You have to listen to the rationale. Only then can you grasp the immense significance of what you see—and appreciate the incalculable peril your presence here means to our society."

Bink shook his head with resignation. "I said I'd listen. I'll listen. But I don't guarantee to believe your story."

"You can not fail to believe," Humfrey said. "But whether you *accept*—that is the gamble. The information comes in this manner: we shall walk about this chamber, intercepting a few of the magic vortexes of the Demon's thoughts. Then we will understand."

"I don't want any more magic experience!" Bink protested. "All I want to know is the nature of the source."

"You shall, you shall!" Humfrey said. "Just walk with me, that is all. There is no other way." He stepped forward.

Still suspicious, Bink paced him, for he did not want to let the Magician get beyond the immediate reach of his sword.

Suddenly he felt giddy; it was as if he were falling, but his feet were firm. He paused, bracing himself against he knew not what. Another siege of madness? If that were the trap—

He saw stars. Not the paltry motes of the normal night sky, but monstrous and monstrously strange balls of flaming yet unburning substance, of gas more dense than rock, and tides without water. They were so far apart that a dragon could not have flown from one to another in its lifetime, and so numerous that a man could not count them all in *his* lifetime, yet all were visible at once. Between these magically huge-small, distant-close unbelievable certainties flew the omnipotent Demons, touching a small (enormous) star here to make it flicker, a large (tiny) one there to make it glow red, and upon occasion puffing one into the blinding flash of a nova. The realm of the stars was the Demons' playground.

The vision faded. Bink looked dazedly around at the cave, and the tremendous, still face of the Demon. "You stepped out of that particular thought-vortex," Humfrey explained. "Each one is extremely narrow, though deep."

"Uh, yes," Bink agreed. He took another step—and faced a lovely she-Demon, with eyes as deep as the vortex of the fiends and hair that spread out like the tail of a comet. She was not precisely female, for the Demons had no reproduction and therefore no sex unless they wanted it for entertainment; they were eternal. They had always existed, and always would exist, as long as there was any point in existence. But for variety at times they played with variations of sex and assumed the aspect of male, female, itmale, hemale, shemale, neutermale and anonymale. At the moment she was close enough to a category to be viewed as such, and it was not a he category.

"————," she said, formulating a concept so vastly spacious as to fail to register upon Bink's comprehension. Yet her portent was so significant it moved him profoundly. He felt a sudden compelling urgency to—but such a thing would have been inexpressibly obscene in human terms, had it been possible or even conceivable. She was not, after all, closest in category to female.

Bink emerged from the thought-eddy and saw Jewel standing transfixed, meshed in a different current. Her lips were parted, her bosom heaving. What was she experiencing? Bink suffered a quadruple-level reaction: horror that she should be subjected to any thought as crudely and sophisticatedly compelling as the one he had just experienced, for she was an innocent nymph; jealousy that she should react so raptly to something other than himself, especially if it were as suggestive a notion as the one he had absorbed; guilt about feeling that way about a nymph he could not really have, though he would not have wished the concept on the one he did have; and intense curiosity. Suppose an itmale made an offer—oh, horrible! Yet so tempting, too.

But Humfrey was moving, and Bink had to move too. He stepped into an eternal memory, so long that it resembled a magic highway extending into infinity both ways. The line-of-sight—though sight was not precisely the sense employed—to the past disappeared into a far-far distant flash. The Demon universe had begun in an explosion, and ended in another, and the whole of time and matter was the mere hiatus between these bangs—which two bangs were in turn only aspects of the same one. Obviously this was a completely alien universe from Bink's own! Yet, in the throes of this flux of relevant meaninglessness, it became believable. A super-magic framework for the super-magical Demons!

Bink emerged from the Thought. "But what do the Demons have to do with the source of the magic of Xanth?" he demanded plaintively.

Then he entered a new flux—a complex one. *If we cooperate, we can enlarge our A,* the pseudo-female Demon communicated seductively. At least, this was as much as Bink could grasp of her import, that had levels and resonances and symbolisms as myriad as the stars, and as intense and diffuse and confusing. *My formula is $E(A/R)^{th}$, yours $X(A/N)^{th}$. Our A's match.*

Ah, yes. It was a good offer, considering the situation, since their remaining elements differed, making them noncompetitive.

Not on your existence! another protested. *Enlarge our E, not our A.* It was $D(E/A)^{th}$, who stood to be diminished by the enlarging A.

Enlarge both D and E, another suggested. It was $D(E/P)^{th}$. $D(E/A)^{th}$ agreed instantly, and so did $E(A/R)^{th}$, for she would benefit to a certain degree too. But this left $X(A/N)^{th}$ out.

Reduce our N, $T(E/N)^{th}$ recommended, and this appealed to $X(A/N)^{th}$. But $T(E/N)^{th}$ was also dealing with the E-raisers, and that gave $T(E/N)^{th}$ disproportionate gain for the contract. All deals fell through for no benefit.

Bink emerged, his comprehension struggling. The names were formulae? The letters were values? What was going on?

"Ah, you have seen it," Humfrey said. "The

Demons have no names, only point-scores. Variable inputs are substituted, affecting the numeric values—though they are not really numbers, but degrees of concept, with gravity and charm and luminosity and other dimensions we can hardly grasp. The running score is paramount."

That explanation only furthered the mystery. "The Demon Xanth is only a score in a game?"

"The Demon whose scoring formula is $X(A/N)^{th}$—three variables and a class-exponent, as nearly as we can understand it," the Magician said. "The rules of the game are beyond our comprehension, but we do see their scores changing."

"I don't care about a score!" Bink cried. "What's the point?"

"What's the point in life?" Humfrey asked in return.

"To—to grow, to improve, to do something useful," Bink said. "Not to play games with concepts."

"You see it that way because you are a man, not a Demon. These entities are incapable of growth or improvement."

"But what about all their numbers, their enlargements of velocity, of viscosity—"

"Oh, I thought you understood," the Magician said. "Those are not expansions of Demon intellect or power, but of status. Demons don't grow; they are already all-powerful. There is nothing that any of them could conceive of, that each could not possess. Nothing any one of them could not accomplish. So they can't improve or do anything useful by our definition, for they are already absolute. Thus there is no inherent denial, no challenge."

"No challenge? Doesn't that get boring?"

"In a billion years it gets a billion times more boring," the Magician agreed.

"So the Demons play games?" Bink asked incredulously.

"What better way to pass time and recover interest in existence? Since they have no actual limitations, they accept voluntary ones. The excitement of the artificial challenge replaces the boredom of reality."

"Well, maybe," Bink said doubtfully. "But what has this to do with us?"

"The Demon X(A/N)th is paying a game penalty for failing to complete a formula-application within the round," Humfrey said. "He has to remain in inertia in isolation until released."

Bink stood still, so as not to intercept any more thoughts. "I don't see any chains to hold him. As for being alone—there are lots of creatures here."

"No chains could hold him, since he is omnipotent. He plays the game by its rules. And of course we don't count as company. Nothing in all the Land of Xanth does. We're vermin, not Demons."

"But—but—" Bink grabbed for meaning, and could not hold it. "You said this Demon was the source of magic!"

"I did indeed. The Demon X(A/N)th has been confined here over a thousand years. From his body has leaked a trace amount of magic, infusing the surrounding material. Hardly enough for him to notice—just a natural emanation of his presence, much as our own bodies give off heat."

Bink found this as fantastic as the Demon's vortex-Thoughts. "A thousand years? Leakage of magic?"

"In that time even a small leak can amount to a fair amount—at least it might seem so to vermin," the Magician assured him. "All the magic of the Land of Xanth derives from this effect—and all of it together would not make up a single letter of the Demon's formula."

"But even if all this is so—why did the brain coral try to prevent me from learning this?"

"The coral has nothing against you personally, Bink. I think it rather respects your determination. It is against *anybody* learning the truth. Because anyone who encounters the Demon X(A/N)th might be tempted to release him."

"How could a mere vermin—I mean, person release such an entity? You said the Demon only remains by choice."

Humfrey shook his head. "What is choice, to an omnipotent? He remains here at the dictate of the game. That is quite a different matter."

"But he only plays the game for entertainment! He can quit anytime!"

"The game is valid only so long as its rules are honored. After investing over a thousand years in this aspect of it, and being so close to success within the rules, why should he abridge it now?"

Bink shook his head. "This makes little sense to me! *I* would not torture myself in such fashion!" Yet a thread of doubt tugged at the corner of his mind. He was torturing himself about the nymph Jewel, honoring the human convention of his marriage to Chameleon. That, to a Demon, might seem nonsensical.

Humfrey merely looked at him, understanding some of what was passing through his mind.

"Very well," Bink said, returning to the main point. "The coral did not want me to know about the Demon, because I might release him. How could I release an all-powerful creature who does not want to be released?"

"Oh, $X(A/N)^{th}$ wants to be released, I am sure. It is merely necessary that protocol be followed. You could do it simply by addressing the Demon and saying 'Xanth, I free you!' Anybody can do it, except the Demon himself."

"But we don't count, on its terms! We're nothings, vermin!"

"I did not create the rules, I only interpret them, through the comprehension gleaned over centuries by the brain coral," the Magician said, spreading his hands. "Obviously our interpretation is inadequate. But I conjecture that just as we two might make a bet on whether a given mote of dust might settle nearer me or you, the Demons bet on whether vermin will say certain words on certain occasions. It does lend a certain entertaining randomness to the proceedings."

"With all that power, why doesn't Xanth cause one of us to do it, then?"

"That would be the same thing as doing it himself. It would constitute cheating. By the rules of the game, he is bound to remain without influencing any other creature on his behalf, much as we would not permit each other to blow on that mote of dust. It is not a matter of power, but of convention. The Demon knows everything that is going on here, including this conversation between us, but the moment he interferes, he forfeits the point. So he watches and waits, doing nothing."

"Except thinking," Bink said, feeling nervous about the scrutiny of the Demon. If Xanth were reading Bink's thoughts while Bink was reading Xanth's thoughts, especially in the case of that shemale memory . . . ouch!

"Thinking is permissible. It is another inherent function, like his colossal magic. He has not sought to influence us by his Thoughts; we have intercepted them on our own initiative. The coral, being closest to the Demon for this millennium, has intercepted more of X(A/N)th's magic and Thought than any other native creature, so understands him less imperfectly than any other vermin. Thus the brain coral has become the guardian of the Demon."

"And jealously prevents anyone else from achieving similar magic or information!" Bink exclaimed.

"No. It has been a necessary and tedious chore that the coral would gladly have given up centuries ago. The coral's dearest wish is to inhabit a mortal body, to live and love and hate and reproduce and die as we do. But it can not, lest the Demon be released. The coral has the longevity of the Demon, without his power. It is an unenviable situation."

"You mean the Demon Xanth would have been freed hundreds of years ago, but for the interference of the coral?"

"True," the Magician said.

"Of all the nerve! And the Demon tolerates this?"

"The Demon tolerates this, lest he forfeit the point."

"Well, I consider this an egregious violation of the Demon's civil rights, and I'm going to correct that right now!" Bink exclaimed with righteous wrath. But he hesitated. "What does the coral gain by keeping the Demon chained?"

"I don't know for certain, but I can conjecture," Humfrey said. "It is not for itself it does this, but to maintain the status quo. Think, Bink: what would be the consequence of the Demon's release?"

Bink thought. "I suppose he would just return to his game."

"And what of us?"

262

"Well, the brain coral might be in trouble. I know I would be upset if someone had balked me for centuries! But the coral must have known the risk before it meddled."

"It did. The Demon lacks human emotion. He accepts the coral's interference as part of the natural hazard of the game; he will not seek revenge. Still, there could be a consequence."

"If Xanth lacks human emotion," Bink said slowly, "what would stop him from carelessly destroying us all? It would be one dispassionate, even sensible way of ensuring that he would not be trapped here again."

"Now you are beginning to comprehend the coral's concern," Humfrey said. "Our lives may hang in the balance. Even if the Demon ignores us, and merely goes his way, there will surely be a consequence."

"I should think so," Bink agreed. "If Xanth is the source of all magic in our land—" He interrupted himself, appalled. "It could mean the end of magic! We would become—"

"Exactly. Like Mundania," Humfrey concluded. "Perhaps it would not happen right away; it might take a while for the accumulated magic of a thousand years to fade. Or the loss might be instantaneous and absolute. We just don't know. But surely there would be a disaster of greater or lesser magnitude. Now at last you understand the burden the coral has borne alone. The coral has saved our land from a fate worse than destruction."

"But maybe the Demon wouldn't go," Bink said. "Maybe he likes it here—"

"Would you care to gamble your way of life on that assumption?"

"No!"

"Do you still condemn the coral for opposing you?"

"No, I suppose I would have done the same, in its place."

"Then you will depart without freeing the Demon?"

"I'm not sure," Bink said. "I agreed to listen to the coral's rationale; I have done so. But I must decide for myself what is right."

"There is a question, when the whole of our Land's welfare is at stake?"

"Yes. The Demon's welfare is also at stake."

"But all this is just a game to $X(A/N)^{th}$. It is life to us."

"Yes," Bink agreed noncommittally.

The Magician saw that argument was useless. "This is the great gamble we did not wish to take—the gamble of the outcome of an individual crisis of conscience. It rests in your hands. The future of our society."

Bink knew this was true. Nothing Humfrey or the brain coral might try could affect him before he uttered the words to free the Demon. He could ponder a second or an hour or a year, as he chose, free of duress. He did not want to make a mistake.

"Grundy," Bink said, and the golem ran up to him, not affected by the Thought vortices. "Do you wish to free the Demon Xanth?"

"I can't make decisions like that," Grundy protested. "I'm only clay and string, a creature of magic."

"Like the Demon himself," Bink said. "You're non-human, not quite alive. You might be construed as a miniature Demon. I thought you might have an insight."

Grundy paced the cave floor seriously. "My job is translation. I may not experience the emotion you do, but I have an awful clear notion of the Demon. He *is* like me, as a dragon is to a nickelpede. I can tell you this: he is without conscience or compassion. He plays his game rigorously by its rules, but if you free him you will have no thanks from him and no reward. In fact, that would be cheating on his part, to proffer you any advantage for your service to him, for that might influence you. But even if reward were legitimate, he wouldn't do it. He'd as soon step on you as smell you."

"He is like you," Bink repeated. "As you were before you began to change. Now you are halfway real. You care—somewhat."

"I am now an imperfect golem. Xanth is a perfect Demon. For me, humanization is a step up; for him it would be a fall from grace. He is not your kind."

"Yet I am not concerned with kind or thanks, but with justice," Bink said. "Is it right that the demon be freed?"

"By his logic, you would be an utter fool to free him."

The Good Magician, standing apart, nodded agreement.

"Jewel," Bink said.

The nymph looked up, smelling of old bones. "The Demon frightens me worse than anything," she said. "His magic—with the blink of one eye, he could click us all out of existence."

"You would not free him, then?"

"Oh, Bink—I never would." She hesitated prettily. "I know you took the potion, so this is unfair—but I'm so afraid of what that Demon might do, I'd do anything for you if only you didn't free him."

Again the Good Magician nodded. Nymphs were fairly simple, direct creatures, unfettered by complex overlays of conscience or social strategy. A real woman might feel the same way Jewel did, but she would express herself with far more subtlety, proffering a superficially convincing rationale. The nymph had named her price.

So the logical and the emotional advisers both warned against releasing the Demon X(A/N)th. Yet Bink remained uncertain. Something about this huge, super-magical, game-playing entity—

And he had it. Honor. Within the Demon's framework, the Demon was honorable. He never breached the code of the game—not in its slightest detail, though there were none of his kind present to observe, and had not been for a thousand years. Integrity beyond human capacity. Was he to be penalized for this?

"I respect you," Bink said at last to Humfrey. "And I respect the motive of the brain coral." He turned to the golem. "I think you ought to have your chance to achieve full reality." And to the nymph: "And I love you, Jewel." He paused. "But I would have respect for nothing, and love for nothing, if I did not respect and love justice. If I let personal attachments and desires prevail over my basic integrity of purpose, I would lose my claim to distinction as a moral creature. I must do what I think is right."

The others did not respond. They only looked at him.

"The problem is," Bink continued after a moment, "I'm not certain what *is* right. The rationale. of the Demon Xanth is so complex, and the consequence of the loss of magic to our world is so great—where is right and wrong?" He paused again. "I wish I had Chester here to share his emotion and reason with me."

"You can recover the centaur," Humfrey said. "The waters of the coral lake do not kill, they preserve. He is suspended in brine, unable to escape, but alive. The coral can not release him; that brine preserves it similarly. But you, if you save the magic of our land, you can draw on the phenomenal power of this region and draw him forth."

"You offer another temptation of personal attachment," Bink said. "I can not let it influence me!" For now he realized that he had not yet won the battle against the brain coral. He had prevailed physically, but intellectually the issue remained in doubt. How could he be sure the decision he made was his own?

Then he had a bright notion. "Argue the other case, Magician! Tell me why I should free the Demon."

Startled, Humfrey demurred. "You should not free the Demon!"

"So you believe. So the coral believes. I can not tell whether that belief is really yours, or merely a function of the will of your master. So now you argue the opposite case, and I'll argue the case for leaving him chained. Maybe that way the truth will emerge."

"You are something of a demon yourself," Humfrey muttered.

"Now I submit that these friends of mine are more important than an impersonal Demon," Bink said. "I don't know what's right for X(A/N)th, but I do know that my friends deserve the best. How can I justify betraying them by freeing the Demon?"

Humfrey looked as if he had swallowed the evil eye, but he came back gamely enough. "It is not a question of betrayal, Bink. None of these creatures would ever have experienced magic, if it had not been for the presence of the Demon. Now X(A/N)th's

266

period of incarceration has been fulfilled, and he must be released. To do otherwise would be to betray your role in the Demon's game."

"I have no obligation to the Demon's game!" Bink retorted, getting into the feel of it. "Pure chance brought me here!"

"That *is* the role. That you, as a sapient creature uninfluenced by the Demon's will, come by your own initiative or accident of chance to free him. You fought against us all to achieve this point of decision, and won; are you going to throw it all away now?"

"Yes—if that is best."

"How can you presume to know what is best for an entity like $X(A/N)^{th}$? Free him and let him forge his own destiny."

"At the expense of my friends, my land, and my love?"

"Justice is absolute; you can not weigh personal factors against it."

"Justice is *not* absolute! It depends on the situation. When there is right and wrong on both sides of the scale, the preponderance—"

"You can not weigh rights and wrongs on a scale, Bink," Humfrey said, becoming passionate in his role as Demon's Advocate. Now Bink was sure it was the Good Magician speaking, not the brain coral. The enemy had had to free Humfrey, at least to this extent, to allow him to play this game of the moment. The Magician's mind and emotion had not been erased, and that was part of what Bink had needed to know. "Right and wrong are not to be found in things or histories, and can not be properly defined in either human or Demon terms. They are merely aspects of viewpoint. The question is whether the Demon should be allowed to pursue his quest in his own fashion."

"He *is* pursuing it in his own fashion," Bink said. "If I don't free him, that's according to the rules of his game, too. I have no obligation!"

"The Demon's honor compels him to obey a stricture no man would tolerate," Humfrey said. "It is not surprising that your own honor is inferior to that perfect standard."

Bink felt as if he had been smashed by a forest-blasting curse. The Magician was a devastating in-fighter, even in a cause he opposed! Except that this could be the Magician's real position, that the coral was forced to allow him to argue. "My honor compels me to follow the code of my kind, imperfect as that may be."

Humfrey spread his hands. "I can not debate that. The only real war between good and evil is within the soul of yourself—whoever you are. If you are a man, you must act as a man."

"Yes!" Bink agreed. "And my code says—" He paused, amazed and mortified. "It says I can not let a living, feeling creature suffer because of my inaction. It doesn't matter that the Demon would not free me, were our positions reversed; I am not a Demon, and shall not act like one. It only matters that a man does not stand by and allow a wrong he perceives to continue. Not when he can so readily correct it."

"Oh, Bink!" Jewel cried, smelling of myrrh. "Don't do it!"

He looked at her again, so lovely even in her apprehension, yet so fallible. Chameleon would have endorsed his decision, not because she wished to please him, but because she was a human being who believed, as he did, in doing the right thing. Yet though Jewel, like all nymphs, lacked an overriding social conscience, she was as good a person as her state permitted. "I love you, Jewel. I know this is just another thing the coral did to stop me, but—well, if I hadn't taken that potion, and if I weren't already married, it would have been awfully easy to love you anyway. I don't suppose it makes you feel any better to know that I am also risking my wife, and my unborn baby, and my parents, and all else I hold dear. But I must do what I must do."

"You utter fool!" Grundy exclaimed. "If I were real, I'd snatch up the nymph and to hell with the Demon. You'll get no reward from X(A/N)th!"

"I know," Bink said. "I'll get no thanks from anyone."

Then he addressed the huge demon face. "I free you, Xanth," he said.

Chapter 13. Magic Loss

Instantly the Demon burst loose. The seeping magic of X(A/N)th's immediate environment was as nothing compared to the full magic of his release. There was a blinding effulgence, a deafening noise, and an explosion that threw Bink across the cavern. He crashed jarringly into a wall. As his senses cleared he perceived the collapse of the cavern in slow-motion sight and sound. Huge stones crunched to the floor and shattered into sand. All the world seemed to be collapsing into the space left by the Demon. This was a demise Bink had not anticipated: not willful destruction by X(A/N)th, not the tedium of loss of magic, but careless extinction in the wake of the Demon's departure. It was true: the Demon didn't *care*.

Now, as the dust clouded in to choke him and the only light was from the sparks of colliding rocks, Bink wondered: what had he done? Why hadn't he heeded the brain coral's warning, and left the Demon alone? Why hadn't he yielded to his love for Jewel, and—

Even in the ongoing carnage, while expecting momentary conclusion of his life, this made him pause in surprise. Love? Not so! He was out of love with Jewel!

That meant the magic really was gone. The love potion had been nullified. His talent would no longer protect him. The Land of Xanth was now one with Mundania.

Bink closed his eyes and cried. There was a great deal of dust in the air that needed washing out of his eyes, and he was wrackingly afraid, but it was more than that. He was crying for Xanth. He had destroyed the uniqueness of the world he knew; even if he survived this cave-in, how could he live with that?

He did not know how the society he had belonged to would react. What would happen to the dragons and tangle trees and zombies? How could the people live, without magic? It was as if the entire population had abruptly been exiled to the drear realm of no-talents.

The action abated. Bink found himself grimed with rock powder, bruised, but with limbs and sword intact. Miraculously, he had survived.

Had anyone else? He peered through the rubble. Dim light descended from a hole far above, evidently the Demon's route of departure. $X(A/N)^{th}$ must simply have shot up and out, forging his path heedlessly through the rock. What power!

"Magician! Jewel!" Bink cried, but there was no answer. The fall of stone had been so complete that only his own section remained even partially clear. His talent must have saved him, just before it faded. He could not depend on it any more, however; it was evident that spells had been the first magic to go.

He stepped out over the rubble. More dust swirled up; it coated everything. Bink realized that though he thought he had been aware of the whole process of the Demon's departure, he could actually have been unconscious for some time. So much dust had settled! Yet he had no bruise on his head, and no headache. Yet again, the physical and magical explosion of the Demon's release could account for many incongruous effects.

"Magician!" he called again, knowing it was futile. He, Bink, had survived—but his friends had lacked his critical protection at the key moment. Somewhere beneath this slope of stone . . .

He spied a glint, a wan reflection, only a glimmer between two dusky rocks. He pried them apart, and there it was: the bottle containing Crombie. Strewn across it was a bit of rag. Bink picked up the bottle, letting the cloth fall—and saw that it was what remained of Grundy the golem. The little man-figure had owed its animation to magic; now he was just a limp wad of material.

Bink closed his eyes again, experiencing another chill seizure of grief. He had done what he had felt was right—but he had not truly reckoned the consequence. Fine points of morality were intangible; life and death were tangible. By what right had he condemned these creatures to death? Was it moral for him to slay them in the name of his morality?

He put the cloth in his pocket along with the bottle. Evidently the golem's last act had been to grab the bottle, protecting it with his body. That had been effective, and so Grundy had given up his life for that of the griffin he served. He had cared, and therefore achieved his reality—just in time to have it dashed by circumstance. Where was the morality in that?

Startled by another thought, Bink drew out the bottle again. Was Crombie still in there? In what form? With magic gone, he could be dead—unless some magic remained corked in the bottle—

Better not open it! Whatever lingering chance Crombie had, resided in that bottle. If he were loosed and the magic dissipated into the air—would Crombie emerge as a man again, or a griffin, or a bottle-sized compressed mass? Bink had just gambled enormously, freeing the Demon; he was not about to gamble similarly with the life of his friend. He repocketed the bottle.

How drear it was, this depth of the hole. Alone with a bottle, and a defunct golem and his own mortification. The ethical principle on which he had based his decision was opaque to him now. The Demon Xanth had lain prisoner for over a thousand years. He could have lain for another century or so without harm, couldn't he?

Bink discovered he was not at the bottom of the hole, after all. The rubble opened into a deeper hole, and at the bottom was dark water. The lake! But the level had lowered drastically; now the dank gray convolutions of a formerly submerged structure lay dimly revealed. The brain coral! It, too, was dead; it could not exist without the potent magic of the Demon.

"I fear you were right, Coral," Bink said sadly.

271

"You let me through, and I destroyed you. You and our world."

He smelled smoke—not the clean fresh odor of a healthy blaze, but the smoldering foulness of incompletely burning vegetation. Evidently the Demon's departure had ignited some brush, assuming there was brush down here underground. The intense magic must have done it, leaving behind a real fire. It probably would not burn far, here deep in the ground, but it certainly was stinking up the place.

Then he heard a delicate groan. Surely not the coral! He scrambled toward the sound—and found Jewel wedged in a vertical crevice, bleeding from a gash on the head, but definitely alive. Hastily he drew her out, half-carrying her to a brighter place. He propped her up against a rock and patted her face with his fingertips, trying to bring her to consciousness.

She stirred. "Don't wake me, Bink. Let me die in peace."

"I've killed everyone else," he said sullenly. "At least you will be able to—"

"To return to my job? I can't do it without magic."

There was something strange about her. Bink concentrated and it came: "You don't smell!"

"It was magic," she said. She sighed. "If I'm alive, I'm alive, I suppose. But I really do wish you'd let me die."

"Let you die! I wouldn't do that! I—"

She glanced up at him cannily. Even through the blood-caked dust on her face, she was lovely. "The magic is gone. You don't love me any more."

"Still, I owe it to you to get you home," Bink said. He looked up, trying to decide on the most feasible route, and did not see her enigmatic reaction.

They checked through the rubble a little longer, but could not find the Magician. Bink was relieved, in a fashion; now he could hope that Humfrey had survived, and had departed before him.

Bink peered up at the Demon's exit. "We'll never make it up there," he said glumly. "Too much of it is sheer cliff."

"I know a way," Jewel said. "It will be difficult,

without the diggle, but there are natural passages—oh!" She broke off suddenly.

There was a monster barring the way. It resembled a dragon, but lacked wings and fire. It was more like a very large serpent with legs.

"That's a tunnel dragon—I think," Jewel said. "But something's missing."

"The magic," Bink said. "It's changing into a mundane creature—and it doesn't understand."

"You mean I'll change into a mundane woman?" she inquired, not entirely displeased.

"I believe so. There really is not much difference between a nymph and a —"

"They usually don't bother people," she continued uneasily. Before Bink could react, she added: "They're very shy dragons."

Oh. A nymphly nonsequitur. Bink kept his hand near his sword. "This is an unusual occasion."

Sure enough, the legged serpent charged, jaws gaping wide. Though it was small for a land dragon, since it was adapted to squeeze through narrow passages, it was still a formidable creature. Its head was larger than Bink's, and its body sinuously powerful. In the conditions of this cavern, Bink could not swing his sword freely, so he held it out ahead of him.

The serpent snapped at the blade—a foolish thing to do, since the charmed blade would likely cut its jaw in two. The teeth closed on it—and the blade was yanked out of Bink's hand.

Then he remembered: without magic, the sword's charm was gone. He had to make it work by himself—completely.

The serpent flung the sword aside and opened its jaws again. There was blood on its lower lip; the blade had done some minor damage. But now Bink faced the monster barehanded.

The head struck forward. Bink danced backward. But as the strike missed, and the head dropped low, Bink struck the serpent on the top of the head with his fist. The thing hissed in furious amazement as its chinless chin bashed into the floor. But Bink's foot was already on its neck, crushing it down. The serpent's

273

legs scraped across the stone as it tried to free itself. But Bink had it pinned.

"My sword!" he cried. Jewel hastily picked it up and extended it point-first toward him. Bink was already grabbing for it before he noticed, and then almost lost his balance and his captive as he aborted his grab. "Other way!" he snapped.

"Oh." It had not occurred to her that he would need to take hold of the handle. She was a complete innocent about weapons. She took it gingerly by the blade and poked the hilt in his direction.

But as he took it, the serpent wrenched free. Bink jumped back, his sword ready.

The thing had had enough. It backed away—an awkward maneuver when slithering—then dived into a side-hole. "You're so brave!" Jewel said.

"I was stupid to let it disarm me," he said gruffly. He was not at all proud of the encounter; it had been fraught with clumsiness, not at all elegant. Just a stupid, indecisive brawl. "Let's get on before I make a worse mistake. I brought you out of your home, and I'll get you back there safely before I leave you. It's only right."

"Only right," she repeated faintly.

"Something wrong?"

"What am I going to do without magic?" she flared. "Nothing will work!"

Bink considered. "You're right. I have wrecked your livelihood. I'd better take you to the surface with me."

She brightened, then dulled. "No, that wouldn't work."

"It's all right. I told you the potion has no effect now. I don't love you; I won't be bothering you. You can settle in one of the villages, or maybe work in the King's palace. It won't be much without magic, but it has to be better than this." He made a gesture, indicating the dismal caverns.

"I wonder," she murmured.

They continued. Jewel did know the labyrinth of the caverns fairly well, once they were out of the Demon's depths, and brought them steadily if circuitously upward. Beyond the immediate region of the

Demon's vacancy there had not been much damage. But everywhere the magic was gone, and the creatures were crazed. Rats tried to zap him with their rodent magic, and failed, and resorted to teeth. They were no more used to naked teeth as weapons than Bink was to using an uncharmed sword, so the sides were fair. He drove them back with slashing sweeps of his sword. There might be no magic in the blade, but the edge remained sharp and it could hurt and kill.

Still, it took a lot of energy to swing that sword, and his arm grew tired. There had been another charm to make the sword lighter and more responsive to direction, without making it self-willed like the one that had attacked Bink in the gardens of Castle Roogna. The rats crowded closer, staying just out of range and coming in to nip at his heels when he climbed. Jewel was no better off; she lacked even a knife of her own, and had to borrow Bink's knife to defend herself. A monster could be killed but these smaller creatures seemed inexhaustible. They weren't nickelpedes, fortunately, but they were reminiscent of them.

. "The way—it will be dark in places," Jewel said. "I hadn't thought—without magic there's no glow, no magic light. I'm afraid of the dark."

There had been some residual glow, but it was fading. Bink looked at the rats, so close. "With reason," he said. "We have to see what we're fighting." He felt naked without his talent, though it only protected him against magic—a protection that was irrelevant now. For practical purposes his situation was unchanged, since no magic threatened him. Not now or ever again. "Fire—we need fire for light. Torches—if we can make torches—"

"I know where some fire stones are!" Jewel said. But she reconsidered immediately. "Only I don't think they are working, without magic."

"Do you know where there's dry grass—I mean straw—something we could twist up tight and burn? And—but I don't know how the Mundanes make fire, so—"

"I know where there's magic fire—" She broke off. "Oh, this is awful! No magic—" She looked as if about to cry. As Bink knew, real sternness of character was not to be found in nymphs. They seemed to have been fashioned by magic to accommodate man's casual dreams, not his serious ones.

Yet he had cried, too, when he first grasped the immensity of what he had done. How much of his perception of the nature of nymphs was human-chauvinistic?

"I know," Bink cried, surprising himself. "There was something burning—I smelled it before. If we went there—picked up some of whatever's burning—"

"Great!" she agreed, with a flash of nymph-enthusiasm. Or female enthusiasm, he corrected his impression mentally.

They soon found it by following their noses: the remains of a magic garden the goblins must have tended, now sere and brown. The dead foliage was smoldering, and the smoke formed layers in the upper reaches of the garden cave. The goblins, of course, were far removed from this region; they had been so afraid of the fire that they had not even tried to put it out.

Bink and Jewel gathered what seemed like the best material, forming it into an irregular rope, and lit the end. The thing guttered and flared and went out in a cloud of awful-smelling smoke. But after several tries they got it working better; it was enough to have it smolder until they needed an open flame, which they could blow up anytime. Jewel carried it; it gave her a feeling of security she sorely needed, and Bink had to have his hands free for fighting.

Now the worst of the enemies were the goblins, who evidently resented the intrusion into their garden. There had been no direct evidence of them before—but of course they had been on the diggle, with protective magic and much light. In the absence of light the goblins grew bolder. They seemed to have been bred from men and rats. Now that the magic was gone, the man-aspect was diminishing and the rat-aspect was becoming more pronounced. Bink realized that this was evident mostly in their habits; physically they still resembled brutish little men, with big soft feet and small hard heads.

The difficulty with the goblins was that they had

the intelligence of men and the scruples of rodents. They slunk just out of sight, but they were not cowards. It was simply that no one, three, or six of them could stand up to Bink's sword, and there was not room for a greater number of them to approach him at one time. So they stayed clear—without giving up.

"I think they know I freed the Demon," Bink muttered. "They're out for revenge. I don't blame them."

"You did what you believed was right!" Jewel flared.

He put his arm about her slender waist. "And you are doing what you believe is right, helping me reach the surface—even though we both know I was wrong. I have destroyed the magic of Xanth."

"No, you weren't wrong," she said. "You had empathy for the Demon, and—"

He squeezed her. "Thank you for saying that. Do you mind if I—" He stopped. "I forgot! I'm not in love with you any more!"

"I don't mind anyway," she said. But he let her go, embarrassed. There was an evil cackle of laughter from a goblin. Bink stooped to pick up a stone to hurl at the creature, but of course it missed.

Bink armed himself with a number of rocks, and hurled one every time he saw a goblin. Soon he got remarkably accurate, and the goblins gave him a wider berth. Stones had a special magic that had nothing to do with real magic; they were hard and sharp and plentiful, and Bink had a much better arm than any goblin possessed. Still, they did not give up. Beauregard's warning had been accurate: Bink had not encountered goblins as brave and tenacious as these before.

Bink wanted to rest, for he was tired, but dared not. If he rested, he might sleep, and that could be disaster. Of course he could have Jewel watch while he slept—but she was after all only a nymph—rather, a young woman, and he was afraid the goblins would overwhelm her in such a situation. Her fate in goblin hands would probably be worse than his.

He glanced at her covertly. This rough trek was taking its toll. Her hair had lost its original sparkle and hung in lusterless straggles. She reminded him somewhat of Chameleon—but not in her beauty phase.

They dragged on, and made progress. Near the surface the ascent became more difficult. "There's not much communication with the topworld," Jewel gasped. "This is the best route—but how you climb it without wings or a rope I don't know."

Bink didn't know either. If this had been a convenient route, Crombie's talent would have pointed it out on the way in. The day sky was visible through a crack in the ground above—but the walls sloped in from the broader cavern-space below, and they were slick with moisture. Impossible to climb, without magic.

"We can't stay here long," Jewel said worriedly. "There's a tangle tree near the exit, and its roots can get ornery." She stopped short, startled. "I'm still doing it! Without magic—"

That was why Crombie's talent hadn't pointed this way, he realized. A tangler! But the bad magic was gone with the good. "Let's go!" he cried.

He found the tangle roots and ripped them out of the rock, and severed them where they would not come free. Quickly he knotted them into a strong if ragged rope. Tangle roots were strong; they were made for holding struggling prey fast. No question: this rope would hold his weight!

"But how can we get it up there?" Jewel asked anxiously.

"There's a major tangle root-trunk crossing at the narrowest section," Bink said. "See, right up there." He pointed.

She looked. "I never noticed! I must have been here half a dozen times before, teasing the tangler and wondering what the world above was like. I was supposed to be planting gems. . ." Her nymphly confession trailed off. "You certainly are observant."

"You certainly are complimentary. Don't worry; you will get to see the surface world this time. I won't leave you until you're safe on the surface and in good hands. Maybe at the magic-dust village."

She looked away, not answering. He glanced at her, peering through the smoke of the smoldering weed rope she held, concerned. "Did I say something wrong?"

She looked back at him with sudden decision. "Bink, you remember when we first met?"

He laughed. "How could I forget! You were so beautiful, and I was so grimy—almost as grimy as we both are now! And I had just taken the—" He shrugged, not wanting to get into the embarrassing matter of the love potion again. "You know, I'm almost sad that's over. You're an awfully nice nymph, and without your help—"

"You loved me then, and I didn't love you," she said. "You were devious, and I was simple. You lured me in close, then grabbed me and kissed me."

Bink fidgeted. "I'm sorry, Jewel. I—it won't happen again."

"That's what you think," she said, and flung her arms about him and planted a passionate kiss on his half-open mouth. Dirty as she was, it was still a remarkable experience; almost he felt the tug of the love potion again. He had loved her before without knowing her; now he knew her and understood her nymphly limitations and respected her for trying so hard to overcome them, and he liked her more than was entirely proper. A genuine affection had been developing beneath the artificial love, and that affection remained. What would Chameleon think, if she saw this embrace?

Jewel released him. "Turnabout's fair play," she said. "I am more complex than I was a few hours ago, and you are simpler. Now get on up your rope."

What did she mean by that? Bemused, Bink weighted the rope with a solid rock and lofted it up toward the root-trunk. It fell short, because of the weight of the rope. He tried again, harder, but the rope was still too heavy. It dragged steadily, its weight becoming greater as the rock got higher. Finally he made a wad out of the rope and hurled the mass of it up; this time it got there—and fell back, having failed to pass over the root. But he was making progress, and after several more tries he got it over. The rock fell down, hauling the rope after it. It snagged before the rock came down within reach, but several jerks on the other end of the rope freed it. Bink knotted the

279

ends together, forming a complete loop of rope that could not come loose.

"I can climb this first, then you can sit in the loop and I'll haul you up," he said. He knew there was no chance of her climbing by herself; her arms were too delicate. "Blow the torch up high, so the goblins won't come too close."

She nodded. Bink took a few deep breaths, feeling his worn system revving up in anticipation of this final effort. Then he took hold and began to climb the rope.

It started out better than he had feared, but soon got worse. His arms tired quickly, since they had been none too fresh to begin with. He clamped his legs about the rope, hanging on, to give his arms a rest, but they recovered reluctantly. Oh for some healing elixir! Still, Jewel was waiting, and so were the rats and goblins; he could not afford to delay too long. Excruciatingly he dragged himself up with smaller and smaller wrenches. His breath rasped, his head felt light, and his arms seemed to turn into waterlogged wood just beyond the elbows, but he kept moving.

So suddenly it seemed a miracle, he was at the top. Maybe his mind had simply gone a bit dead too, cutting out the agony of the continuing effort, and revived when he arrived. He clung to the big root, which was somewhat furry: the better to grip its prey, perhaps, He had never, before this adventure, anticipated gladly embracing a tangle tree!

He flung a leg over, missed, and felt himself falling. It was almost a relief, this relaxation! But the rope was still there, and he wrapped himself about it and hung, panting. So little to go, so hard to do!

There was a knot up near the apex. Bink braced his feet against it and used his relatively fresh leg muscles to push him up, and somehow scrambled around the root. Now he perceived that rough bark underlay the fur on top, making it good for clinging to, good for scrambling. He clung and scrambled, and finally inched over to the top of it and lay there, panting weakly, too worn out even to feel proper relief.

"Bink!" Jewel cried from below. "Are you all right?"

That roused him. His labor was far from over! "I should be asking you that! Are the rats staying back? Can you get in the seat, to come up?" He didn't know how he would pull up her weight in his present state, but he couldn't tell her that.

"I'm not all right. I'm not coming up."

"Jewel! Get up the rope! The rats can't reach you there, if you pull the end up after you!"

"It's not the rats, Bink. I've lived down here all my life; I can handle the rats and even the goblins, as long as I have my light. It's you. You are a handsome man."

"Me? I don't understand!" But he was beginning to. She was not referring to his present appearance, which was homelier than Chester's face. (Oh, noble centaur —in what state was he now?) The signs had been there; he had merely refused to interpret them.

"When you took the potion, you remained an honest person," Jewel called. "You were strong, stronger than any nymph could be. You never used the potion as an excuse to betray your quest or your friends. I respected and envied that quality in you, and tried to use it as a model. The only exception was that one kiss you stole, so I stole it back. I love you, Bink, and now—"

"But you never drank that potion!" he protested. "And even if you had, now that the magic is gone—"

"I never drank that potion," she agreed. "Therefore the loss of magic could not take my love away. Growth was forced upon me, driving out my nymphly innocence. Now I can perceive reality, and I know there can be no antidote but time, for me. I can not go with you."

"But you have no life down there!" Bink cried, appalled. His love for her had been magic; hers for him was real. She loved better than he had. Her nymphhood was, indeed, behind her. "There must be some way to work it out—"

"There is, and I am utilizing it. When I saw how you sacrificed me when the spell was on you, I knew there could be no hope at all when it was off. It is ironic that my love bloomed only when you gave me up, *because* you gave me up. Because you were true to your principles and your prior commitment. Now I shall be true to mine. Farewell, Bink!"

"No!" he cried. "Come out of there! There has to be some better way—"

But the rope was sliding and bumping over the root. She had untied it at the bottom part of the loop and was drawing it free. He grabbed for it, too late. The end passed over the root and dropped into the darkness.

"Jewel!" he cried. "Don't do this! I don't love you, but I do like you. I—" But that was a dead end. She was right: even when he had loved her, he had known he could not have her. That was unchanged.

There was no answer from below. The nymph had done the honorable thing, and gone her way alone, freeing him. Exactly as he would have done, in that circumstance.

There was nothing he could do now but go home. "Farewell, Jewel!" he called, hoping she would hear. "You may not have my love, but you do have my respect. You are a woman now."

He rested, listening, but heard nothing more from her. Finally he got off the root and looked about. He was in a deep cleft that he now recognized as a section of the Gap, the great chasm that cleft the Land of Xanth in twain. The tree was anchored in the bottom, but reached up toward the top, and a branch extended over the rim. In the absence of magic, the tree was safe to climb. In fact, the terrain would hold few direct threats for him now. He could proceed directly to the King's palace, arriving there within a day.

He spied some inert bugs. They were lying in a patch of sunlight, their pincers twitching. Bink felt compassion, and nudged them gently toward the nearest shadow with one foot. Poor little things!

Then he recognized them. These were nickelpedes, shorn of their magic! What a fall they had taken!

But when he swung himself from the last tentacle of the tangler and reached the surface, he discovered it to be unfamiliar. This crevice ran north-south, not east-west, unless the loss of magic had somehow turned the sun around. It had to be a different chasm, not the Gap. He was lost after all.

Now that he thought about it, he doubted he could have come as far north as the Gap. So he was probably somewhere south of it, and south of the palace. His best bet was to travel north until he encountered the Gap, or some other familiar landmark.

The trek was more difficult than he had anticipated. There was no hostile magic, true—but there was also no beneficial magic. The nature of the landscape had changed fundamentally, becoming mundane. There were no flying fruits, no shoe-trees or jean-bushes to replace his ragged apparel, no watermelons to drink from. He had to find ordinary food and water, and hardly knew what to look for. The animals, stunned by their loss of magic, avoided him; they weren't smart enough to realize that he, too, had been shorn of magic. That was a blessing.

It was late afternoon. How many hours or days he had spent below he could not be sure, but here in the sight of the sun he would be able to keep track again. He would have to spend the night in the forest. It seemed safe enough; he could climb a tree.

He looked for a good one. Many of the trees of this forest seemed dead; perhaps they were merely dormant, in this new winter of the absence of magic. It might take months or years for the full ravages of that winter to become known. Some trees flourished; they must be the mundane varieties, freed from the competition of magic. Would he be better off in a healthy mundane tree, or a defunct magical one?

Bink shivered. It was getting chill, and he could find no blanket bushes. However, it was not merely temperature that affected him. He was tired and lonely and full of remorse for what he had done. Tomorrow he would have to face his friends at the palace and tell them—

But surely they would already have guessed his guilt. It was not confession that bothered him, but punishment. Jewel had been wise to avoid him; he had no future at home.

There seemed to be a certain vague familiarity about this region. There were trails through the brush like those of ant lions, and brambles, and regions of odoriferous plants—

"That's it!" he exclaimed. "Where we intersected the magic highway to the magic-dust village!"

He peered up through the languishing foliage. There it was—a walkway fashioned from logs and vines, suspended from the stoutest trees. It made no loops in air, but of course it wasn't magic now.

He climbed aboard the lowest loop and walked along it. The thing seemed dangerously insecure, sagging beneath his weight and swinging sidewise alarmingly, but it held. In due course it brought him to the village.

He had feared a scene of gloom. Instead, the entire village seemed to be celebrating. Another great bonfire was blazing, and men and women of all types were dancing around it.

Men? How had they gotten here? This was a village of women! Could it be another Wave of conquest from Mundania, with the brutish men reveling in this village of helpless women?

Yet there seemed to be no threat. The men were happy, of course—but so were the women. Bink walked on into the village, looking for Trolla, its leader.

A man spied him as he stepped off the hanging walk. "Hello, friend!" the man called. "Welcome home! Who's your widow?"

"Widow?" Bink asked blankly.

"Your woman—before the gorgon got you. She'll be overjoyed to have you back."

The gorgon! Suddenly Bink understood. "You're the stone men! Freed by the loss of magic!"

"And you weren't?" The man laughed. "You'd better come see the head man, then."

"Trolla," Bink said. "If she's still here—"

"Who's looking for Trolla?" someone demanded. It was a huge, ugly troll. Well, an average troll; they were all huge and ugly.

Bink's hand hovered near the hilt of his sword. "I only want to talk with her."

"'Sokay," the troll said genially. He cupped his mouth with his hands. "Bitch, get over here!"

A dozen young women glanced his way, startled, thinking he meant them. Bink covered a smile. "Uh, the gorgon," he said. "What happened to her?"

"Oh, we were going to string her up, after we, you know . . ." the troll said. "She was a good-looking slut, except for those snaky tangles in her hair. But she jumped into the lake, and before we realized there weren't any more monsters in it, she was too far off to catch. Last we saw she was headed north."

North. Toward Magician Humfrey's castle. Bink was glad she had escaped, but knew she would not find Humfrey at home. That was another aspect of the tragedy Bink had wrought.

Trolla, responsive to the summons, was arriving. "Bink!" she exclaimed. "You made it!"

"I made it," he agreed gravely. "I abolished magic from the Land of Xanth. I converted it to Mundania. Now I return home to pay the penalty."

"The penalty!" the troll cried. "You freed us all! You're a hero!"

This was an aspect Bink hadn't considered. "Then you aren't angry at the loss of magic?"

"Angry?" Trolla cried. "Angry that my husband is back, good enough to eat?" She hugged the troll to her in an embrace that would have cracked normal ribs. He was well able to sustain this, though he seemed momentarily uneasy about something.

A female griffin glided up. "Awk?" she inquired.

"And here's the one who guided you, released from the midas-spell," Trolla said. "Where is your handsome griffin?"

Bink thought it best not to tell about the bottle. "He is . . . confined. He was actually a transformed man. He spoke well of the lady griffin, but he . . . sends his regrets."

The griffiness turned away, disappointed. Apparently she did not have a male of her own. Perhaps she would find a male of her kind soon—though with the alteration of form that was slowly taking place in such magical creatures, Bink wondered whether that male would be more like an eagle or more like a lion. Or would the present griffins retain their shapes, while their offspring would be eagles and lions? Suppose

Crombie emerged from the bottle, but retained his griffin form; would he then find this griffiness worthwhile? If so, what would *their* offspring be? The loss of magic posed as many questions as the presence of magic!

"Come, we shall fête you royally tonight, and you shall tell us the whole story!" Trolla said.

"I, uh, I'm pretty tired," Bink demurred. "I'd rather not tell the story. My friend the Good Magician—is missing, and so is the centaur, and the memories—"

"Yes, you need distraction," Trolla agreed. "We do have a few leftover females, daughters of older villagers. They are very lonely at the moment, and—"

"Uh, no thanks, please," Bink said quickly. He had broken too many hearts already! "Just some food, and a place to spend the night, if there's room—"

"We're short of room; our population has just doubled. But the girls will tend to you. It will give them something to do. They'll be glad to share their rooms."

Bink was too tired to protest further. But as it turned out, the "girls" were an assortment of fairies and lady elves who paid him flattering attention, but were not really interested in him as a man. They made a game out of feeding him odds and ends, each one putting her morsel in his mouth with her own little hands, twittering merrily. They wouldn't let him have a plate; everything had to be trotted in from another room, piecemeal. Then he lay in a bed made out of thirty small colored pillows, while the fairies flitted around, the breeze from their gossamer wings fanning him. They could no longer fly, of course, and soon their wings would fall off as they reverted to mundane forms, but at the moment they were cute. He went to sleep counting the creatures that leaped merrily over him in the course of their game of follow-the-leader.

But in the morning he had to face reality again: the bleak journey home. He was glad his quest had done at least this little bit of good; perhaps his talent had planned it this way, before being nullified by the loss of magic, so as to provide him with a good, safe place for this night. But as for the rest of Xanth—what hope remained for it?

The griffiness accompanied him for a distance, guiding him again, and in a surprisingly brief time he was up to the dead forest: halfway familiar territory. It was no longer so different from the rest of the wilderness. He thanked her, wished her well, and continued on alone, northward.

The loneliness closed in about him. The lack of magic was so pervasive and depressing! All the little amenities he was accustomed to were gone. There were no blue toads sitting on their squat vegetable stools, no Indian pipes wafting their sweet smoke aloft. No trees moved their branches out of his way, or cast avoidance-spells on him. Everything was hopelessly Mundane. He felt tired again, and not merely from the march. Was life really worthwhile, without magic?

Well, Chameleon would be locked in her "normal" phase, the one he liked best: neither pretty nor smart, but rather nice overall. Yes, he could live with that for some time before it got dull, assuming that he was allowed to—

He paused. He heard a clip-clop, as of hooves on a beaten path. An enemy? He hardly cared; it was company!

"Hallooo!" he cried.

"Yes?" It was a woman's voice. He charged toward it.

There, standing on a beaten path, was a lady centaur. She was not especially pretty; her flanks were dull, her tail tangled with burrs (naturally a lady would not be able to curse them off), and her human torso and face, though obviously feminine, were not well proportioned. A colt followed her, and he was not only unhandsome, he was downright homely, except for his sleek hindquarters. In fact he resembled—

"Chester!" Bink exclaimed. "That's Chester's colt!"

"Why, you're Bink," the filly said. Now he recognized her: Cherie, Chester's mate. Yet she was in no way the beauty he had ridden before. What had happened?

But he had enough sense to express himself obliquely. "What are you doing here? I thought you were staying in the centaur village until—" But that was a trap, too, for Chester would never return.

287

"I'm trotting to the palace to find out what is responsible for the miracle," she said. "Do you realize that obscenity has been banished from Xanth?"

Bink remembered: Cherie considered magic obscene, at least when it manifested in centaurs. She tolerated it as a necessary evil in others, for she regarded herself as a liberal-minded filly, but preferred to discuss it only clinically.

Well, he had the detail on it! He was glad that at least one person liked the change. "I'm afraid I'm responsible."

"*You* abolished magic?" she asked, startled.

"It's a long story," Bink said. "And a painful one. I don't expect others to accept it as well as you will."

"Get on my back," she said. "You travel too slow. I'll take you in to the palace, and you can tell me the whole story. I'm dying to know!"

She might be dying literally, when she learned the truth about Chester. But he had to tell her. Bink mounted and hung on as she broke into a trot. He had anticipated a daylong march, but now this would be unnecessary; she would get them to the palace before dark.

He told her the story. He found himself going into more detail than strictly necessary, and realized this was because he dreaded the dénouement—where Chester had fought his dreadful battle and lost. True, he might have won, had the evil eye intended for Bink not stunned him—but that would be scant comfort to her. Cherie was a widow—and he had to be the one to tell her.

His narrative was interrupted by a bellow. A dragon hove into view—but it was a miserable monster. The once-bright scales had faded into mottled gray. When it snorted fire, only dust emerged. The thing was already looking gaunt and ill; it depended on magic for its hunting.

Nevertheless, the dragon charged, intent on consuming centaur, rider, and colt. Bink drew his sword, and Cherie skittered lightly on her feet, ready to kick. Even a bedraggled dragon of this size was a terror.

Then Bink saw a scar on the dragon's neck. "Say— don't I know you?" he exclaimed.

The dragon paused. Then it lifted its head in a signal of recognition.

"Chester and Crombie and I met this dragon and made a truce," Bink said. "We fought the nickelpedes together."

"The nickelpedes are harmless now," Cherie said. "Their pincers have lost their—" She pursed her lips distastefully. "Their magic. I trotted right down inside the Gap and stepped on them and they couldn't hurt me."

Bink knew. "Dragon, magic is gone from Xanth," Bink told it. "You'll have to learn to hunt and fight without your fire. In time you will change into your dominant mundane component, or your offspring will. I think that would be a large snake. I'm sorry."

The dragon stared at him in horror. Then it whipped about and half-galloped, half-slithered off.

"I'm sorry too," Cherie said. "I realize now that Xanth isn't really Xanth, without magic. Spells do have their place. Creatures like that—magic is natural to them." This was a considerable concession, for her.

Bink resumed his narrative. He could stall no longer, so nerved himself and said what he had to. "So I have Crombie here in the bottle," he concluded. And waited, aware of the awful tenseness in her body.

"But Chester and Humfrey—"

"Remain below," he said. "Because I freed the Demon."

"But you don't know they are dead," she said, her body still so tense that riding her was uncomfortable. "They can be found, brought back—"

"I don't know how," Bink said glumly. He didn't like this at all.

"Humfrey's probably just lost; that's why you couldn't find his body. Dazed by the collapse. Without his informational magic he could be confused for a goblin. And Chester—he's too ornery to—to—he's not dead, he's just pickled. You said that was a preservative lake—"

"So I did," Bink agreed. "I—but it was drained, so that I could see the convolutions of the brain coral."

"It wasn't drained all the way! He's down there,

deep below, I know it, like the griffin in the bottle. We can find him, revive him—"

Bink shook his head. "Not without magic."

She bucked him off. Bink flew through the air, saw the ground coming at his head, knew that his talent would do nothing—and landed in Cherie's arms. She had leaped to catch him at the last moment. "Sorry, Bink. It's just that obscenity bothers me. Centaurs don't . . ." She righted him and set him on his feet, never completing her statement. She might not be beautiful now, but she had the centaur strength.

Strength, not beauty. She had been a magnificently breasted creature, in the time of magic; now she remained ample, but she sagged somewhat, as most human or humanoid females of similar measurement did. Her face had been delightfully pert; now it was plain. What could account for the sudden change—except the loss of magic?

"Let me get this straight," Bink said. "You feel all magic is obscene—"

"Not *all* magic, Bink. For some of you it seems to be natural—but you're only human. For a centaur it is a different matter. We're civilized."

"Suppose centaurs had magic too?"

Her face shaped into controlled disgust. "We had better be on our way before it gets too late. There is a fair distance yet to cover."

"Like Herman the hermit, Chester's uncle," Bink persisted. "He could summon will-o'-the-wisps."

"He was exiled from our society," she said. Her expression had a surly quality that reminded him of Chester.

"Suppose other centaurs had magic—"

"Bink, why are you being so offensive? Do you want me to have to leave you here in the wilderness?" She beckoned to her colt, who came quickly to her side.

"Suppose you yourself had a magic talent?" Bink asked. "Would you still consider it obscene?"

"That does it!" she snorted. "I will not endure such obnoxious behavior, even from a human. Come, Chet." And she started off.

"Damn it, filly, listen to me!" Bink cried. "You

know why Chester came on my quest? Because he wanted to discover his own magic talent. If you deny magic in centaurs, you deny him—because he does have magic, good magic, that—"

She spun about, raising her forehooves to strike him down. A filly she might be, but she could kill him with a single blow.

Bink danced back. "Good magic," he repeated. "Not anything stupid, like turning green leaves purple, or negative, like giving people hotfeet. He plays a magic flute, a silver flute, the most lovely music I ever heard. Deep inside he's an awfully pretty person, but he's suppressed it because—"

"I'm going to stomp you absolutely flat!" she neighed, smashing at him with both forefeet. "You have no right even to suggest—"

But he was cool, now, while she was half-blinded by rage. He avoided her strikes as he would those of a savage unicorn, without ever turning his back or retreating more than he had to. He could have stabbed her six times with his sword, but never drew it. This debate was all academic now, since magic was gone from Xanth, but he was perversely determined that she should admit the truth. "And you, Cherie—you have magic too. You make yourself look the way you want to look, you enhance yourself. It's a type of illusion, restricted to—"

She struck at him with both forefeet at once, in a perfect fury. He was affronting her deepest sensitivities, telling her that she herself was obscene. But he was ready, anticipating her reactions, avoiding them. His voice was his sword, and he intended to score with it. He had had too much of delusion, his own especially; he would wipe the whole slate clean. In a way, it was himself he was attacking: his shame at what he had done to Xanth when he freed the Demon. "I challenge you," he cried. "Look at yourself in a lake. See the difference. Your magic is gone!"

Even in her fury, she realized she was not getting anywhere. "All right I'll look!" she cried. "Then I'll kick you to the moon!"

As it happened, they had passed a small pond recently. They returned to it in silence, Bink already starting to be sorry for what he was doing to her, and the lady centaur looked at herself. She was certain what she would find, yet honest enough to have her certainty disrupted by the fact. "Oh, no!" she cried, shocked. "I'm homely, I'm hideous, I'm uglier than Chester!"

"No, you're beautiful—with magic," Bink insisted, wanting to make up for the revelation he had forced on her. "Because magic is natural to you, as it is to me. You have no more reason to oppose it than you do any other natural function, like eating or breeding or—"

"Get away from me!" she screamed. "You monster, you—" In another fit of fury she stamped her hoof in the pond, making a splash. But the water only settled back, as water did, and the ripples quieted, and the image returned with devastating import.

"Listen, Cherie!" Bink cried. "You pointed out that Chester can be rescued. I'm just building on that. I don't dare open Crombie's bottle because the process requires magic, and there is none. Chester must stay in the lake for the same reason, in suspended animation. We *need* magic. It doesn't matter whether we *like* it. Without it, Chester is dead. We can't get anywhere as long as you—"

With extreme reluctance, she nodded agreement. "I thought nothing would make me tolerate obscenity. But for Chester I would do anything. Even—" She gulped, and twitched her tail. "Even magic. But—"

"We need a new quest!" Bink said with sudden inspiration as he washed himself in the pond. "A quest to restore magic to the Land of Xanth! Maybe if we all work together, humans and centaurs and all Xanth's creatures, we can find another Demon—" But he petered out, realizing the futility of the notion. How could they summon $X(A/N)^{th}$ or $E(A/R)^{th}$ or any other super-magical entity? The Demons had no interest in this realm.

"Yes," Cherie agreed, finding hope as Bink lost it. "Maybe the King will know how to go about it. Get on my back; I'm going to gallop."

Bink remounted her, and she took off. She did not have the sheer power Chester had, but Bink had to

292

cling to her slender waist to stay on as she zoomed through the forest.

"And with magic, I'll be beautiful again . . ." she murmured into the wind, wistfully.

Bink, tired, nodded sleepily as Cherie charged on through the desolate wilderness. Then he was almost pitched off as she braked.

They faced a huge shaggy pair of creatures. "Make way, you monsters!" Cherie cried without rancor. They were, after all, monsters. "This is a public easement; you can't block it!"

"We not block it, centaur lass," one monster said. "You give way to let we pass."

"Crunch the Ogre!" Bink exclaimed. "What are you doing so far from home?"

"You know this monster?" Cherie asked Bink.

"I certainly do! What's more, now I can understand him without translation!"

The ogre, who now resembled a brute of a man, peered at Bink from beneath his low skull. "You man we met, the one on quest? Me on gooeymoon with she loved best."

"Gooeymoon?" Cherie murmured.

"Oh, so that's Sleeping Beauty!" Bink said, contemplating the ogress. She was as ugly a creature as he cared to imagine. Yet beneath her hair, which resembled a mop just used to wipe up vomit, and her baggy coarse dress, she seemed to have rather more delicate contours than one might expect in an ogress. Then he remembered: she was no true ogress, but an actress, playing a part in one of the fiend's productions. She could probably look beautiful if she tried. Why, then, was she not trying? "Uh, one question—"

The female, no dummy, caught his gist before he got it out. "True, me once have other face," she told Bink. "Me glad get out of that rat race. Me find man better than any fiend; me like it best, by he be queened."

So the prima donna had found a husband worthy of her attention! After meeting the fiends, Bink found himself in agreement with her choice. She was maintaining the ogress guise, which was in any event merely a physical reflection of her normal personality, while teaching Crunch to speak more intelligibly. One savvy lady fiend, there! "Uh, congratulations," Bink said. Aside, he explained to Cherie. "They married on our advice. Humfrey and Crombie and Chester and the golem and I. Except that Humfrey was asleep. It was quite a story."

"I'm sure," Cherie agreed dubiously.

"Yes, me bash he good," the fair she-ogre said. "He head like wood."

"Ogres are very passionate," Bink murmured.

Cherie, after her initial surprise, was quick to catch on. "How do you keep his love?" she inquired with a certain female mischief. "Doesn't he like to go out adventuring?"

Bink realized she was thinking of Chester, perhaps unconsciously.

"Me let he go, me never say no," the ogress said, full of the wisdom of her sex. "When he come back, me give he crack." She struck the ogre with a horrendous backhand wallop by way of example. Just as well, for Bink had been about to misunderstand the reference. "Make he feel like beast, then give he feast."

Crunch's face contorted into a smile of agreement. He was obviously well satisfied. And probably better off, Bink thought, than he might have been with a natural ogress, who would have taken his nature for granted. Whatever faults the actress might have, she certainly knew how to handle her male.

"Does the loss of magic interfere with your lifestyle?" Bink inquired. Both ogres looked at him blankly.

"They never noticed!" Cherie exclaimed. "There's true love for you!"

The ogre couple went on its way, and Cherie resumed her run. But she was thoughtful. "Bink, just as a rhetorical example—does a male really like to feel like a beast?"

"Yes, sometimes," Bink agreed, thinking of Chameleon. When she was in her stupid-beautiful phase, she seemed to live only to please him, and he felt extremely manly. But when she was in her smart-ugly phase, she turned him off with her wit as well as her appearance. In that respect she was smarter when she was stupid than when she was smart. Of course now all that was over; she would stay always in her "normal" phase, avoiding the extremes. She would never turn him off—or on.

"And a centaur—if he felt like a real stallion at home—"

"Yes. Males need to feel wanted and needed and dominant, even when they aren't. Especially at home. That ogress knows what she's doing."

"So it seems," Cherie agreed. "She's a complete fake, a mere actress, yet he's so happy he'd do anything for her. But lady centaurs can act too, when they have reason . . ." Then she was silent as she ran.

Chapter 14. Paradox Wish

Bink, nodding again, was suddenly jolted awake. Cherie was braking so hard he was being crushed against her human back. He threw his arms about her waist, hanging on, careful not to grab too high. "What—?"

"I almost forgot. I haven't nursed Chet in hours."

"Chet?" Bink repeated dazedly. Oh, the foal.

She signaled to her young one, who promptly came up to nurse. Bink hastily excused himself for another kind of call of nature. Centaurs were not sensitive about natural functions; in fact they could and did perform some of them on the run. Humans were more squeamish, at least in public. It made him realize one reason why Cherie did not seem as lovely now: her breasts were enlarged to the point of ponderosity, so that she could nurse her foal. Little centaurs required a great deal of milk, especially when they had to run as much as this one did.

After a decent interval Bink cautiously returned. The foal was still nursing, but Cherie spied Bink. "Oh, don't be so damned human," she snapped. "What do you think I'm doing—magic?"

Bink had to laugh, embarrassed. She had a point; he had no more occasion to let his squeamishness interfere with business than she did. His definitions of what might be obscene made no more sense than hers. He came forward, albeit diffidently. It occurred to him that centaurs were well adapted to their functions; had Cherie had an udder like a horse, the foal would have had a difficult time. He was an upright little chap, whose human section did not bend down like the neck of a horse.

"We're going the wrong way," Cherie exclaimed.

Oh, no! "You strayed from the path? We're lost?"

"We're on the path. But we should not be going toward Castle Roogna. Nobody there can help."

"But the King—"

"The King is just an ordinary man, now. What can he do?"

Bink sighed. He had just assumed King Trent would have some sort of answer, but Cherie was right. "What can *anyone* do without—" He was trying to spare her the use of the obscene word, though he knew this was foolish.

"Nursing Chet started me thinking," she said, giving the foal a loving pat on the head. "Here is my foal, Chester's colt, a representative of the dominant species of Xanth. What am I doing running away from Chester? Chet needs a real stud to teach him the facts of life. I could never forgive myself, if—"

"But you're not running away!" Bink protested. "We're going to the King, to find out what to do in the absence of—how we can—"

"Oh, go ahead, say it!" she exclaimed angrily. "Magic! You have shown me in your blundering human way that it is necessary and integral to our way of life, including my own private personal life, damn you. Now I'm taking the rationale further. We can't just go home and commiserate with former Magicians; we have to *do* something. Now, immediately, before it's too late."

"It's already too late," Bink said. "The Demon is gone."

"But maybe he hasn't gone far. Maybe he forgot something, and will return to fetch it, and we can trap him—"

"No, that wouldn't be right. I meant it when I freed him, even though I don't like the result of that freedom."

"You have integrity, Bink, inconvenient as it sometimes is. Maybe we can call him back, talk to him, persuade him to give us back a few spells—"

Bink shook his head. "No, nothing we can do will

influence the Demon Xanth. He doesn't care at all about our welfare. If you had met him, you'd know."

She turned her head to face him. "Maybe I'd better meet him, then."

"How can I get it through your equine brain!" Bink cried, exasperated. "I told you he's gone!"

"All the same, I want to see where he was. There might be something left. Something you missed. No offense, Bink, but you *are* only human. If there were some way we could—"

"There is *no* way!" Bink cried. Chester had been stubborn enough, but this filly—!

"Listen, Bink. You rubbed my nose in the fact of my need of magic. Now I'm rubbing yours in the fact of your need to *do* something, instead of just giving in. You may tell yourself you're going to fetch help, but actually you're just running away. The solution to our problem is at the prison of the Demon, not at the King's palace. Maybe we'll fail—but we do have to go back there and try." And she started back the way they had come. "You've been there; show me the way."

Involuntarily, he ran along beside her, very much like the foal. "To the cave of the Demon?" he asked incredulously. "There are goblins and demagicked dragons and—"

"To hell with all that obscenity!" she neighed. "Who knows what is happening to Chester now?"

There it was: her ultimate loyalty to her mate. Now that he thought of it that way, his own attitude seemed inferior. Maybe his humanity did make him imperfect. Why hadn't he stayed at least long enough to locate his friend? Because he had been afraid of what he might find. He had, indeed, been running away!

Maybe Chester could be hauled out of the brine and saved without the aid of magic. Maybe Good Magician Humfrey yet survived. A small chance, certainly —but so long as there was any chance at all, Bink was derelict in his duty to his friends by not making every possible effort to find them. He had the sick certainty that they were dead, but even that confirmation would be better than his hiding from the truth.

He climbed back aboard Cherie, and she launched

herself onward. They made amazingly good progress. Soon they had passed the place where they had encountered each other, and were galloping across the terrain in the direction Bink indicated. A centaur could really move—but even so, it was almost as if there were some magic enchantment facilitating their progress. That was an illusion, of course, and not a magical one. It was just that Cherie was now goaded by her eagerness to rescue her stallion, foolish as that ambition might be. Bink directed her to the tangle-tree cleft, bypassing the magic-dust village.

As they galloped up, it seemed to Bink that the tangler quivered. That had to be a trick of the fading light, since without magic the monster was impotent.

Cherie drew up to the branch that overlapped the rim of the chasm. "Climbing down a tangle tree—I find that hard to—" She broke off. "Bink, it moved! I saw it!"

"The wind," Bink cried with abrupt illumination. "It rustles the tendrils!"

"Of course!" she agreed, relieved. "For a moment I almost thought—but I knew it wasn't so."

Bink peered down into the crevasse, and spied the crack in its base where the tree's big root crossed. He really did not want to go down there again, but didn't want to admit it. "I—uh—I can swing down on a vine. But you—"

"I can swing down too," she said. "That's why centaurs have strong arms and good chest muscles; we have greater weight to support. Come, Chet." She grasped a large tentacle and stepped off the brink.

Sure enough, she was able to let herself down, hand under hand, with her front legs acting as brakes. Her posterior swung grandly around in a descending spiral until she reached the base. The colt followed her example, though with such difficulty that she hastened to catch him at the base. Embarrassed by their examples, Bink swung down himself. He should have led the way, instead of letting fillies and foals do it!

At the base of the tree, gazing down into the looming black hole that was the aperture to the underworld, Bink had further misgivings. "This descent is worse;

I don't think Chet can make it. And how could you climb up again? It nearly killed me getting to the top, and your weight—no offense—"

"Chester could climb it," Cherie said confidently. "Then he could haul the rest of us up."

Bink visualized the muscles of Chester's human torso, and remembered the colossal power of the centaur. Only a monster like the ogre had more strength of arm. Maybe, just maybe, it was possible, especially if they set up a double rope so the rest of them could haul on the other end and help Chester lift himself. But that presumed they would actually find and rescue Chester. If they failed, Cherie herself would be lost, for Bink could never haul her up. He might handle the foal, but that was the limit.

Cherie was already testing tangler tentacles for strength. She had faith that banished doubt, and Bink envied her that. He had always thought of Chester as the ornery one, but now he understood that the true strength of the family lay in Cherie. Chester was mere magic putty in her hands—oops, obscene concept!—and so also, it seemed, was Bink. *He* did not want to return to the horrors of the depths, to battle uselessly against the half-goblins and snake-dragons in the dark. But he knew he would do it, because Cherie was going to rescue her poor dead stallion, or else.

"This one's good," she announced, tugging at a particularly long, stout tentacle that dangled from the very top of the tree. "Bink, you climb up and sever it with your knife."

"Uh, yeah, sure," he said with imperfect enthusiasm. Then he was ashamed of himself. If he was going to do this thing, at least he should do it with some spirit! "Yes, of course." And he started to climb the dread trunk.

He experienced a strange uplift and exhilaration. It was as if a burden had been lifted from his body. In a moment he realized what it was: conscience. Now that he had made his decision, and knew it was right even if suicidal, he was at peace with his conscience, and it was wonderful. This was what Cherie had experienced, which had made her almost fly through the wilderness, her strength expanded. Even without magic, there was magic in a person's attitude.

He reached the point where the tentacles sprouted like grotesque hairs from the apex of the trunk, braced himself with his legs looped about it, and slashed into the base of the selected tentacle. And felt a shudder in the tree reminiscent of the one made by the tangler Crombie had attacked so long ago.

No! he reminded himself immediately. It was not magic. The tree was still alive, it had merely lost its magic and become as Mundane trees. It might feel the pain of the cut, and react, but would not be able to move its tentacles about consciously.

He severed the tentacle and watched it drop. Then he cut a second and a third, to be sure they had enough.

Yet the tree was still shuddering as he descended, and the hanging tentacles seemed to be quivering more than might reasonably be accounted for by the wind. Would it be possible for a tangler to revive without magic? No; it must be the effect of his climbing, shaking the trunk, sending ripples through the vines.

They tied the first tentacle to the root, knotting it with difficulty because of its diameter, and dangled it down. It seemed to swing freely, marvelously limber, so they hauled it back up. With some care they knotted another tentacle to its end, extending its effective length. This time they heard the thump as it struck the rock below.

"I'll go first," Bink said. "Then I'll stand guard with my sword while you lower Chet. There are goblins— uh, have we anything for a light? We need fire to scare away the—"

Cherie gave him a straight stare. "If you were a goblin, would you mess with a centaur foal?" She tapped one forefoot meaningfully.

Bink remembered how he had foiled her attack, not long ago, when he forced her to face the obscene concept. But he was twice the height of a goblin, and armed with a sword, and familiar with centaurs. Most important, he had known that whatever Cherie's rage of the moment, she was his friend, and would not really hurt him. No goblin had any such assurance—

and a centaur filly protecting her young would be a terror. "I would not mess with a centaur foal even if I were a dragon," he said.

"I can see in the dark a little when I have to," she continued. "I can hear the echoes of my hooves, so I'll know the approximate contours to the caves. We'll get there."

Without another word Bink leaned down, grasped the tentacle rope, and swung himself into the hole. He handed himself into the depths rapidly, feeling much stronger than he had during the ascent. With surprising suddenness he was past the knot and at the floor. He peered up at the wan illumination above. "Okay —I'm down!"

The rope writhed up as Cherie hauled it. Centaurs had excellent balance for this sort of thing, since they could plant four feet on the ground and devote the full strength of their arms to the task. Soon Chet came swinging down, the rope looped about his middle while he held on tightly with his hands. In all this time he had spoken no word and made no demand or complaint; Bink was sure that would change drastically as Chet matured. Bink untied the little fellow at the base and gave him a pat on the back. "Chet's fine!" he called.

Now it was Cherie's turn. She had made it into the crevasse all right, but this was a narrower, darker, longer haul, with a less secure rope, and Bink was privately worried. "Stand clear, in case I should— swing," she called. Bink knew she had almost said "fall." She was well aware of the hazard, but she had courage.

She swung down without event, handing herself along until she neared the floor. Then the narrowing tentacle snapped, dropping her the last few feet. But she landed squarely, unhurt. Bink relaxed. "All right, Bink," she said immediately. "Get on my back and tell me where to go."

Silently Bink went to mount her—and in that silence he heard something. "Something's moving!" he snapped, surprised to discover how nervous he was. "Where's Chet?"

"Right here beside me," she said.

302

They listened—and now it was plain. A scraping, rustling sound off to the side and up. Definitely not any of them. Yet it didn't sound like goblins, either.

Then Bink saw a snakelike thing writhing between them and the hole, silhouetted by the light. "A tangler root—it's moving!" he exclaimed.

"We must have jarred it loose from the earth," she said. "It's own weight is pulling it free, and its shape makes it twist as it drops."

"Yes." But Bink was uncertain. That looked too much like conscious motion. Could the tangler be animating again? If so, there would be no escape this way!

They started along the cavern trail. Bink found he remembered it fairly well, even in the dark—and he found he could see a little. Maybe some glow remained. Actually, it seemed to get brighter as his eyes adjusted.

"The glow—it's returning," Cherie said.

"I thought it was my imagination," Bink agreed. "Maybe there is some residual magic down here."

They moved on, more rapidly. Bink couldn't help wondering: if the tangler was coming back to life, and the glow was getting brighter, could that mean that magic was returning? The implications were—

Suddenly the passage debouched into—a palace chamber so large he could not readily compass it with his gaze. Jewels sparkled on every side, hanging brilliantly in air. A fountain of scintillating water spread out upside down, its droplets falling back toward the ceiling. Streamers of colored paper formed whirls and whorls that traveled as if by their own volition, tilting sidewise or curling into spirals, only to straighten out again. On every side were fresh wonders, too many to assimilate; in all it was a display of the most phenomenal magic Bink had seen.

There had been no cave like this in this region before! Cherie looked around, as startled as he. "Is—could this be the work of your Demon Xanth?"

As she spoke the name, the Demon $X(A/N)^{th}$ materialized. He sat in a throne of solid diamond. His glowing eye fixed on Bink, who still bestrode Cherie, while the foal pressed closely to her side.

"You are the one I want," X(A/N)th exclaimed. "You stupid nonentity who threw yourself and your whole culture into peril, for no likely gain to either. Such idiocy deserves the penalty it brings."

Bink, awed, nevertheless tried to defend himself. "Why did you return, then? What do you want with me?"

"They have changed the nomenclature system," X(A/N)th replied. "They are into differentials now. I shall have to study that system for an eon or two, lest I apply it with gaucherie, so I am returning to this familiar place for the moment."

"An eon-moment?" Bink asked incredulously.

"Approximately. I brought you here to ensure that my privacy will be preserved. Every entity of this world that knows of me must be abolished."

"Abolished?" Bink asked, stunned.

"Nothing personal," the Demon assured him. "I really don't care about your existence one way or the other. But if my presence is known, other vermin may seek me out—and I want to be left alone. So I must abolish you and the others who are aware of me, preserving my secret. Most of you have already been eliminated; only you and the nymph remain."

"Leave Jewel out of it," Bink pleaded. "She's innocent; she only came because of me. She doesn't deserve—"

"This filly and her foal are innocent too," the Demon pointed out. "This has no relevance."

Cherie turned to face Bink. Her human torso twisted in the supple manner he remembered of old, and her beauty was back to its original splendor. Magic became her, without doubt! "You freed this thing—and this is his attitude? Why doesn't he go elsewhere, where none of us can find him?"

"He's leaked a lot of magic here," Bink said. "It is quiescent without him, but so long as magical creatures like dragons and centaurs remain, we know it hasn't departed entirely. The whole of the Land of Xanth is steeped with it, and this must be more comfortable for him. Like a well-worn shoe, instead of one fresh from the shoe-tree that chafes. The Demon is not of our kind; he has no gratitude. I knew that when I freed him."

"There will be a brief delay before I terminate you," the Demon said. "Make yourselves comfortable."

Despite his immediate peril, Bink was curious. "Why the delay?"

"The nymph has hidden herself, and I do not choose to expend magic wastefully in an effort to locate her."

"But you are omnipotent; waste should have no meaning to you!"

"True—I am omnipotent. But there is proportion in all things. It bothers my sensitivities to use more magic than a given situation warrants. Therefore I am minimizing the effort here. I have amplified your persona. She loves you—I do not pretend to know the meaning of that term—and will come to you here, believing you to be in a danger she can ameliorate. Then I can conveniently abolish you all."

So the return of magic to the Land of Xanth meant the end for Bink and his friends. Yet the rest of Xanth profited, so it was not a total loss. Still—

"I don't suppose you would be satisfied if we simply promised not to reveal your presence, or took a forget-potion?"

"No good," a voice said from Bink's pocket. It was Grundy the golem, back in form with the restoration of magic. He climbed out to perch on Bink's shoulder. "You could never keep such a promise. Magic would have the truth out of you in a moment. Even if you took a forget-potion, it would be neutralized, then the information would be exposed."

"A truth spell," Cherie agreed. "I should have trusted my original judgment. Magic is a curse."

Bink refused to give up. "Maybe we should reverse it," he told the Demon. "Spread the word to all the land that you are down here, and will destroy anyone who intrudes—"

"You'd encourage ninety-nine nuts to rise to the challenge," Cherie pointed out. "The Demon would be constantly annoyed, and have to waste his magic destroying them one by one."

The Demon looked at her approvingly. "You have an equine rear, but a sapient head," he remarked.

"Centaurs do," she agreed.

"And what do you think of me?"

"You are the absolute epitome of obscenity."

Bink froze, but the Demon laughed. The sound blasted out deafeningly. The magically ornate palace shattered about him, filling the air with debris, but none of it touched them.

"Know something?" Grundy remarked. "He's changing—like me."

"Changing—like you," Bink repeated. "Of course! While his magic was leaking out, infusing the whole Land of Xanth, some of our culture was seeping *in*, making him a little bit like us. That's why he feels comfortable here. That's why he can laugh. He *does* have some crude feelings."

Cherie was right on it. "Which means he might respond to a feeling challenge. Can you come up with one?"

"I can try," Bink said. Then, as the Demon's mirth subsided, he said: "Demon, I know a way to protect your privacy. We have a shieldstone, formerly used to protect the whole Land of Xanth from intrusion by outsiders. We valued our privacy as much as you value yours. Nothing living can pass through that shield. All I need to do is tell our King Trent about you, and he will set up the shield to prevent anyone from coming down here. The shield worked for us for over a century; it will work for you too. Then it won't matter who knows about you; every fool who tries to reach you will die, automatically."

The Demon considered. "The notion appeals. But the human mind and motivation are largely foreign to me. How can I be sure your King will honor your request?"

"I know he will," Bink said. "He's a good man, an honest one, and a savvy politician. He will immediately appreciate the need to protect your privacy, and will act on it."

"How sure of that are you?" the Demon asked.

"I'd stake my life on it."

"Your life is insignificant compared to my convenience," the Demon said without humor.

"But my talent is significant in human terms," Bink

argued. "It will act in my interest by encouraging the King to—"

"Your talent is nothing to me. I could reverse it by a simple snap of my fingers." The Demon snapped his fingers with a sound like the detonation of a cherry bomb. Bink felt a horribly disquieting internal wrench. "However, your challenge intrigues me. There is a certain element of chance involved that can not occur when I myself undertake a challenge. Therefore I must indulge myself to a certain extent vicariously. You say you shall stake your life on your ability to preserve my privacy. This is really no collateral, since your life is already forfeit, but I'll accept it. Shall we gamble?"

"Yes," Bink agreed. "If that's what it takes to save my friends. I'll undertake any—"

"Bink, I don't like this," Cherie said.

"Here is the testing laboratory," the Demon said, indicating a huge pit that appeared as he gestured. Around it were spaced half a dozen doorways. The walls were vertical stone, too high and slick to climb. "And here is the intruder." A monster appeared in the center, a minotaur, with the head and tail and hooves of a bull and the body of a powerful man. "If he escapes this chamber alive, he will intrude on my privacy. You will stop him if you can."

"Done!" Bink cried. He jumped down into the arena, drawing his sword.

The minotaur surveyed him coolly. The return of magic had invigorated Bink, making him feel strong again—and he had never been a physical weakling. The muscles of his arms showed through the tattered shirt, and his body was balanced and responsive. His sword moved with smooth proficiency, buoyed by its magic, and the charmed blade gleamed. The monster decided to pass up the pleasure of this quarrel. It spun on one hoof and walked toward the exit farthest from Bink.

Bink pursued it. "Turn about and fight like a monster!" he cried, unwilling to cut it down from behind.

Instead the creature broke into a run. But Bink's momentum carried him forward faster, and he caught the minotaur before it reached the exit. He hauled on its tail, causing the thing to crash into a wall. Bink put his sword to its throat. "Yield!" he cried.

The minotaur shivered—and became a monster bug, with tremendous pincers, stinger, and mandibles. Bink, startled, stepped back. He was fighting a magic monster—one that could change its form at will! This was going to be a much more formidable challenge than he had, in his naïveté, supposed.

What a fool he had been to hold back his sword, expecting this thing to yield! Surely its life, like his own, would be forfeit if it lost. He had to kill it in a hurry, before it killed him—or got away, which amounted to the same thing.

Even while he realized this, the bug was skittering toward the exit. Bink leaped after it, his sword swinging. But the bug had eye-stalks that looked back at him—in fact, it was now a giant slug, sliding along on a trail of slime. Bink's sword swished over its head harmlessly.

He could, however, move faster than a slug, even a large one. Bink jumped over it and reached the exit first, barring the way. He took careful aim and made a two-handed strike at the slug's head, to slice it lengthwise. But his blade clanged off the shell of a snail. The monster had changed again, to the nearest variant that would protect it. Either it was hard-pressed, or it lacked imagination.

Bink gave it no chance to think. He thrust directly into the opening of the shell. This time he scored—on the substance of a big green jellyfish. His blade sliced through it and emerged from the far side, dripping, without really hurting the blob. He carried his stroke on up and out and shook the blade off, disgusted. How could he kill a mass of jelly that sealed up after his cut?

He sniffed. Now he recognized the odor of the thing: lime. Lime-flavored jelly. Was it edible? Could he destroy the monster by eating it?

But as he pondered, the monster changed into a purple vulture the size of a man. Bink leaped for it, trying to slay it before it flew up beyond his reach—and skidded on the remaining patch of lime goo. What a disastrous coincidence!

Coincidence? No—this was his talent operating—in reverse. The Demon had negligently switched it. Now seeming coincidence would always work against Bink, instead of for him. He was his own worst enemy.

Still, he had done all right for himself when his talent had been largely canceled out by the brain coral's magic. What he needed to do now was to minimize the element coincidence played in this battle. His talent never revealed itself openly, so was restricted, awaiting its chance to operate. Everything he did should be so carefully planned that it left virtually nothing to chance. That way, chance could not operate against him.

The bird did not fly. It ran toward the center of the arena. Bink scrambled to his feet and pursued, watching his step. Here was a pebble that he might have tripped over; there was another spot of grease. His prior slip in the jelly had been mainly carelessness. He could minimize that. But why didn't the bird simply fly, while Bink was being so careful of his motions?

Probably because the monster was not a Magician. Each form it assumed was about the same mass, and landbound. A good talent, but not an extraordinary one. There were definite limits. King Trent could change a fly into a hephalumph, or a worm into a flying dragon; size and function were of no account. But this monster only changed its form, not its abilities. Good!

Bink stalked the vulture, alert for any move it might make toward the exit. To flee him it would have to turn its back, and then he would strike it down. No element of chance involved there, so no way for his reversed talent to intercede. Bink's early life, when he had not known about his talent, had prepared him for operating without it. His recent adventures, when it had been either neutralized or eliminated entirely, had served as a refresher course. The monster would have to stand and fight, rather than depending on Bink to foul up.

Suddenly it was a man—a burly, tousle-haired brute in tattered clothing, carrying a gleaming sword. The man looked as if he knew his business; in fact he looked familiar.

In fact—it was a replica of Bink himself! The monster was getting smart, fighting sword with sword. "Fair enough!" Bink said, and launched his attack.

As he had guessed, the monster was no swordsman. He might look like Bink, but he couldn't *fight* the way Bink could! This battle would soon be over!

Bink made a feint, then engaged the other's sword and knocked it out of the monster's hand. He backed the monster up against the wall, ready for the finish.

"Bink!" a woman cried in despair.

Bink recognized that voice. It was Jewel! Drawn by the spell the Demon had made, she had arrived just at the wrong moment. It had to be the machination of his reversed talent, interfering just in time to save his enemy from destruction. Unless he acted immediately—

"Bink!" she cried again, jumping down into the arena and throwing herself between him and the monster. She smelled of a summer storm. "Why didn't you stay out of the caverns, where you would be safe?" Then she stopped, amazed. "You're *both* Bink!"

"No, he's the monster," the monster said before Bink spoke. "He's trying to kill an unarmed man!"

"For shame!" Jewel flashed, facing Bink. The storm had become a hurricane, with the odors of sleet and dust and crushed brick, windborne. "Begone, monster!"

"Let's get out of here," the monster said to her, taking her by the arm and walking toward an exit.

"Of all the nerve!" Cherie cried from above. "Get that fool nymph out of there!"

But Jewel stayed with the cunning monster, escorting him toward safety—and a disaster she could not imagine. Bink stood frozen, unable to bring himself to act against Jewel.

"Bink, she'll die too, if you let him go!" Cherie screamed.

That nerved him. Bink launched himself at the pair, catching them each about the waist and hauling them down. He intended to separate them, stab the monster, and explain to Jewel later.

But when he righted himself, he discovered that he had a nymph on each arm. The monster now resembled Jewel—and Bink couldn't tell them apart.

He jumped to his feet, sword ready. "Jewel, identify yourself!" he shouted. The monster could hardly have been smart enough to think of this on its own; Bink's talent had probably decreed such a fortuitous choice of appearances. Bink had not given it any opportunity to catch him in an accident, so it had acted on the monster instead. Coincidence took many forms.

"Me!" the two nymphs cried together, getting to their feet.

Oh, no! They sounded alike, too. "Jewel, I'm fighting a change-shape monster," he cried to them both. "If I don't kill him, he'll kill me. One way or another. I've got to know which one he is." Assuming the monster was male. Bink had to assume that, because he didn't want to kill a female.

"Him!" both nymphs cried, pointing at each other. The scent of skunk cabbage filled the air. Both backed away from each other, and from him.

Worse and worse! Now his talent had the bit in its teeth, determined not to let him prevail. Yet he had to kill the monster, and to spare Jewel. He could not afford to choose randomly.

The nymphs were heading for different exits. Already it was too late to catch both. Upon his choice rested the fate of himself and all his friends—and his infernal talent would surely make him choose wrongly. No matter which one he chose, it would be the wrong one. Somehow. Yet to make no choice would also spell doom.

Bink realized that the only way he could be sure of salvaging anything was to kill them both. The monster, and the nymph-woman who loved him. Appalling decision!

Unless he could somehow trick the monster into revealing itself. (Call it *it:* that would be easy to kill!)

"You are the monster!" he cried, and charged the nymph on the right, swinging his sword.

She flicked a glance over her shoulder, saw him, and screamed in mortal terror. And the smell of dragon's breath, the essence of terror, was strong.

Bink completed his swing, avoiding her as she cowered, and hurled his sword at the second nymph, who was almost at the other exit. The one he had decided was really the monster.

But the near-nymph, in her terror, threw up her hands defensively. One hand brushed Bink's sword arm, just as he threw the weapon, fouling his aim. His talent again, using his friend to balk his attack on his enemy!

Yet it was not over. The monster, seeing the approaching blade, leaped to the side—right into the misthrown sword. The blade struck the chest and plunged through, such was the force of Bink's throw and the charm of the weapon. Transfixed, the monster fell. Two bad lucks had canceled each other out!

Bink, meanwhile, crashed into Jewel, bearing her to the floor. "Sorry," he said. "I had to do it, to make sure—"

"That's quite all right," she said, struggling to get up. Bink got to his own feet and took her by the elbow, helping her. But his eyes were on the dead or dying monster. What was its natural form?

The monster didn't change. It still looked exactly like Jewel, with full bosom, slender waist, healthy hips, ideal legs, and sparkling hair—and blood washing out around the embedded sword. Strange. If the monster was mortally injured, why didn't it revert to form? If it were not, why didn't it scramble up and out the exit?

Jewel drew away from him. "Let me go clean up, Bink," she said. At the moment she smelled of nothing.

Of nothing? "Make a smell," Bink said, grabbing her arm again.

"Bink, let me go!" she cried, pulling toward the exit.

"Make a smell!" he growled, twisting her arm behind her back.

Suddenly he held a tangle tree. Its vines twisted to grab him, but they lacked the strength of a real tangler, even a dwarf species. Bink clamped both his arms about the tree, squeezing the tentacles in against the trunk, hard.

The tree became a squat sea serpent. Bink hunched his head down and continued squeezing. The serpent became a two-headed wolf whose jaws snapped at

312

Bink's ears. He squeezed harder; he could afford to lose an ear in order to win the battle. The wolf became a giant tiger lily, snarling horrendously, but Bink was crushing its stem.

Finally it got smart. It changed into a needle cactus. The needles stabbed into Bink's arms and face—but he did not let go. The pain was terrible, but he knew that if he gave the monster any leeway at all it would change into something he couldn't catch, or his talent would arrange some coincidental break for it. Also, he was angry: because of this creature, he had cut down an innocent nymph, whose only fault was loving him. He had assumed that jinxes had canceled out when his misthrown sword cut her down, but that had not been the case. What an awful force his talent could be! His hands and face were bleeding, and a needle was poking into one eye, but Bink squeezed that cactus-torso with the passion of sheer hate until it squirted white fluid.

The thing dissolved into foul-smelling goo. Bink could no longer hold on; there was nothing to grasp. But he tore at the stuff with his hands, flinging gobs of it across the arena, and stomped the main mass flat. Could the monster survive dismemberment, even in this stage?

"Enough," the Demon said. "You have beaten it." He gestured negligently, and abruptly Bink was fit and clean again, without injury—and somehow he knew his talent was back to normal. The Demon had been testing *him,* not his talent. He had won—but at what cost?

He ran to Jewel—the real Jewel—reminded of the time Chameleon had been similarly wounded. But the Evil Magician had done that, while this time Bink himself had done it. "You desire her?" the Demon asked. "Take her along." And Jewel was whole and lovely, smelling of gardenias, just as if she had been dunked in healing elixir. "Oh, Bink!" she said—and fled the arena.

"Let her go," Cherie said wisely. "Only time can heal the wound that doesn't show."

"But I can't let her think I meant to—"

"She knows you didn't mean to hurt her, Bink. Or

313

she *will* know, when she thinks it out at leisure. But she also knows that she has no future with you. She is a creature of the caverns; the openness of the surface world would terrify her. Even if you weren't married, she could not leave her home for you. Now that you're safe, she has to go."

Bink stared the way Jewel had gone. "I wish there were something I could do."

"You can leave her alone," Cherie said firmly. "She must make her own life."

"Good horse sense," Grundy the golem agreed.

"I will permit you to perform the agreed task in your fashion," the Demon said to Bink. "I hold no regard for you or your welfare, but I do honor the conditions of a wager. All I want from your society is that it not intrude on my private demesnes. If it does, I might be moved to do something you would be sorry for—such as cauterizing the entire surface of the planet with a single sheet of fire. Now have I conveyed my directive in a form your puny intellect can comprehend?"

Bink did not regard his intellect as puny, compared to that of the Demon. The creature was omnipotent, not omniscient: all-powerful, not all-knowing. But it would not be politic to remark on that at the moment. Bink had no doubt that the Demon could and would obliterate all life in the Land of Xanth, if irritated. Thus it was in Bink's personal interest to keep the Demon happy, and to see that no other idiots like him intruded. So his talent would extend itself toward that end—as X(A/N)th surely was aware. "Yes."

Then Bink had a bright flash. "But it would be easier to ensure your privacy if there were no loose ends, like lost Magicians or pickled centaurs—"

Cherie perked up alertly. "Bink, you're a genius!"

"This Magician?" Xanth inquired. He reached up through the ceiling and brought down a gruesome skeleton. "I can reanimate him for you—"

Bink, after his initial shock, saw that this skeleton was much larger than any Humfrey could have worn. "Uh, not that one," he said, relieved. "Smaller, like a —a gnome. And alive."

"Oh, that one," X(A/N)th said. He reached

through a wall and brought back Good Magician Humfrey, disheveled but intact.

"About time you got to me," Humfrey grumped. "I was running out of air, under that rubble."

Now the Demon reached down through the floor. He brought back Chester, encased in a glistening envelope of lake water. As he set the centaur down, the envelope burst; the water evaporated, and Chester looked around.

"So you went swimming without me!" Cherie said severely. "Here I stay home tending your colt while you gad about—"

Chester scowled. "I gad about *because* you spend all your time with the colt!"

"Uh, there's no need—" Bink interposed.

"Stay out of this," she murmured to him with a wink. Then, to Chester, she flared: "Because he is just like you! I can't keep *you* from risking your fool tail on stupid, dangerous adventures, you big dumb oaf, but at least I have him to remind me of—"

"If you paid more attention to me, I'd stay home more!" he retorted.

"Well, I'll pay more attention to you now, horsehead," she said, kissing him as the arena dissolved and a more cosy room formed about them. "I need you."

"You do?" he asked, gratified. "What for?"

"For making another foal, you ass! One that looks just like me, that you can take out for runs—"

"Yeah," he agreed with sudden illumination. "How about getting started right now!" Then he looked about, remembering where he was, and actually blushed. The golem smirked. "Uh, in due course."

"And you can run some with Chet, too," she continued. "So you can help him find his talent." There was no hint of the discomfort she must have suffered getting the word out.

Chester stared at her. "His—you mean you—"

"Oh, come on, Chester," she snapped. "You're wrong ten times a day. Can't I be wrong once in my life? I can't say I like it, but since magic seems to be part of the centaur's heritage, I'll simply have to live with it. Magic does have its uses; after all, it brought you back." She paused, glancing at him sidelong. "In fact, I might even be amenable to a little flute music."

Startled, Chester looked at her, then at Bink, realizing that someone had blabbed. "Perhaps that can be arranged—in decent privacy. After all, we are centaurs."

"You're such a beast," she said, flicking her tail at him. Bink covered a smile. When Cherie learned a lesson, she learned it well!

"Which seems to cover that situation sufficiently, tedious as it has been," the Demon said. "Now if you are all quite ready to depart, never to return—"

Yet Bink was not quite satisfied. He did not trust this sudden generosity on the part of the Demon. "You're really satisfied to be forever walled off from our society?"

"You can not wall *me* off," the Demon pointed out. "I am the source of magic. You will only wall *you* off. I will watch and participate anytime I choose—which will probably be never, as your society is of little interest to me. Once you depart, I forget you."

"You ought at least to thank Bink for freeing you," Cherie said.

"I thank him by sparing his ridiculous life," X(A/N)ᵗʰ said, and if Bink hadn't known better he might have thought the Demon was nettled.

"He earned his life!" she retorted. "You owe him more than that!"

Bink tried to caution her. "Don't aggravate him," he murmured. "He can blink us all into nothingness—"

"Without even blinking," the Demon agreed. One eyelid twitched as if about to blink.

"Well, Bink could have left you to rot for another thousand years, without blinking himself," she cried heedlessly. "But he didn't. Because he has what you will never understand: humanity!"

"Filly, you intrigue me," X(A/N)ᵗʰ murmured. "It is true I am omnipotent, not omniscient—but I believe I could comprehend human motive if I concentrated on it."

"I dare you!" she cried.

Even Chester grew nervous at this. "What are you

trying to do, Cherie?" he asked her. "Do you want us all extinguished?"

The Demon glanced at Grundy. "Half-thing, is there substance to her challenge?"

"What's in it for me?" the golem demanded.

The Demon lifted one finger. Light coalesced about Grundy. "That."

The light seemed to draw into the golem—and lo, Grundy was no longer a thing of clay and string. He stood on living legs, and had a living face. He was now an elf.

"I—I'm real!" he cried. Then, seeing the Demon's gaze upon him, he remembered the question. "Yes, there is substance! It's part of being a feeling creature. You have to laugh, to cry, to experience sorrow and gratitude and—and it's the most wonderful thing—"

"Then I shall cogitate on it," the Demon said. "In a century or so, when I have worked out my revised nomenclature." He returned to Cherie. "Would one gift satisfy you, feeling filly?"

"I don't need anything," she said. "I already have Chester. Bink is the one."

"Then I grant Bink one wish."

"No, that's not it! You have to show you understand by giving him something nice that he would not have thought of himself."

"Ah, another challenge," the Demon said. He pondered. Then he reached out and lifted Cherie in one hand. Bink and Chester jumped with alarm, but it was not a hostile move. "Would this suffice?" The Demon put her to his mouth. Again Bink and Chester jumped, but the Demon was only whispering, his mouth so large that the whisper shook her whole body. Yet the words were inaudible to the others.

Cherie perked up. "Why yes, that would suffice! You *do* understand!" she exclaimed.

"Merely interpolation from observed gestures of his kind." The Demon set her down, then flicked another finger. A little globe appeared in air, sailing toward Bink, who caught it. It seemed to be a solidified bubble. "That is your wish—the one you must choose for yourself," the Demon said. "Hold the sphere before you and utter your wish, and anything within the realm of magic will be yours."

Bink held up the globe. "I wish that the men who were restored from stone by the absence of magic, so they could return to the village of magic dust, will remain restored now that magic is back," he said. "And that the lady griffin will not turn back to gold. And that all the things killed by the loss of magic, like the brain coral——"

The Demon made a minor gesture of impatience. "As you see, the bubble did not burst. That means your wish does not qualify, for two reasons. First, it is not a selfish one; you gain nothing for yourself by it. Second, those stone and gold spells can only be restored by reapplication of their inputs; once interrupted, they are gone. None of those people have returned to stone or gold, and none of the similar spells in your land have been reinstated. Only magic *life* has been restored, such as that of the golem and the coral. The other spells are like fire: they burn continuously once started, but once doused remain out. Do not waste my attention on such redundancy; your wish must go for a selfish purpose."

"Oh," Bink said, taken aback. "I can't think of any wish of that kind."

"It was a generous notion, though," Cherie murmured to him.

The Demon waved his hand. "You must carry the wish until it is expended. Enough; I become bored with this trivia."

And the party stood in the forest that Bink and Cherie and the colt had left. It was as if the Demon had never been—except for the sphere. And Bink's friends, restored. And the reviving magic of the forest. Even Cherie seemed satisfied with that magic, now.

Bink shook his head and pocketed the wish-globe. All he wanted to do now was to get home to Chameleon, and he needed no special magic for that.

"I'll carry Bink, as usual," Chester said. "Cherie, you carry the Magician—" He paused. "Crombie! We forgot the loud-beaked griffin!"

Bink felt in his pocket. "No, I have him here in the bottle. I can release him now——"

"No, let him stew there a while longer," Chester decided. Evidently he had not quite forgiven the soldier for the savage fight the two had had.

"Maybe that's best," Cherie agreed. "He was in a life-and-death struggle when he was confined. He might come out fighting."

"Let him come!" Chester said belligerently.

"I think it would be better to wait," Bink said. "Just in case."

It was dusk, but they moved on rapidly. The monsters of the night seemed to hold no terror, after their adventure. Bink knew he could use his stored wish to get them out of trouble if he had to. Or he could release Crombie and let him handle it. Most of the more dangerous wilderness entities were still recovering from the shock of the temporary loss of magic, and were not aggressive.

Chester had a problem, however. "I have paid the fee for an Answer," he reminded the Good Magician. "But I found my talent by myself. Now I could ask about Cherie's talent——"

"But I already know it," Cherie said, coloring slightly at this confession of near-obscenity. "Don't waste your Question on that!"

"You know your talent?" Chester repeated, startled. "What——"

"I'll tell you another time," she said modestly.

"But that leaves me without a wish—I mean without an Answer," he said. "I paid for it with my life, but don't know what to ask."

"No problem," Humfrey said. "I could tell you what to ask."

"You could?" Then Chester saw the trap. "But that would use it up! I mean, your telling me the Question would use up the Answer—and then I wouldn't have the Answer to my Question!"

"That does seem to present a problem," Humfrey agreed. "You might elect to pay another fee——"

"Not by the hair of your handsome tail!" Cherie cried. "No more adventures away from home!"

"Already my freedom is slipping away," Chester muttered, not really displeased.

Bink listened glumly. He was glad to be getting home, but still felt guilt about what had happened to Jewel. He had a wish—but he knew he could not simply wish Jewel out of love with him. Her love was real, not magical, and could not be abolished magically. Also, how would Chameleon react to this matter? He would have to tell her. . . .

They galloped up to the palace as night became complete. The grounds were illuminated by shining luna moths whose fluttering green radiance gave the palace an unearthly beauty.

Queen Iris was evidently alert, for three moons rose to brighten the palace as they entered, and there was a fanfare from invisible trumpets. They were promptly ushered to the library, the King's favorite room.

Without ceremony, Bink told his story. King Trent listened without interrupting. As Bink concluded, he nodded. "I shall make arrangements to set the shield as you suggested," the King said at last. "I think we will not publicize the presence of the Demon, but we shall see that no one intrudes on him."

"I knew you would see it that way," Bink said, relieved. "I—I had no idea there would be such a consequence to my quest. It must have been terrible here, without magic."

"Oh, I had no trouble," the King said. "I spent twenty years in Mundania, remember. I still have a number of little unmagic mannerisms about me. But Iris was verging on a nervous breakdown, and the rest of the kingdom was not much better off. Still, I believe the net effect was beneficial; citizens really appreciate their magic, now."

"I suppose so," Bink agreed. "I never realized how important magic was, until I saw Xanth without it. But here in our group we're left with distressing magical loose ends. Chester has a surplus Answer, and I have a wish I can't use, and Crombie is confined—"

"Ah, yes," the King agreed. "We'd better reconstitute him now."

Bink uncorked the bottle, releasing Crombie. The griffin coalesced. "Squawk!" he proclaimed.

"About time," Grundy translated.

King Trent looked at the griffin—and it became a man. "Well," Crombie said, patting himself to make certain of his condition. "You didn't need to leave me bottled up. I could hear what was going on, all the time." He turned to Chester. "And you, you hoof-headed hulk—I only fought you because the coral controlled me. You didn't have to be scared of me once that was settled."

Chester swelled up. "Scared of you! You feather-brained punk—"

"Anytime you want to try it again, horsetail—"

"That will suffice," the King said gently, and both shut up, albeit with imperfect grace.

King Trent smiled, returning his attention to Bink. "Sometimes you miss the obvious, Bink. Let Chester give his Answer to you."

"To me? But it's *his*—"

"Sure, you can have it," Chester said. "I don't need it."

"But I already have a wish I can't use, and—"

"Now you use Chester's Question to ask the Good Magician what to do with your wish," the King said.

Bink turned to Humfrey. The man was snoring quietly in a comfortable chair. There was an awkward pause.

Grundy went up and jogged the Magician's ankle. "Get with it, midge."

Humfrey woke with a small start. "Give it to Crombie," the Magician said before Bink opened his mouth, and lapsed back into sleep.

"What?" Chester demanded. "The Answer I sweated for only brings a free wish to this bird?"

Bink marveled himself, but handed the wish-bubble to Crombie. "May I ask what you mean to use it for?"

Crombie fidgeted a moment, an unusual perform-ance for him. "Uh, Bink, you remember that nymph, the one who—"

"Jewel," Bink agreed. "I dread trying to explain about her to—"

"Well, I—uh, you see, I had this fragment of the magic mirror in the bottle, and I used it to check on Sabrina, and—"

"I fear constancy was never her strong suit," the King interposed. "I don't believe you two were right for each other anyway."

"What about her?" Bink asked, perplexed.

"She was two-timing me," Crombie said, scowling. "Right when she had me on the verge—but the other guy is married, so she was going to let on the kid was mine, and—I knew I couldn't trust a woman!"

So Sabrina had deserted Crombie, as she had deserted Bink himself, before he knew Chameleon. Yet she connived to marry Crombie anyway—and it had been fated that he would have to marry her unless he married someone else first. "I'm sorry," Bink said. "But I think it would be best simply to let her go. No sense wasting a wish for vengeance."

"No, that's not what I had in mind," Crombie assured him. "I wouldn't trust *any* woman now. But I think I could love a nymph—"

"Jewel?" Bink asked, amazed.

"I don't expect you to believe this," Crombie said seriously. "I don't really believe it myself. But a soldier has to face realities. I lost the battle before it started. There I was, lying in that cleft where you had slain me, Bink. I don't blame you for that; it was a hell of a good fight, but I was really hurting. Suddenly she came, smelling of pine needles and gardenias, bringing the healing elixir. I never saw anything so sweet in my life. She was weak and hesitant, just like a nymph. No threat to any man, least of all a soldier. No competition. The kind of female I could really get along with. And the way she stood by you—" Crombie shook his head. "That's why I went back in the bottle, after pointing out the antidote for you. I wouldn't do anything to hurt that nymph, and killing you would have torn her up. And if you got the antidote, you'd get out of love with her, which was how I wanted you. She's lovely and loyal. But since she still loves you—"

"That's hopeless," Bink said. "I'll never see her again, and even if I did—" He shrugged. "There can be nothing between us."

"Right. So if you don't mind, I'll just take this wish and wish her to drink some of that love potion—and to see me next thing. Then she'll feel about me the way you felt about her. Only I'll be available, seeing as I have to marry someone anyway."

And Crombie was a dashing soldier and a handsome man. Inevitably the love the potion started would become real. The hurt Jewel felt for what Bink had done to her, striking her down with his sword, would make the transition easier. Except—

"But you like to travel about," Chester said before Bink could formulate the same objection. "She lives below, planting precious stones. That's her job; she wouldn't leave it."

"So we'll separate—and rejoin," Crombie said. "I'll be seeing her part-time, not all the time. That's the way I like it. I'm a soldier."

And that, neatly, solved Bink's problem.

"What about me?" Grundy demanded. "Without birdbeak, I have no job. I'm real, now; I can't just disappear."

"There is occasional need for translation around this court," the King said. "We shall find employment for you." He glanced about. "That about suffices for tonight. Quarters have been arranged for all of you, here at the palace." With that he ushered them out.

Bink was last to go. "I—I'm sorry I caused all this trouble," he said. "The Good Magician tried to warn me, and so did Beauregard the demon, but I wouldn't listen. Just because I wanted to know the source of magic—"

"Have no concern, Bink," the King said with a reassuring smile. "I was aware that there was an element of risk when I sent you—but I was as curious about the source of magic as you, and I felt that it was best to have the discovery made by you, protected by your talent. I knew your talent would see you through."

"But my talent was lost when the magic went, and—"

"Was it, Bink? Didn't it strike you that the Demon's return was unusually fortuitous?"

"Well, he wanted a private place to—"

"Which he could have arranged anywhere in the universe. What *really* brought him back? I submit that it was your talent, still looking out for your long-range interests. Your marriage was in trouble, so your magic indulged in an extraordinary convolution to set it straight."

"I—I can't believe my talent could operate to affect the origin of magic itself!" Bink protested.

"I have no such difficulty. The process is called feedback, and it can and does reflect profoundly on the origin. Life itself may be regarded as a feedback process. But even if that were not the case, your talent could have anticipated the chain of events, and established a course that would inevitably bring magic back to the Land of Xanth, much as an arrow shot into the air inevitably returns—"

"Uh, when we fought the constellations, Chester's arrows didn't—"

The King shook his head. "Forgive an inept analogy. I shall not bore you further with my Mundane perspective. I am satisfied with the result of your quest, and you should be satisfied too. I suspect that had any other person released the Demon, $X(A/N)^{th}$ would never have returned to our realm. At this point the matter is academic. We shall have to find another occupation for you, but there is no rush. Go home to your wife and son."

"Son?"

"Oh, did I forget to inform you? As of dusk you became the father of a Magician-class baby, my likely successor to the throne—in due course. I suggest that infant's talent is the Demon's selected gift to you, and perhaps another reason your own talent put you through this adventure."

"What talent does the baby have?" Bink asked, feeling giddy. His son—an overt Magician at birth!

"Oh, I wouldn't spoil the surprise by telling you! Go home and see for yourself!" King Trent clapped him heartily on the shoulder. "Your home life will never be dull again!"

Bink found himself on his way. Talents never repeated in the Land of Xanth, except maybe among fiends, so his son could not be a transformer like the King or a storm master like the prior King, or a magic-adapter like King Roogna who had built Castle

Roogna, or an illusionist like Queen Iris. What could it be, that showed so early?

As he approached the cabin at the edge of the palace estate, and smelled the faint residual odor of cheese from the cottage, Bink's thoughts turned to Chameleon. It had been only a week since he had left her, but it seemed like a year. She would be in her normal phase now, ordinary in appearance and intelligence: his favorite. Their mutual worry about the prospects of their baby was over; the boy was not variable like her, or seemingly without talent like him. His love for her had been tested most severely, by the love potion and availability of a most desirable alternative. What a relief to have Crombie going after Jewel ... though that could be another action of his talent. At any rate, now Bink knew how much he loved Chameleon. He might never have realized, had he not had this adventure. So the King was right; he—

Someone emerged from the cabin. She cast a triple shadow in the light of the three moons, and she was beautiful. He ran to meet her with an exclamation of joy, grabbed her and—discovered it was not Chameleon.

"Millie!" he exclaimed, turning her hastily loose. She had phenomenal sex appeal, but all he wanted was Chameleon. "Millie the ghost! What are you doing here?"

"Taking care of your wife," Millie said. "And your son. I think I'm going to like being a nursemaid again. Especially to so important a person."

"Important?" Bink asked blankly.

"He talks to things!" she blurted enthusiastically. "I mean, he goo-goos at them, and they answer back. His crib sang him a lullaby, his pillow quacked like a duck, a rock warned me not to trip over it so I wouldn't drop the Magician—"

"Communication with the inanimate!" Bink breathed, seeing the significance of it. "He'll never get lost, because every rock will give him directions. He'll never be hungry, because a lake will tell him the best place to fish, or a tree—no, not a tree, that's alive—some rock will tell him where to find fruit. He'll be able to learn more news than the Good Magician Humfrey, and without consorting with demons! Though some of my best friends are demons, like Beauregard . . . No one will be able to betray him, because the very walls will tell him about any plots. He—"

A grim shape loomed out of the dark, dripping clods of earth. Bink gripped his sword.

"Oh, no, it's all right!" Millie cried. "That's only Jonathan!"

"That's no man—that's a zombie!" Bink protested.

"He's an old friend of mine," she said. "I knew him back when Castle Roogna was new. Now that I'm alive again, he feels responsible for my welfare."

"Oh." Bink sensed a story there—but at the moment he only wanted to see his wife and son. "Was he the zombie I met—?"

"In the garden," she agreed. "He got lost in the Queen's maze, the night of the anniversary party. Then he came to me, inside, and got pickled. It took quite a spell to undo that! Now we're looking for a spell to make him alive again, too, so we can—" She blushed delicately. Obviously the zombie had been more than a friend, in life. Millie had displayed an embarrassing interest in Bink himself, during that party, but it seemed the appearance of the zombie ended that. Another loose end Bink's talent had neatly tied up.

"When my son gets older we can have him ask about that," Bink said. "There must be some rock, somewhere, that knows where a spell to restore zombies would be."

"Oh, yes!" Millie cried ecstatically. "Oh, thank you!"

Bink faced the zombie, but did not offer to shake hands. "I think you were another omen for me, Jonathan. When I met you the first time, it signaled death with all its horrors: the death of magic. But through that death I found a kind of rebirth—and so will you."

Bink turned to the door of the cottage, ready to join his family.